FIREBRAND

FIREBRAND

Copyright © 2017 by A. J. Hartley

A Tor Teen Book
Published by Tom Doherty Associates
175 Fifth Avenue
New York, NY 10010

www.tor-forge.com

Tor® is a registered trademark of Macmillan Publishing Group, LLC.

The Library of Congress Cataloging-in-Publication Data is available upon request.

ISBN 978-0-7653-8813-1 (hardcover)
ISBN 978-0-7653-8814-8 (e-book)

Our books may be purchased in bulk for promotional, educational, or business use. Please contact your local bookseller or the Macmillan Corporate and Premium Sales Department at 1-800-221-7945, extension 5442, or by e-mail at MacmillanSpecialMarkets@macmillan.com.

First Edition: June 2017

Printed in the United States of America

0 9 8 7 6 5 4 3 2 1

For my family

FIREBRAND

CHAPTER

1

THE THIEF HAD BEEN out of the window no more than a minute but had already shaken off the police. The only reason I could still see him was because up here we got the full flat glare of the Beacon two blocks over, because I knew where to look, and because he was doing what I would be doing if our positions were reversed. Moments after the theft had been reported and the building locked down, he had emerged from the sash window on the fourth floor of the War Office on Hanover Street—which was probably how he had gotten in in the first place—and had climbed up to the roof. Then he had danced along the steeply pitched ridgeline and across to the Corn Exchange by way of a cable bridge he had rigged earlier. The uniformed officers in the pearly glow of the gas lamps below blocked the doorways leading to the street, milling around like baffled chickens oblivious to the hawk soaring away above them. If he hadn't shot one of the guards on his way into the strong room, they wouldn't have even known he had been there.

But he had, and he was getting away with a roll of papers bound with what looked like red ribbon. I didn't know what they were, but I had seen Willinghouse's face when the alarm had been raised and knew how badly he needed them back.

Not Willinghouse himself. Bar-Selehm. The city needed them back, and I, Anglet Sutonga, former steeplejack and now . . . something else entirely, worked for the city. In a manner of speaking.

The thief paused to disassemble his cable bridge and, in the act of turning, saw me as I rounded a brick chimney stack. His hand went for the pistol at his belt, the one that had already been fired twice tonight, but he hesitated. There was no clearer way to announce his position to those uniformed chickens below us than by firing his gun. He decided to run, abandoning his dismantling of the bridge, betting that, whoever I was, I wouldn't be able to stay with him up here on the ornamented roofs and towers of the government district.

He was wrong about that, though he climbed expertly. I gave chase, sure-footed in my familiar steel-toed boots, as he skittered down the sloping tiles on the other side and vaulted across the alley onto a metal fire escape. He moved with ease in spite of his formal wear, and the only time he looked away from what he was doing was to check on my progress. As he did, he smiled, intrigued, a wide hyena grin that made me slow just a little. Because despite the half mask he was wearing over his eyes, I knew who he was.

They called him Darius. He was a thief, but because he was also white, famously elegant, and limited his takings to the jewelry of wealthy society ladies—plucked from their nightstands as they slept inches away—he was known by the more romantic name of "cat burglar." I had never been impressed by the title. It seemed to me that anyone whose idea of excitement—and it clearly was exciting for the likes of Darius—involved skulking inside houses full of people was someone you needed to keep at a distance. I've stolen in the past—usually food but sometimes money as well—and I wouldn't trust anyone who did it for sport, for the thrill of standing over you while you slept. For all his dashing reputation and the breathless way in which the newspapers recounted his exploits, it did not surprise me in the least that he had killed a man tonight.

I was, I reminded myself, unarmed. I didn't like guns, even when I was the one holding them. Especially then, in fact.

I too was masked, though inelegantly, a scarf of sooty fabric wrapped around my head so that there was only a slit for my eyes. It was hot and uncomfortable, but essential. I had a job that paid well, which kept me out of the gangs and the factories that would be my only tolerable options if anyone guessed who I really was. That would be easier if anyone realized I was Lani, so my skin stayed covered.

I crossed the wire bridge, slid down the ridged tile, and launched myself across the alley, seventy feet above the cobbled ground, dropping one full story and hitting the fire escape with a bone-rattling jolt. Grasping the handrails, I swung down four steps at a time, listening to Darius's fine shoes on the steps below me. I was still three flights above him when he landed lightly on the elegant balcony on the front of the Victory Street Hotel. I dropped in time to see him swinging around the dividing walls between balconies, vanishing from sight at the fourth one.

He might just have hidden in the shadows, waiting for me to follow him, or he might have forced the window and slipped into the hotel room.

I didn't hesitate, leaping onto the first balcony, hanging for an instant like a vervet monkey in a marulla tree, then reaching for the next and the next with long, sinewy arms. I paused only a half second before scything my legs over the wall and into the balcony where he had disappeared, my left hand straying to the heavy-bladed kukri I wore in a scabbard at my waist.

I didn't need it. Not yet, at least.

He had jimmied the door latch and slipped into a well-appointed bedroom with wood paneling and heavy curtains of damask with braided accents that matched the counterpane.

Fancy.

But then this was Victory Street, so you'd expect that.

I angled my head and peered into the gloom. The bed was, so far as I could see, unoccupied. I stood quite still on the thick dark carpet, breathing shallowly. Unless he was crouching behind the bed or hiding in the en suite, he wasn't there. The door into the hotel's hallway was only thirty feet away, and I was wasting time.

I took four long strides and was halfway to the door when he hit me, surging up from behind the bed like a crocodile bursting from the reeds, jaws agape. He caught me around the waist and dragged me down so that I landed hard on one shoulder and hit my head on a chest of drawers. For a moment the world went white, then black, then a dull throbbing red as I shook off the confusion and grasped at his throat.

He slid free, pausing only long enough to aim a kick squarely into my face before making for the hallway. I saw it coming and turned away from the worst of it, shrinking and twisting so that he connected with my already aching shoulder. He reached for the scarf about my head, but I had the presence of mind to bring the kukri slicing up through the air, its razor edge flashing. He snatched his hand away, swung another kick, which got more of my hip than my belly, and made for the door.

I rolled, groaning and angry, listening to the door snap shut behind him, then flexed the muscles of my neck and shoulder, touching the fabric around my head with fluttering fingers. It was still intact, as was I, but I felt rattled, scared. Darius's cat burglar suaveness was all gone, exposed for the veneer it was, and beneath it there was ugliness and cruelty and the love of having other people in his power. I wasn't surprised, but it gave me pause. I'd been kicked many times before, and I always knew what was behind it, how much force and skill, how much real, venomous desire to hurt, cripple, or kill. His effort had largely gone wide because it was dark and I knew how to dodge, but the kick had been deliberate, cruel. If I caught up with him and he thought he was in real danger, he would kill me without a second's thought. I rolled to a crouch, sucked in a long, steadying breath, and went after him.

The hallway was lit by the amber glow of shaded oil lamps on side tables, so that for all the opulence of the place, the air tasted of acrid smoke, and the darkness pooled around me as I ran. Up ahead, the corridor turned into an open area where a single yellowing bulb of luxorite shone on intricate ceiling moldings and ornamental pilasters.

There were stairs down, and I was aware of voices, lots of them, a sea of confused chatter spiked erratically with waves of laughter.

A party.

More Bar-Selehm elegance and, for me, more danger. I had no official position, no papers allowing me to break into the hotel rooms of the wealthy, nothing that would make my Lani presence among the cream of the city palatable. And in spite of all I had done for Bar-Selehm—for the very people who were sipping wine in the ballroom below—I felt the pressure of this more keenly than I had Darius's malevolent kick. Some blows were harder to roll with.

I sprang down the carpeted stairs, turning the corner into the noise. The hallway became a gallery running around the upper story of the ballroom so that guests might promenade around the festivities, waving their fans at their friends below. Darius was on the far side, moving effortlessly through the formally dressed clusters of startled people. He was still masked, and they knew him on sight, falling away, their mouths little Os of shock. One of the women fainted, or pretended to. Another partygoer, wearing a dragoon's formal blues, took a step toward the masked man, but the pistol in Darius's hand swung round like an accusatory finger and the dragoon thought better of his heroism.

I barreled through the crowd, shoving mercilessly, not breaking stride. The party below had staggered to a halt, and the room was a sea of upturned faces watching us as we swept around the gallery toward another flight of stairs. As I neared the corner, I seized a silver platter from an elegant lady in teal and heaved it at him, so that it slid in a long and menacing arc over the heads of the crowd below and stung him on the shoulder. He turned, angry, and found me elbowing my way through the people as they blew away from him like screws of colored tissue, horrified and delighted by their proximity to the infamous cat burglar. And then his gun came up again and they were just horrified, flinging themselves to the ground.

He fired twice. The gilded plaster cherub curled round the

balustrade in front of me exploded, and the screaming started. Somewhere a glass broke, and in all the shrieking, it wasn't absolutely clear that no one had been seriously hurt, but then someone took a bad step, lost their balance, and went over the balustrade. More screaming, and another shot. I took cover behind a stone pillar, and when I peered round, Darius had already reached the stairs and was gone.

I sprinted after him, knocking a middle-aged woman in layers of black gauzy stuff to the ground as I barged through. My kukri was still in my hand, and the partygoers were at least as spooked by the sweep of its broad, purposeful blade as by Darius's pistol, though it had the advantage of focusing their attention away from my face and onto my gloved hands. A waiter—the only black person in the room that I could see—stepped back from me, staring at the curved knife like it was red-hot. That gave me the opening I needed, and I dashed through to the stairs.

Darius had gone up. I gave chase, focusing on the sound of his expensive shoes. One flight, two, three, then the snap of a door and suddenly I was in a bare hall of parquet floors, dim, hot, and dusty. A single oil lamp showed supply closets overflowing with bed linens and aprons on hooks. The hall ended in a steel ladder up to the roof, the panel closing with a metallic clang as I moved toward it.

He might be waiting, pistol reloaded and aimed. But he had chosen this building for a reason. Its roof gave onto Long Terrace, which ran all the way to the edge of Mahweni Old Town, from where he could reach any part of the northern riverbank or cross over into the warren of warehouses, sheds, and factories on the south side. He wouldn't be waiting. He was looking to get away.

So I scaled the ladder and heaved open the metal shutters as quietly as I could manage. I didn't want to catch him. I wanted to see where he went. It would be best if he thought he'd lost me. I slid out cautiously, dropped into a half crouch and scuttered to the end of the roof like a baboon. Darius was well away, taking leaping strides along the roof of the Long Terrace, and as he slowed to look back, I leaned behind one of the hotel's ornamental gargoyles out of sight. When next I peered round, he was moving again, but slower, secure in the knowledge that he was in the clear.

I waited another second before dropping to the Long Terrace roof, staying low, and sheathing my kukri. The terrace was one of the city's architectural jewels: a mile-long continuous row of elegant, three-story houses with servants' quarters below stairs. They were fashioned from a stone so pale it was almost white and each had the same black door, the same stone urn and bas-relief carving, the same slate roof. Enterprising home owners had lined the front lip of the roof with planters that, at this time of year, trailed fragrant vines of messara flowers. The whole terrace curved fractionally down toward the river like a lock of elegantly braided hair. For Darius it provided a direct route across several blocks of the city away from prying eyes.

The nights were warming as Bar-Selehm abandoned its token spring, and the pursuit had made me sweat. We had left the light of the Beacon behind, and I could barely keep track of Darius in the smoggy gloom, even with my long lens, which I drew from my pocket and unfolded. At the end of the terrace, he paused to look back once more, adjusting the tubular roll of documents he had slung across his back, but I had chosen a spot in the shadow of a great urn sprouting ferns and a dwarf fruit tree, and he saw nothing. Satisfied, he shinned down the angled corner blocks at the end of the terrace and emerged atop the triumphal arch that spanned Broad Street, then descended the steps halfway and sprang onto the landing of the Svengele shrine, whose minaret marked the edge of Old Town. I gave chase and was navigating the slim walkway atop the arch when he happened to look up and see me.

I dropped to the thin ribbon of stone before he could get his pistol sighted, and the shot thrummed overhead like a hummingbird. He clattered up the steps that curled round the minaret and flung himself onto the sand-colored tile of the neighboring house. He was running flat out now, and I had no choice but to do the same. I jumped, snatched a handhold on the minaret, and tore after him, landing clumsily on the roof so that I was almost too late in my roll. Another shot, and one of the tiles shattered in a hail of amber grit that stung my eyes. I sprawled for cover, but Darius was off again, vaulting from roof to roof, scattering tile as he ran, so that they fell, popping and crackling into the street below. Somewhere behind us, an elderly black man emerged shouting, but I had no time for sympathy or apologies.

As the narrow street began to curl in on itself, Darius dropped to the rough cobbles and sprinted off into the labyrinth which was Old Town. The streets were barely wide enough for a cart to squeeze through, and at times I could touch the buildings on either side of the road at the same time. There was a pale gibbous moon glowing like a lamp in Bar-Selehm's perpetual smoky haze, but its light did not reach into the narrow ginnels running between the city's most ancient houses. Down here his footfalls echoed in the dark, which was the only reason I could keep up with him as he turned left, then right, then back, past the Ntenga butchers' row and down to the waterfront, where I lost him.

The river wasn't as high as it had been a couple of weeks before, but it filled the night with a constant susurration like wind in tall grass. As the carefully maintained cobbles gave way to the weedy gravel around the riverside boatyards and mooring quays, any footfalls were lost in the steady background hiss of the river Kalihm. I clambered down the brick embankment that lined the riverbank and revolved on the spot, biting back curses as I tried, eyes half shut, to catch the sound of movement.

There. It may have been no more than a half brick turned by a stray foot, but I heard it, down near the shingle shore only fifty yards away. It came from the narrow alley between a pair of rickety boathouses that straddled a concrete pier. I made for the sound, opting for stealth rather than speed, one hand on the horn butt of my kukri, picking my way over the rounded stones, my back to the city. Even here, in the heart of Bar-Selehm, when you faced the river, you stepped back three hundred years, and there was only water and reeds and the giant herons that stalked among them.

I heard the noise again, different this time, more distinct, but in this narrow wedge of space between the boathouses, almost no light struggled through. The river itself was paler, reflecting the smudge of moon in the night sky and touched with the eerie phosphorescence of glowing things that lived in its depths, but I could see nothing between me and it.

Or almost nothing.

As I crept down the pebbled slope, I saw—or felt—a shape in front of me as it shifted. Something like a large man crouching no more than a few feet ahead. A very large man. I slid the kukri from its sheath, and in that second, the shape moved, black against the waters of the Kalihm. It turned, lengthening improbably as it presented its flank to me. It was, I realized with a pang of terror, no man. It was as big as a cart, and as it continued its slow rotation to face me, a shaft of light splashed across its massive, glistening head. I felt my heart catch.

The hippo rushed at me then, its face splitting open impossibly, eyes rolling back as it bared its immense tusks and bellowed.

CHAPTER
2

I SCRAMBLED UP THE riverbank, knowing the hippo could easily outrun me and that those jaws would fold and break me like a steam hammer. My boots slid on the wet stones. I was falling.

I felt the mad, blood-rushing horror of dropping to the ground in front of the great beast. I knew how it would trample me, toss me, rip me apart.

And then, somehow, I was recovering my balance.

In a blind madness of terror, I vaulted the embankment, feeling the hippo snapping its great coal-hatch door of a mouth inches behind me. Then I was clear and shooting up the slope toward the dim huddle of domes and spires that was the edge of Old Town.

The hippo roared again: a tremendous, window-rattling wall of noise that raised every hair on my head. I squeezed my eyes shut and slammed my hands against my ears, even though I knew it couldn't get over the embankment. Or not there, at least. In places where the brick had crumbled, it was not unheard of for hippos to blunder into the outskirts of the town. I needed to move on.

My feet took me instinctively away from the snorting hippo in the dark of the riverbank, but I had no conscious idea where to go next. I had lost Darius completely.

Or so I assumed. In fact my detour to the river had taken only seconds. As I looked back, I caught the movement of a distant figure standing alone on one of the long brick jetties.

It couldn't be.

But it was. He must have lost me when I went down to the river, and he was no longer hiding. He was, in fact, waiting.

I dropped into a balled crouch, then skulked crablike along the embankment wall to the head of the jetty and peered over. The hippo was grunting restlessly below me, some twenty yards to my left. Darius was perhaps three times that distance away. I watched as he drew something from inside his jacket and adjusted it. A white light leapt from his hand, vanished, then came back.

Luxorite. Probably a signet ring or locket he had purloined from some opulent bed chamber.

The light came again, then went. He was signaling.

I pulled out my long lens and started scanning the water, still aware of the heavy, shuffling breaths of the hippo in the dark, but I saw nothing beyond Darius's dim silhouette. On the far side of the river, a half mile away, there was a distant glow of firelight: some large warehouse or factory on the south bank was ablaze. I smelled the smoke despite the distance, a strange and unpleasant stench quite unlike wood fires. I checked my surroundings, my eyes fastening on the rusty scaffold of a crane that loomed over the nearest boathouse. Its gantry stuck out over the river, the end well past Darius's spot on the jetty.

Perhaps from there I would have a better view. . . .

I moved, stepping carefully, not looking back to Darius till I had reached the foot of the girdered tower. He had resumed signaling, his attention elsewhere. I grabbed the rust-bitten edges of the iron struts and began to climb. Pushing my boots into the triangular holes where the support beams intersected, I worked my way up, thirty feet, forty, till I reached a catwalk that gave onto the operator's winch. In use, the chains would be connected to a steam engine below, but the pulleys and cables were brown and furred with rust, as if the crane hadn't been used for months, even years. The great arm of the main boom stuck out over the water into the night, pointing indistinctly toward the burning building on the other side. If it wasn't structurally sound, I might not know till it was too late.

I pulled my way up over the cab and onto the lattice boom through which the main hoist ran. It had a triangular cross section, a yard wide on top, the bottom a single beam, the whole crisscrossed by supports like the rungs of a ladder. I crept out on my hands and knees, staring through the boom as I left the wharf and inched out over the dark and steadily moving water.

I was halfway along before I saw the rowboat approaching Darius's position from the south bank of the river, and two thirds of the way along when someone stepped onto the arm of the crane behind me.

I stared as he hauled himself up. Not Darius, who was still down on the pier. Someone else. This new person, a white man in an incongruous suit and tie, stood tall on the girders of the boom, hands at his side, a revolver in one and what looked like a small pickax in the other. It sparkled coldly. Even at this distance, I could see that he was smiling as he took his first step toward me.

It was a cautious step, but he seemed quite composed, staring fixedly at me, his blond hair blowing slightly in the breeze that came up off the river, and as he took another, his confidence seemed to grow. Soon he was walking toward me with easy, measured strides, despite being fifty feet up in the air. It felt less like the skill of a steeplejack and more like the carelessness of someone who thought himself beyond harm.

It was frightening.

I kept crawling, though I had no idea where I would go when I reached the end of the crane's jib. Maybe the cable would be hanging, and I would be able to swing to safety. . . .

Maybe. Probably not. But the alternative was the man with the gun and the pickax and the smile. It was the last that scared me most. He came on, a man who could not fall, eyes locked on mine. I struggled to my feet and drew the kukri, knowing that it was futile against a man with a gun. His smile widened, and I was first baffled, then terrified, as he slipped the pistol into his pocket and kept coming.

He wanted to fight me.

I felt the breeze stir my clothes as I stood up on the narrow boom, my weight balanced over my feet. I held the kukri by my right ear and extended my left hand toward him. He didn't even slow. He took three more steps, slightly faster now, and I swung the kukri at him, a broad, slashing chop at his shoulder. He leaned away from it fractionally. The blade cut through the air, and I almost overbalanced as my arm came round. Instantly, he reached and tapped me on the side of the head with the pick as if he were striking a bell in a temple.

The blow stung like a wasp. I clapped my free hand to it. It came away slick with blood. He smiled again, and I knew that to him, this was sport. Entertainment. I stepped back unsteadily, then dropped to the boom, grabbed it with my hands, and scythed a kick at him.

He jumped. High up above the river and with nothing but two slim rails of metal to land on, he actually *jumped* over my kick, landed, and tagged me again with the spike of the pickax, this time in the small of my back. I cried out at that, less in pain—though it was real—and more in terror.

This, I thought with absolute certainty, *is how I die.*

I stepped forward and swung wildly at his face with my balled fist. He pivoted back out of range, and my momentum turned me away from him. As he closed in, I regained my balance and seized his outstretched wrist, trying to tug him off the boom, but I succeeded only in plucking his cuff link free. It arced through the night, sparkling bluish, and bounced on the iron frame before falling out of sight. He felt blindly at his flapping cuff, and a pulse of irritation went through his hard, pale eyes. He would kill me for that alone.

I couldn't fight him. That much was clear. He was too strong, too fast, too skilled. Nor could I get past him. My only choice was to scramble to the very limit of the crane's boom. I turned and half stepped, half jumped to get out of his range. He did not lunge after me, not right away. Seeing how futile my retreat was, he approached more cautiously. I backed away as far as I could, but in a few feet, I was out of room and there was nothing below me except a long fall into deep water.

There was a flash in my peripheral vision and an almost instantaneous bang. I looked down. The boat had reached the jetty, but as Darius had stooped to extend a hand toward it, the boatman had shot him down. The cat burglar crumpled, and the man in the boat reached up to tug the document roll Darius had been carrying free. The dead man spilled softly off the jetty into the water, his luxorite lamp lighting the river up with a greenish, dreamlike haze from below, as the boatman pushed off and rowed away.

I tore my gaze away and turned to the man on the crane, who moved almost close enough to touch. He held the pistol loosely at his side once more, but his right hand, the one with the pick, was taut and ready. Its spike was already tipped with the smallest touch of crimson. My blood. He was making no attempt to hide his face. A very bad sign. He did not intend for me to live long enough to tell anyone who I had seen. He was still smiling, a bland, unsettling smile at once ordinary and terrible. Though he could easily have shot me where I was, I knew instinctively that he would prefer to use the pick.

I jumped.

In fact it was more a fall, a desperate lunge into the airy nothing above the water, and I had just enough time to remember the hippo before I hit the surface.

Hit the surface I did. Hard. I have always been healthily afraid of water, because I can't swim and I know what lives in and around the Kalihm, yet it had never occurred to me that falling into water would feel like falling onto concrete. I slammed into the river, my left knee, thigh, hip, and shoulder taking the full impact. The pain shocked the air out of me. For a second I was incapable of my own distress, stunned into inaction, turning over and over as I sank.

Then I was drifting to the surface again, borne toward the ocean by the current. All I felt was pain, so that I was not even able to keep my eyes and mouth closed. Before I broke the surface, my throat was full of the warm, soiled water of the Kalihm. I coughed it up and promptly swallowed more. My body screamed with the agony of impact and my lungs filled.

I was dying.

CHAPTER

3

"WELL, OBVIOUSLY I SURVIVED," I said.

Willinghouse watched me, his face stern, while the man I had known as Detective Andrews—now Inspector Andrews, thanks to his part in the Beacon affair—motioned one of his men to replace the sopping blanket around my shoulders with another.

My left arm was dislocated, and they had strapped it in place till someone from Saint Auspice's could tend to it properly. My face throbbed. Most of my left side was suffused with a deep and coloring bruise that made the slightest movement painful. More to the point, as Willinghouse's very first question had made clear, I had neither the stolen plans nor any clue to the identity of who had orchestrated the theft. The police had recovered Darius's body and were planning to put notices in the papers requesting assistance from the public to confirm the cat burglar's real name.

I had described the man with the pick, but he was nondescript in everything but the strange detachment with which he had planned to kill me, and I couldn't put that into words they understood.

"He was white," I said. "Blond. Ordinary-looking but well dressed."

Willinghouse, never a man to hide his disappointment in me, scowled and looked away across the river to where a thick smudge of smoke hung over the remains of whatever had burned the night before. I had drifted only a few hundred yards down the river, my barely conscious body pulled into a central channel too deep—mercifully—to run afoul of the nearby hippo pod. I had snagged upon a raft of driftwood on the central stanchion of the shifting and rickety Ridleford pontoon bridge and been spotted by Mahweni longshoremen on their morning ferry ride to work. They had alerted the coast guard, who were out in unusual numbers.

"What burned last night?" I asked, following Willinghouse's green eyes.

"What?" he asked, as if just remembering I was there. "Oh. Nothing. An abandoned factory. It's not relevant."

And that was Willinghouse. There was work—which was relevant—and there was everything else. I hopped from one category to the other like a secretary bird hunting snakes.

"Why all the coast guard boats?" I asked. I could see three this side of the Ridleford pontoons. They had armed men in their bows, and one seemed to be towing another vessel—actually more a raft bound together with rope and buoyed up unevenly on rusted barrels—crowded with people. Black people. Thin and ragged looking. Almost all women and children.

"Illegals," said Andrews. "Trying to sneak into the economic paradise that is Bar-Selehm."

I watched the people on the raft as they gazed from one shouting officer to another, uncomprehending and scared, the children huddled around their mothers, their faces tear streaked.

"How are you feeling?" asked Andrews. He was a thin-faced, clean-shaven white man whose eyes had a predatory intensity, but his voice was soft, and his concern sounded genuine.

I reached for my injured shoulder with my right hand, but couldn't grasp it before the pain became too much. I winced, and he nodded.

"Anything other than your shoulder?" he asked. "That was quite a fall."

"Just my pride," I said, still watching the children as they were lifted from their listing raft and into the arms of the police who clustered around in the thigh-deep water. One of the women—wearing a filthy and soaking orange sarong that stuck to her sticklike limbs—was nursing a tiny infant.

"Why did you jump?" asked Willinghouse, peering at me from

behind his wire-rimmed spectacles. "You couldn't have, I don't know, fought them off or something?"

"No," I said.

"I thought you were more adept at this kind of thing." He didn't sound critical as much as curious, and when I glared at him, he shrugged. "What?"

"The one who came after me was too strong, all right? Too skilled."

"And you saw nothing to identify either him or the gunman in the boat?" Willinghouse pressed.

I shook my head, feeling stupid and useless, looking back to the ragged immigrants, then caught myself.

"There was something," I said. "He lost a cuff link as we fought on the crane. It might have fallen in the river, but it might not."

"Where?" asked Andrews.

"I'll show you," I said, getting to my feet with the inspector's help. I scowled at Willinghouse, but he was watching the raft and seemed to have forgotten me entirely, so I led Andrews along the riverbank to the steps and the pier and the crane, a uniformed officer trailing us, uninterested. The hippo was still there, its back turned to the water, pinking in the sun.

"There," I said. "We were at the midpoint of that boom when he lost the cuff link. It went behind him and hit metal on the way down."

I shrugged apologetically. It wasn't much of a clue.

"Benson!" called Andrews to the uniformed officer, pointing.

"Down there, sir?" protested Benson. "There's a bloody great hippo!"

"Well, keep your distance from it," said Andrews, not very helpfully.

Benson gave me a baleful look.

"Was it luxorite?" said Willinghouse suddenly.

"What?"

"The cuff link your assailant dropped. Did it contain luxorite?"

"I don't think so. It was bright but only by reflection. Why?"

"If it was luxorite, he would have had an easier time finding it in the dark," Willinghouse said with a noncommittal shrug. "Unless it fell into the river, in which case the point is rather moot."

He said it sourly, the scar on his cheek tightening, as if where the item had fallen was somehow my fault. I talked to push away the sense of failure.

"Probably just crystal or enamel," I said, "but large and blue."

It took a moment for this to register in my employer's face, but the transformation was marked.

"Blue?" snapped Willinghouse. "You're sure? What shape?"

"I didn't get a good look at it—"

"Diamond shaped?"

I thought hard, sensing how much he needed me to remember more than I had seen. I shrugged, and my shoulder cried in protest.

"I don't know for sure," I said. "Could have been."

"On a white background?"

"White or silver, yes," I said. "You know it?"

"Oh yes," said Willinghouse, and there was something more than pleasure in his face. His jaw was set in grim resolution. He hurried away and was soon poring over the ground behind Andrews and Benson, who was peering into the water below the crane's piers, keeping a watchful eye on the hippo some thirty yards away. I joined the hunt, but only for a moment. Willinghouse suddenly straightened up with a cry of "Huzzah!" He held the cuff link aloft, and his face was full of grim triumph.

"What is it?" asked Andrews.

"Elitus," said Willinghouse, holding out the cuff link for Andrews to inspect it. It was indeed a blue crystalline diamond on a silvery white enamel background. "A club. Very exclusive."

"Never heard of it," said Andrews.

"No," Willinghouse answered. "You wouldn't have. No offense meant. If it's any consolation, they wouldn't have me as a member either."

Andrews raised his eyebrows. Willinghouse was only a junior

member of Parliament, but he was a man of considerable means, which was how he was able to employ me.

"Excuse me!"

We all turned to look down to the shore, where Benson gazed up at us with a look of considerable unease. "Did you find what you were looking for? Only, this hippo is eyeballing me something awful . . . ?"

"Oh, for crying out loud, man!" exclaimed Andrews. "Yes, we found it. Get up here." He turned back to Willinghouse irritably. "You were saying you wouldn't be allowed to join this Elitus club. Why not?"

Willinghouse smiled mirthlessly.

"Well, I'm not a member of the right party for one thing, but . . ." He hesitated. "Let's just say that the cuff link's white background is . . . symbolic."

Andrews looked taken aback, embarrassed even. He knew that Willinghouse was a quarter Lani, though it wasn't clear from his appearance. His hair was jet-black like mine, but his eyes were green, and most people would assume he was merely a little tanned by the Feldesland sun. His socialite sister, Dahria, passed even more completely for white.

"Did he see your face? Your skin?" asked Willinghouse.

I bit back my irritation.

"Are you asking if he saw who I was or what I am?" I said.

"Both. Either."

I looked away.

"My face was masked," I said. "He didn't get a good look at me. Whether he could tell I was Lani . . . I don't know. Maybe."

Willinghouse scowled, dissatisfied.

"There's no need for that, old fellow," said Andrews. "Miss Sutonga has had a singularly trying experience—"

"I don't dispute that," Willinghouse shot back. "I'd just like to know whether our enemy realizes the government has a Lani agent working for them."

"Your concern is noted," I said, frostily, "but I can look after myself."

"My *concern*," said Willinghouse, "is that if they do, in fact, know that the person who pursued their agent was Lani or, for that matter female, then your use value just went into a sharp decline, wouldn't you say?"

Fury got the better of me.

"My *use value*?" I spat.

"Your function as a government operative."

"You're not the government," I said, swinging wildly now. "You're a member of Parliament in the opposition's back benches."

"Who serves the interests of the city with the means available to him," Willinghouse retorted.

"Meaning me? I'm the means available to you?"

"Meaning . . . no," he said, stuttering to a frustrated halt. "I meant using my family's fortune, a small part of which has been used to secure your services."

"And excellent services they are too," inserted Andrews, trying to keep the peace.

We both glared at him. There was a long silence.

"I'll also remind you," said Willinghouse pompously, "that while my party is not currently in power, this is an election year and the Brevard membership has high hopes of—"

"This Elitus place," I said. "How do I get in?"

Andrews frowned.

"Miss Sutonga," he said, "these people, whoever they are, have already demonstrated they are quite ruthless. Two people have already died trying to stop them. The documents are gone. The enemy have them, and nothing we do now will change that."

"What are they?" I asked.

"That is confidential information," said Andrews. "Even I don't know—"

"Plans for a new machine gun," said Willinghouse.

Andrews and I both gaped at him. I had seen a machine gun in use once before. I did not know how they could be made more lethal than they already were, but if someone had that knowledge, someone I had failed to stop . . .

"The documents were stolen from the War Office," said Willinghouse. "I was in a meeting across the street when the alarm was raised, which is why I was able to alert you to what was going on before the thief made his escape. The shadow secretary for defense spoke to me in the heat of the moment and was, you might say, unguarded in his speech. Something he now regrets. Anyway, yes, the plans are for a new machine gun, and word in government circles is that it's the Grappoli who took them."

"Of course," said Andrews. "They always suspect the Grappoli."

The Grappoli were the city's colonial rivals, and they controlled considerably more of Feldesland, the continent of which Bar-Selehm was the jewel, than we did. Bar-Selehm had been established three centuries ago by King Gustav II of Belrand, a country on the northern continent of Panbroke: a process equal parts military conquest, barter, and legal sleight of hand. The city-state eventually became an industrial sprawl unrivaled in Feldesland, but pretty isolated from its neighbors. It had leeched parcels of land away from the indigenous Mahweni over the years, but Bar-Selehm's total holdings still amounted to no more than a few thousand square miles. The Grappoli's native lands were in southeast Panbroke, their people still white, but tending to darker hair and eyes than the Belrandians, and their expansion across the sea to Feldesland had been a more concerted effort to dominate the continent. They had taken over whole countries in the north and west and seemed to be perpetually looking to expand farther. It was one of those bitter colonial jokes that when anyone referred to the "Feldish," they meant the white colonists from Belrand, not the Mahweni who had always lived on the continent and who had called the land something different. I didn't know what.

Willinghouse nodded.

"I know," he said. "But this time . . . the Grappoli are moving east, north of the Hagrab desert. They are claiming obscure legal precedent based on settlements made a century or more ago. Reports suggest that they are fuelling tribal conflicts that are driving the locals off the land, and the only modern military resistance they are encountering comes from local warlords who are fighting only to protect their opium fields. The people who live there are caught in the middle. We don't know for sure what is happening yet, and there is no suggestion that the conflict might expand south toward Bar-Selehm, but it's a mess, and a bloody one. Trade routes are being watched; sanctions against the Grappoli are being drawn up. Potential deals between Bar-Selehm and the Grappoli that might in any way augment their military capacity are being debated even as we speak. Some of my more hawkish colleagues are suggesting we send troops north to support the cartels, while others say that the drug lords are clearly the lowest of the very low, and that if we are to take sides at all, we are better lining up alongside the Grappoli. My party's position is that the Grappoli's current landgrab may not involve us at all, but we must ensure that Bar-Selehm does not support it, however indirectly. In the long term, the consequences could be dire."

"The long term?" I said. "What about the northern tribes whose land is being taken now?"

"Miss Sutonga, let's not make this a crusade, shall we?" he said. His eyes flashed to the now-empty raft surrounded by the coast guard, and I made the connection.

"Them?" I demanded. "That's what this is? You said they were illegal immigrants."

"They are!" said Willinghouse.

"But they are also refugees?"

"The lands north of the Hagrab desert are not Bar-Selehm's concern," said Willinghouse. "The people who live there have sovereignty over their own territory. Interference on our part would merely spark diplomatic discomfort. The results could easily escalate into trade sanctions, the closing of embassies, the collapse of international trade agreements—"

"We're talking about the Quundu, yes?" I said.

"There are various tribal territories involved," said Willinghouse wearily, "but yes, the Quundu, the Delfani, the Zagrel—"

"Who all have their own sovereignty," said Andrews.

"Yes," I said. "You know what else they have? Spears. Shields covered with buffalo hide. Knives. While the Grappoli have machine guns. But let's be sure not to spark diplomatic discomfort."

"You can't take things like this personally," said Willinghouse. "It impairs your judgment."

I watched where the police and coast guard were gathering the weary huddle of women and children together on the shore. Some of them had collapsed. How long had they been at sea? Days? Weeks? There were bodies on the raft that I had thought were sleeping, but they had not moved after the others disembarked. One wailing woman splashed through the water toward a small body, while a policeman pulled her back. . . .

"How do I get into Elitus?" I asked again, turning back to Willinghouse, my tone neutral.

"I really don't think—" Andrews began, but I cut him off with a look.

"How do I get in?"

"If someone of my status can't get into Elitus," said Willinghouse, "how on earth am I going to get a full-blood Lani girl in?"

"I have no idea," I said. "But I can't wait to find out."

CHAPTER

4

I WAS NOT ALLOWED in the Drowning, so after my visit to the hospital, I took my weekly meeting with my sister Rahvey at the old monkey temple where my father's remains were buried. I waited for her under a sambar tree a few yards from where I had first met Mnenga, the Mahweni herder who, with his brothers, had saved my life only three months before.

I had not seen him since. Though I had sat down to write letters to him twice, I never sent them. Where would he be? Would he even be able to read Feldish? His absence felt the way I imagined a much older, dearer friend's would. My forced separation from the Drowning was doubly hard without him, and underscored my isolation—something which normally suited my temperament, but now felt strangely disorienting. I had never been one to find much comfort in community, particularly when I felt constrained by it. Not long ago, I would have imagined my current independence from the gang and the Drowning as a kind of paradise. But perhaps because the Drowning was now forbidden to me, I found that, for the first time I could remember, I actually missed it.

If so, I told myself, *it is because you've forgotten what living there was really like.*

I breathed in, catching the edge of spice on the air drifting up from the shanty's cooking fires—cardamom, I thought, and something sweet and woody like cinnamon. I frowned, considered sharpening my kukri, and cursed when I remembered that it had been lost in the river. I would need to get another.

The summer seemed to be already upon us. The land lay under a dry, searing heat, which built as the day went on, broken only by afternoon storms that blew in like angry gods, railed and stamped for an hour or two, and then vanished. Nights remained warm, and the temple air held a sweet rankness that hung about the trees and flowers thick as incense. It smelled of life, which was quite an achievement for a cemetery.

It was all very Lani: circular and timeless, balanced, bittersweet, and unchanging. Or rather, almost unchanging. I was not welcome in the Drowning because I had caused the death of my eldest sister, Vestris, and broken my blood oath: in the right light, the traces of that promise could still be seen scored into my cheeks. Rahvey had four daughters living with her now, and that had been my doing too. More balance, more tears blended with the laughter. I had wept for Vestris, even though she had tried to kill me and had killed others. I knew as I dried my eyes that I was really weeping for myself, for a version of my past, an image of the world which had turned out not to be true. Maybe grief was always like that. I had lost a sister, but Rahvey got to keep a daughter who would otherwise have been given up to the hard life of the Pancaris orphanage. I took that as a kind of victory, even if my banishment meant that I was now the orphan.

Balance, I mused, one child finding a home while I was cut adrift, sent to stay in rented rooms paid for by somebody else, no longer even the steeplejack I had been in the gang on Seventh Street. For a moment, I almost missed that too. Not the place itself, dirty and teeming with noisy boys as it always was, but a sense of belonging and a corner of the old weavers' shed which, however fiercely I'd had to protect it, I had called mine.

Home.

I brushed the thought away like a hogfly, seeing it for the absurdity it was. If I could get nostalgic for Seventh Street and the brutal life I had endured there under Morlak, I was getting soft and stupid.

I spat into the dusty earth and rubbed the soot-speckled wetness in with the toe of my boot.

Normally I would have done my Kathahry exercises as I waited, but just walking there had taken me twice as long as usual, and every part of me ached and throbbed. My shoulder, painfully wrenched into place by a burly doctor at the hospital, had been strapped up in a sling. It could have been much worse, they told me, as if I had won a prize, but it would be days before I could get rid of the sling and weeks before I got a full range of motion in the joint again. At any other time, I would have resented their diagnosis: I lived, after all, to climb, to test my muscles and sinews till I felt my blood sing. Yet the man with the pick and the smile had scared me. I had been utterly powerless, incapable of defending myself against someone so skilled and so deliberate, and I had retreated into my head. My body could not be trusted, and I was glad of the excuse not to use it. Instead, I lay on the dusty ground on my back, my right hand palm down, my left crossed over my chest, eyes shut, listening to the vervet monkeys chattering in the treetops and feeling the earth breathe.

"Auntie Ang!"

I opened my eyes and lifted myself up onto my right elbow. I tried to keep the hurt out of my face, but Jadary, Rahvey's second-youngest daughter, gave my sling a shrewd look.

"What happened to you?"

"I had a fall, but I'm all right," I said.

Rahvey looked me up and down, refusing to give away any sign of concern as she cradled Kalla in her arms. I got to my feet.

"Let me see her," I said, stooping to the warm bundle and kissing the child on her forehead. She squirmed vaguely in her sleep. She wasn't a person yet, or at least not one I could see, but she was also not the helpless infant she had been during my erratic and incompetent "care." Before, she had been all fragility and potential. Now, she was a stirring, curious awareness that seemed to age and mature before my very eyes. Her growth was beautiful and terrifying and felt both right and sad, in the best Lani tradition. "And the rest," I added, going from daughter to daughter and kissing them each in turn.

Lastly, on strange impulse, I did the same to my sister, who stepped back with a quizzical look.

"What happened?" she asked.

"Nothing," I said, shaking my head at my obvious injuries, and pushing away the image of the weeping black woman straining to get to her dead child on the raft. "I'm just glad to see you all. Here."

I fumbled in my pocket for the purse of coins I had brought, but Rahvey glared at me and shooed the three older girls away.

"Go and play," she said. "See who can find the oldest grave."

"What?" I said, as soon as they were out of earshot.

"I don't want them to know you are giving us money," she said, still frowning as if I had done something wrong. "I don't want them thinking they are living off charity."

My turn to frown. This was typical of Rahvey. She didn't want handouts, but neither would she acknowledge that her husband was shiftless and qualified for nothing that would put food on the table.

"This was part of the arrangement," I said. "So no one can complain that a fourth daughter is too much of a drain on your household."

"You don't have to wave it like a flag," she shot back. Her pride was stung.

"I'm sorry," I said. "Maybe one day the girls will find work of their own and you won't need my . . . whatever I can bring."

Rahvey harrumphed and sat on the ground beside me, gathering her skirts. Maybe her annoyance wasn't really about the money. I saw the way her eyes lingered on my sling.

"Doing what?" she said, as if to make sure I hadn't guessed she was concerned about me. "I had thought that Radesh might find a place at Sorenson's, but they are saying that no child under ten can work there anymore. Is that true?"

It was. The law was newly passed, pushed by a bipartisan committee on which Willinghouse sat. He said this was a breakthrough in labor law designed to prevent the exploitation of the poor. I didn't know about that, but a lot of families in the Drowning counted on the meager income from positions that would now be closed to them. I shifted in my seat and just said, "That's what I heard too."

"Mrs. Singh's girls both lost their jobs," said Rahvey. "They don't know what they will do. You can't blame Sorenson's. They have always been a good employer. It's the government."

"Weren't the children being paid a fraction of what adults would get for the same work?"

"So? They were being paid. That's the point," said Rahvey. "Now they have nothing. Mr. Singh hasn't been able to work since the accident, and Mrs. Singh was already working at the fruit stall on the Etembe market *and* cleaning houses. In *Morgessa*," she added, as if that showed the full indignity of the situation. Morgessa was a respectable working-class district in the northwest corner of the city, but it was also largely black. "And her with mouths to feed and a house to keep. It's scandalous!"

I watched a red hornbill, its beak as long as its body, take flight across the cemetery and alight on a roughly carved grave marker. I didn't know what to say to Rahvey. The thought of trying to talk to her about the city's various ills wearied me. But there was something I wanted to discuss and now seemed as good a time as any.

"The other part of the arrangement," I said, "when I brought Kalla to you, I mean, was that she would one day go to school."

Rahvey was immediately on her guard. She turned to watch the laughing children as if suddenly concerned for their safety.

"Yes," she said. "So? Not now."

"Well, obviously," I replied, "but maybe, since the older girls can't work, it might be worth considering for them."

"Send Radesh to school?" she repeated, incredulous. "Where?"

"Hillstreet or Truth Mountain," I ventured.

"Black schools," said Rahvey dismissively. "And Truth Mountain is run by Pancaris. I thought you didn't like them?"

It wasn't a real question. She was merely throwing up roadblocks.

"If the girls were educated, they would have more options when they are old enough to work," I said. "In the process, they are off your hands, learning about the world, learning to read and do math—"

"They can learn about the world right here," said Rahvey, her faced closed. "Or is that not the world you want them to learn about?" I couldn't think of a response to that. Rahvey nodded thoughtfully as if I had said something hurtful. "Right," she said. "You just keep the money coming, doing . . . whatever it is you do, and I'll look after my daughters."

"I'm not trying to take them away from you, Rahvey," I said.

"You couldn't," she snapped back.

"I know that," I said. "You are a good mother. I've told you that before."

"Then why do you always question the way I raise them?"

"Because you are too much a slave to habit," I said, my anger blossoming suddenly. "Because you still assume the old ways are the best even as the world changes around us. Some people travel halfway across the country to be in the city specifically so they can send their children to school and build a better life for them—"

"Different," said Rahvey. "You don't know it will be better."

Something in her tone stripped me of my fury. She looked down at the sleeping baby in her arms, and her face held not defiance, but doubt and fear.

"That's true," I said, softening my voice. "Different is not necessarily better. But when what you see ahead is—" She shot me a warning glance, and I changed tack. "Sometimes a change is worth the risk."

No reply. She seemed to think about this as her gaze slid back to Kalla. She smiled faintly, like someone catching the distant strains of an old, familiar song.

THE CITY PROPER WAS packed with factories where the Lani girls could work one day. I was wary of being seen there, around my old stomping ground, and decided to cross the river using the incom-

plete suspension bridge. Under a sooty pall that hung over the riverbank like a shroud, I walked up to Dagenham Steps, almost directly
across from the spot where I had been attacked the previous evening.
I looked out toward the city side, scanning the bank with my pocket
spyglass. The fog hadn't thickened yet, but I could make out a pod of
about fifteen hippos, one of which may have been the one that had
menaced me the night before. Down by the jetty, the coast guard
boats were moored and quiet. There was no sign of either the refugees or the makeshift vessel they had arrived on, and I wondered
whether they had perhaps crossed over to this side. Considering this
as I looked up and down the south bank shingle, I saw something out
of place. Three pairs of water-stained sandals were lined carefully up
on the shore, as if their owners—children, judging by the size—had
just gone swimming. But no one was in the water, and the sandals
each had a clutch of flowers in them.

I wandered to where a lone, helmeted white police officer kept
watch over the scene. He ignored me till I spoke.

"What happened to them?" I asked.

"Who?"

"The people who arrived this morning."

"Friends of yours, were they?" he said. A joke, of sorts. "Rounded
up and ferried over to this side and a camp in Blackstairs till the politicians decide who's going to pay their transit back. Well out of the
way so they don't stink up the city."

"There was a woman," I said, not sure how to phrase it. "She
seemed . . . I think her child . . . Did any of them die?"

He looked at me directly then and shrugged deliberately, defiantly.

"Rusty pieces of *kanti*," he said, daring me to argue. "What kind
of idiot would think you could go hundred of miles at sea in those?"

"I don't suppose they get a lot of boat choices," I said.

The policeman flexed his back and tipped his head from side to
side. His neck made a sharp popping sound while he thought of a
witty comeback.

"Should find better travel agents, shouldn't they?" he said, smirking.

I bit the inside of my cheek till I could taste blood.

He glanced down at me. "What?" he demanded. "I don't recall inviting them, do you? I don't see why law-abiding citizens of Bar-Selehm should have to deal with the likes of them. Coming here," he muttered scornfully, "taking our jobs, bringing their drugs, their thieving, hooligan children—"

"Maybe if you knew more about what they were running *from*—" I began. He stepped toward me, one hand dropping to the truncheon he wore on a leather thong at his waist. "You questioning the judgment of a uniformed officer?" he asked with studied pleasantness, as if I was fulfilling something he had dearly wanted to do for weeks. "A Lani street urchin—or worse—with the brass to contradict a member of the city's constabulary! Tempting fate, little girl."

"Is there a problem, Constable?"

The voice—male, authoritative—came from behind me. I turned to see a black man in a navy blue soldier's uniform trimmed with gold and crimson. He did not smile when he saw me, but that was because of the policeman. He knew me well enough. His name was Tsanwe Emtezu, Corporal in the King's Third Feldesland Infantry Regiment, and we had had dealings before.

"No, sir," said the policeman, slightly discomfited. "This girl was being a mite impertinent, but I see no reason to pursue the matter."

"Really?" said Emtezu. "In my experience, Miss Sutonga has been nothing but respectful."

"You know her?" he said, his voice mixed with incredulity and a disdain for the soldier as well as for me.

Emtezu's chiseled face tightened as if he had bitten down hard, then flickered into the briefest and most knowing of smiles.

"I have that privilege," he said.

The policeman's smirk was barely concealed. "In *my* experience,"

he said, "getting to know a Lani street whore doesn't take much privilege."

Emtezu didn't speak, and his face did not change. He took a single
long stride and, with an extraordinary economy of movement,
gripped the policeman by the throat with one hand and twisted his
truncheon arm up behind his back with the other. The constable's
eyes widened like dinner plates.

"That," said Emtezu, his voice low and conversational, "was disrespectful. I believe you owe the young lady an apology."

"That's not necessary," I said, meaning it.

Emtezu glanced at me, held the helpless policeman for one long
second, then released him. The man crumpled, coughing, and when
he looked up his face was murderous.

"I'll report you!" he hissed, backing away. "You see if I don't."

Emtezu said nothing as the policeman finally turned from us and
began a blundering retreat, massaging his throat.

"You shouldn't have done that," I said.

"The name of the Glorious Third still carries some weight," he said
with a half shrug. "He won't report me."

"I mean you didn't need to do it," I said, torn between pleasure at
seeing him again and irritation at his high-handed defense of my
honor. "I was perfectly fine."

"He was rude."

"If you arrest every man in the city who is rude to Lani women,
you're going to need a lot more prisons."

"True," he said, adding stiffly, "I apologize if I overstepped my
bounds."

I shook my head.

"It is good to see you," I said, beaming. "How is your wife? Your
children?"

"Well," he said, stooping to brush a fine gray dust from his regu-
lation boots, "Clara, my wife, is looking for work. That's why I am

here." He paused and checked the stained clock on the tower of the Sarnulf paper mill. "She should be finished. Walk with me. I am sure you have many interesting things to tell me. I confess, I have looked for your name in the papers many times since we last spoke, but it seems you have managed to keep what they call a *low profile*. I doubt this means you have been inactive."

I just grinned at him, matching his measured step as we moved up from the river and into the street behind the waterfront factories, which was choked with wagons pulled by blinkered horses and orleks. The river at our backs vanished behind ungainly brick structures. Once red, now tar-black with ingrained soot, uneven, and marked with clumsy towers and eccentric cupolas, the whole thing looked like a landscape thrown together by a child with blocks.

"I see," he said, with a shrug and half smile. "I will let you keep your secrets. There is this," he added, tapping the stripes on his shoulder. "Sergeant."

"Everyone's getting promoted," I said. He gave me a sidelong look, and I shook my head, smiling. "Congratulations. It was well deserved."

"Not everyone thinks so," he said, "but it spares their blushes."

The commanders of Emtezu's regiment had been involved in some shady business, which had reflected badly on the outfit.

"Can I ask you something?" I said.

"Certainly."

"What do you know about machine guns?"

He gave me a curious glance and another half shrug.

"What do you want to know? We have four at the regiment. I do not like them particularly."

"Why not?" I asked.

"Wasteful weapons," he said. "A rifleman knows he has one bullet before he has to reload, so he makes it count. Machine gunners think that since they can fire three or four times for the rifleman's one, they don't need to be accurate."

"If someone was to make a better machine gun, what would they focus on?"

"Speed of fire," he said. "You could make the weapon lighter, more accurate, or with greater range, but to make it fire faster without overheating or jamming is what the soldiers want."

"Jamming?"

"The cartridges go into a hopper above the gun," he said. "You turn a handle to feed each round into the weapon, but the cartridges get turned around or go in two at a time. . . . They lock up the mechanism and make it impossible to fire. Wait here for one moment."

We were standing outside a great brick building with high windows and a tall, round chimney from which dark smoke drifted on the morning air, feeding the infamous Bar-Selehm smog. Emtezu had hurried to where his wife stood with another black woman, bigger, stronger looking. I watched the three of them talking, remembering that awful night when I had seen one of those hopper-fed machine guns in action, the noise, the deadly efficiency of the thing. . . .

And then Emtezu was hugging his wife and waving me over.

"She got the job!" he said. "Clara, you remember Miss Sutonga."

"I do," she said, offering me her hand. "And this is our neighbor, Bertha Dinangwe. She arranged my interview."

"Pleased to meet you," I said, offering my hand to the woman.

"What?" she shouted back.

"I said I'm pleased to meet you," I repeated.

The woman looked vaguely at Clara.

"She says she's *pleased to meet you*," Clara yelled. Turning back to me, she said apologetically, "it is so *loud* inside. I hadn't realized it would be so loud. The machines. You can't hear yourself think."

She ended with a look at her husband that was loaded with something more complex than the simple joy which had been there a moment before: resignation, perhaps, sadness? It was good that she had gotten the job, but she didn't want it. Not really.

"What does the factory make?" I asked, trying to bring something of her delight back.

"Cloth," she said simply. "Cotton cloth. In two weeks, I will be a weaver."

"What?" asked Bertha.

"A WEAVER," said Clara.

"No," boomed Bertha, smiling. "You'll be a WEAVER."

"Yes," said Clara, her smile tiring. "I will. It's good to have work."

"Yes," I said. "It is."

I turned and caught Sergeant Emtezu watching me shrewdly, his eyes full of questions. He said nothing, but I knew he was thinking about machine guns.

CHAPTER

5

I WANTED TO HEAR all Willinghouse had learned about the circumstances surrounding Darius's theft of the machine gun plans, but I knew he would not be home yet, so I decided to do something I had never done before: see him at work. Discreetly, of course. It would do his reputation no good at all—as well as blowing my cover as a detective, spy, or whatever I was—for him to be seen whispering in doorways with a Lani steeplejack.

The Parliament House stood at the end of the broad stone-paved and statued thoroughfare which was Grand Parade between Cannonade and Occupation Row and I arrived as an army of Lani street sweepers were being replaced by men in suits and a squad of ceremonial guardsmen. The building was 120 years old, built on the site of the old Administrative Center as the government had swelled to meet the demands of the similarly swollen, and increasingly independent, city. Bar-Selehm was just too far from Belrand, separated by too much ocean, Feldish jungle scrub, desert, and rival entities, human and animal. It had gorged itself like a leech, growing ponderous and unwieldy, so that though we remained a nominal part of Belrand, they acted less like the proud parent they had once been and more like an older sibling: stronger, wiser, perhaps, but without our vigor. If we hadn't stopped paying our taxes into their administrative systems a century ago, we would, like most siblings, have surely come to blows. The Parliament House modeled the city's curious separateness, its halls and towers shaped from a russet and pink local stone, but fashioned and trimmed in the old and fussy Belrandian style. The result, though dark now from the perpetual smoke of the city, was as unique as it was imposing, an architectural anthem breathing grandeur and formally restrained power.

I stood in the blacks and coloreds line for the public entrance under the watchful eye of a half dozen armed dragoons who took our bags and gave us reclamation tickets. They operated with an officiousness designed to make us feel small and irrelevant, as if the great stone portico alone was insufficient. They counted us in to the public galleries which, combined, amounted to less than a quarter of the space allocated to the whites' section, and then divided us into male and female. I was the only woman in the colored section: a solitary bench at the back of the gallery.

I should have felt outraged, I supposed, but I could not quite escape a sense of confused awe, which filled the air like cigar smoke, heady and aromatic. The staircases and hallways were lined with monumental oil paintings of both heads of state and abstract ideas personified: liberty, justice, and fortitude, all modeled by women with spears and shields, their white nakedness discreetly draped with swaths of fabric like curtains or flags. The galleries looked down into the parliamentary chamber. Three hundred seats were arranged around a podium and desk where two men sat, one with a stack of large leather-bound books, the other beside a stand holding a ceremonial gold-hilted sword. The seats showed their party affiliation with a braided cord: Red—the most numerous—for the ruling National party, led by the prime minister, Benjamin Tavestock. Blue for the Brevard opposition (Willinghouse's party). There was a handful of silver, which stood for an affiliation I did not know, and a solitary green cord for the recently appointed leader of the Unassimilated Mahweni Tribes, the only black man on the floor. I did not know his name and wondered suddenly if Mnenga had been involved in his selection.

You should find him and ask, I thought.

I had first thought Mnenga just a stray villager with a flock of nbezu to tend, but it had become clear that he had been sent to monitor events affecting his people. I never found out how he had been selected for that task or whether he might one day be more than the herder I had taken him for.

You never found out, a bitter voice in my head reminded me, *because you never asked.*

I frowned at the truth of the observation.

The man sitting beside the sword got to his feet and called for order, banging a little wooden hammer on the desk until the burble of conversation dropped to nothing. He consulted his notes and announced, "The Honorable MP for Eldritch North, Mr. Norton Richter, Heritage party, to present Bill 479—the so-called Bar-Selehm First Act—for final debate and voting."

I watched as a slim, middle-aged man got out of one of the silver-trimmed seats and approached the podium, taking a pair of spectacles from his pocket and slipping them on.

Heritage party.

I realized that the gray suits they all wore were curiously similar, less, in fact, like suits and more like uniforms with silver buttons and black trim. They wore ties with enamel shield-shaped pins in red and silver, though I could not make out the details.

Norton Richter, the Heritage party leader, cleared his throat and read from a sheet.

"Thank you, My Lord Secretary," he said. "The third reading of the bill having met with sufficient support to merit a general vote, I hereby present Bill 479 for the House's consideration. The bill's summary—the full text of which has been circulated among all members—reads thus: 'That in response to the dramatic increase in foreign immigration into Bar-Selehm, much of it illegal; to race-related protests, often violent and destructive; and according to a time frame to be decided by the House, all people living within two miles of this estimable House shall have ancestry demonstrably rooted in Panbroke, and that those failing to prove such ancestry shall be relocated outside the city walls or to the south bank of the river Kalihm.'"

He lowered the paper and whipped off his glasses as a murmur went round the chamber.

The man Richter had called "My Lord Secretary" looked up and said, "Bill 479 is now open for final debate, which will be limited to one half hour before voting commences." Several men left their seats immediately, but in the shuffling that followed, the lord secretary identified one in the Brevard ranks who had raised his hand.

"The Honorable MP for Tulketh Brow, Jeromius Truit, Brevard," said the secretary.

"I wonder," said Truit, "if the honorable gentleman from Eldritch North has looked at a map of the city lately. If he had, he would realize that much of the district he has specified contains the abodes of citizens of Mahweni and Lani origin, many of whom work locally. Far from being an anti-immigration bill as he suggests, this would seem to be an attempt to create an all-white enclave within the city."

"Your question?" prompted the secretary.

"Certainly," said the MP. "Did the honorable gentleman think we wouldn't notice?"

There was much chuckling at this. Richter smiled knowingly, and replied in the same measured tones. "I can't say that I had noticed that particular implication," he said, to much laughter and jeering from the Brevard side, "though I think we might consider it a happy accident. Bar-Selehm is a thriving city with many places of employment outside the recommended limits should the current factories prove inconvenient for those required to relocate."

More laughter. I glanced around. Richter's companions in the silver braided seats looked pleased with themselves, which was—I suppose—to be expected, but I was alarmed at how many in the red seats seemed to find the matter jolly amusing. I looked up and scanned the faces in the public galleries. The whites were divided in their mood, but the black and colored were all watchful and somber. A handful of Lani men I did not know—one was dressed as an elder—sat motionless on the other side of the divide from me, faces set, eyes boring into the chamber below us.

"The Honorable MP for Bar-Selehm Northeast, Josiah Willinghouse, Brevard," said the secretary.

Willinghouse's name brought my focus back to the floor. I sensed a ripple of interest pulse through the room, a slight leaning forward in the colored gallery, and a slight leaning back in the red seats. Either way, they thought something interesting was coming. Willinghouse was, as I said, one quarter Lani.

"Speaking as one of only two people currently on the floor likely to feel a personal impact from this bill," he said, his tone full but frosty, his eyes hard, and with the smallest of nods toward the representative of the unassimilated Mahweni, "I would like to register not so much my doubts about its fiscal or administrative difficulty, which cluttered previous debates on this matter, but its essential moral wrongness. I am appalled that this house believes the matter worth serious consideration, and I urge my colleagues on both sides of the aisle to decisively and unequivocally reject the proposed bill on the grounds of its fundamental inhumanity." This brought murmurs of agreement from his own party and applause from the black men in the public gallery, which earned three loud strikes of the secretary's gavel.

"May I remind the public that their role here is strictly observational," said the secretary, eyeing the upper story sternly. "Further disruption will force me to clear the galleries. You have been warned. Mr. Willinghouse, you may conclude your question, assuming there is one."

Another ripple of amusement, which Willinghouse had to override.

"There is," he said, "though it is less, perhaps, for the Honorable MP for Eldritch North, who has proved himself unwilling or incapable of any scrutiny of beliefs so heinous—"

He did not get to finish the sentence, as the Heritage party roared their fury, supported by many of the National party members, and order was only restored with more thumping of the secretary's gavel followed by another strident warning.

"I would remind the honorable gentleman of the rules of conduct of this chamber," he said, eyeing Willinghouse. "Personal attacks and other forms of incivility will not be permitted. Pray conclude your question."

"I apologize for my *incivility*," said Willinghouse, biting off the last word like a jackal and spitting it out. "I sometimes forget the way that House decorum takes precedence over honesty—"

Another boiling of discontent erupted, and the secretary beat his desk once more.

"Mr. Willinghouse," he exclaimed, "you will follow the procedural norms of this chamber, or you will be removed, sir. Ask your question."

"My question," said Willinghouse, composing himself, "is this. What kind of world do we want to live in? The strength of Bar-Selehm is its people, regardless of color or creed. You speak of illegal immigration, of racially based resentments that have sparked protests and yes, sometimes, violence, but we do not end the root causes of that discontent by closing our doors against the unfortunate who wish to build a better life here or by pushing those who once owned this land aside, turning a blind eye to their concerns, and adding to the daily injustices they suffer by banishing them from the city they have helped to build. This assembly should yoke its energies to redressing the grievances of those less fortunate and of those who, though less well represented by this chamber, have to live by the consequences of its decisions. It is abominable, sir! And the day we must prove our ancestry to gain any kind of privilege is the day we shelve our common humanity. To vote for this bill assumes that you are more important than the Mahweni, the Lani, or those who flock to our shores daily to escape the horrors of their own world, but such a vote does not make you more. Indeed, it shows you to be less!"

And then the chamber exploded in shouting. Defiant applause rang down from the black and colored galleries; boos and hisses rang out from the chamber below, particularly from the silver seats, but also from many in the red, and even a few in the blue who were more than a little affronted. The secretary rose and, getting no peace with his gavel, raised the golden-hilted sword, whereupon the great doors of the chamber boomed open and dragoons marched in. As one went to escort Willinghouse from the room, others appeared in the galleries, ordering us out, truncheons drawn.

"SO," I SAID TO Willinghouse. "That went well."

We were sitting outside in a rear courtyard, waiting till it was Willinghouse's time to vote and watching the brown industrial fog of the city thickening around us as the day warmed up.

"Stupid of me," he muttered, though his face showed no contrition, only the burning anger that had flared when he made his speech. "Madness. But what did they expect? How can we sit around debating such things as if we are civilized people? It's monstrous."

"How will the vote go?" I asked.

"Richter will lose," said Willinghouse. "This time. There are enough men of good conscience among the Nationals to ensure he does not get their full support, but it will be closer than I would like, and he will be back soon enough. He already has another bill on the docket proposing increased trade with the Grappoli."

"But he's a nationalist. I'd think he would hate the Grappoli."

"He says they are our *natural allies* on the continent," said Willinghouse bitterly. "Meaning racial allies. Anyone from Panbroke, however greedy and merciless, is—to him—a more suitable ally than anyone—"

"Brown," I concluded for him. "Or black."

Even in his anger, the baldness of the statement seemed to embarrass him. He nodded and sighed. "We have a noninterference treaty with the Grappoli, which basically says that so long as what either of us does doesn't directly involve the other, we stay out of each other's way."

"Which is why we're sitting on the sidelines while they tear through the tribal lands in the north," I said.

"Richter wants to expand the treaty," said Willinghouse. "Turn it into an alliance. And we have an election coming. Look to see the Heritage party make greater inroads into the House until the Nationals feel more and more compelled to take them seriously."

"That would be good for you, wouldn't it, dividing their supporters?"

"In the short term," he said. "But one day we may find ourselves looking at a National-Heritage Alliance with Richter at the head, and that would be calamitous for the city." He paused to reflect on this, then turned back to me, as if just realizing who I was. "Why are you here?" he asked. "We should not be seen together, especially since I have attracted so much . . . attention."

"I wanted to get more details about the theft of the—"

"Not now," he said, looking quickly around. "I have to vote, and then I have been summoned to the whip's office, where I will be lectured on maintaining the dignity of the Brevard party."

"I will go," I said. "You have enough to worry about."

He nodded, his green eyes thoughtful and sad, and then said, "Thank you."

CHAPTER

6

I WROTE TO MNENGA at last, figuring I could send it care of the Mahweni trading post near Thremsburg. Someone would know where he was. I sat at my writing desk, staring at the blank sheet of paper, slightly ragged down the left side, and dipped my pen in an inkwell I had borrowed from my landlady.

My Dearest Mnenga, I wrote.

I stared at the words, then snatched the paper up and crumpled it into a ball. I took out a new sheet and began again.

Dear Mnenga, I wrote. *I do not know if this will reach you, so I will be brief. It seems like it has been years since I saw you last, and I think there are things I should say, things I meant to say before but didn't. I am sorry for that. I never thanked you properly for your help, your support, and I fear you will think me ungrateful, even rude. Worse, I fear that you might have thought that I exploited or otherwise manipulated your feelings for me . . .*

I stopped, rereading what I had written. The words were all wrong. My handwriting looked childish in its formal care, as if I was some Clock Street girl writing home for an advance on her allowance. I dipped the pen and wrote with quicker, more fluid strokes. *What I mean to say is that I miss you and hope that I see you soon. You are still very dear to me*—that word again, I thought, annoyed at my own incompetence—*which is to say I like you very much, even if I don't exactly feel the way I think you might prefer*—

I cursed, snatched up the letter, screwed it into a tight ball, and thrust it into the waste basket on the floor, shoving the chair back and getting to my feet, muttering expletives. It was hopeless. However much I had grown in confidence, in presence, since entering

Willinghouse's employ, I still found that I would rather scale a two-hundred-foot chimney without rope or harness than unpack my heart in words.

I moved to the window.

MY AFORESAID EMPLOYER HAD put me up in rented rooms across the street from the Market Street Koresh, where some of the city Mahweni worshipped, called to prayer twice daily with the tolling of a gonglike bell up in a cobalt blue, tulip-topped minaret. They would file in silently in their drab work clothes, the men and women entering by separate doors. What they did in there I didn't really know, though it seemed sedate, unlike the Lani religious festivals I had known growing up. So far as I understood it, their religion—Bashtara, it was called—was in many ways closer to the northern beliefs of the white Feldeslanders than it was to the fertility, ancestor, and animal worship practiced by the Unassimilated Tribes. I found it all a bit bemusing, and—when their bells woke me at first light on days I really could have used the rest—a little tiresome.

I parted the thin curtains and looked down into the street, the quiet crowd flowing steadily into the Koresh, and I rolled my injured shoulder experimentally. It ached, if less fiercely, and I wondered how many hours of sleep I had actually been able to get. The hospital staff had sent me home with a paper of powders to numb the pain, but I had opted not to take them. Yawning and gazing out into the rapidly warming morning with bleary eyes, feeling my shoulder begin to grumble with the slightest movement, that was beginning to look like a bad decision.

I washed with a jug and basin and dressed, the twinge in my shoulder slowing me, making me cautious. It was annoying. I had not intended to keep wearing the sling, but that looked like another bad idea. I put it on, took the powders after all, locked my room, and trudged wearily down to the dining room, where I helped myself to honey, yogurt, flat bread, and starfruit washed down with two cups of spiced chai. After years of gruel, crusts, and what I could pilfer from the market, this breakfast, simply—almost magically—laid out by Mrs. Topesh, the landlady, felt like a feast, a secret and luxurious discovery, as if someone had mistaken me for an adult. Or a white person. It never failed to raise my spirits.

The boardinghouse was famously quiet. Mrs. Topesh insisted upon it, demanding a kind of civility better suited to rather more respectable lodgings. There were eight rooms, all singles: three black girls who worked as servants in neighboring houses and shops; two older women who were part of the weavers' guild and had positions at one of the Fourth Street factories; two unmarried black men, one a steel worker, the other a butcher for the Bashtara community; and an elderly white man, widowed. Mrs. Topesh spoke to them all with the same benevolent politeness—her manner as rare as the mere existence of the boardinghouse she maintained. Chitchat, especially between the sexes, was frowned upon, however. That suited me just fine. My life had changed drastically since I had been a steeplejack for the Seventh Street gang, but I was no more social now than I had been. I relished my privacy, even if I felt like an imposter in the scrubbed silence of Mrs. Topesh's rooms.

My temperament and lack of social skills could be, however, a liability—one Willinghouse was apparently looking to solve so that I could find my way into Elitus. A note, folded discreetly and brought to my table on a tarnished silver tray by a wordless Mrs. Topesh, told me to report to Willinghouse's town home at ten. I knew better than to thank the landlady in words and merely inclined my head a fraction. She returned the gesture and slid away, as if she was waiting on some dowager duchess.

That Willinghouse wanted to see me right away suggested he had an idea, which made me feel both a thrill of anticipation and a hint of panic. I wanted to get a look at the inside of Elitus and see if the bland assassin with the pick would show his face there, but if the club was as exclusive as he had suggested, I would be badly out of my element, and not only because I was brown. The world of silks and jewelry and sophisticated banter was something I had only read about in books or seen dimly reflected in Vestris.

The association made me uneasy. I had looked up to my eldest sister, idolized her, but she had not been the person I had taken her for. She had been, in fact, my opposite, and with no other options left to me—or so I continued to tell myself—I had left her to die for it. I would not become her just to get into some fancy club.

The stand in the gloomy downstairs hallway, its air already smudged by tendrils of the city's penetrating smog, held the morning's paper. I saw the headline—DARIUS IDENTIFIED—and picked it up.

The infamous cat burglar who captured the imagination of Bar-Selehm until his mysterious death has been identified as one Karl Gillies, 31, a sign writer from the Hastingford District, by his tearful fiancée, Leticia Jones, 22. His employer, David Vandemar of Vandemar Paint and Signage, expressed his considerable surprise and disillusionment at the revelation of his erstwhile employee's nocturnal activities and hoped that the city would not hold it against a company with a reputation for fine and reasonably priced work.

I considered this, feeling the paper's palpable disappointment that the "gentleman thief" had turned out to be among the city's poorest white people, no more than a jobbing day laborer who had used the climbing skills developed while painting hoardings and advertising panels to pilfer from the rich and respectable. I knew that the people who had discussed Darius's exploits with such breathless excitement would have no interest at all in Karl Gillies. A chapter of the city's history had just closed forever. The headline below it read HERITAGE

SUPPORTERS PROTEST DEFEAT OF SEGREGATION BILL. That chapter was still very much open.

I scanned the paper throughout, but saw no reference to the flower-filled sandals on the riverbank, or what might have happened to the people who had owned them.

AS USUAL, I MADE my way to Willinghouse's home by a series of back streets that took me all the way from Szenga Square almost to the north wall and east, approaching the elegant town house from the rear. The scullery maid let me in through the tradesmen's entrance and showed me into the kitchen; the butler—there was no other suitable name for him—told me to go through to the drawing room, where I was to begin my instruction. In spite of my former anxieties, I followed him down the carpeted hall with mounting excitement. That was doused the moment I knocked on the paneled door and stepped inside. The room was empty save for a single person perched on an overstuffed love seat and smirking like a cat that had gotten into a cage full of songbirds.

Dahria.

She was poised and elegant, beautiful in a chill, aristocratic way, and dressed in a cream-colored tea gown with dainty shoes and preposterous elbow-length gloves.

"You?" I exclaimed.

"You may call me Professor," she cooed, delighted by my outrage.

"Do you think I'm likely to?"

"I think you are in my brother's employ," she said, smiling wider still, "and that if you hope to remain so, you will undergo this course of instruction with focus and deliberation, lest you fail to attain passing marks."

"I can't do this," I said. "Not with you."

"Now, that's the Lani street brat in you talking. An aristocratic lady can do anything she puts her mind to."

I bristled at the remark, and she beamed.

"Why doesn't he just send you?" I demanded. "You are much paler than me."

"Because, Miss Sutonga, while a member of Bar-Selehm's ruling class despite being tainted by my grandmother's Lani blood, I am known. You are not."

She said it matter-of-factly, used to the idea that the people she spent much of her time with probably thought her somehow less than they were. She smiled again, and this time it was a brittle, knowing look that made her brown eyes hard.

"Then he should find someone else," I said. "There must be some suitable white person he could pay as an informant."

"Possibly," she answered, "but my brother puts a lot of store in trust. He trusts you. I'm not entirely sure why, but there it is."

"His trust won't get me into Elitus," I said.

"No," she agreed, "but some training and a little creativity might."

"Creativity?"

"You will go in not as Anglet Sutonga, but as Lady Ki Misrai—"

"That won't help!"

"From Istilia."

That stopped me. Istilia is a small kingdom in the northeast of Lanaria, the ancestral homeland of the Lani, a vast subcontinent located hundreds of miles off the eastern coast of Feldesland. I knew little about it, my people having left centuries before I was born, brought to Feldesland to help the white colonists build the infrastructure of Bar-Selehm. They were imported as something as close to being slaves as was technically possible and driven with the promise of a better life, which for most of them, had never materialized. I thought of the Lani as poor, downtrodden, and politically powerless, but that was because I knew only what we were here. Istilia was a different world entirely.

"Would that make a difference to Elitus?" I asked.

"Let's call this lesson one," said Dahria. "Elitus, like all subsets of high society, is driven by self-interest and exclusivity. Racism is endemic in such places of course, but among such people it usually bows before snobbery. As you are now, they would bolt the doors to keep you out. But as a young Istilian princess trailing the exotic whiff of a distant land where she sleeps on beds of rubies? Yes, I think we might just get you in. If you can learn not to fart in public or put your work boots up on the supper table."

"I do *not*—" I began, catching myself at her grin. This was going to take patience.

"Why don't you have a seat," she said. "You loom. Did you know that? It's not very ladylike."

A lot of patience.

I sat in the wingchair opposite her. She pulled a face.

"Let's try it again," she said, "only this time, let's try to settle into the chair like a person, not like a sack of root vegetables being dumped into a cellar."

I bit my tongue, got awkwardly to my feet, and sat again.

"Hmmm," she mused. "Sitting is apparently too advanced. Let's save that for another day. Let's practice standing. No, not like a statue. Not like that either," she said, watching as I adjusted self-consciously. "Are you made of steel? And must you have your feet so far apart? It's really most unseemly. I'm sure I don't know where to look. No, not with your weight on one hip! You look like you're about to light a pipe and offer to carry my case. Good grief, woman, look at yourself! You look like an off-balance crane poised to fall and kill the bystanders."

"That has a kind of appeal," I said.

"Then let us hope I die at the hands of an Istilian aristocrat, and not a Lani steeplejack. I don't think I could bear the shame." She got to her feet, a fluid, easy movement that left her straight but composed, elbows drawn in, hands crossed demurely below her waist.

"Perhaps if you did things other than sitting and standing around," I remarked, "you'd be less particular about them."

"I suppose we'll never know," she replied. "Relax your shoulders and straighten your back. Chest up, stomach flat. Chin level with the floor, head centered over your feet."

"This hurts."

"Good. We learn nothing in life from what comes easily. Keep still. I'm going to balance a book on your head."

"Or you could put a knife through my ribs," I muttered through clenched teeth.

"All in good time," she said. "Now, keep your chin up."

She set a heavy book on top of my head and carefully drew her hands away.

"Better," she said, smiling. "Doesn't that feel better?"

"No."

"Well, it looks better, and that's what counts. Now take a step toward the fireplace."

The book fell. Of course the book fell. I considered picking it up and throwing it at her, but I knew that would just give her more opportunities to criticize my posture. Dahria gave me a withering look, and at that moment, we heard the distant creak and thud of the front door. Her expression slipped back into secret pleasure.

"What?" I asked, immediately suspicious. "Who is here?"

"Your dressmaker," said Dahria, looking my old, masculine clothes up and down scornfully. "Didn't think you were going to Elitus dressed like that, did you?"

Though I had not actually been a steeplejack for months, I still wore the clothes of one: charcoal gray jacket and trousers, heavy leather belt, heavier boots. I tipped my head back, eyes closed, and exhaled showily.

"Oh, spare me the theatrics," Dahria said, going to the door. "Most girls your age would kill to get to dress as you will be doing."

"I'm not most girls," I shot back.

"On that, Miss Sutonga, you have my complete agreement."

It wasn't a compliment.

The door opened, but it wasn't the dressmaker. It was Willinghouse. His sister's momentary joy was instantly replaced by bored irritation, and she threw herself into a chair, closely mimicking my earlier performance of root-vegetables-going-into-the-cellar.

"What do you want?" she demanded. "We were just about to have a little fun for once."

His eyes flicked to mine and his face managed to acknowledge that my idea of fun and Dahria's might be different.

"I sent the dressmaker away," he said.

"You did what?" Dahria demanded, her spine stiffening.

"I'm not comfortable with Miss Sutonga's comings and goings to this house being observed by every servant and street person in the district," he said. "I include your gossipy dressmaker. We should reconvene at the estate, away from prying eyes."

"The *estate?*" Dahria exclaimed, disbelieving. "And who there, pray, has the skills to dress an Istilian princess?"

Willinghouse took a breath and gave her a level look.

"You must be joking," said Dahria with a disbelieving stare.

"It's safer this way," said Willinghouse. "We can't have Miss Sutonga associated with this house."

"Joss!" she exclaimed. It took me a moment to realize that she meant him. Josiah. The nickname humanized them both, and for a second he looked ordinary and abashed.

"It's the only way, Dahria," he said, recovering his dignity. "You'll need to go too, of course," he added, not looking at her.

"No!" said Dahria. "You wouldn't. You will not send me to that place with . . . her."

Again it took me a second to realize that the pronoun was not directed at me.

"Her?" I inquired.

Dahria glowered at her brother and there was a long, smoldering silence.

"Fine," she said at last, ignoring me. "I will babysit the steeplejack in the wilderness with *that woman,* but don't expect me to like it."

She swept out, slamming the door behind her.

"My dear sister," muttered Willinghouse after her, "I would expect nothing less."

"Er . . . ?" I began. "Who is *that woman*? And . . . wilderness?"

CHAPTER

7

I WAS, AS I have said, a city girl. Yes, the Drowning, and the other edges of Bar-Selehm blurred the idea of city to breaking point. And yes, the riverbanks were almost always wild places even when they fell within the limits of the town, but I had spent the bulk of my life surrounded by brick and iron, cobbles and concrete. The bush and, more particularly, the creatures that called it home, frightened me.

As they should have. Mine was no irrational phobia, nor was it the paranoid anxiety of the cossetted and civilized. I knew danger, after all, in all its city forms, from the long fall that haunted all steeple-jacks to the footpads and degenerates who might be skulking in any dark alley. They were the monsters I had grown up around and, since they were predictable perils, I had learned strategies for keeping them at arm's length.

The beasts of the grasslands and scrub forest, however, were any-thing but predictable, and I avoided them by staying away from the places they called home. Some of the white city folk romanticized wild animals, but if the Lani had learned anything from the black Mahweni who were native to this land, it was a healthy—and fearful—respect for the elephants, weancats, clavtar, snakes, and one-horns that roamed the land around Bar-Selehm. I had spent my life avoid-ing what Dahria had referred to as the wilderness. The prospect of venturing into it in order to learn how to better play a civilized lady at an elite club was more than ironic. It was terrifying.

Just once, I thought, *it would be good for my task to be somewhere familiar, somewhere I belong. . . .*

In my pocket I still had a single sorrel nut, a gift from Mnenga, and I took it out now and felt it, hard and smooth between my fingers. I told myself I carried it as an emergency ration, a tiny mouthful that would give me a little strength if I had no other food, but that was a lie. I kept it because it reminded me of him, a young man who seemed to take his village with him everywhere he went, always at ease, always sure of who he was. Or so it seemed to me. Maybe he was as lost as I was. Maybe his people thought of home less as a place and more as a set of relationships. I didn't know, and I couldn't ask him because I didn't know where he was, and that was my fault too. He had wanted to be closer, and when I did not reciprocate his feelings—*decided* not to reciprocate his feelings—he had slipped away, and I had let him. Perhaps when I returned to my rooms, I could recover my aborted letter to him, smooth it out, make it right. . . .

Willinghouse, Dahria, and I sat in silence in the family's horse-drawn carriage as we left the city behind in the softening light of the late afternoon and headed north. My employer cradled a shotgun uncertainly in his lap, his eyes fixed on the landscape outside as it rolled slowly past. Slowly, because the road deteriorated fast. Within minutes of leaving the city, we had joined an uneven turnpike paved with river rock, and a half hour after that, we took a rutted dirt road, which narrowed till the dry shrubs on either side brushed the sides of the carriage. I leaned out and looked back toward the smoggy sky over the receding city, watching its towers and chimneys through the leaves of thickening marula and thorn trees, listening to the way the distant sounds of machinery and steam engines were steadily replaced by the whine and screech of insects and birds in the tall grass. With each quarter mile I felt more uneasy, more lost, and I eventually drew my head back inside and pulled the blind down, preferring the cramped interior to all that uncluttered sky. For a while I listened to the driver murmuring encouragingly to the horses, and then we were slowing, slowing, stopping.

"What is it?" asked Dahria.

Willinghouse shook his head and leaned out to look down the

track. I had been glad of the carriage's roof and small windows, but now I felt blind and trapped. The air inside was stuffy and thick. I was reaching for the paper blind on the window when something large outside moved and cast its shadow on the translucent screen. For a moment my hand froze. I could hear Dahria and Willinghouse breathing. My hand moved again, unsteady fingers grasping the cord below the blind, releasing it, so that it furled up in a tight curl and the carriage was suddenly filled with light.

In the stillness, the snap of the blind sounded like a pistol shot. Suddenly the world outside the carriage was a chaos of leaping tan fur, pronglike antlers and dainty black hooves, perfect eye-shadow and mascara faces. Impala. Perhaps thirty of them, bolting as a herd, wheeling left and right like a flock of starlings, boiling briefly around the carriage and then vanishing into the undergrowth.

Except one. One looked back at us, at me, still and seemingly thoughtful while the others fled as if it was guarding their retreat, and something in its elegant composure made me feel better, stronger.

Willinghouse chuckled his relief and sat back, but Dahria continued to look about her, in case we might have disturbed something stalking the herd. For a second, nothing happened, and then the carriage rocked forward and recovered its former rolling pace. I found I was sweating unduly, and was grateful that I had not yet been confined to the layers of fabric, the crinoline and corsetry Dahria wore. Nonetheless, I kept the face of the sentinel impala in my mind and found myself easing out of the tension that had so gripped me since we left the city.

I had known vaguely that the town house in Bar-Selehm was not Willinghouse's ancestral home, and he had referred to the estate before, but I had assumed it was some remote ranch in the hinterlands far from the city, or somewhere close to one of the mining settlements where his family had made their fortune. I did not expect to see the stone walls, with their wrought-iron gates into which the Willinghouse crest had been woven, only an hour and a half from the city.

The driver got down and unlocked them with a heavy key taken from his waistcoat, and as we began to move again, I gave the siblings opposite me a look.

"Why don't you live here?" I asked.

"Out here?" asked Dahria, aghast. "Your sense of humor needs as much work as your posture."

"It seems nice enough," I said, feeling safer now that we were within the walls of the estate. The carriage had gone just far enough to get through the gates before the driver had climbed down again and locked them behind us.

"I prefer to be closer to the parliamentary offices," said Willing-house, "and to my constituents."

Dahria rolled her eyes.

"And I prefer neighbors who don't want to eat me," she added, leaning out and gazing down the long, straight road to where a majestic three-story house built in the white, northern style sat like a castle, waiting for us. "Ah, the ancestral pile," she observed dully. "I can feel myself getting less civilized the closer we get."

I couldn't understand her response. The house was grand, monumental. It lacked the whimsy of some of the fashionable new construction in the city, but it had a sense of weight and purpose that almost compensated for its being alien to the wildness of the Feldesland terrain around it. In the old north, such a house might have risen above ornate formal gardens with green lawns and stone cherubs in fountains, but here the grounds retained their native irregularity and intense color. What order there was came from the carefully spaced mbeco trees that lined the approach to the front door, but each one had grown in its own tangled way, and their branches had intertwined so that they formed two unbroken walls of trailing blue-white flowers. Riding between them was like being flanked by fragrant waterfalls.

"Ugh," said Dahria sourly, as she pulled the veil of her hat down over her face. "The mbecos are flowering."

"So?" I asked.

"Milk flies," she said. "In an hour, there'll be clouds of them all over the garden."

The evening was already gathering about the house, the sun painting the sky with red and gold as it dipped below the horizon.

"I think it's beautiful," I said. "All of it." It wasn't defiance. The words just came out because they were true. My love of the city was momentarily forgotten, and I felt only awe and an envious delight in what my traveling companions had grown up with. Dahria tipped her head to one side and considered me, her brow furrowed as if I had started speaking a foreign language.

"Funny," she mused. "What with all your running around and fighting for justice and whatnot, I forget that you're still basically a child."

"I'm the same age as you, near enough," I said.

"Only in years, Miss Sutonga," she replied sagely. "Only in years."

I glanced at Willinghouse.

"Do you know what that means?" I asked him.

He shook his head wearily, but Dahria had reverted to her usual, blank-eyed stare out of the window, as if she was bored by the world, exasperated by its failure to entertain her.

We pulled up to the front door, and Willinghouse urged Dahria and me into the cool, carpeted hallway while he saw to the luggage with an athletic young Lani man who made eye contact with no one but him.

"I'll send for some tea," he said, holding the door open to a well-appointed drawing room.

"Not for me," said Dahria. "I have a headache coming on. I think I'll go to bed."

"Very well," said Willinghouse. "Might I have a word first?"

She scowled at him, as if having to retrace the three steps she had taken into the room was more than any reasonable person could expect of her, sighed, then went after him. The door latched closed behind her, and I was alone in the silence.

I was reminded forcibly of the night I had been taken—blindfolded—to see Willinbghouse for the first time only a few months ago. That had been the night that changed my life. How long I could expect to put food in my belly and a roof over my head by doing odd jobs in service of the city's out-of-power political elite I had no idea, nor could I imagine what might come next. After sitting in rooms such as this, perching on the edge of an overstuffed sofa waiting for tea in fine porcelain cups and saucers to be brought by a respectful butler, it would be difficult to rejoin the steeplejacks in the smog and soot of the city's great chimneys.

Difficult, I thought, *but not impossible.* I would not allow myself to believe that I had been utterly changed by my brush with life among the aristocracy. I got up and paced the room, idly picking up the elegant, decorative knickknacks and studying the paintings on the walls, each one of which was worth more than my entire working life and probably that of everyone in my family.

Except Vestris, of course.

That was the second time I had thought of my sister today. I generally tried not to, which was probably healthy, but her face came forcibly to mind now. Had this been her world? Elegant withdrawing rooms lit by luxorite lamps, brooding family portraits, and fine carpets? Had she spent her days in chambers like these and slept in silk and down besides . . . ? Had Von Strahden been her only lover? Again, I had no idea.

I mused on this for a while, then checked the clock on the mantel. Willinghouse and Dahria had been gone ten minutes, and in their absence, I had heard no sound at all beyond the ticking. I didn't know that I had ever experienced such total silence. In the city there was always the rumble of distant machinery, trains, drunken singing, the footsteps of the night watchmen. In the Drowning, the walls of the huts were so thin and full of holes you could hear the river, the animal pens, and the snoring of people two buildings over. Here there was nothing. No sigh of wind in trees, no animal howls, no bustle of labor. Nothing at all. It was like being in a dream, a place outside reality.

I recommenced my pacing, then checked the clock again. I had now been alone almost twenty minutes. I knew nothing of white person etiquette, but surely this was odd.

My nervousness was returning. I sat down again. I got up. I checked the clock.

Something is not right.

That was the trusted instinct I used to feel up on the chimneys when a ladder gave just a little more than it should. I went to the door, opened it quietly, and peered out into the hall.

There was a luxorite chandelier in the high ceiling, but it had been covered for the night, and the hall was lit only by what little bleed escaped the hanging, so the carpeted corridor and its silent doors brooded in the gloom.

"Hello?" I said, softly. "Mr. Willinghouse?"

Nothing.

I took a few steps down the hall, pausing to listen at some of the doors as I went, but there was absolutely no sound from within. I moved farther, my boots noiseless on the rich carpet, till I reached the door at the other end.

I tried it, and went through silently, finding myself in an open area with a broad staircase to my right and a pair of corridors that led to different parts of the house. Figuring that Willinghouse had gone to a kitchen or pantry, I chose the hallway that looked the most functional. The one that led directly away from the front of the house had less elaborate moldings, and the door at the far end showed more wear, as if it had been repeatedly pushed open by people whose hands were full.

The door was hinged to open in both directions and had no latch. The corridor on the other side was painted simply and tiled with plain but clean ceramic. An iron bracket held a small luxorite globe, its light soft and verging on amber. There was no sign of Willinghouse,

Dahria, the driver, or the silent manservant, the only person I had seen so far who appeared to live in the house. I remembered Dahria's bitter hostility to coming here and being with "that woman," and I couldn't help but be curious. It would take someone remarkable to jar Dahria out of her world-weary unflappability.

"Hello?" I tried again, aware that my sense of the uncanny was swelling unsettlingly. "Sorry to disturb you, but I was looking for Mr. Willinghouse."

But there was no one to disturb, and I was getting more and more uneasy.

Something is wrong.

I moved more slowly now, more cautiously. The corridor smelled different from the rest of the house. Old cooking smells, some of it, the metal and stoneware of the kitchen, but there was something else, something that didn't belong. I stopped for a moment and closed my eyes, inhaling, and caught it again: dirt and musk and grass. It wasn't an unpleasant smell, but it was a hint of the outside world that the rest of the house seemed at pains to banish. With it came a movement of night air.

An open window, I thought.

I turned the corner at the end of the hall and found myself in another junction of doors, all black and simple, lit by another aging luxorite bulb. I tried one of the doors and it revealed a pantry, all shelves and cupboards and racks of drying herbs and peppers. Another larder had stone walls that lowered the temperature considerably, and in it were trays of butter and cooked meats, summer sausages and game birds hanging from hooks.

There was still no sign of anybody, but as I considered the larder, I heard what seemed to have been the first sound in ages that I hadn't made myself. It came from beyond the largest door. I forced myself to stop and make sense out of the noise.

It had been a soft clunk, dull but with a fractional metallic tinkle somewhere inside the sound. I had no idea what it might be, but as I stood there, trying to understand it, the sound came again. There was an almost inaudible sweeping before the clunk. I closed my eyes again, trying to focus on the noise, wondering if I could connect it to the sound of a servant making tea for unexpected guests.

It came once more, and this time there was a different sound in the silence between the noises, one that raised the hair on the back of my neck. A grunt, I thought. There were no words in it, so I couldn't be sure it was human, but it sounded like . . . effort.

Caught between fear and embarrassment, I set my hand against the door and pushed very gently. It opened a crack, almost weightless against the pressure of my hand. I peered in.

Inside was a large, stone-flagged kitchen. There was no visible luxorite, though there was a pair of gas lamps turned very low, their light soft and blue so that everything in the room was drained of color: sinks and countertops with cutting boards and knife blocks, a vast gas-fired stovetop, a pair of ovens in one wall, and a huge soot-stained fireplace, the only thing in the room that did not look scrubbed.

I opened the door wider and stepped inside. Then the sweep and thunk came again, and my ear traced it.

For a moment, my heart flooded with relief. At the far end of the kitchen was an external door that had been left unlatched. It was swinging softly in the breeze from outside, thunking shut but never latching, so that the next rush of air pushed it wide, then sucked it closed again.

I took an instinctual step toward it along the side of the long island where the stove was mounted, but stopped. Perhaps it had been left open on purpose. Perhaps the manservant had stepped out to some cellar which was inaccessible from inside the house.

The stillness of the place continued to unnerve me, and I immediately doubted such easy explanations. I didn't know the layout of the house or grounds and couldn't be sure that the high-gated wall we had entered didn't go all around the house, protecting it from the bush beyond. Surely it would. So the open space through the kitchen door would be merely a kind of courtyard. Surely. No one would leave an external door open out here, particularly after sunset. That would be madness. I frowned, then took another step. I would call out, and if no one came, I would close it. If I accidentally locked someone out, they could knock at the front door.

I took three more steps and saw movement in the shadows outside. I froze, staring.

There was a soft splash of the kitchen's gaslight playing over the threshold, but it faded to nothing only a couple of yards beyond the doorframe. Something had passed the entrance only feet from the house. Something large. Something that loped in uneven bounds. I kept very still, uncomfortably aware that the gaslight would reveal me to whatever was outside far better than the other way around.

Perhaps if I rushed the door and slammed it shut, I could find a way to latch it before whatever was out there chose to come in. . . .

And then, in spite of the warmth of the night, I felt a chill run the full length of my spine. Out of the dark had come the sound of a child's laughter. A strange, mad child.

I knew what that meant long before the creature loped into view only a yard beyond the door.

Hyena.

I felt my eyes widen and my nostrils flare. The animal moved into the light, its gaze on me, nose high, bat-wing ears wide and alert. It was a huge brute of a beast, probably my own weight, maybe more. Its legs were delicate, almost spindly, but its haunches were powerful and its back sloped up to hulking shoulders and a long, thick neck, all muscle and sinew. Its head was pointed, eyes glass-hard and alight with the milky glow of the gas lamp, muzzle black, jaws lolling.

It was absolutely still. When my eyes caught the next flicker of movement, it wasn't the animal in front of me, but another one a few feet behind.

So there's a pack.

One hyena was dangerous, lethal even, but a pack could kill anything that walked on land. I had heard about them all my life—the way they stole prey from weancats, the way they coordinated to bring down one-horns. There wasn't a creature in the world that scared me more.

I could slam the door, I thought, but that would mean taking two substantial steps toward it, toward *them,* and that was beyond me. Without taking my eyes off the lead hyena, I began a slow step backwards. The maniacal chuckle came again, and this time it was behind me.

They were already inside.

CHAPTER
8

FOR A MOMENT I did not move. Could not. Then I pivoted slowly at the waist, revolving a few degrees, terrified of taking my eyes off the hyena in the doorway, but desperate to see the one that was already in the kitchen.

It slunk out from behind the stove island, head low, eyes watchful. There was another behind it, skittering out where it could see, and producing that unnerving giggle. It was a chilling sound, and it spread through the pack like madness. There were at least three more outside.

I could smell them clearly now, a rank musk that shifted in the hot air.

I had to get out.

I inched back toward the door through which I had come, but the hyenas responded, circling back around me. Two more came in from the yard, trotting almost casually, though their eyes were fastened on me. Suddenly unsure I could reach the door without a fight, I let my gaze rake the countertops for something I might use as a weapon. I had left my satchel of tools in the sitting room. The knives were agonizingly far away, heavy handles sticking out of their blocks over by the ovens. If I went around the island . . .

Before the thought could complete itself, the nearest hyena shifted, cutting off my route as if it had read my intent. It bared pointed teeth crowded behind thin black lips. The chuckling began again.

My heart was hammering, and the blood sang in my ears. There was a coppery taste in my mouth, and my knees felt unsteady. I had no idea what to do.

Another hyena, leaner than the others, edged in from the darkness, turning its striped flank on me as it moved to the wall. They were spreading out, surrounding me, noses held high, drinking in my terror.

I had to move, but my feet refused to shift. I considered shouting, but had no idea what that would do. It seemed more likely to incense them than scare them off.

The pantries.

If I could get out of the kitchen and get those larder doors open, surely all that aging meat would hold their attention while I got behind a lockable door.

The idea was what I needed to stir my legs into action. I began to move slowly, but even my fractional start alerted them. For a split second they froze, staring, calculating, and then the yipping chuckle began again. I could stand it no longer.

Thought evaporated.

I sprang for the door. Three long strides and I was smashing it open, racing out into the orange glow of the corridor, knowing they were at my heels. I dragged one larder door open, but dared not wait to do more, as the first hyena gave chase. It hesitated only a second at the open pantry, then came galloping after me. The others followed.

I ran, bellowing Willinghouse's name.

Down the corridor I pounded, exploding through the swinging door into the open lobby with the staircase, and into the front hall. I could hear them coming after me, gibbering hysterically, blundering through the doors. I saw the main entrance directly ahead, no more than fifteen yards away.

It might as well have been a thousand.

It was fastened shut with two heavy bolts, and there was no key in the lock. If I got to the door and couldn't get it open, I would be trapped. I needed to buy myself some time.

"Willinghouse!" I shouted. "Dahria!"

I tried the nearest side door and found myself in another elegant sitting room. The windows were high and small, but I ducked inside, pulling the cord that released the shades on the luxorite chandelier so that the room was instantly bathed in hard white light. I closed the door behind me, making sure it latched, then moved quickly to the hearth, where I selected a brass poker with a pointed hook that swept out just below the tip. Not much of a weapon against the jaws of a hyena, perhaps, but it would have to do.

The room was decorated in cream and ivory, the prim chairs and sofa trimmed with lace and brocade. There was a pair of decanters on a highly polished sideboard, a tray of crystal goblets, and a silver flask with a bulb, but the chamber was otherwise sparsely decorated. There was nowhere to hide.

Maybe they would return to the pantry, or even to the kitchen door and out into the night. I just needed to stay still and quiet until they gave up looking for me, and that, I thought, couldn't take long.

There was a distinctive creak from the door. It was a familiar sound, but my mind didn't process it until I saw the handle move.

No.

It snapped back into position, and I heard a grunt from the hall. Then there was the muffled thump of weight being thrown against the door and the handle shifted again. More this time.

I stared, hardly able to believe it. The door handle was the long, bar kind, not the round knobs that would surely have defeated an animal's paw.

It flicked back into place once more, and now I heard the mad giggle of the hyenas echoing down the hallway.

The handle began to move again.

There was nowhere to go. If only one of them got in, we could chase each other around the couch a few times, but if there were more than one of them, even that brief absurdity would be prevented. They knew how to hunt as a pack, and they would have caught my scent by now, even if they hadn't actually seen me come in.

Scent.

I looked wildly round the room, and my eyes focused on the silver flask on the cabinet. The bulb where its stopper might have been was the size of a small lemon, covered in glossy fabric. I strode over and snatched it up. Liquid swilled inside it. Then I moved behind the door as the handle twisted again, stuck for a second, then tipped all the way down. The latch snapped, and the door juddered.

For a moment it just cracked a little, and then the black nose of the lead hyena nudged it open. It entered cautiously, shoving the door wider with its striped shoulder. I braced myself, the perfume bottle in one hand, the poker in the other, not breathing as the beast committed to its search and moved all the way into the room. My body ached and twinged from my fall into the river. I was not ready for a fight.

The sense of being inside a dream came back like a heady aroma as the great hyena, tawny and black striped with a pale splash across the ridge of its spine, moved around the elegant, cream-colored furniture. Everything in the room denied the wildness outside these walls, yet here it was, moving with low menace between the end tables of crystal decanters.

I waited till it was as far from the door as it would get before making my break, but it saw me. It turned snarling, lips fluttering as a deep rumbling growl came up from its throat, eyes narrow and fixed, ears flattening to the sides of its head. It was less than ten feet from me. Its haunches rippled and flexed as it prepared to spring—

I sidestepped around the door, hoping against hope that there wasn't another hyena poised to come in, leveled the perfume bottle, and squeezed the bulb. It sprayed a fine mist, finer than I would have liked, but the scent of roses and lavender filled the air, and the hyena flinched away, eyes stinging, nostrils momentarily overwhelmed. In its instant of hesitation, I slid out of the door and slammed it shut.

I knew that wouldn't hold it for more than a few seconds, but that might be all I needed to get the front door open. I checked the hall for the other animals, but there was no sign of them. I didn't pause to examine my good fortune and flew along the hall to the entrance.

The scream came from above. A female voice.

And at once I knew where the missing hyenas were.

They had gone upstairs.

I hesitated for a second, feeling the inadequacy of the poker in my hand, and then I turned sharply and ran back into the house. I was halfway up the stairs before I heard the second scream.

CHAPTER

9

THE HOUSE WAS WARMER upstairs, the musky tang of the hyenas sharper on the still air. To move into it, to run to where they were, meant shutting off all instinct, all thought, in the pursuit of a single flickering certainty: someone was going to get killed unless I could get to them. The poker shifted in my slippery grip, but I ran on.

There was a carpeted landing at the top. A single shaded luxorite bulb showed four paneled doors, then a turn in the corridor. One of the doors was ajar. I was almost through it when a hyena rounded the corner, doubling back toward the stairs. Its gaze fell on me, and it stuttered to a halt, hackles rising, teeth bared.

I didn't hesitate, blundering into the darkened room to find three hyenas already inside. Dahria was crouching on the bed against the far wall, sheets drawn up to her throat, eyes wide and horrified under the thin veil of the mosquito netting. The hyenas were clustering around her, watching her, till my arrival caught their attention and they hopped away, chuckling.

I brandished the poker at the nearest of them, and it bounded easily out of range. The one from the landing had slunk into the doorway at my back. I gave it a warning lunge, but it barely moved.

Their chittering laugh rippled around the group again as they sized me up, and I made another slashing motion with the poker at the nearest of them, shouting wordlessly. It was as if they were calculating the odds. Dahria was frozen, whimpering. If they attacked, she would be no use.

My eyes flashed around the dim chamber. I had only come up one story, but the room's sole window was behind the headboard and looked to be heavily shuttered. We would have to leave the way we came in.

"Move toward me," I said. "Quickly."

Dahria stared at me. In the gloom she looked mad with panic, paralyzed. I reached a hand toward her, looking for a gap in the mosquito netting. The hyenas reacted, forgetting her entirely and giving me all their attention. Two of them took little mincing steps toward me, heads lowered. I was now the center of a tightening circle whose radius was the reach of the poker.

The one in the doorway hopped closer, and I swung at it, knowing even as it stepped lightly away that the two by the bed were closing in. I felt the brush of fur against my legs and turned, shouting out in terror.

Dahria had not moved, but even in the horror of the moment, I saw something in her eyes that seemed . . . wrong.

Not scared. Curious. Even amused.

Her look distracted me, and I was too slow to react when the hyena from the doorway pounced.

Its weight caught me off balance, and I went down hard, dropping the perfume bottle and catching my elbow on the end of the bed. There was pain, but I was too aware of the crowding hyena muzzles to feel it. I rolled onto my back and they were there, their paws on my chest, their narrowed eyes inches from mine. Their scent was overpowering, and as their faces dipped and bobbed toward my throat, it struck me in the wild madness of the moment that their fetid rankness was the last thing I would ever smell.

I flailed wildly with the poker, catching one of them on the side of the head, but another caught my arm in its jaws and wrenched it aside. I writhed and kicked, but it was over.

I didn't recognize the voice for what it was until the hyenas pulled back, shrinking away.

There was an elderly Lani woman in a dressing gown standing in the doorway, looking down at me, her face hard, her arms spread wide in command. She was shouting words I didn't understand.

Names.

One by one, the hyenas pulled away and dropped like dogs, panting, to the floor.

The woman gave them an imperious glare and one of them whimpered.

"Keep still, girl," she demanded, staring at me. "You are alarming them."

For a moment, I just looked at her, caught between relief and bewilderment. The woman seemed angry. With me. The hyenas had stopped their giggling, and when she pointed out onto the landing and barked their names, they trotted out. She caught one of them, stooping to it, and parting the fur around a thin wound on the back of its head.

"What did you do?" she said, fixing me with her baleful stare. Her eyes found the discarded poker. "You hit her?"

"Her?" I echoed.

"Yavix," said the old woman. "The hyena."

I sat up, rubbing my arm. It was bloody, and there were four clear puncture wounds near the elbow, but they did not look deep.

"I asked you a question," said the woman. She looked like she was eighty, but her eyes blazed. "Answer it."

"I was defending myself!" I shot back, aghast. "And protecting her!"

I turned to face Dahria, who had not moved from the bed. There was no trace of terror in her face now. She was leaning back against her pillows, smirking.

The thought came to me as it had before.

This is all wrong.

"What is going on?" I demanded, getting awkwardly to my feet.

There was a creak from a wardrobe in the corner. I flinched, expecting another hyena, but when the door opened, I saw Willing-house standing inside, looking nonchalant and a little bored.

"Satisfied, Grandmamma?" he said.

The old woman turned her glare on him for a moment, then re-turned it to me.

"In part," she said, in a low voice, unimpressed. "Took her a long time to start exploring."

"But she did what she was supposed to," said Willinghouse. "She passed the test."

I stared at him.

A test?

"I felt like I was screaming for about half an hour before you came, Miss Sutonga," said Dahria, back to her laconic self. "If it had gone on much longer, I might have lost my voice."

I gaped at her.

"You were acting," I said.

She bowed extravagantly, first to one side, then to the other, as if the bed was a stage surrounded by people.

"Thank you! Thank you!" she said to her imaginary audience.

Willinghouse nodded with a benevolent smile and gave a little polite applause, first for her then, to my amazement, for me.

"My little sister, ladies and gentlemen," he said.

"Good evening, Grandmamma," said Dahria politely to the old woman. "A pleasure, as always, to see you. I trust you are suitably impressed by my discharge of the role assigned to me."

There was no attempt to make the formality sound heartfelt, but I didn't care. I was too busy trying to make sense of what had just happened. My heart was still pounding, my arms and legs trembling with exertion and fear, but those feelings were quickly giving way to outrage.

"You were *testing* me?" I said, glaring at Willinghouse.

"Not him," said the old woman who was, apparently, their grandmother. "Me. I heard you were afraid of wild animals. I wanted to see how you would react under pressure, particularly when others were in peril."

"I beg your pardon?" I said, my rage mounting.

The woman waved away my outrage with a flick of her hand.

"You were never in real danger," she said, dismissively. "The pack was hand reared from birth. Better than guard dogs out here in the bush, and they do as I tell them."

I glared at her.

"I'm supposed to be . . . ," I began, too blind with fury and humiliation to find the words. "How is this helping me to . . . ? I'm leaving," I concluded, striding for the door.

The old woman blocked my path.

"On foot?" she demanded coolly. "That would be unwise."

"I'll take the carriage back to town," I blustered.

"Think again, Miss Sutonga," she said. "I will not risk the horses after dark. Not all the hyenas around here are tame."

That was a kind of bleak joke that turned one corner of her mouth up a fraction. The four hyenas sprawled untidily on the carpet were eyeing me.

"They won't hurt you," she said. "I will have Namud make up a room for you."

She had lost the edge in her voice, but her face was still patrician hard, her eyes appraising.

"I will not be your pet," I said to whoever was listening. "Your trained animal."

The old woman took a slow step toward me. When I did not shrink away from her touch, she raised my injured arm so that the luxorite glow fell on it, turning it slightly as she considered the damage.

"Let us get this wound dressed before it becomes infected," said the old woman.

She gestured to the hyenas, flicking her wrist and uttering a handful of words in a language I did not recognize. The animals got to their feet and trotted down the stairs. I watched, amazed, reminded again of the strange sense of being inside a dream.

"This way," she said.

She led the way along the landing to another door which she opened, showing me into a spacious bathroom, all porcelain and glossy ceramic tile. I was glad to leave Willinghouse and Dahria behind, and I burned with anger and humiliation still. Picking up an earthenware jug of clear water, their grandmother nodded at a basin. I held my arm out, and she poured water over it. As she took a clean towel and dabbed at the wound, I considered her brown, papery, and wrinkled skin, her silver hair. Lani in the Drowning rarely lived to such an age, and I doubted even the frailest of our elders had seen as many years as she had, though she seemed strong in mind and body.

Privilege has its advantages, I reminded myself.

"I'm sorry that my little test went so far," she said. "But it speaks to your character that you passed."

"If I'd known who I was trying to rescue, I might not have bothered," I muttered.

She shot me a sideways look, and for a moment, her eyes flashed and the corner of her mouth buckled into a knowing smile. A second later, the look was so completely gone that I could barely remember it.

"You dislike Dahria?" she asked.

"Yes," I said quickly. "No. I don't know. I just didn't think . . ."

"She would pull such a stupid and mean-spirited trick on someone who thought her a friend," said the old woman shrewdly. "Yes. But then she was doing as I told her and my granddaughter has the emotional maturity of Yavix."

I gave her a questioning look.

"The hyena," she explained. "Don't take it personally. Dahria keeps the world at arm's length. It's how she lives with herself for being so utterly useless to that world's needs." She said it simply, without malice but with a certainty that shocked me. When I looked down, unsure, she added, amused, "In your mind you just risked your life to save someone who spends her days gossiping and taking tea with friends, someone who would not acknowledge you in the street for fear of damaging her own reputation."

"That's not true," I said, not sure if I believed it.

"Isn't it?" said the old woman.

I looked down, abashed.

"Be courageous, by all means," the woman continued, "but make sure you can achieve what you set out to. Dead heroes are no use to anyone."

She said that last bitterly, and I found myself confused.

"You don't think I should be working with your grandson," I said.

She replaced the water jug and handed me a clean towel.

"I think you did not survive this long on the towers and chimneys of Bar-Selehm by taking unnecessary risks," she said. "Believe me when I say that now is not the time to start. I hear you have done good work for my grandson, for the region, which is in need of it, but understand the danger of your situation. Be careful who you trust and what you believe. Nothing in Bar-Selehm is what it seems, and the deeper you penetrate what we are pleased to call high society, the more you need to be on your guard."

I bridled slightly at her tone.

"I can look after myself," I said.

She gave me a level look.

"Yes?" she said. "Josiah thinks you passed the test tonight, and that is good, but if the test had been to see if you could discern truth from lies, what was real from what was merely staged, you would have failed. In a place like Elitus, that error would cost you dearly."

I felt the rush of blood to my face, but said nothing. I could see that she was right, but the fact of it gave me no clarity, nor did it ease my annoyance. It was a relief when Willinghouse appeared in the doorway. There was no sign of Dahria.

"I'm sure the point has already been made," he said, avoiding his grandmother's eyes, "but I feel I should apologize for what happened. It was inappropriate."

"It doesn't matter," I said, meeting his gaze and, like him, avoiding that of the old woman. "I understand."

I felt his grandmother's eyes on me.

"Thank you," he said. His manner was still formal, his posture rigid, but there was a fractional change in his sharp green eyes that might have been relief. "And I must commend you on your use of the perfume bottle. Most resourceful. Even Dahria was impressed."

I blushed.

"We were watching the whole time," he added. "If things had gone badly . . ."

"You were watching?" I interjected. "How?"

"My father was a cautious man," he said. "Paranoid, even."

"With good cause," said his grandmother crisply.

Willinghouse gave a nod of acknowledgment that was also a shrug, turning his head and closing his eyes for a moment, but he did not look at her directly.

"The house is a warren of ventilation ducts," he said, "many of which contain carefully positioned mirrors. From the central rooms upstairs, it is possible to glimpse activity all over the house. A security measure."

"So you saw everything I did?" I said, feelingly suddenly exposed, as if I might have betrayed my most private thoughts without realizing it.

"It was all very impressive," he offered, kindly. "As I had expected. A room has been prepared for you. We breakfast at seven, though I may have to be on the road before then. For work."

"And I will be doing what?" I demanded, still on my dignity.

"You will begin the training we should have started three months ago," said Willinghouse's grandmother.

I turned to her, taken aback, and her lips flexed with something like satisfaction.

"Yes," she said, reading my surprise. "I am Madame Nahreem. I will be your tutor."

CHAPTER

10

I WAS IN THE Drowning for the rice festival. It was raining, a fine, misting rain refreshing on the skin. The river was swollen up around the makeshift paddy fields where the green sprouts broke through the wet mirror reflecting a purple sky and the girls smeared with the saffron-colored powder paint as they danced for the harvest. Rahvey was there, happy as I almost never saw her, swaying from her neck to her hips in time with the shrill, wild music. And Vestris, radiant at the head of the dance in a fire-red sari.

I was holding Papa's hand and wishing I was old enough to join in, but when I asked my father if I could, he looked warily at the sky.

"Rain's getting harder, little one," he said.

And it was. The steady drizzle had become a downpour, and suddenly the music had stopped while everyone ran for cover, looking for their sandals amidst the piles of flowers on the ground. We made for higher ground, but a policeman in white gloves said we couldn't go that way. At first everyone was laughing in the chaos, but then the mood shifted and I was overcome with a strange and powerful dread.

Something awful had happened.

It was the river. It had burst its banks, and now we were awash in flowers, chasing our sandals as they floated away. I reached for mine, and in that instant I let go of Papa's hand. I turned, frantic, but he was lost in the crowd of flailing, crying people. I saw Rahvey splashing through the water, screaming the names of her daughters, her face a mask of horror and fear.

The waters rose still higher, around our knees, our waists, our necks. We were all washing away, and now the colorful Lani crowd were mainly black, half-naked people I did not know, their eyes wide and desperate. I was lifted on a great brown wave. The river rolled like an ocean. Among the crocodiles and hippos, sharks circled, their dorsal fins knifing through what had been rice paddies, flower petals shredding in their wake. I was overcome by a desperate desire to find Mnenga amidst the black faces, but they did not understand me when I asked for him, and were too afraid of the sharks.

I took refuge on a shrinking island, scrambling up its shore as the tide rose, and climbing onto a rock only a couple of yards across, suddenly alone in a vast mud-colored sea. There was a terrible silence. All the people who had been there—family, friends, Lani, and the nameless black people I did not know, had vanished inexplicably. There were only the sharks and the blank, surging waters of what had been the river. And then I looked down and found that the slope I had climbed was not rock at all, but bone: a pile of human skulls that was sinking into the water, eye sockets filling with brown murk as the ground beneath me crumbled. I cried out, but my scream turned into the dawn shriek of a go-away bird, and I woke with a start, unsure of where I was and how I had gotten there.

I sat on the bed, sweating, waiting for my heart to slow, then plunged my face—after only a moment's dreadful hesitation—into a basin of water, to wash the dream away. Taking a series of ritual breaths such as I would before performing my Kathahry exercises, I blew the air from my lungs like smoke.

Just a dream. It doesn't mean anything.

I decided to believe that. I had real dangers enough without wasting energy on others that only existed in my head. And there were things I had to do today.

Another deliberate splash of water, and the dream was gone.

FOR ALL ITS STOLID opulence, the estate was sparsely furnished and drafty, but I slept in a vast, quilted bed so comfortable that, if not for my unsettling dream, I might have forgotten my anger at Madame Nahreem's test. I had feared the chamber would be stuffy, since—remembering what Willinghouse had said about mirrors in the air shafts—I had thrown clothes and rugs over every vent I could see, but it was quite pleasant. The room was in a corner of the house, and the shuttered windows looked out upon a range of hills, some fenced and sprouting orderly crops, but most wild and untended brush. I had woken several times in the night to the sound of animal calls, one of which was surely the repeated grunting roar of a lion, and morning had come with a cacophony of screaming birds and chattering monkeys. Before going downstairs, I sat at the window scouring the countryside for elephants or one-horns. Apart from a solitary, browsing giraffe, I saw nothing, but given that I knew to expect hyenas *inside* the house, that wasn't much consolation.

My shoulder felt better than it had, but it was still tight and ached when I rolled it. Whatever training I had coming today, I hoped it would not be unduly taxing on my already bruised and battered body.

For someone used, until very recently, to snatching a roll of bread from a bowl before the rest of the gang took it all, breakfast was bizarre. A white maid greeted me on the landing with a bobbing curtsy and an apparently unsarcastic "good morning, miss," then led me down to a formal dining room where a long table draped in a starched white cloth was laid with plates and assorted cutlery. The others—Willinghouse, Dahria, and their grandmother, Madame Nahreem—were already there, eating in silence as a second maid, this one black, ministered to them under the watchful gaze of the young Lani butler I had seen the night before. They looked up from their food, and Willinghouse nodded me into a chair opposite Dahria, who was smirking at the way I refused to look her in the eye.

I helped myself to a dish of curried rice with smoked fish and hard-boiled eggs, and tried not to eat like it was the last meal I might get. That such plates of delicious food were mine for the taking still struck me as strange, and though I reveled in it all, I could not quite escape a lingering sense of guilt when I thought of Tanish, my erstwhile apprentice, and what he might be eating this morning.

"Miss Sutonga," said Willinghouse brightly, "I trust you slept well. Your training will begin in one hour. I hope to return later today with an update from Inspector Andrews on the theft from the war department."

His manner was businesslike, and as he spoke, he laid down the newspaper, checked his pocket watch, and got to his feet. He kissed Dahria lightly on the top of her head as she spread marmalade on her toast, nodded to Madame Nahreem with a polite "Grandmamma," dithered in front of me, and left the room.

There was an awkward silence while Dahria swallowed.

"Just us girls together, then," she deadpanned. "What japes we shall have."

Madame Nahreem checked the clock on the mantel and turned to me.

"Meet me here in . . . thirty-seven minutes," she said. Dahria rolled her eyes and went on eating as her grandmother left, the servants following in her wake.

"I haven't forgiven you," I said to Dahria, as soon as the door was closed and we were alone.

"However will I live with myself?" she remarked. "Oh, come off it. It was only a joke. You weren't in any true danger."

"It was cruel," I said. "And humiliating."

"Ah," said Dahria, sitting back and smiling. "Your pride is wounded. Understandable, if a little surprising in one such as . . ."

I glared at her over the rim of my teacup, and she grinned wider than ever.

"Another joke," she said.

"You should be a low comic in the music halls," I remarked. "You clearly belong onstage."

"You wound me, my dear steeplejack," she said. "You wound me."

I finished my food in silence, palmed a dusk peach on my way out, and left her sitting at the table looking sardonically amused. When I got back to my room, I found that clothes had been laid out for me: a tea gown in pale lustrous green with white lace trim. It wasn't perhaps as fine as what Dahria wore, but it outstripped anything I had ever owned by a considerable distance, and I felt a peculiar confluence of powerful feelings at the prospect of putting it on. At first I was angry, resentful at the impertinence, but then I reminded myself that I was being trained to pass as a society lady—albeit one from far away—and this was doubtless a part of that. That hurdle past, I allowed myself the prospect of enjoying the dress, the softness of its material, the way it seemed to shift in the light, and finally the way it made me look when I put it on and stood in front of the mirror that had been set up for the purpose.

I looked . . . different. Like someone I had never seen before. Delighted, fearful. Pretty.

It was a strange feeling. Too strange. I hurriedly took the dress off, flung it over the back of a chair feeling increasingly foolish, and put my old things back on.

I was almost ten minutes late getting back downstairs, and Madame Nahreem was waiting for me. She stared as the butler showed me in and shot a pointed look at the clock.

"I know," I said. "I'm sorry. I've just been—"

"I don't care," she said. "Follow me. We will begin immediately."

She led me through the door behind the desk, and down the carpeted hallway where I had run the night before, but at the foot of the stairs, instead of going through to the kitchen and servants' quarters, we took the other corridor past polished doors and out into a sunlit courtyard with a stone fountain, where one of the hyenas sprawled like a housecat. I gave it a wary look, and Willinghouse's grandmother shot me a brittle smile.

On the far side of the courtyard, we entered another wing of the house entirely. The place was huge, far larger than I had realized. This portion was, however, less luxuriant, the floor matted with woven grass, the walls simple wood and plaster. We arrived at what seemed to be a kind of locker room with a sunken alabaster bath, a pair of benches, and an array of shelves and cupboards on the walls.

"You may leave your . . . clothes here," said Madame Nahreem. The hesitation, and the critique it implied, suggested she knew about the green dress that had been left for me. I flushed and looked away. "Put these on."

She nodded to a shirt and trousers made of what felt like heavy raw silk, smooth and pliable and gray. I frowned all the same. Why was everyone suddenly so concerned with what I wore?

"No jewelry," she said.

I had Berrit's sun disk around my throat with Papa's coin.

"And take your boots off," said Madame Nahreem. "You will perform this first exercise barefoot."

I did as I was told, tottering as I plucked the first foot free so that she gave me a withering look, as if I was proving to be as incompetent as she had expected. I scowled, and when she did not look away as I prepared to undress, turned my back on her. When I finished dressing and looked at her again, she was giving me a disdainful smile.

"Modesty intact, I see," she said.

"Is that a problem?" I responded. Her critical stare was getting on my nerves.

"Not if you are trying to spare my blushes," she said, "though there is no need to do so. If it is a matter of your own embarrassment, however, then yes, it's a problem."

"How can my not wanting to parade around naked be a problem?" I scoffed.

"No one asked you to *parade*," she said, her voice low and even, in pointed contrast to mine.

"If you had lived only a thin partition from a dozen teenage boys, you'd understand," I retorted.

"Quite," she said. "But you no longer live like that and need to put it out of your mind if you are to learn the deportment of a lady."

"That's just playacting," I said. "Just tell me what to do."

"No," she said. "This is about being a lady. *Being,* not *playing.* You are used to being judged by your appearance as a Lani steeplejack—condemned for it even—and the result is that you don't care what you look like, since nothing you do will counterbalance the assumptions made about you because of your skin. Believe me, I know."

I stared at her, taken off guard by this moment of apparent solidarity, but her look of wry understanding slid away like a pit viper, and her face was as it always seemed, implacably hard and laden with scorn.

"So you have given up," she said. "Your body rebels against civilization because civilization is for white people. The way you slouch, the way you roll your eyes when you are feeling superior, the curl of your lip when you are feeling resentful, the way you hang your head when you feel abashed—all of which you have done in the last thirty seconds—are beyond your conscious mind. They are not things you choose to do, so to stop doing them you must learn to think differently. To *be* different. So first I want you to be a body without a self," she said, turning to a cabinet and opening it. On a shelf inside was a wooden box about a foot square. "Look here."

She took the box down, unsnapped the clasp, and opened it.

Inside, sitting on velvet gray as my training clothes, was a mask.

It was an elegant thing, finely worked from some plain, almost grainless wood, smooth to the touch and remarkably light. It had eye, ear, and nostril holes, but the mouth was closed, and the face—the color of which matched my own skin almost perfectly—was blank. Two black ribbons were attached at the ears.

Disguise, I thought, unexpectedly pleased.

"I am going through this door," said Madame Nahreem, nodding to a panel on the wall beside her. "When you are ready, you will follow me, and you will be the mask."

I blinked at her.

"What do you mean?" I asked.

"I mean what I said," she answered. "You will study the mask. You will wear the mask. You will be the mask."

"I don't understand," I said. "How can I *be* the mask? If it had a jackal or a vulture face or something, I could be the mask, but this is . . . nothing."

"It is not *nothing*," said Madame Nahreem, irritation flashing in her eyes. "It is neutral. That is what you must be. When you are ready, tie the mask so it sits on top of your head—that is the *mask off* position—when I give you the command, you lower it over your face—*mask on* position. From that moment on, everything you do must fit the mask."

And without another word, she opened the almost invisible door, stepped through it, and closed it behind her.

I stared after her, then sat on the bench and considered the mask, weighing it vaguely in my hands.

Stupid, I thought. *And a waste of time. How will this help me in Elitus?*

I sighed my exasperation, then—realizing that the old bat could probably hear me through the walls—snatched up the mask, laced the ribbons around the back of my head, and tied it in place. It felt odd. I had expected to smell the wood or the oil it had been treated with, but I smelled nothing. My vision contracted a little, and my jaw felt constrained by the mask's chin, but it wasn't too bad. I pushed it up onto my forehead—what Madame Nahreem had called the *mask off* position—and stepped through the door.

I had expected a climbing apparatus or exercise equipment, but the room was quite empty, save for its matted floor and Madame Nahreem sitting on a solitary chair at the far end. I took a step inside.

"Stop there," said Madame Nahreem. "Turn to face the door."

I did so, feeling ridiculous and annoyed.

"Mask on," the old woman barked.

I pulled the mask down over my nose and waited.

"Breathe," said Madame Nahreem—as if I might have forgotten to—"and, when you are ready, turn to face me, as the mask."

I waited for a dutiful second, then began to turn.

"No," she interrupted. "Stop. Do it again. Be the mask."

I paused, then did it again.

"No!" she shouted. "Again."

I returned to my starting position with mounting anger, but I had barely even begun to move when she shouted at me again.

"No! Mask off."

I snatched it from my face and stared her down.

"Did you study the mask?" she demanded.

"Yes," I said.

"So why aren't you being the mask?" she returned.

"What does that even mean?"

"Look at it!"

I forced my eyes onto the wooden face in my hands, its empty eyes and blank expression.

"Is that how you feel?" she demanded, still sitting haughtily twenty feet away.

"What?"

"Look at the expression on the mask," she said, her voice rising now. "Does its expression match your feelings?"

"Of course not!"

"Why not?"

"Because I'm angry!" I shouted back at her.

"Exactly. You are supposed to be the mask, but your feelings won't let you. The mask is neutral. You must be neutral."

"I am being."

"No, you are not. You are *behind* the mask. You must *be* the mask."

"This is absurd."

"No, it is not. You merely cannot do it. The two are not the same."

The barb struck home like a scorpion's tail, and I winced, then flung the mask at her, as hard as I could. It arced oddly, half floating, missing her, and bouncing comically against the wall.

I stood stock-still, my anger boiling, and she watched as if she had been waiting for just such a moment.

"It seems," she said, "that we need to work on your throwing." When I said nothing, she added, "Your temper will get you killed, Miss Sutonga."

I stared at her, fists balled, for a long moment, then I took a breath, held it, and blew it slowly out.

"Fine," I said. "Show me how to be neutral in the stupid mask."

It was more challenge than request. She said nothing, but got up from her chair, crossed the room in a series of brisk strides, and stooped to the spot where the mask lay. She picked it up, her back to me, and bowed her head, as if in prayer, though I think she was merely looking at the mask in her hands.

She raised it to her face, belting the ribbons around the back, and paused.

The room was utterly silent, redolent of the slight aroma of the dry grass matting, light filtering in through high, shaded windows. I watched her irritably, her back to me, and then she changed.

It happened before she turned, and I could not say exactly how it happened, but it did, and she became something different. Her posture shifted, straightening and softening at the same time, she became somehow balanced, and the anger I had seen only moments before leached out of her even though I could not see her face. When she turned, it was with a fluid grace, and there was no trace of her own personality in the person standing in front of me. She turned her head to one side, then the other, the blank face of the mask showing nothing but its own neutral equilibrium, and then she took two steps, a fractional hop, and moved into three poses from the Kathahry: weancat, river rock, and pine. Each motion was like wind or air or water moving her body from within. I gaped. Madame Nahreem had vanished. She had become the mask.

She moved toward me, close enough to touch, stood for a silent moment, then with the same uncanny ease, lifted the mask from her face. Her eyes, which had been so full of fire before she began the exercise, were empty, unreadable.

"Now you," she said, offering me the mask.

I could not do it. I knew that. But I at least understood what I was trying to achieve, even if its purpose was still dark to me. So I did it, and when she stopped me, corrected me, I started again. Over and over. She pointed out the tension in my shoulders, the way I twisted my neck before I turned, the stiffness of my arms, and with each adjustment, I tried again. She told me I was too self-conscious, too deliberate, that I was thinking too hard, and at one point she made me step back into the locker room and consider the mask in silence, before trying again.

For two hours, we worked like this. She did not say I had improved. She offered no encouragement or support. But she criticized with less irritation, and that, I supposed, was as much as I could hope for.

"Why are we doing this?" I asked. I didn't speak caustically or even skeptically, but I wanted to know.

"To be a lady, you must unlearn seventeen years of thinking yourself an underling. That is a difficult thing to do, perhaps an impossible one. So for now I want you to turn off your mind. But this is not merely about being a princess so you can fit into some ridiculous private club. This is also about survival."

"How so?" I asked.

"My grandson said you were unsure of your combat skills."

I flushed and looked down.

"And there it is again," she said, reading my look. "The collapse of poise, of self in the face of powerful feeling. You must learn not to be a victim to your emotions, your little rages and embarrassments, and not only because an aristocratic lady would not suffer such self-doubt. They put your life in peril."

She saw the doubt in my face and came close.

"Some of what you are going to do will require you to think, to process, to analyze. Some of it won't. In fact, some of it will demand the opposite, that you do not think or feel or even simply react. It will require you to *be* in your body. To act without thought, to move in the most efficient and fluid manner possible, and in ways that will not reveal your intentions to your enemies."

"Enemies?" I cut in, uncertainly.

She ignored me, continuing as if I had not spoken at all.

"It will require balance. It will require the elimination of passion and personality. It will require you to do what your body alone requires, what it needs, what it demands."

"You want me to have no personality?" I said, not liking the sound of this. "My feelings make me strong."

"No," she said. "They make you *feel* strong because you are caught up in them. But that does not mean you *are* strong. They do not give you control, or poise, and when you rely on your body for your work, your life, these are essential. You must strive to be neutral."

"I'm not sure I want to be," I said.

"What you want is irrelevant," she answered flatly.

"Are you going to be like this all the time?" I said, tipping my chin up and glaring down my nose at her.

"If it helps to keep you alive," she replied, "yes. Mask on."

CHAPTER

11

FOUR DAYS I SPENT with Madame Nahreem, and in that time I saw Willinghouse only twice, both times at dinner, which, for all its opulence, was a harrowing affair that I came to think of as trial by fish knife. Each place serving was set with upward of a dozen knives, forks, and spoons of various shapes and sizes, all bafflingly arranged like the tools of an overly meticulous watch repairman. On the first night, I ignored them all, jabbing with a single fork, slicing what needed to be sliced with the sharpest available knife, and using my hands to scoop up the rest.

"Oh my God," breathed Dahria, spearing me with her fascinated stare. "I have, and I mean this quite literally, seen baboons with better table manners. It's like watching a jackal in a dress. If you would prefer, we could just put the food on the floor in a bucket."

"Shut your face," I said, raising my balled fist, "before I shut it for you."

"Oh yes," said Dahria. "An Istilian princess. The resemblance is uncanny."

"I mean it, Dahria," I said, through a mouthful of food. "I'll take that whole plate and ram it down your reeking neck in a minute."

"You will do no such thing!" said Madame Nahreem, her eyes alight. "And if you use language like that once more in this house, you will be sent packing back to the city, and I don't care what Josiah thinks about it."

"That's your third helping!" Dahria remarked, eyeing my plate. "You should be the size of the house."

"The trick is moving around," I shot back. "Maybe you'd be able to eat more than a handful of crackers if you got off your arse occasionally."

"Language!" exclaimed Madame Nahreem. "And Dahria is right in at least one thing, Miss Sutonga. You must stop eating as if each meal may be the last food you will ever see."

Dahria grinned at me secretly, and I stuck my tongue out at her. I hadn't yet swallowed all that was in my mouth.

Dahria made a disgusted face, and Madame Nahreem roused herself again.

"Are you an eight-year-old boy in a slum?" she demanded. I wasn't, of course, but most of the people I had eaten with for the past decade or so were, near enough. "You must treat mealtimes as part of your training."

"Scriously though, Grandmamma," said Dahria. "This is impossible. She's a guttersnipe. The original sow's ear from which no one could realistically expect to make a silk purse."

I gave her a halfhearted lunge so that she flinched away and got to her feet.

"I think I'll finish my dinner in the kitchen," she said. "With the rather more sophisticated hyenas."

As she stalked out, banging the door behind her, Willinghouse and his grandmother just sat there. I was stripping a mutton bone with my teeth and slurping up the tender filaments of meat.

"What?" I asked, feeling their eyes on me. "It's food. I was hungry."

"You make the mistake," said Madame Nahreem, "of thinking that a formal dinner is about nourishment. It is not. It is a social activity, not a biological one."

And so it went on. Everything I did, everything I was, had to be unlearned, rebuilt, while Dahria stayed in her room reading or walking the path around the garden in a gauzy veil to keep the insects off. When I wasn't actively training or being dressed by Dahria, I studied a book of Istilian Lani phrases on which Madame Nahreem grilled me over dinner, correcting my pronunciation and inflection till I was ready to fling my food at her. Namud, the butlerish young manservant, took me running every morning and stood over me while I lifted weights, before banishing me to a bathroom fed by hot, sulfurous water from an underground spring, where I washed and soaked till my muscles felt supple again. Throughout, he kept a respectful and largely silent distance, so that I became convinced that he found the arrangement even more awkward than I did, and though I had reason to think myself—in many ways—his social inferior, he insisted on treating me as if I was an extension of Madame Nahreem.

From the lady of the house herself, however, and in spite of my obvious progress, I got only criticism.

"How many times do I have to tell you, child?" said Madame Nahreem at dinner on the fourth day. "The tone rises at the end of the sentence, like a question. To stay flat is very rude."

"I thought I was doing," I said, trying not to show my resentment and—once more—failing.

"Not enough," said Dahria cheerfully. "You have to sing it."

"I'll never get any of this," I muttered.

"Not with that attitude," said Madame Nahreem.

"It's not about attitude!" I shot back. "You expect the impossible. I cannot master half a dozen different skills in under a week, and it is unreasonable of you to expect me to, so kindly refrain from insinuating that this is somehow *my* failure!"

I did not shout. I was composed and measured in my delivery, and I was surprised to find, at the end of my speech, that Madame Nahreem held my eyes for a moment, then smiled.

"At last," she said.

"What?" I demanded.

"That was the first time you sounded like an Istilian lady."

I looked from her to Dahria in bemusement.

"She's right," Dahria agreed. "You even did the inflection right."

I stared at her.

"And not a moment too soon," said Willinghouse. "You need to go to Elitus tomorrow night."

"Tomorrow?" I exclaimed. "I can't."

"The Grappoli ambassador returns to his home country next week," said Willinghouse, "and it is essential that you see who he is most intimate with. It's now or never."

"I'm not ready."

"First you should see if your attacker is a member." Willinghouse went on as if I hadn't spoken. "We don't even know for sure who frequents the place. Very hush-hush. But a former colleague who was invited as a guest once suggested there was an office containing a ledger of the members' names. It's kept away from the more social areas, so reaching it may prove tricky, but if you can get a look at the complete list—"

"I said, I'm not ready!" I repeated.

"You are," said Madame Nahreem. I gaped at her. "We could practice for weeks, months, and you would improve, but I think we have achieved enough to maintain the illusion for a short period."

She held my eyes for a moment—it was as close to praise as she was likely to get—and then turned to Willinghouse.

"How short?" he said. "The situation is bound to be fluid. I can't say how long she will need."

"An hour if no one present knows much about Istilia," said Madame Nahreem. "Less if anyone does."

Willinghouse looked unhappy.

"Perhaps if she's quick—," he began, but Madame Nahreem cut him off.

"Any attempt at speed will destroy the illusion utterly. Miss Sutonga needs to take her time without risking overexposure."

"Oh goody," said Dahria. "A paradox."

"Then we should postpone," said Willinghouse, ignoring her. "But . . ." He reached beneath his chair and produced a newspaper. "Grandmamma generally prohibits reading at the table, but I believe today she will make an exception." He glanced at Madame Nahreem as he unfolded the paper—the *Bar-Selehm Standard*—and pushed it to where we could see the headline.

REFUGEE CRISIS DEEPENS.

"Five boats came last week," he said as we read. "Twelve so far this week. Those are just the ones which made it. Wreckage and bodies wash up on the northeast coast daily. Dozens. Mostly women and children because the men are already dead or conscripted by the drug cartels to fight."

More sandals stuffed with whatever weedy flowers they could scrape together on the oily riverbank. . . .

"There's also this," he added, pushing the top paper aside to reveal another beneath it whose block capitals were bigger, more strident than anything in the *Standard*. Its headline was simpler.

SEND THEM BACK!

"The sentiment expressed by the *Clarion* has a lot of support in the government," said Willinghouse wearily. "There's talk of a naval blockade. The opposition will try to derail it, of course, but we don't have the votes in the house. Even in our own ranks there are some who will argue that we should put Bar-Selehm's needs before meddling in foreign affairs, especially in the light of our nonintervention treaty with the Grappoli, and Richter's Heritage people are getting more vocal by the day."

"But the more the Grappoli expand across northern Feldesland . . . ," I began.

"The more refugees will risk everything to get out, yes," he said. "I don't know if we can prevent those machine gun plans from reaching Grappoli manufacturers or not—it may already be too late—but it's clear that they have agents here at home who are going to continue to aid them. We must find out who those people are and stop them."

I considered him, then looked at Madame Nahreem. As I did so, I thought of the mask, and in place of the grief and anger I had felt rising within me, there was only a serene and mysterious confidence.

"I'll do it," I said. "Madame Nahreem is right. I'm ready."

The table fell silent, and everyone looked at me, mildly taken aback by the forcefulness, the finality of my decision. It was, I dare say, aristocratic.

I INSISTED ON ONE visit to my sister's family before I adopted my new guise, and though Madame Nahreem said that she found my "sentimentality" annoying, she admired the hauteur with which I stated that I had made my decision, and left it at that.

It was a hot day, and I could smell the Drowning's stagnant sourness long before I reached it. Rahvey and her girls met me outside the sprawling shanty itself, and we sat by the river on an overgrown pier where the village girls drew water. The hippo pod which sometimes ventured down here had moved upstream for now and could be seen sunning themselves pink on the bank amidst reeds where ospreys soared. I thought again of the abandoned sandals down by the harbor and gave my sister five shillings. She thanked me with a tight little nod, spirited them into her simplified sari, and looked at the water.

I considered the group of children there smilingly, and realized that one of the girls—the one holding the infant Kalla—was a stranger to me. Even for a Lani girl, she was shy, and she kept her eyes down to the baby even when I asked her name. In fact, she didn't respond at all till Rahvey reached over and tugged at her filthy sleeve.

"She's deaf," my sister explained. "Born that way. Can't hear or speak."

I smiled at the little girl, who must have been about seven or eight, and raised my hand in greeting. The girl, whose face was splashed with mud, considered my gesture then repeated it warily.

"What's her name?" I asked.

"Aab," said Rahvey. "Aab Samir. You remember Mrs. Samir? Works at the laundry with me. Her husband is sick and she's staying home with him. I said I'd keep an eye on the girl. She's no trouble. Actually, she's not much of anything. Not very bright. She tries to play with my girls, but she's always behind, always left out when the rules change." Rahvey shrugged, but her lips were pursed grimly. "You have to watch her because she doesn't hear if someone shouts that they've seen a snake or a crocodile. She's not allowed out if there are hyenas about." She shook her head. "What she'll do when she grows up I just don't know. If she gets to grow up. It's impossible to explain anything to her, and she can't leave the Drowning. But Mrs. Samir is no spring chicken, and what the girl would do if she had to fend for herself . . ." She shook her head again and broke off, shooting me a bleak, knowing smile.

"Life, eh, sister mine?" she said. "It's no place to be poor."

The remark stayed in my head, humming like an old temple bell, as I made my circuitous way back to Willinghouse's town home, and Madame Nahreem's remarks about unlearning my own body came back to me. We of the Drowning and the streets wore our past, our place in the world, like a cloak we could not shed. It muffled us, shaped us, weighed us down. It stuck to our arms, tangled around our feet, and laced itself into our hair till it became a second skin, all we had been defining what we were, what we might be. To shake it off, to become someone else as I had to now, demanded a kind of surgery, a splitting open of the skin, a bitter, bloody birthing in which the new self pushed its way out of the old and lay gasping between life and death on the midwife's floor.

I was not sure it could be done.

CHAPTER

12

THE NEWSPAPERS, WHICH HAD so decried the cluttering of Bar-Selehm's harbor with homeless and unskilled immigrants, were now reporting that the Grappoli advance had temporarily slowed, though no one had any good explanation as to why. Conditions in the northern part of the continent were, they said "difficult," an understatement offered to explain why their stories contained little more than rumor and conjecture. More interesting to me was a discreet announcement in the society pages. It revealed the arrival of one Lady Ki Misrai, a princess from Istilia, who was touring the region before returning home to a marriage arranged between her family and that of an Antrioan landowner of excellent pedigree and considerable wealth. The visit was, said the paper, strictly recreational. The invitation to attend Elitus had arrived at the post office box Willinghouse had quietly established for that purpose almost immediately.

"You will be staying at the Royal Palace Hotel," said Madame Nahreem.

I should have expected as much, but the name of the place clearly registered in my face.

"You must not show yourself intimated or impressed by anything," said Madame Nahreem. "Take everything in stride. Remember the mask."

She did not wish me good luck.

I rode in Willinghouse's carriage back to the city accompanied by Namud, who was to be my escort for the evening. A lady would never attend a venue such as Elitus unaccompanied. But Namud was no mere chaperone. He was also my bodyguard, and while he would have to turn in the ostentatious pistol he wore at his side to the door-man when we arrived, he had, he assured me, other weapons con-cealed about his person that he intended to keep.

I liked Namud. He was perhaps thirty, quiet, and, I felt, gentle, in spite of his physical strength. He said very little, but there was a wry amusement that sometimes surfaced in his face, like a dolphin breaching unexpectedly. The dolphin dived quickly, as if showing itself would violate Namud's private sense of decorum, and when it did, the waters of formality would close so completely over the top that it became hard to believe you had actually glimpsed that glis-tening playfulness only moments before.

We left the carriage on the corner of Deerfeld Avenue, waiting in the cool shade of a chapel with my luggage, till we were collected by a cab and driven to the Royal Palace. It was important that no one there connect us to Willinghouse. I asked Namud if there was any chance of his being recognized.

"I rarely venture into the city, my lady," he said, quite poised. "But even if I did, I am told that one Lani servant looks much like another."

With the faintest flicker of a smile, the dolphin vanished once more.

I wore a demure veil over a long black dress and elbow-length gloves, which was supposed to be suitable Istilian travel wear for a lady, but was uncomfortably hot and restrictive. I did not speak to the check-in clerk, allowing Namud to confirm my reservation and or-chestrate the army of uniformed bellhops who would ferry my lug-gage to my room, while I stood in a little globe of silence like an ominous statue under dust sheeting.

The Royal Palace had been fitted with a steam-driven elevator that took the form of a small, square sitting room, beautifully furnished and upholstered with plush red fabric and gold cord. I took my place on a padded bench, turned slightly sideways, legs together and hands clasped at my waist, glad that the veil concealed my panic as the at-tendant closed the gated door and adjusted the ropes that controlled the engine below. There was a distant hiss, a whir, and a clank, and the room rose smoothly and steadily up. I kept my hands locked tightly together and held my breath till we reached the fifth floor and slowed.

I inclined my head to the attendant, all the thanks a lady in my position was expected to bestow, and followed the solicitous bellhop to what would be my room for the night. In fact, it wasn't so much a room as a suite: a luxurious bedchamber, a separate bathroom with running water, an opulent sitting room and a private bar, which would be staffed at my request. Namud had an adjoining room. It was all extraordinary.

I had only an hour to enjoy it, however, before I had to change, and this I could not do alone, since I would be going out in one of the complex Istilian saris which I had seen only in their simple, impoverished, and it had to be said, more convenient forms in the Drowning. After forty minutes reveling in my solitude, there was a knock at the door and Namud showed Dahria in.

"My, my," she exclaimed. "We have moved up in the world! And not by climbing like a bush baby with its tail on fire."

"Did it have to be you?" I asked, secretly pleased to see her.

"Josiah wants to keep this within the family. So *I* get to be *your* maid for a while. Imagine my delight."

"I wish you were coming with me tonight," I confessed.

She looked momentarily surprised, then shook her head.

"You'll do better without me," she said.

"Why?"

"Because I know who you really are and that would make you self-conscious, like you're pretending. Success depends on you believing your own lie. Better that there's no one there to remind you of the truth."

It could have been a half joke at my expense, but it wasn't. She was sincere, thoughtful even, and when I held her gaze, she looked away, as if the remark had meant something more than the words alone suggested.

More masks, I thought, *more playing until it becomes true, and your new self outgrows your old.*

"Notes from my dear brother," she said, producing a fold of paper. "There's little on the club's layout—because he doesn't know much, though that has never prevented him from writing a detailed report. It's a government thing."

I glanced at it. There was a carefully lined diagram containing almost no detail, but conveying one salient point.

"The office with the membership list is on the top floor?" I said.

"And probably not accessible from inside the building," said Dahria. "You may have to climb in through a courtyard window. Well within your steeplejack abilities, I'm sure."

"So when he said I was the only one he could send because I was the one he trusted . . ." I began.

"That was a lie, yes," said Dahria. "Sorry. He does that."

"I see," I said simply, and left it at that.

Elitus was a members-only club. It was also all white and all male. Unless you were employed in its service sector or brought in for entertainment value, there would be no way for a woman to cross its threshold, particularly if you were black or Lani. I expressed my furious bafflement to Dahria, but she just shrugged.

"You're not a society lady," she said, "so you don't understand, but I actually see the appeal."

I stared at her.

"Of what?"

"A club where I could be with people like me," she said. "Women's clubs are not as common as men's, not as politically powerful, but if you'd grown up among only your own kind, been sent to an all girl's school, and been shuffled into the women-only drawing room whenever the meal was over, you might see that a lot of women don't actually want to have to deal with men who, for the most part, they neither understand nor like. Even their romantic entanglements are largely scripted and occasional affairs. I seriously doubt that any husband and wife are as close as are two old acquaintances of the same sex who do not have to hide their thoughts for fear of violating what might be considered genteel. My dear steeplejack, this may come as a surprise to one raised as scandalously as you, but Bar-Selehm is full of married men and women who want nothing more than to retreat into the company of those with whom they grew up."

"White people," I said, shaking my head in bewilderment.

"I wish you wouldn't take that disagreeable tone," she said. "It is extremely tiresome. And stop fiddling with your veil."

"It's in the way. I can't see properly."

"Leave it. An Istilian lady rarely removes her veil in mixed company."

I scowled. However much Dahria wanted to characterize the clubbable world of the city as a kind of hankering after childhood simplicities uncomplicated by the opposite sex, there was no denying that many of the agreements, deals, policy changes, and alliances that were at the heart of the city's economic and political life were cobbled together in the private rooms of those exclusive clubs. Elitus was a prime example, and its exclusivity had a tang of secrecy about it. While certain aristocrats, high-ranking politicians, diplomats, financiers, and industrialists were known, or assumed, to be members, there was no precise list of who was allowed in and who wasn't, nor—and this was more troubling—was there a clear sense of what went on within the club itself. I had prepared to behave as an Istilian lady, but what exactly I was going into, I had no idea.

Half an hour later Namud, a square suitcase in one hand, presented my card at the ornate but discreet door on Rethmina Avenue, turned in his pistol with his coat, and led me into I knew not what.

The entrance was deceptively ordinary—a flight of stone steps up to a black lacquered door indistinguishable from half a dozen others on the same block. The building was four stories aboveground and a basement, so that it looked to all the world like a well-appointed town house with ground floor rooms for entertaining and servants' quarters below. It was not until I had made my way along an elegant hall that I realized the walls dividing this house from those on either side had been knocked through. Elitus wasn't on the block between numbers 22 and 34. It *was* the block.

I could hear music and voices coming from the end of the hallway.

"Lady Misrai, if you would do me the honor of stepping this way?"

The voice came from a silver-haired white man in a tailcoat with gold braid on the oversized cuffs and a perfectly knotted white cravat at his throat. The shirt he wore beneath showed a pair of familiar cuff links: a blue diamond on a silver field. He stood ramrod straight, one hand extended thumb side up like a statue.

"I am Wellsley, Elitus's doorman," he said. "Your man will follow me." It was a statement of fact, and he followed it with another. "All the rooms on this floor—including the Imperial Library, the Satin Lounge, and the King Gustav suite—are at your disposal. A retiring room has been assigned to you on the second floor, though all other chambers on the upper floors are by prior booking and invitation only. You will be notified if such an invitation is forthcoming. Through this door to the Great Hall, if you would be so kind."

Namud gave me an encouraging look and, so quietly I barely heard it, breathed, "Be calm. Keep your veil on."

I approached the end of the carpeted hallway where a pair of white footmen stood on either side of a set of double doors. Without a word or gesture, they opened them in perfect unison, revealing a wood-paneled chamber with a high ceiling in which the air—gray with cigar smoke—moved slowly like fog. It felt more like a lobby than a hall, and I was a little let down by its lack of opulence. The central area was open, but around it was a disorder of armchairs and end tables, couches and newspaper racks, potted palms and drinks carts, around which a dozen or more men had gathered like elderly flies.

Wellsley stepped through and presented my calling card to a liveried servant in a uniform that evoked a military parade ground, crimson with brass buttons and a white silk sash. He wore a saber at his side. He was white, but then they all were, some reading, some playing backgammon, some considering their drinks as they listened to a young man playing a stately piece on the pianoforte.

"Lady Ki Misrai!" boomed the liveried swordsman in a voice so loud and commanding that I started, realizing too late that every face in the room had turned to look at me.

The music continued, but only for a moment. Nothing else did. And eventually, thrown by the sudden silence, even the musician broke off. Everyone stared.

For a second, I felt not merely an imposter, but an attacker, an insurgent deep behind enemy lines, in the very heart of their command headquarters. The room was not grand, but it was old and tasteful, layered with tradition. But then I knew what that tradition meant and what it had cost. The chairs these worthy gentlemen sat on may have been lacquered by Lani craftsmen, the gleaming tiled floor on which they stood had been swept, scrubbed, and mopped by Lani servants for two hundred years, the very stone of which the building had been raised had been quarried by forgotten Lani laborers who ended their lives poor and cast off as their bodies gave in to the ravages of age and they found they had nothing else to show for decades of work. Not just the Lani, of course—the Mahweni too, and the poorest whites, but for a second, I could see only the remains of my own people scattered like dust among the brass and stone of the Great Hall. It was like feeling the ache of a forgotten wound.

And just as quickly as it had come, I buried it. I drew myself up to my full height, met their appraising blue eyes, and held them as if I was wearing Madame Nahreem's neutral mask, shedding my past, my identity like so much snake skin. I was dressed in a sari of amber silk, worn in the Istilian style—eight yards of lustrous fabric wrapped around my waist and wound up over one shoulder, baring my slim, brown midriff. It was paired with a close-fitting blouse called a choli and a lace shawl, which doubled as the veil I wore over my face. The silk glowed and shimmered like fire reflected on gold. In the center

of my forehead, I wore the red bindi mark around which were positioned four minute grains of old, yellow luxorite held in place with
spirit gum, and just bright enough to give a warm and gentle radi-
ance.

There was a ripple through the gathering of drab, formally dressed
white men as they looked up from their newspapers and got to their
feet. At least one of them gasped. I left Namud and strode purposefully into the room, the sari trailing behind me, the shawl billowing
slightly like wings, and as I did so, I smiled about me through the veil,
each glance a little scattering of gold in a crowd of peasants and for a
moment, a tiny, shining moment, I was a princess and the Great Hall
had been built with the sweat of *their* backs for me and my kind.

They came to me, stopping what they were doing and gathering
about me like hummingbirds to nectar, bowing and smiling and murmuring how charmed they were to make my acquaintance. I smiled
and inclined my head a fraction and smiled some more, and in my
heart I fought a war between blind panic and wild, savage triumph
as they introduced themselves, proffering their cards, which Namud
took and stored in a silver case.

I recognized some of their names, and I suspected that Dahria
would have known them all, at least by repute, so I tried to remember who was who as best I could, filing their titles away while continuing to glide like a swan on water, its unseen feet paddling furiously
below.

Nathan Horritch.

Something or other Ratsbane? Rathbone?

Lord Elwin.

Thomas Markeson.

Eustace Montresat.

A Mr. Vandersay . . .

Someone who might have been called Byron. Or was it Brian?

It was impossible.

I was offered drinks and selected a cordial in a tiny crystal glass shaped like a rose hip. It was rich and thick as syrup and I did little more than moisten my lips with it beneath my veil before setting it down, seeking with each movement to mirror that languid grace Madame Nahreem had modeled for me. As I did so, I considered my solicitous companions, all at least twice my age and pale as paper. None of them resembled the man with the pick and the bland smile, though they all wore his blue diamond cuff links. The thought of that gave me pause. The old men who seemed so delighted by me were, I had to remember, potentially very dangerous.

"Lady Misrai," said one who had introduced himself as Nathan Horritch, twinkling over the rim of his glass, "do tell us all you have planned for your visit to our fair city."

Another—Rathbone? Ratsbane?—pulled out a chair, and I settled carefully into it, thereby giving them permission to sit too.

"Well," I began, speaking quietly but with clarity and decision, head very slightly cocked, planning the upward lilt of the statement even as I made it, "I have heard wonderful things about your great buildings, structures whose like we do not have in Istilia. A great bridge suspended by chains?" I said to Horritch. He was perhaps sixty, silver haired but robust, and his eyes were a deep blue and alive with thought and a watchfulness that felt different from the others, as if he were considering me from a great distance through some kind of lens.

"The jewel of Bar-Selehm," said one Thomas Markeson, a florid-faced man who was beaming with pride as if he had built it himself. "A rare spectacle indeed."

"And the Beacon?" I added. "I believe I saw its light from the carriage."

"You may well have done," said another, smaller than the others, a wheedling, ferretlike man called Montresat, who clasped his hands before his chest like a squirrel with a nut. "The Trade Exchange is indeed a marvel, and as for the Beacon itself, I suspect it is alone worth crossing oceans for!"

"Perhaps we should arrange a tour for you," wheezed Markeson, leaning back as if to see over his gargantuan stomach. "I am sure we could find you suitable escorts who would ensure you saw only the best of the city."

"That is most kind," I said, feeling thoroughly overwhelmed, "though I'm keen to see the entirety of so wondrous a settlement. Bar-Selehm is renowned throughout the world for its industry, and I find myself driven to see the machinery that makes it work."

"You may find," chuckled the scarlet-faced Markeson, "that such places are full of noise and filth, and populated by entirely the wrong sort of people. I think we can find a lady such as yourself more suitable pastimes."

"Perhaps," I replied, "but I find that to truly understand a place, to know its heart, you need to see what feeds it, what makes it move, wouldn't you say?"

"Absolutely," said Vandersay, as if speaking on behalf of the group, though they seemed unsettled by the idea.

"I think I can survive a little noise," I added, still smiling beatifically. "As to the people, one never knows quite who the wrong sort are till one meets them, don't you think?"

Another chorus of hurried agreement.

"Gentlemen," said Markeson, his voice booming, "I think *we* know when we have met at least one of the right kind of people." He bowed his head slightly to me and raised his glass. "My dear and most exquisite lady, welcome to our club and to our city." As he took a drink, the others burbled their agreement and followed suit.

"Well," said Lord Elwin, a man with an almost comically aristocratic air and a drawling voice that made every word sound like it was coming out midyawn, "we must not keep you to ourselves, much as we would like to. I am sure the ladies are waiting breathlessly to hear all about Istilian fashion and courtly gossip."

I blinked.

"Ladies?" I said.

"The ladies of Merita," said Lord Elwin. "Our sister institution. They are expecting you in the east wing. Activities here that take place in mixed company are rare and all too brief. You will spend most of the evening with our esteemed female companions. If that accords with your wishes, of course."

"Certainly," I said, covering my surprise and frustration. It had not occurred to me—or indeed to Dahria or Willinghouse—that the club had a woman's wing, however nominally separate. The prospect of sitting around on uncomfortable chairs making small talk with a gaggle of Bar-Selehm's elite flower arrangers and tea drinkers while we waited for whatever absurd ritual of social niceties would permit us to interact with the men in the building was maddening.

Unsure just how much of my face they could see through the veil, I forced a smile—the strain on my cheeks was becoming painful— and turned to where Namud was waiting to escort me out of the room I had only just entered. I found the man with the intense blue eyes—Nathan Horritch—watching me shrewdly, and as my gaze met his, his lip twisted into a knowing smile. Despite his years, he had something of the focused energy I saw in Willinghouse.

"I fear," he said, "that we have caught Lady Misrai out."

I hesitated, feeling my pulse quicken and my color rise.

"How so, sir?" I managed.

"This is not, I think, why you came," said Horritch, his eyes narrow. "Confess yourself, my lady. We shall not judge you too harshly."

"I'm sure I don't know what you mean," I said, lowering my hands so that their fractional quaver would not attract attention.

"I think," said Horritch, "that you did not come to talk to other ladies. Indeed," he said, raising his forefinger, "I do not believe you knew there were ladies here. I would go so far to say, that you dread the company of such light and silly creatures as you have no doubt encountered on your travels. I can only assure you that the ladies of Merita are most accomplished and that"—and here his stern countenance gave away the punch line he had been holding off—"we will do our utmost to rescue you as soon as decorum permits."

His remark was greeted with laughter and agreement while I nodded and smiled again, though in my case it was relief that I felt rather than mirth, and I was glad to follow Namud to the door.

"Directly along the hall toward the street door," said the uniformed swordsman who had announced me, "then keep walking directly across. An attendant will greet you at the far end." He handed a key on a brass fob numbered 236 to Namud. "The lady's retiring room."

I stayed in character with each measured step I took down the hall, but my heart was racing, and I was unnerved by how quickly we had been forced off script. How could there be a women's club here that Dahria had never heard of? It changed everything and meant, I suspected, that I'd be under even more scrutiny than I had anticipated while learning even less. I gritted my teeth, infuriated by how—in spite of all my finery—I felt powerless to do anything useful.

I glanced at Namud, and he flicked his eyebrows, a minuscule but expressive gesture of exasperation. We passed the entrance to the street door where Wellsley, the silver-haired doorman, was overseeing a young Mahweni as he swept the stoop with a broom of twigs and straw. Wellsley nodded respectfully, gesturing in the direction we were walking.

"The ladies' hall is directly at the end of this gallery," he said.

And once in, I thought, *I am stuck till summoned.*

"Perhaps there are other parts of the club I could explore first," I said to Namud, hopefully.

"I'm afraid you are expected," said the manservant.

"Fine," I muttered, recovering my aristocratic poise as I walked on down the hall. "I'm sure this will be gripping entertainment."

"I suggest," whispered Namud at my elbow, "that you leave your sarcasm at the door. You are beginning to sound like Mistress Dahria."

I couldn't help but grin at that.

But then, back along the hall behind me, came the sound of men laughing and talking. I turned, gazing past Namud toward the entrance. Three men in evening wear were exchanging pleasantries with the doorman as they stepped inside, removing their top hats.

Him.

I took four hurried steps along the corridor, remembering at the last moment to force myself into some more stately gait, glad of the shawl that still veiled my face.

I did not need to see his mismatched cuff links. I knew his eyes, his bland smile. I knew the man who had tried to kill me on the crane over the river.

CHAPTER

13

"MY LADY . . . ?" VENTURED NAMUD as I strode past him.

I was halfway along the hall, only yards from the entrance. The voices were louder, clearer though they had stepped back into the lobby to finish their good-humored banter with the doorman: jovial fellows, these, men who did not stand on ceremony, men who took pride in their bonhomie, their easy comfort with their inferiors. And one of them was a killer of the most sick and ruthless kind.

They stepped back into the hall just as I reached the entry alcove, turning in surprise at my golden exoticism so that for a moment they just gaped. One of them might perhaps have been one of the men from the boat, the one who had felled the unfortunate cat burglar, Darius. There could be no mistaking the other, with those eyes, cool even in impressed surprise.

"Our esteemed visitor from Istilia, no doubt," he said, extending his hand. I hesitated only a second, but it gave him pause. "Forgive my forwardness," he remarked, smiling the same bland smile that had been plastered across his face as he had prepared to put a pickax through my skull, "we are less formal in Bar-Selehm than you are, perhaps, accustomed to. Even here. My apologies."

His voice had an edge of local accent under its cultured polish.

"Not necessary," I managed, offering him my hand, brown fingers unfamiliar in gold rings with sparkling stones. He took it in his, bent slightly, and kissed it just above the knuckle. It took all my presence of mind not to yank it away and bring it hard back across his face, though my aggression came from fear, and not simply of discovery.

The mask. Remember the mask.

"Lady Ki Misrai," said Namud, materializing at my elbow and managing to loom just a little, so that my admirer released my hand with a fractional and all too familiar smile.

"James Barrington-Smythe," he said, with a little swagger. "Enchanted."

I said nothing to that, but gave a tiny nod of acknowledgment, glad of the veil between us as I combed his face for any sign that he recognized me. I saw none, but I found that the hand he had kissed was trembling very slightly. Even here, when he was being suave and urbane, when the killer I had seen that night by the river was as carefully hidden as it could be, I sensed what he was and could not stand to be in his company a moment longer.

I turned toward the doorman, looking for an escape, and only then did I see the third man. He was clad in a slim gray suit with black trim and silver buttons which had a whiff of the military about them. I did not need to ask his name. It was Norton Richter, head of the Heritage party, the man whose Bar-Selehm First Act had so incensed Willinghouse.

Up close he was lean and mirthless, and the hardness of his face did not thaw at the sight of me. The red and silver badge he wore on his lapel was the same as I had seen on his supporters in Parliament, and now I could make out its emblem: an upraised gloved fist clutching what looked to be a lightning bolt. I would have stopped Namud from introducing me if I could, but I was a fraction of a second too late in turning away, and I was forced to look the man in the face, even as he turned his blank, unimpressed stare from Namud to me.

"Charmed, I'm sure," he said, cursorily, turning even as he did so to Barrington-Smythe. "James, I believe we are late for our meeting. Excuse us."

This last was to me, a terse dismissal, but one I was all too eager to embrace.

"I'm sorry," I managed, addressing the doorman. "I seem to have become disoriented. The ladies' parlor is . . . ?"

"At the end of the hall, my lady," said the doorman.

"Of course," I said, turning.

"It is a large house," said the doorman kindly. "Easy to get turned around in."

"Indeed," I said, standing on my dignity. "If you will excuse me, Mr. Barrington-Smith—"

"Smythe," he corrected, stung.

"Quite so," I said. "These Bar-Selehm pronunciations are tricky." I turned and walked away, once more repressing the urge to run, to get as far from that man as I could. The company of women, whoever they were, suddenly seemed very appealing.

Merita boasted its own lobby, a miniature version of its Elitus counterpart. The architectural features and decorative trim were all on a slightly smaller, finer scale, and the color palette was softer, paler. The guard on the door was accompanied by a middle-aged woman, matronly of dress and demeanor. Her austere, slightly hard face melted only fractionally as I approached, but her careful bow was respectful.

"Lady Misrai, I presume," she said. "I shall announce you. Gentlemen," she remarked, eyeing Namud pointedly, "are not permitted within the confines of the club."

Namud caught my eye, but his nod of acknowledgment was formally polite, and he turned on his heel as if he had expected no less. As he walked away, I felt once more that momentary panic, as if I was high on a chimney stack and had just unclipped the carabiner of a safety rope. I half turned toward his retreating back, but the door was open, and my name rang out from the mouth of the rather dour housekeeper, if that was what she was.

The room, like the foyer, was smaller than its equivalent in Elitus, more like a drawing room, with walls of deep mauve set off by bright white trim and molding. The furniture, all restrained elegance and soft curves, was old-fashioned, formal, and less comfortable-looking than what the men had. The effect was like a gilded frame that had been designed to complement the image within, though in this case the painting was the ladies of Merita artfully perched on the various chairs and love seats.

There were eight of them. Three were only a few years my senior, four were nearer forty than thirty, and one was at least sixty. They were, of course, all white and made more so through what I took to be a well-managed regimen of lead or arsenic cosmetics, which left them ivory pale, their skin translucent and bluish like watered milk. They wore fashionable evening gowns with short sleeves, low neck-lines, and voluminous skirts buoyed up on crinolines. They rose with a rustle of expensive fabrics—one of the middle-aged ladies wobbling on heels high and narrow as railroad spikes—and turned their eyes on me. They were cautious, appraising eyes, eyes keen to determine my interest value, my worth to them.

Or so it felt. What was really going through their minds I could not guess, but I was used to being invisible, ignored, and this sudden scrutiny made me feel like a butterfly in a jam jar, albeit one with golden wings. They took in my dress with eager fascination. The eldest lady seemed to linger on my exposed navel and her eyebrows arched fractionally, as if she had steeled herself against the shock of Istilian attire but it had proved too much for her after all. In a moment she would have to sit down, overcome by all that brown skin open to the air.

I clenched my teeth, then ceremoniously lowered my veil and gave my practiced aristocratic smile. Where the gentlemen of Elitus had been effusive and titillated in their hurry to greet me, the ladies of Merita were subdued, cautious even, and several seemed to be standing on their dignity, so that I wondered how many of them had objected to my being invited. They stood, smiling politely rather than warmly, extending gloved hands, and murmuring their names as if I really ought to already know who they were.

Except one. She was, I suspected, the youngest of the group, a fresh-faced, blue-eyed doll of a girl with blond ringlets spilling with sheer exuberance out of her demure cap. Her eyes were as wide as her smile when she took my hand—the first to do so, as she had been the first to her feet as I was announced—and while the others merely offered their names like diners passing the salt, she opened her mouth and the person she was spilled out in a rush of delighted glee.

"Lady Ki! Such a pleasure to meet you," she gushed. "Can I call you Lady Ki? Or should I call you Lady Misrai? I'm not terribly good at etiquette when it comes to foreign dignitaries, but I mean well. Do tell us all bout your journey! I just can't wait to hear all about your travels and about Istilia. It must be so beautiful! I want to go there *so much,* but Father won't let me. Not till I'm twenty-five, he says, which I think is absolute rot, don't you?"

It was like standing beneath a waterfall.

"Your father . . . ?" I inserted.

"Oh, what a clodpoll I am!" she said. "I'm Lady Alice Welborne. But you can call me Alice. Everyone does."

"No, Lady Alice, they don't," said the next woman, another pale-skinned beauty who might have been twenty-four, twenty-five, but who had an aura of wry-amusement in her gray eyes.

"Well, Constance, I ask them to," said Alice, "and that amounts to the same thing."

"Oh *do* stop talking, you silly girl," said the elderly, lace-veiled matron, pushing her way into the conversation like a haughty tug on the river. "I'm afraid, you must forgive our more exuberant member, Lady Misrai. Doesn't have the brains God gave a sparrow, bless her. But she does, as she says, mean well. I am Serafina Dearbeloved. My husband, as I'm sure you know, is MP for Skevington East."

"Is he in the Brevard party?" I asked, settling into the gracefully designed armchair and doing my best not to sit on the pleats of my sari. The Merita ladies followed suit.

"I should think not," exclaimed Mrs. Dearbeloved, a large, opulent woman who—at least in this moment—gave the impression of just having eaten a considerable meal which rendered her bloated and disinclined to movement. Her eyes swiveled as she spoke, but the rest of her might have been held to her chair with a number of well positioned straps. "Brevard party, indeed! Reginald is a cabinet minister! A member of the National party, the ruling party of the city-state of Bar-Selehm. One would think a foreign dignitary would know such things. I'm afraid that the Brevard party are really not our kind of people at all," she added with a chuckle at the others, which rippled around the group like the chittering of Madame Nahreem's hyenas.

"Why is that?" I asked innocently.

"Yes, Mrs. Dearbeloved," said Lady Alice, her brow puckered with confusion as if the question had never occurred to her before, "why *is* that?"

"Because the Brevard party would hand the country over to the blacks in a heartbeat!" declared Mrs. Dearbeloved, still moving nothing but her eyes and lips as if someone was performing a species of surgery on her spine. "Not that they will ever be elected into power," she added, calming. "Thank God."

"You lean more to Mr. Richter's party," I said.

I sensed the unease around me, but Mrs. Dearbeloved seemed oblivious to it.

"Well, he's hardly of the noblesse," she said, musingly, "and it is widely thought that the practicality of his policies would require more than can be currently spent, but he has some very sound ideas."

"Segregation by color," I said.

"It's really not so very different from what we have now," said Mrs. Dearbeloved loftily, "but I wouldn't expect an outsider like yourself to understand. You don't have our problems."

"Because her country is not ruled by people who conquered it, you mean?" said one of the younger women, who had introduced herself as Violet Farthingale. She was a slight, pretty thing in an ordinary sort of way, with a mass of chestnut curls and a shapely bosom. She had smiled as she asked the question, but there was steel inside the velvet, and it stung the older woman in the high-heeled shoes like a dagger fly.

"Don't speak about things you don't understand, girl," the woman who had introduced herself as Agatha Markeson snapped. She was, I thought, surely the wife of the blustery fellow I had just met in Elitus. She had a shrewd, pointed face which had the curious effect of looking permanently startled and accusatory, as if she had just interrupted you pilfering her jewelry box. "Mr. Richter is merely pointing out that we were best to follow nature in such matters. The lion does not befriend the antelope."

"And which are we?" asked the younger woman.

"I beg your pardon?" demanded Agatha Markeson.

"The white people," said Violet, sweetly. "Are we the lion or the antelope?"

"Don't be ridiculous," snapped Agatha. "You know how dangerous the city has become. A *respectable* lady can barely cross the street in safety."

I thought her emphasis curious, and said, "So the Mahweni are the lions?"

Agatha gave a just-as-you-say nod, lips pursed, but Violet said, "We must be a remarkable species of antelope to have entirely subjugated a race of lions and confiscated all their territory."

It took all Madame Nahreem's mask work for me to show no flicker of amusement and surprise, and in my head I suddenly saw Mnenga grinning broadly, that unrestrained delight of his, which—

"The past is past," said Mrs. Dearbeloved returning to the conversation with a flick of one finger which, given her immobility to this point, was as potent as if she had leapt onto the table and bellowed, thereby rendering three centuries irrelevant. "We must now look to stabilizing the future."

I wondered if that was a phrase her husband had used in Parliament.

"Which the Brevard party could not accomplish?" I inquired.

"Well, they have their sympathizers," said Mrs. Dearbeloved. "The various Mahweni *tribes*," she said, disliking the word, "though they, of course, can't vote."

I saw the flash of annoyance in Violet Farthingale's eyes, though she said nothing.

"But the city blacks can participate in elections?" I asked, my tone neutral.

"Oh yes," she said. "They can't run for office themselves, of course. That would hardly be appropriate. Yet they can vote for the candidate of their choice like everyone else."

"Well, perhaps not like everyone else," said the woman who Alice had called Constance. As before, her tone was amused, as if she alone had noticed something funny, and her gray eyes flickered with intelligence. I had thought her beautiful, but she had none of Alice's girlish softness or Violet's furvor, and her beauty—"handsomeness" was perhaps a better word—might have looked better on a statue placed somewhere high up, a feature that reminded me a little of Dahria. I gave her a puzzled look, and she explained her remark. "The city's black voters can only vote in certain districts."

"It's more than fair," said Mrs. Dearbeloved.

"No doubt, Serafina," said Constance, "but while the city's white districts have several government seats allocated per few thousand residents—and some seats are elected by only a few hundred voters—black districts such as Morgessa, Nbeki, and Old Town have only one seat per ten thousand voters. The result is that even when the Mahweni are of one mind—"

"Which hardly ever happens," inserted Mrs. Dearbeloved dismissively.

"Their votes cannot have a meaningful effect on the election," Constance concluded. She spoke with that same dry amusement as before, and the effect was disorienting. The point she was making suggested outrage at a palpable, if time-honored, injustice, and I saw as much in Violet Farthingale's face, but Constance delivered it with such ironic detachment that she seemed not to care at all. It occurred to me that she was merely needling Mrs. Dearbeloved for her own private amusement and, feeling like I had been made a pawn in whatever socially acceptable spitefulness was in play, I felt stung.

"Isn't that rather appalling?" I asked, still sweet, still sedate, but only just. "That so many people have no practical voice in their own governance strikes me as deeply unjust."

"Well, as an outsider," said Mrs. Dearbeloved—and there was that trace of distaste again as she looked me up and down, "you can't be expected to understand, but it is, I assure you, a kindness. Better that those who *can* govern do so. As we say here in the city, we don't look to the infant to plan its own breakfast."

More knowing smiles, which I attempted to match.

"On these matters," she added, "I think Mr. Richter very sound, and I would like to see the Nationals adopt something closer to his position. Indeed, a merger of the two parties might prove most fruitful for the city, perhaps even under his leadership. Tavestock is a decent enough prime minister, but Richter speaks the truth without worrying about what is popular or whom he might offend. We need that kind of integrity."

"If you are concerned about unequal representation," added Constance, "I might add that no one in this room can vote at all, so black men have one better on us."

"Oh, please don't start on that women's suffrage business again, my dear," said Mrs. Dearbeloved. "It is quite tedious."

Constance smiled her private smile, and her eyes lingered on mine.

"Tedious it may be," said Violet Farthingale stiffly, "but until Bar-Selehm allows women—"

"I wouldn't want to vote," Lady Alice interrupted guilelessly. "I can't abide politics. It is so terribly boring, and it never has anything to do with me. If I was given the vote, I'm sure I'd choose the gentleman who wore the nicest hat or—"

"Perhaps you might vote for a lady like yourself," asked Constance. More needling.

Lady Alice's doelike eyes got wider still.

"A lady MP!" she gasped. "Now I think you are teasing me, Constance. You really shouldn't."

"That is very true," said Mrs. Dearbeloved. "I suggest we change the subject before our visitor concludes that we have no conversation at all. Agatha, tell us about that glorious shawl. It is quite becoming."

I couldn't tell if she was still irritated with Constance or at something else entirely, but her compliment to Mrs. Markeson seemed somewhat halfhearted. The woman in question—whose last contribution to the debate had been to spar with Violet Farthingale over lions and antelopes—was perhaps next in age to Mrs. Dearbeloved, and she wore a royal stillness like an achievement. Her shawl, it had to be admitted, was indeed lovely. It was draped around her shoulders over a conventional, even old-fashioned, dress. The color of the shawl—a misty gray, almost silver—was not especially out of the ordinary, but the fabric itself was astonishingly fine, even compared to my own lustrous silk. It hung with such softness about her that the slightest movement stirred it, so that in brightness and texture, it seemed almost liquid, and looking at it was like beholding moonlight on water.

Despite her queenly demeanor, it was clear that Agatha Markeson had been waiting for this very moment, and though she affected a politely self-deferential tone as she showed off the shawl, she was delighted by the attention.

"It is rather special, isn't it?" she said. "And it complements these shoes so nicely." The shoes in question were the ones with the three-inch dagger-point heels usually worn by women half her age. They looked absurd and lethal, and though I could shin up a two-hundred-foot chimney without batting an eye, those dizzying heights would have been beyond me. "I take no credit, of course, but I am proud to be, I believe, the first to wear so remarkable a cloth."

There was something in her manner that was more than snobbery or smugness—a hint, perhaps of defiance, even of anger, which I did not understand. She pointedly did not look at anyone in the room, but I felt a shuffling of attention, an awkwardness like embarrassment, and when one of the ladies rose abruptly, I felt that the rest avoided her eyes.

Violet Farthingale was pink in the face.

"Excuse me, ladies," she said, not looking at them. "I believe I need a little air or a lie down."

No one said anything, and as the door closed behind her hurried exit, the uneasiness in the room seemed to deepen for all but Agatha Markeson, who inflated a little. There was color in her cheeks, and the glitter in her eyes looked oddly like triumph.

"What is the shawl made of?" I asked to fill the silence.

"I like to call it Bar-Selehm silk," said Agatha Markeson with feigned indifference that could not conceal her glee, "though I think that rather sells it short, don't you? Forms of the material have been around for a long time, and the western tribesmen used to weave a version of it for their ceremonies. Not like this, naturally, but using the same basic material. It was always quite heavy and coarse, but this has a considerably finer thread. Of course, with these new child labor laws, it is frankly astounding that anyone is able to produce anything, but the best in the city have always risen to a challenge, as I think this material demonstrates. You might expect it to be very fragile, but it is remarkably strong. I can't tell you where I got it, but I'm sure you will be able to find its equal in the shops eventually."

As the other ladies purred their resentful admiration, my gaze fell on Constance, who rolled her eyes fractionally, so that I grinned back before I could stop myself. The momentary breach in my performance of the aloof Istilian princess shook me, and I took hold of myself, determined to make all this subterfuge worth the trouble. I had not, after all, come here to listen to society women prattle about their dresses.

"Whatever happened to that charming Mr. Sandringham?" asked Mrs. Dearbeloved, changing the subject. "I haven't seen him all week."

Alice looked guilessly at Constance, and though she looked quickly away again, the damage was apparently done, and Constance was forced—against her wishes, I would say—to reply.

"Ephraim has left the city," she remarked. "On business. I do not know when he will return."

"That is a shame," remarked Mrs. Dearbeloved with exquisite venom. "So sad when young couples cannot find ways to resolve their personal lives. But never mind, my dear. You have several good years in you yet, and I'm sure someone will find you most beguiling."

Constance's face clouded, and she gritted her teeth but managed to smile broadly.

"I'm quite sure Constance knows her own mind," said Alice, "and that pity is not called for."

It was a gallant attempt to stand up for someone she clearly admired, but Constance's irritation seemed to increase. I cleared my throat delicately.

"I was surprised to find that Elitus and Merita shared the same house," I remarked, reemphasizing the Istilian lilt. "I even met some of the gentlemen members just down the hallway."

"Oh?" said Mrs. Dearbeloved. "Which ones?"

The switch in the matron's attention redirected the focus of the whole room, so that Mrs. Markeson looked put out that her moment of glory had been cut so short.

"Let me see," I said, pretending to reach into my memory. "Ratsbane?"

"Rathbone," Mrs. Dearbeloved corrected, ignoring—or not seeing—Constance's flash of mischievous delight at my error, "a most respectable gentleman, with family in the old country. His grandfather was chamberlain to the last king before moving to our humble colony."

"Mr. Markeson," I said, acknowledging his wife with a smile, which went some way toward banishing the cloud of pique that had descended on her when we stopped discussing her shawl. "Mr. Barrington-Smythe . . ."

I laid the name out like the snares some of the Lani use to trap woodcock, though I wasn't sure what I was trying to catch. Its effect, however, was instantaneous. Mrs. Dearbeloved draw herself up to her full height and snorted with indignation.

"*Barrington-Smythe*," she repeated in a voice loaded with all the disdain she could muster.

"You do not like the gentleman?" I asked.

"I do not *know* him!" snapped Mrs. Dearbeloved, as if that was condemnation enough. "No one does. He has no family in the city, no crest, no old school friends. The man is a kind of nothing. Yet here he is, lounging with the very best of us."

I was surprised by her candor, and it was clear from the faces of the younger women that they were shocked by how much she was confiding, but Agatha Markeson showed the same hauteur.

"Three nights ago," she said, leaning forward and lowering her voice a fraction, but spitting the words as if they might contaminate her, "I saw him slap my husband on the back like some Southend dockworker and call him 'mate.'"

Several of the ladies put hands to their mouths.

"What did Mr. Markeson say?" asked a staggered Lady Alice.

Something strange came over the older woman, a sudden worried discomfort that registered in her face even as she tried to brush the question away with a flick of her hand.

"Well, what could he say?" said Agatha. "You know Thomas. He's the soul of decorum and politeness. He gave the fellow a stern look, and I fancy he had words with him in private later."

"Scandalous!" huffed Mrs. Dearbeloved. "I never thought I would see such people in this building."

The room fell into a thoughtful and uneasy hush.

"How does one become a member of the club?" I asked.

"Recommendation by existing members," said Mrs. Dearbeloved. "Followed by a vote."

"So Mr. Barrington-Smythe must have had some friends inside the club?" I said, as if I was smoothing things over.

The thoughtful silence returned, and there was a tension to it now that registered especially in Agatha Markeson's face.

"Sometimes when a senior member is especially insistent," said Constance meaningfully, "the vote becomes something of a formality."

"Ah," I said. "A bit like your city elections, then."

Someone gasped. I had overstepped my bounds. The tension thickened, and I felt Mrs. Dearbeloved swelling, like a steam boiler about to burst. Only Constance seemed delighted by my observation, or the outrage it had caused.

"Of course, in Istilia we have a very large royal family," I said, "and no elections at all, so this is all quite strange to me."

This seemed to open the stopcock on Mrs. Dearbeloved, and her steam began to drain harmlessly away.

"Oh, do tell us about life in the Istilian court!" said Lady Alice. "Do you live in a palace? How many servants do you have? Do you change your clothes many times a day?"

Whether anyone else cared to hear such stuff or not, they seemed glad not to be discussing politics, and for the next ten minutes, I responded to Lady Alice's gleeful questions with everything I had studied over the last few days, embroidering in a few fanciful details when the mood took me. I saw no sign that anyone doubted my account, and I was careful to give them what I thought they wanted: an Istilia that was romantic and luxuriant, but fundamentally primitive, lacking both the decorum of Bar-Selehm's high society and its industrial might. This seemed to please, but I was glad when a light supper was served and the bland northern food received more of their attention than they could spare for me.

They gossiped about minor scandals, about debutante balls, about which musicians and painters were being extolled by the society papers, and about where they might spend the hottest months of the summer or the coldest months of the winter. Mrs. Dearbeloved remarked upon the scandalous influx of all those brown and black people trying to come to Bar-Selehm from north of the desert to leech off the state. I said nothing, trying not to think of the little sandal shrine by the river, focusing instead on making sure I was using the right knife. I pretended that my ignorance of all they thought worthy of discussion came from the fact that I was as elevated and remote as an exotic bird instead of a sewer rat they would cross the street to avoid if they saw me in my normal clothes. Mrs. Markeson tried to draw me into a conversation about the terrible falling off of "our poor Lani" from the nobility of their origins, but I dodged like a prizefighter and, more to the point, managed not to stab her through the hand with my salad fork. The young woman who had left us to get some air, Violet Farthingale, did not reappear, and no one mentioned her.

I declined an after-dinner sherry by claiming I had a headache and wanted a moment to relax before whatever passed for after-dinner excitement in Elitus or Merita. Constance gave me a shrewd look at this and, not for the first time, I thought she had seen through all my playacting, but the others seemed blissfully unaware of my desire to escape. Indeed, they were probably glad of the opportunity to discuss me in extended terms.

I would have wanted to get out even without a mission to complete, but I was acutely conscious that for all their talk around the subject—some of it suggestive—I still didn't know who had brought Barrington-Smythe—or whatever his real name was—into the heady ranks of Elitus. It was time I got a look at those membership records.

CHAPTER

14

EXCUSING MYSELF, I LEFT the room, managing not to pause and listen at the door as the discussion of their illustrious guest began, and found Wellsley, the liveried doorman, who summoned Namud from a servants' smoking room off the lobby.

"Will you be rejoining the gentlemen?" asked Wellsley.

"I believe I will take a few moments to myself first," I said.

"Certainly, ma'am," said Namud, offering me the key to my retiring room. "I will bring your things."

I nodded again, took the key, and ascended the stairs, shoulders back, spine straight, chin and eyes level for the benefit of the doorman. I kept that up till I got to my little room, which faced an ornate floral display in a huge urn, unlocked the door, stepped inside, and closed it behind me. Then I threw myself onto what was probably called a fainting couch and screamed my silent frustration into a bolster.

Namud's discreet tap roused me a few minutes later. He offered me the suitcase, checked the hallway, and stepped quickly inside, half closing the door behind him. Given how careful he had been to maintain a very Feldeslandian decorum, I was surprised, more so when he reached into his breast pocket and drew out a slim bundle bound with cord. He untied it and unrolled a pouch of slender tools.

"You know what these are?" he said in an undertone.

I nodded.

"And you know how to use them?" he pressed, giving me a level stare.

I had been a steeplejack in the Seventh Street gang. Plain and simple. But not all my gang mates had been so exclusively legitimate, and I had seen lock picks before. Morlak had kept some in a toolbox—along with three different padlocks for practice—and some of the boys had picks of their own refinement, carefully modified with file and hacksaw. They would pass the padlocks around and challenge each other to see who could get them all open fastest. I generally only tried when the others had gone to bed, and I was no expert, but yes, I knew how to use them.

"Why do you have these?" I asked.

"The room may be locked—," he began.

"No," I said. "I mean why do *you* have these?"

He hesitated, then reopened the door behind him, his face blank.

"I will attend your ladyship downstairs," he said. "Please do not hesitate to call if you need me. There is a bellpull by the bed."

There was indeed. He bowed, cracking not the smallest of smiles—the consummate professional—and walked away. I closed the door behind him and unlatched the case.

It should have contained a change of formal wear and whatever absurd cosmetics ladies went armed with to places such as this, and it did indeed have a few vials and toiletries nestled in a pink satin gown trimmed with silver thread. All these I dumped onto the carpet in pursuit of what lay underneath: charcoal gray trousers, close-fitting smock shirt, sturdy boots, a work belt with pouches, a pair of well-forged crowbars, a hammer, a hacksaw blade, a chisel, a paper of matches, a stub of candle, and a coil of rope with a grappling iron on one end. After everything I had been through this evening, it felt like coming home.

I changed hurriedly, noting the way the sari's pleats and folds were gathered so I could get it back on unassisted later. Fastening my hair back, I pulled a black silk mask—basically a bag with a letter-box slit for my eyes—over my head, pocketed Namud's lock picks, then un-shuttered the room's single window. It looked down upon a court-yard lined with dwarf trees to form a small cloister with a bronze statue on a plinth in the middle. This was the heart of the Elitus block. I checked Willinghouse's paltry notes. The records office was on the corner of the uppermost floor, which was, I supposed, intended to maintain their confidentiality. Approaching from the inside, up stairwells, along corridors, and through locked doors would afford Elitus's officers plenty of opportunities to apprehend anyone who wasn't welcome.

Which is why I was going in via the window.

I considered the courtyard. It was cobbled. Hard enough to do real damage if I fell from my window, and enough to kill if I fell from the fourth floor. I coiled the rope and slipped my head and one arm through it, so it hung diagonally to my waist. A pair of canvas awnings had been set up in the courtyard beneath the formal trees, but the center with the bronze was open to the sky. As I watched, a black servant came out of the ground-floor door and moved a handcart under one of the awnings. Another, a woman, appeared with an armful of long-stemmed flowers. Something was being prepared, an event of sorts. I had to move quickly, before the courtyard was bustling with people, any one of whom might look up and see an Istilian princess, cunningly disguised as a Lani steeplejack, breaking into their records office.

Ledges of decorous stone ran around the courtyard below every window, and there were downspouts from the gutters in each corner. With care, I might not need the rope at all. I checked the traffic below, leaned out of the window, and grasped the top of the shutters as I lifted first one leg, then the other out and onto the ledge. It was a little over two inches wide. Enough for no more than the toes of my boots. I sucked my belly in, spread my arms, and found just enough purchase in the mortar lines with my fingers to stop myself swaying backwards. Then I turned my head so that my cheek was flush to the wall. I had no fear of heights, but a fear of falling was— as the steeplejacks always used to say—just common sense. Closing my eyes, I thought about Madame Nahreem's mask. My heart rate slowed. Everything that wasn't the feel of the ledge beneath my feet and the texture of the mortar lines under my fingers faded away. Slowly, I inched my way along.

Maybe the maddening old woman wasn't so crazy after all.

I paused at the first shuttered window, looking for light through the crack, moving more swiftly to the next and the one after that as I got used to my surroundings. I heard a snatch of conversation from the courtyard below, but no panic or alarm. I relaxed a little as I reached the deep shade of the corner and could straddle the gap, gripping the drainpipe. It was quality iron, well maintained and anchored. For someone like me, it was as good as a ladder.

I made it up to the fourth floor in a half minute. The store room's window was shuttered and bolted, but I had come prepared. I found the wooden lip of the shutters where it closed over the seam in the middle, satisfied myself that the room beyond them was totally dark and therefore empty, then splintered the wood away from the gap with my chisel. I slipped the hacksaw blade in and slid it up and down until I found the bolt, which I cut, the metal dust blowing away in a little silver plume. After that, the shutters opened easily, and seconds later, I was inside.

Once I had the shutters closed again, I removed the stifling mask and lit my candle, hoping against hope that the membership ledger was in some desk drawer or cupboard, rather than a safe. In fact, though there was indeed a safe and there was a heavy lock on the door to the corridor, the ledgers themselves were sitting on the desk. One marked ELITUS, one marked MERITA. Their large, leather-bound covers were open and the page set to today's date.

No need for Namud's lock picks after all.

Probably just as well. I was a steeplejack, not a housebreaker. I wondered what my chaperone had been before he became a butler. Something different, that was for sure.

I lit the candle and bent over the Elitus volume, tracing the lines recording who was present till I found my own name, or rather that of my Istilian alter ego. My arrival time had been recorded and a note made: *Special guest of the club, invited by the leadership.* That meant someone had to come up here to sign people in and out constantly.

I didn't have much time.

Three lines below my own entry was one for Barrington-Smythe, but the note beside his name said merely *M.* Member? Perhaps. I riffled through the previous pages, but they were no more than a catalog of comings and goings. Struck by a possibility, I turned to the back and flipped the book upside down. The first page was titled "Membership."

It was not so long a list as I might have expected, particularly given the fact that it went back over twenty years, and I saw several names which had been bracketed and marked *Deceased.* Living members seemed to total about forty. Each one showed the date they were admitted and who had sponsored them. Barrington-Smythe had been a member for only three months. His sponsor was Thomas Markeson, the booming, red-faced man I had met with the others in the Great Hall, husband to Agatha, the woman in the unusual shawl who had expressed such outrage at the dangerous man with the bland smile calling her husband *mate.*

Interesting.

I put the books back as I had found them, snuffed out my candle, and opened the shuttered window once more. The sound from the courtyard rose up immediately. People. Rather more than there were before, all bustling about. Worse, the central area by the statue now held a series of standing braziers all blazing merrily and throwing light around the courtyard. I would not be leaving the way I had come in.

I took a steadying breath and considered my options. I could make my way to the front of the building, find a window onto the street, and make a run for it, but that would mean leaving Namud to face the music when it became clear that the Istilian princess had vanished into the night and the club's precious records had been broken into.

The alternative was to leave through the door, make my way through the galleries and staircases to my own room—dressed as the Lani steeplejack I was—and hope I didn't meet anybody. One thing seemed certain: Lady Ki Misrai had made her final social appearance.

I flattened myself against the door and listened.

Nothing.

I tried the handle. Locked from the outside.

I felt the aristocratic steely calm I had been so careful to cultivate melting away as my heart rate quickened. Someone could come at any moment, and there was nowhere to hide if they did. I checked the shuttered window and found the courtyard brighter and busier than ever. I had to get through that door and quickly.

If I hadn't been worried about alerting anyone outside the door, I'd have shoved the pinch point of my pry bar in between the door and the jamb and wrenched it, clearing the rest with my hammer and chisel, but this was not the time for that. Breath quickening, I unrolled Namud's picks and considered them. Some were little thicker than wire with angled bends, others were more like skeleton keys, sturdy but slim with bevels and flanges slender enough to enter the keyhole and unlatch the tumblers if used with a steady hand. I imagined Madame Nahreem's mask once more and tried to shut out the swelling bustle of the courtyard outside. It sounded like musicians were warming up down there. Of traffic in the hallway beyond the door, I could hear nothing.

Maybe everyone is gathering outside, I thought. I could use a little luck.

The first key I tried fit into the lock but was too big to turn inside. I went three sizes smaller but had to angle it to connect with anything. I tried the next largest one, forcing myself to breathe . . .

Neutral . . .

And rotated the shaft between thumb and forefinger till I felt something engage inside. It turned, then slipped.

Almost.

I tried again, ears straining for footfalls in the hallway only inches from my head, and this time turned the pick all the way. The thunk of the lock disengaging reverberated through the timber, and I felt it sag slightly. I put my tools away, replaced the silk mask over my head, and cracked the door open.

The hallway was wood floored with a worn carpet runner, and the sconces on the walls were powered by gas, not luxorite, suggesting that this story was not meant to be seen by club members or their guests. If the servants were busy below, that meant I might just get the luck I needed.

I left the room, nudged the door shut behind me, and walked briskly past a series of unmarked doors toward a narrow staircase. The stairs creaked as I scuttled down to a landing and the next staircase down—wider than the previous flight, its balustrade shaped from dark, elegant wood—and had just set foot on the first stair when I heard the distinctive snap of a door below me. I hesitated, conscious that while I was invisible to whoever had opened the door, I was now perfectly obvious to anyone who might appear on the fourth floor. Should the newcomer below me be on his way up . . .

I dropped into an ungainly crouch, thanking the gods I wasn't wearing that damned sari, and slid crablike down another stair, head as low as I could get to see the corridor below.

Someone was there.

He was no more than ten yards away from the stairwell. I shrank back instinctively, but when I heard no further movement, risked another cautious look.

There was a man in evening wear, but minus his jacket and tie. And his shoes. He was standing barefoot and quite still with his back to the door he had surely come through, looking for all the world like someone who had forgotten what he intended to do next. He was perhaps fifty, gaunt, his gaze unfixed, and his body very slightly unsteady. As I watched, he seemed to waver in place, his head lolling slightly like he was drunk or stunned.

All my desperate need to get down to my second-floor room faded in the strangeness of the moment. I kept very still, knees drawn to my chest in a froglike hunker, and watched as he reached back vaguely for the door handle. As he reached it, he turned absently and, for a fraction of a second, seemed to look right at me, though his eyes seemed unfocused, and he moved like a man in a dream. He pushed the door open, and just stood there before lurching his way into the room. In that moment, I saw the blue haze of smoke billowing out. Once he was inside, I got to my feet again and began to slink down the stairs, but not before I caught the strange tang of the smoke, sweet and sickly. I breathed it in, trying to decide if it was a kind of incense, and almost instantly felt my senses fog, so I blew it out and shook my head to clear it.

Opium. It had to be. I had seen such places in the garrets and derelict warehouses of the city. They were noisome, squalid, and dangerous places full of the lost and the desperate. Their clientele was, I had always assumed, the very poor, either because the drug offered the kind of relief from the miseries of the world that especially appealed to those with no other means of escape, or because their addiction had a way of making them poor in the long run. That Elitus might be running an exclusive version of the illicit back-alley pipe rooms for the use of its members was, to me at least, extraordinary.

Astounded, I forced myself to continue my descent, listening for signs of anyone moving about. I reached the second floor as quickly as I dared. My room was at the end of the long gallery near another corner staircase, marked by the great vase of lilies on its stone plinth. I was halfway there, my eyes fixed on the nondescript door of number 236 when someone came round the corner ahead. It was Wellsley, the doorman from the lobby.

I saw the certainty in his face immediately, and I froze. He reached round to the small of his back as if to draw a weapon, and his mouth opened in a cry of anger and alarm.

CHAPTER
15

THE DOORMAN'S CRY NEVER came.

Instead, he folded at the knees, crumpling into a heap and revealing, behind him, cosh raised where he had bounced it precisely on the back of Wellsley's head, Namud.

The manservant said nothing, but set to dragging the unconscious doorman behind a potted palm in a large stone urn. I made for my retiring room, tearing the steeplejack grays from my body the moment I crossed the threshold. My mask off, I leaned back into the corridor and gave an urgent jerk of my head to summon Namud. He rushed over, but hesitated at the door, uncertain and embarrassed.

I gaped at him, and he stepped reluctantly into the chamber.

"I need to be downstairs now," I said, closing the door behind him, "and in that sari. Help me."

"I hardly think that appropriate, my lady."

"You just laid out the doorman!"

"It seemed the expedient thing to do," he said. "The gentleman will awake with a headache and a confused memory of seeing an intruder, but I do not believe he will connect said intruder with their esteemed foreign visitor."

"Unless I don't show my face as Lady Ki downstairs in about a minute," I said, exasperated. "Avert your eyes."

He turned comically away, eyes screwed shut as if his life depended on it, and I undressed.

"Hold this," I said, stuffing the end of the sari's fabric into his hand as I wriggled into the choli and began turning myself into the long skein of silk. "Now this," I said, pushing another bit of the elaborate skirt into his free hand while I got the rest in place and secure. "Unlace my boots," I added, then kicked them off as he finished and began searching for the delicate slippers with my toes. "Now go."

I pushed the door open and swept past him, almost running to the staircase, flinging the shawl-veil over my face as I sped along. I was still adjusting, Namud breathing heavily in my wake, as I reached the lower level, where I met a mixed crowd of revelers from both clubs, flowing in a steady, excited stream out into the courtyard above which I had been hanging only minutes before. I took a deep, steadying breath, thought again of the neutral mask, and became the Istilian princess once more.

Not a moment too soon. My arrival in the courtyard, which was now packed with glittering people, was greeted with polite applause and a little fanfare from the band at the far side of the square. This, it seemed, whatever it was, was at least partly in my honor. As the music stopped, I was beckoned forward by the florid-faced man called Markeson—husband to the indomitable Agatha and sponsor to the killer she so disliked—who had surmounted a specially erected podium in front of the statue. He was not alone there. Beside him, flanked by an honor guard of the clubs' private sentries in their scarlet tunics, stood a white man, but darkly complexioned and with slicked-back, crow-black hair. This, like his dress, which was formal and similarly black, but augmented with color and sparkle—a crimson sash with gold braid, matching epaulettes on his shoulders, and an unfashionably large ring with a gigantic emerald—marked him as foreign: judging by the ornamented crest on the pocket of his blazer, this was the Grappoli ambassador. His eyes glittered with pride and amusement as he surveyed the crowd and alighted on me like a heron selecting the plumpest frog from a pool.

"Lady Misrai," he said clicking his heels together in the way the comedians in the music hall did whenever they played Grappoli. He extended a gloved hand to help me onto the podium. "I am Count Alfonse Marino, Grappoli Imperial Ambassador to the Court of His

Royal Highness King Gustav, serving the city-state of Bar-Selehm."
He bowed, a sort of sideways nod that lowered his eyes, then kissed
the back of my hand and came up, smiling. "I regret not being
present for your earlier entrance. I had to take a rather important
meeting."

With Richter, I thought.

His Feldish was superb. Only a fractional lilt spoke of his own
native and more musical language.

"I hear these are trying times," I said, as if I was remarking on the
warmth of the evening.

"But not here," he said, closing the matter with a smile. "Not
tonight."

Our entire conversation had been conducted in low voices, but
even so, the crowd that now packed the courtyard had grown still
enough to overhear anything further we might say. Agatha Markeson, imperial in her shimmering shawl, pressed her way to the front
and up onto the platform beside her husband, where she gave me a
serene smile and waved vaguely to her friends in the audience. At the
back, alone in a corner, I spotted Violet Farthingale, her makeup
smeared and her eyes red. I thought back to our maddeningly innoc-
uous gathering in the Merita sitting room and tried to imagine what
could possibly have happened to so upset the woman.

"Gentlemen of Elitus, Ladies of Merita," boomed Agatha's husband. "It is my great honor to welcome not one but two illustrious
visitors to our humble club. I am—as some of you know—alas, incapable of making the kind of speech such worthy guests deserve, but
I am sure you will, as they say, make allowances for my imperfections, and trust that we greet them in honor and in joy. I speak, of
course, of the Grappoli ambassador, Count Marino, whom many of
you have met before but who is no less welcome for all that, and to
our somewhat more mysterious and, might I say, radiant, visitor from
the kingdom of Istilia, Lady Ki Misrai."

The sea of white faces broke into polite applause, and some of the gentlemen murmured "hear, hear." I felt naked, transparent, and not just because I wasn't an Istilian princess. I did not belong here, and under all their politeness and their awe at my fake riches and spurious nobility, I suspected most of them hated me a little and would have liked nothing more than to see my fraud exposed so that I could be thrown out in ignominy. For a moment I almost ran, more unnerved by being looked at like this by the cream of the city than I had been forcing my way into the office window. But as I scanned the crowd, I saw one by the door who fit in no better than I did. Namud caught my eye, took a breath, and nodded once, small but encouraging. I kept my veil in place, but I smiled to the crowd, bowed fractionally, and said nothing.

"I confess," Markeson went on, "that I find myself quite overawed by the prospect of saying anything suiting the occasion, but"—he raised a finger and smiled—"we trust that the visitors in question will not take our attempts amiss, and fireworks are, I am assured, always welcome. You'll be pleased to hear that that's all I have to say, other than to ask that you join me in a toast." He raised his glass, and the honor guard behind him drew their sabers and held them formally upright. "The king," he said, "and foreign guests."

I stood there, smiling, heart rate slowing, as the assembly repeated his toast. There was another round of applause, and the first rocket went up, a great soaring stream of light that burst with a cannon roar and an explosion of golden fire like a massive trena flower leaping into bloom. The crowd aahed and gasped as more fireworks went off overhead, great blazes of light and color popping in the night sky, but I tore my eyes away and looked at the people, faces upturned with admiration and delight, save for a single person, who had blundered out into the courtyard holding his head.

The doorman.

He staggered, gesturing as first one servant, then another stopped what they were doing and rushed to his side. Two of the club's elderly members forced their way through the throng to speak to him and then one, the skeptic who had unnerved me earlier—Nathan Horritch—raised his right hand and looked directly at the podium where I was standing. In the corner of my eye, I saw the two guardsmen, their sabers still drawn, step forward.

I flinched, and as I half turned, I found the Grappoli ambassador's black eyes on me, his mouth turned into a smile of interest.

"And I thought all the excitement would be about the fireworks," he remarked. I blinked and opened my mouth to speak, but nothing would come out. I was glad I'd kept my veil down.

The guardsmen stepped forward, one on my side, one on the ambassador's, and with their nonsword hands, they gripped each of us by the elbow and moved us steadily to the steps down from the podium.

"This way, if you don't mind," said the nearest.

"What is happening?" I demanded, recovering my voice and something of my aristocratic persona.

But the guard said nothing, propelling me down and into the crowd, who were parting unevenly before us as the fireworks continued to boom their floral fire overhead.

"I demand to know what is happening!" I sputtered. Namud had joined the huddle around the injured doorman, and when he looked around at me as I plowed through the sea of wealth and power, his face was hard, unreadable. He met us midway.

"This rough handling of a foreign guest demands explanation," he barked.

"Sorry, sir," said the first guardsman. "Orders."

"Of what nature?" inquired the ambassador. He looked less put out, more amused, but his manner was brusque. "The lady's gentleman is correct. You owe us an explanation. Horritch?"

The keen-eyed man, who seemed to have taken charge of the situation, took two purposeful steps toward us and said, "The club's security has been breached. An intruder, perhaps more than one. Take our guests to the library and lock them in, one of you inside with them, the other outside the door."

One of the guards gave a very military "sir!" and set me in motion once more, practically lifting me off the ground as he led me into the house.

"Oh I say!" exclaimed the ambassador. "Is this really necessary?"

"Until the house has been thoroughly swept for undesirables, I'm afraid so," said Horritch flatly.

We were met in the hall by two more guards, these with shouldered rifles. One went in front of us, and one joined the rear behind Namud. At the double doors of the parlor, the lead guard barked, "Wait," then stalked into the room, unslinging his rifle. As we waited, absurdly in the hall, he paced the room, checking behind sofas and parting the window curtains with the muzzle of his weapon.

"Clear," he announced, stepping to the window and taking up a watchful stance like a sentry as we were herded in and the doors shut upon us.

The library faced the street, but its windows had bars across them. Anywhere else, the room might have been too dim for reading, but this was Elitus, and that meant a luxorite chandelier burned in the center of the room with a pair of matching standing lamps with green shades. The walls were books, floor to ceiling, elegantly bound and housed in dark wood cases. The only furnishings were leather wing chairs with side tables and a pair of desks with inlaid tops, inkwells, and blotters. In any other circumstance, I would have been in my element, but as it was, I was scared. They said I was being protected, but the room would serve just as well as a cell if they suspected I was not who I claimed to be.

What did Wellsley remember? How much of me had he seen before blacking out?

It wouldn't take long for the break-in to the office with the membership ledgers to be discovered. Perhaps they would assume some thief had been intent on getting access to the club's funds, been foiled by the safe, and made the best of their escape. Perhaps.

I studied a pair of oil paintings so that no one would see my face, heroic scenes depicting huddles of crimson-uniformed white soldiers in pith helmets fighting off hordes of spear-wielding Mahweni warriors. I wasn't sure if it was supposed to represent one of the original conquests of the lands around Bar-Selehm or one of the later native rebellions. The black men wore loincloths of weancat skin and somehow all seemed to have the same face.

I turned round.

The ambassador looked less amused now, and though he selected a book from the shelves and flung himself into one of the leather chairs to read, he quickly slammed it shut and exclaimed, "Oh, but this is intolerable."

"I'm sure it is only meant to protect us," I said, trying to convince myself as much as him.

"If their security were worth a damn, they wouldn't need to," he shot back.

Before I could respond, the door opened again, and though the guard's hand went to his weapon, it was only Lady Alice who peered in, pink faced and anxious.

"They said I should be with you, to be on the safe side," she said, slipping in and moving toward us, avoiding the eyes of the guards.

She looked scared for sure, but there was something else, a kind of acute embarrassment, which, in spite of everything, was almost funny. She took a step toward the ambassador, thought better of it, pulled a book from one of the shelves at random, and buried her face in it. It was so extreme and ridiculous a ruse that I turned my bafflement on the ambassador, only to find him doing something similar, not so much reading his book as staring fixedly at the page.

Again, interesting.

"Why did they think you might be a target, Alice?" I inquired.

She looked up, and her face was as transparent as the look she stole at the ambassador before she began her lie.

"Well, I am the daughter of Harrolf Welborne," she said. "He's a very wealthy industrialist. Someone might want to kidnap me."

"Has that happened before?" I asked, moving to her and taking her trembling arm in mine.

"No," she said in a small voice, "but Father says one never knows."

"That is very true," I said. She was trying, unsuccessfully, not to look at the ambassador. "Should I introduce you?"

Her flushed hesitation was all the confirmation I needed, and before she could venture another lie, I said as much. "But then you already know each other," I said. "Well."

The ambassador got up at that.

"Now, just one moment," he began, full of righteous indignation, "I don't know what you are implying, but—"

"Yes," I said, smiling sweetly and speaking in my gentle Istilian accent, "you do, and while you clearly don't want your relationship discussed, the fact that people in the club are sufficiently aware of it that they fear any threat to you may also be a threat to Lady Alice here suggests that ship has already sailed."

The ambassador's entire body language altered. He seemed to crumple, like a marionette when all the tension is taken out of its strings, and the hand he put to his face was visibly unsteady. In the next instant, he had crossed the library to Alice's side and enfolded her in a tender embrace. She clung to him, squinting warily at me over his shoulder.

"I beg you not to tell anyone," she whispered.

"Who would I tell, and why?" I said, shrugging. It felt like the first genuine gesture I had made in hours. "Your secret, such as it is, is safe with me."

"Only Wellsley, the unfortunate doorman, is fully aware," said the ambassador. "One or two of the senior members may suspect, but no one knows for sure."

"And I've told no one," said Alice quickly. A little too quickly, in fact, and I suspected the girl was lying again. She had boasted of the ambassador's interest in her to someone. Maybe to more than one person. I recalled Serafina Dearbeloved telling Alice she was a silly girl and thought, with a flash of irritation, that the old battle-ax was right. In the current political climate, any kind of relationship between a Bar-Selehm society lady and a Grappoli ambassador, however innocent, could be extremely dangerous to more than their reputations. "Frankly, I don't know why we don't tell people. We are friends," she said primly, "dear friends, perhaps. But nothing untoward has gone on. Not like some of the guests here."

"Have they learned anything about the intruder?" asked the ambassador.

Alice shook her head earnestly.

"They think he came in while we were at dinner," she said, "and made his escape during the fireworks display."

I liked that "he."

"An assassin?" I wondered aloud.

"More likely to be a common thief," she said, "but a clever one. Mr. Wellsley thinks it's someone trying to take the place of Darius, the cat burglar who died last week. Whoever it was broke into the office upstairs but couldn't get into the strongbox."

Despite her panic and embarrassment, something of her girlish excitement was starting to show again. A part of her was thrilled at the prospect of having been in the same building as the thief whose exploits—like Darius's—would soon be all over the gossip pages.

"No one saw him?" I asked, trying to sound mildly outraged.

"Mr. Wellsley saw him briefly," she answered, "but doesn't remember any details, and the man was disguised. He must have been big and strong to overpower Wellsley, though."

I turned away so they couldn't see the ghost of a smile I couldn't quite suppress.

"Probably one of the servants," Alice added. "They only let whites work on the member floors, but Wellsley says they have all sorts working in the kitchens."

"Lani?" I asked pointedly.

"Blacks too," she said, realizing only after she had said it what I had been driving at. "Not Lani like you!" she said, horrified. "I mean, the ones here aren't like you at all, are they? You are so sophisticated and beautiful and . . . well, you know."

Silly girl.

I nodded, biting the inside of my cheek, wanting more than ever that evening to tell her what I was—what I *really* was—under this thinnest veneer of fabric, cosmetics, and secondhand manners.

This mask.

But I did not.

The door opened again, and the two of them broke apart like startled monkeys, each furiously pretending to be doing things by themselves, so that a mean-spirited part of me wanted to point and laugh at their absurd charade.

It was the doorman, his head bandaged, another ridiculous sight that made me want to giggle. I needed to get out of there before I unravelled what remained of my disguise. That impulse was fueled further by the man who followed the doorman in. Richter.

"Apparently the people who might be targets are being gathered here," he said, amused by the idea that his reputation made him worthy of assassination.

"I think I would like to leave now," I said, millpond calm. "Kindly notify my man."

"The constabulary are on their way, my lady," said the doorman.

"Oh, I can't have that!" I said, suddenly struck by real panic. Any conversation with the police would surely expose that I was not who I claimed to be. "I will not be interviewed like some common criminal when I have done nothing wrong."

"No, my lady," Wellsley agreed. "No one thinks you are in any way—"

"Then fetch Namud to prepare my things. I want nothing more to do with the whole sordid business."

"Yes, my lady," he said, retreating to the door and ducking out.

I waited, stilling my nervous fingers when I realized they had begun to tap rhythmically on my thigh. The room felt stuffy, the ceiling too low. I turned to Alice to distract myself from the delay and to avoid Richter's imperious stare. He in turn shot a question to the ambassador.

"What's all this about, Marino?"

The ambassador shrugged and looked away. His manner was embarrassed, even furtive, as it had been when he had tried to play down his relationship with Alice.

Curious.

"Do you think we're safe here?" Alice asked me. It wasn't a real question. The girl—she was about my age, but her demeanor reminded me of one of Rahvey's children—just wanted reassuring.

"That lady before," I said, "Violet Farthingale. Did something happen to upset her?"

Alice's doelike anxiety evaporated, replaced by a stiffness that would have suited Mrs. Dearbeloved.

"Well, I wouldn't like to say," she said, "but I've always thought that you can be happy or you can be moral. Not both."

She stared at me, daring me to question or contradict her extraordinary pronouncement, and in the next instant, the door opened again and Wellsley appeared.

"Your man, my lady," he said.

I met Namud in the hallway.

"We're leaving," I said, haughty as before in the hope that people would see only my indignation at being thrust into criminal proceedings, not my fear.

Namud nodded gravely, and I privately noted that I owed him a good deal of thanks when this was all over. I gave a smiling nod to the ambassador and Alice, and something rather more perfunctory to Richter, who merely watched as I slipped out.

We walked past the lobby and up to the stairs while a cab was summoned. I should probably have waited where I was, but I needed to be doing something and not talking to anyone, so I went with Namud. As a result, it was my hand that turned the handle to room 236, my hand that pushed it open, my eyes that were the first to see Agatha Markeson sprawled across my bed, the pillow stained and stiff with blood.

CHAPTER

16

THE BODY WAS STILL warm. I knew because I touched the woman's pallid, hawkish face, an almost instinctive act, which horrified me even as I did it. I felt for a pulse, but Agatha Markeson's eyes—though still aristocratically haughty—were quite sightless. Dead, but not long dead. Minutes, maybe. No more than that.

While I was in the library for my own "protection," then. That's when it had happened. Whoever had killed her had known this room would be empty. The suitcase was still locked, so there was no reason to think that whoever had done it had also discovered my disguise and tools. She looked exactly as she had done last time I had seen her—accusatory and affronted, as if at the audacity of someone killing her—except that the high heel of one of her new shoes was missing.

"What do we do?" asked Namud.

He had been silent as usual since we came in, but he had been shocked out of his habitual equilibrium and looked, for once, quite young. I thought fast and decided.

"We leave," I said. "Now. We get our things and go as if nothing has happened."

Namud gaped.

"With her lying here?" he asked.

"There is nothing we can do for her. If we stay, we'll be detained, and things will get very complicated very quickly."

"Can't you explain things to Inspector Andrews?"

"Later," I said, "yes, but not now, not without exposing who we are and who we work for."

That did it. Namud's nervous uncertainty evaporated like rain on

hot metal. He was the loyal retainer once more, as if I really was someone in authority who knew what I was doing.

"Very well," he said. "After you."

As he picked up the suitcase, I set to putting on the Istilian persona and drew my shawl up over my head. The action gave me pause.

"Her shawl," I said, turning back to the body on the bed. "Where
is her shawl?"

There was no sign of it.

"Does it matter?" asked Namud.

"Probably not," I replied. "Come on."

And we left her. As Namud locked the door behind us, I glanced
up and down the hall. On the wall opposite the door was the vase of
lilies sitting on a plinth no higher than the lip of a fireplace. One of
the flowers was bent over, its stem broken, and there was water on
the ground, as if someone had spilled the vase and then carefully re-
set it. I stooped to it, running my fingers along the cold, hard edge of
the plinth, but then Namud was finished and we were moving to the
stairs. All of my former anxieties, all the imposter's baggage I had
been dragging around since I set foot in the building, felt heavier and
more cumbersome than ever.

The cab had arrived.

So had the police. Three uniformed officers were standing in the
lobby as Wellsley explained the situation to them. Namud gave me an
uneasy look, but I shook my head fractionally and smiled at the doorman. It was good that the police were there. That meant they'd find the
body quickly and would be able to estimate when Mrs. Markeson had
died. The longer she lay there, the harder that would become and
the more possible that Namud and I might become suspects. In this
case, accuracy and truth were my best alibi.

"Good evening, my lady," said Wellsley, halting the irritated officer he was talking to with a single raised finger. "I regret the circumstances of your departure."

"As do I," I said, "though I hold you innocent of any responsibility."

He smiled at that, grateful, and a moment later, we were out in the street and climbing into our cab.

"Well done, my lady," whispered Namud in the dark of the taxi, as he reached out and rapped on the roof with his knuckles so that the driver stirred the horses into action.

"Pass me the suitcase," I said, watching through the window as Elitus fell behind us.

Namud did so, giving me a questioning look as I flipped it open.

"I'm changing," I said.

"Here?" he said, disbelieving.

"Lady Ki Misrai has to vanish for a while," I said. "Maybe forever. Look away."

This time he did not protest and pressed his face to the upholstered headrest like a frightened child. As I undressed, shimmying into my dark smock and pants, I recalled Madame Nahreem's making me change in front of her and wondered if she had somehow known how my evening would go.

Modesty intact, I see, she had remarked.

Quite. I unsnapped the latch on the cab door.

"What are you doing?" asked Namud.

"Disappearing," I said. "Check out of the hotel. I'm going to Willinghouse's town house. We'll meet there, and you can tell me why you carry lock picks."

"I wasn't born a servant," said Namud, in the dark.

"I'm beginning to see that. Does Madame Nahreem know?"

There was an odd silence, and I could almost sense his raised eyebrows.

"You don't know her very well, do you?" he said.

It was a taut, loaded remark that hinted at . . . I didn't know what.

"Not yet," I said.

"You will," he said. "I think you'll find it worth waiting for."

"We'll see," I said, trying to recover a little of my defiant swagger and then thinking better of it. "Namud?" I added.

"Yes?"

"Thanks."

I was out before I realized the scent that I caught on my fingers, a dull and unsettling smell with a metallic edge, was Agatha Markeson's blood.

WHATEVER HAD HAPPENED TONIGHT at Elitus involved Markeson, and the sooner I learned all I could about him, the better. The city was asleep, but I knew at least one person who wouldn't be.

Bar-Selehm's major daily newspaper was the *Bar-Selehm Standard*, produced in morning and evening editions, which meant that there were reporters hard at work at all hours. The *Standard*'s offices sat in an ornate, white-fronted stone building facing Szenga Square, its relief carving of a woman representing Truth glowing a frosty blue in the gaslight. There were lights on in the upper stories, but the lobby was quiet and the doorman wasn't for letting me in.

"I'm here to see Sureyna," I said, when he finally eased the glass-paneled front door open a fraction. "She's a reporter."

"I know who she is," said the doorman.

He was white, midtwenties, and he didn't take kindly to being disturbed from his reading by a Lani girl dressed like a steeplejack. The fact that the person I was asking for—Sureyna, formerly Sarah—was the only black reporter of her age in the building probably didn't help.

"So?" I said, something of my recent aristocratic attitude resurfacing as he looked me over. "Are you going to let me in or not?"

"Why should I?" he said.

"Because I asked nicely," I said, "and there's no reason why you shouldn't."

"Maybe I don't need a reason," he said.

"And maybe I, after I have found a way to speak to Sureyna—who is a friend of mine—will tell her how you treat the people who bring her news."

His eyes narrowed at that. He might have had some standing in the office, but I was guessing that the reporters—even the junior ones—outranked him. Still he managed a sneer.

"The likes of you bringing news that regular people want to read?" he said.

"You'd be amazed at what the likes of me can do," I said. It didn't mean anything, but I said it with certainty and took a step toward him that seemed to give him pause.

"Fine," he said, opening the door. "But see that you're out within the hour."

"Or what?" I asked, hesitating in the door and giving him a level stare. An hour or so ago, I had been a princess. I had broken into and out of a locked room. I had held my own over dinner with Bar-Selehm's social elite, and I had walked through a cordon of police officers, leaving a dead body in my room. I would not be intimidated by this insignificant weasel.

He took a step back as if I had threatened to punch him, and his eyes looked troubled. Something that he could not quite put his finger on was subtly wrong with the universe.

"Thank you," I said pointedly, and made for the stairs.

SUREYNA DIDN'T SEE ME till I was looming over her desk, and her face when she looked up was tired and irritable. That changed immediately, splitting into a delighted grin. She leapt to her feet and folded me in a tight embrace. She does that occasionally. I stood there, embarrassed, and waited for her to finish, then we sat down.

The newsroom was a large open area that took up almost the entire third floor of the building. One end had a series of rooms with doors, all closed and dark, which I assumed belonged to the senior editors who were not in yet. It was a dour environment smelling of old coffee and older cigar smoke. There were half a dozen other reporters at work at their desks, all white, all twice Sureyna's age or more, though I doubted any of them had her extraordinary memory. Everything she saw got stored away in some cabinet in her brain, ignored till summoned and then reproduced with photographic accuracy.

"What are you working on?" I asked, twisting my head to peer at her great typewriter.

She groaned and showed me, nudging the long-handled bag that she called a reticule—overflowing with books and papers—out of the way.

Cucumber award to Hannah Stewart for 4th year running!

"Ah," I said. "Yes, I see. *The stories that matter.*" The paper's marketing tag. She gave me a bleak smile, so I said, "Want to help me bring about the downfall of the ruling class?"

"Always," said Sureyna. She was wearing a brown dress with black ribbons, and her hair was concealed beneath a demure white cap so that she looked something between a shopgirl and a kitchen maid. "What have you got?"

"Questions, mainly, about the members of an exclusive club," I said. "And maybe some connections."

"How exclusive?"

"Ever heard of Elitus?"

Her eyes widened. "Fire away," she said.

"What do you know about Thomas Markeson?"

"The shipping magnate?" said Sureyna, head cocked. "Not much. Should I?"

"Not sure," I said.

"Well, he's in trade. Import-export, mainly foodstuffs. Well connected but not overtly political so far as I know. Rich, of course."

"Of course."

"What about Nathan Horritch?"

"Industrialist, mainly soft goods. Inherited a fortune made by his father through the mechanization of weaving. That was his factory that burned last week," she added.

"It was?" I asked. "Huh."

"Is that important?"

"I have absolutely no idea," I said. "I doubt it."

"Who's next?" I mused, consulting a list I had made. "Rathbone."

"Abel Rathbone, the cabinet secretary?"

"I think so," I said.

"You *think* so?" said Sureyna, eyebrow raised. She shuffled through some previous editions and flapped one open to a picture of a familiar lean, serious man with a funereal air.

"Yes," I said. "Him."

"He's one of the most powerful men in the country!"

"Oh," I said, feeling my ignorance about politics and wondering anxiously what I might have missed because of it. "Right."

"Professional civil servant," said Sureyna, reverting to that encyclopedic mode that had so amazed me when we first met. "Well educated, entered the service directly from university, working his way up the ranks in the War Office. Was made head of domestic policy—an advisory position to the prime minister—six years ago, a position he held for two years before rejoining the civil service. Became cabinet secretary six months ago. Not a popular man with your employer's party."

"Norton Richter was there too," I said.

Sureyna's face darkened.

"Richter," she snarled. "You know who he is, I take it? What he stands for?"

"I heard him speak in Parliament," I said. The hatred was coming off my friend like heat. "Where did he make his money?"

"Iron and manufacturing," she said. "Never heard of the Richter process? His people developed a system for mass-producing steel."

"He's *that* Richter?" I exclaimed. You couldn't spend as much time around construction as I had without knowing something of Bar-Selehm's steel industry and its dependence on the Richter process. Half the factories in the city used machines rolled and forged from

Richter's furnaces, and there were catalogs of his wares on the desks of the other half.

"The city contracted him to supply the platform canopies for the Pump Street underground station," said Sureyna, "and I think he's about to start rail production too."

"Any weapons?" I asked.

"Not that I know of."

"But if someone wanted to build something from blueprints," I said, liking the idea, "he might be a useful man to know."

Someone, I thought, who had already advocated for more open trade with the Grappoli, whom he considered the city's natural— which is to say racial—allies.

"Have you ever read his party's manifesto?" she asked. While I had been thinking about Richter's part in the death of Darius and the theft of government documents, she had been rooting through her reticule of notebooks and papers, and now—with a kind of furious triumph— she produced a slim, dog-eared pamphlet emblazoned with the lightning-fist motif. She brandished it. It was titled *The Dilemma of the White Man: A Heritage Party Publication.* Then, with unsteady fingers, she opened it to a page heavily scored with pencil markings, underlinings and astonished exclamation marks. I leaned in to the small, close type, focusing on a passage she indicated with a word-less stab of her nail-bitten finger.

. . . which is certainly true of the various black races, their being evidently closer to apes than to white humanity, a fact which goes some way to accounting for their low intelligence and in-stinctive barbarism. While their innate savagery—directed frequently and spitefully among themselves, as well as with resentment toward their white superiors—is evidence of their patent failings and inability to build anything resembling civili-zation, it is not—properly considered—a strictly moral defi-ciency. Morality, as the authorities and religion of our culture have long told us, is the realm of the human and the elevated. To bewail the morality of the black man is to complain about water for seeking out its own level. This is not opinion; it is science, and one must inevitably conclude that the error manifested in a city such as Bar-Selehm is not one made by the blacks, of whom no better can be expected, but by the whites, who have deluded themselves into treating lower creatures as if they were people.

I pushed the pamphlet away, sickened, and looked into the face of Sureyna, whose anger had burned through whatever restraint she had left so that hot tears shone in her eyes.

"See?" she managed.

"Yes," I said. "Why do you carry it around with you?"

She thought about that and shrugged.

"Know your enemy," she said. "Understand the way they think, what they say, the things they want to do to you. That way you never let your guard down."

I nodded, though I was not sure I could live like that.

"But you remember everything," I said. "Why keep it written down?"

She scowled.

"Some things I choose not to remember," she said. "Keep them . . . outside."

I nodded.

"Tell me about Lord Elwin," I said, deliberately changing the subject and plucking the name at random from my list of who I had met at Elitus.

She blew out a long breath and whisked the pamphlet away, stowing it carefully as if afraid it might get damaged.

"Socialite," she said, blinking her way back to business. "Distantly related to Belrandian royalty. Wealthy and well connected, but his family hasn't done any actual work for about a hundred and fifty years."

"Last one," I said. This was getting me nowhere. "Eustace Montresat."

"Arms dealer and manufacturer."

That got my attention, and I tried to remember the man I had met so briefly while surrounded by others, conjuring the image of a small mongoose of a man who kept his hands in front of his chest and gave the impression of someone finicky, nervous. Not an obvious killer, but if he dealt in weapons, he wouldn't need to be. He would have connections.

But then they all did. That was why they were in Elitus to begin with.

"What does he make?" I asked. "Who does he trade with?"

"Another family business," she said. "Used to be swords and bayonets, but he deals in explosives now too, and has a factory that produces field guns and carriages for the military."

"Ours?"

"Government contract, yes," said Sureyna. "But he trades with Belrand directly as well, and is licensed to sell to a limited range of allies, mainly minor principalities. Bar-Selehm will be his biggest market."

"Not the Grappoli," I said.

"Not unless he wants to hang for treason," said Sureyna. "His merchandise gets a full military escort everywhere he ships, and that makes him squeaky clean. He has another factory that builds agricultural machinery, but unless we plan on defeating our enemies by riding over them with steam tractors, I suspect that's a blind alley. Now, about this story you are supposed to be bringing me?"

"Markeson's wife is dead," I said. "Murdered last night at Elitus."

All sleepiness and impatience fell away from her in a second.

"Murdered?" she exclaimed. "Are you sure?"

"Saw the body myself."

"You were in Elitus? How?"

"That doesn't matter for now," I said.

"Not to you, maybe," she said, snatching up a pencil and testing its point on a scrap of paper. "I heard the police had been dispatched because of reports of an intruder, but there were no injuries I heard of."

"Separate incidents," I said.

"Separate? The police are never called to Elitus. They are famous for their security. Two criminal acts in one night there is quite a coincidence."

"Isn't it?" I mused. "Ever heard of a Violet Farthingale?"

The reporter flicked through whatever her unconscious mind might have filed away, eyes half closed, and shook her head.

"Who is she?"

"I don't know," I said. "Maybe no one important."

"What's this about?"

"Not sure yet, but I think it's about Darius."

"*The cat burglar?*" gasped Sureyna. Her eyebrows had slid almost to the top of her head.

I nodded.

"You've got to give me something I can print," she said. "If I have to write one more flower show or 'Discontent in Morgessa' story, I may kill someone myself."

"I will, I promise. But I have to do my job first."

"Which is what exactly? You still working for Willinghouse?"

I looked around and put a finger to my lips.

"No one knows," she said, and there was a question in her look. "You should be famous, but you're not."

"Better that way, " I said. "Montresat's factories. Do they make machine guns?"

"Machine guns? They might. Why?"

"What about the other industrialist I mentioned: Horritch? Does he make anything that could be used in guns? Steel? Machine parts? Anything like that?"

"No," said Sureyna. "He's all about textiles, carpet, sacking."

"Uniforms?" I tried.

"So far as I know, he produces fabric, not garments. What is this about?"

"I'm not sure," I said, feeling suddenly stupid and annoyed at how little I had come away from Elitus with. "The factory that burned was one of these, spinning or weaving and such?"

"May have been once," she said. "But it was derelict. Worthless. The fire brigade weren't called out till other buildings in the neighborhood were threatened. By the time they got there, it was too late to save the structure, so they just closed off the streets around it and let it burn."

"Do you know how the fire started?"

"I don't think anyone really asked," said Sureyna. "The police were busy that night with the Darius incident, so they didn't go over there till the next morning, by which time it was all over. As I heard it, even Horritch didn't much care what had happened."

"Are they going to rebuild?"

"What for? It was empty. I think he's looking to sell the land once the remains have been bulldozed. Maybe he'll build another warehouse, since it's between the docks and railway sidings."

I scowled. It felt like another blind alley.

"Why are you asking about guns?" Sureyna prompted, her voice even lower.

"The plans Darius stole that night," I said.

"A weapon?" said Sureyna. "Are you sure?"

"Pretty sure."

"So he was working for a foreign power?" said Sureyna, the story taking shape in her head. "The Grappoli!"

I shushed her.

"When I know for sure, I'll tell you what I can," I said. My eyes strayed to a bulletin board where headlines and stories had been pinned up so that someone could plan the layout of the page. The word *Grappoli* leapt off several of the stories. "They're saying that the

Grappoli advance across the north has slowed down. Do we know why?"

Sureyna made a face and waggled her head noncommittally.

"Our war correspondent thinks they are just pausing for breath," she said. "Regrouping to make sure their supply lines hold, but his contacts say they have also suffered what he calls *unexpected reversals*."

"Military losses?" I said, surprised.

"Maybe," she said. "Seems unlikely. Probably they're just preparing for another big push. The people, I mean the tribes . . ." She faltered and shook her head.

"I know," I said. "It's awful."

"No one here cares," she said. "We've tried to cover the refugee crisis, show what the people are running from and what happens, but no one wants to know. Our rival's circulation has gone up significantly since they started printing those 'Kick Them Out' stories. People don't want information. They want justification for what they already believe."

She stared hopelessly at the scraps of paper pinned up on the board. Not knowing how to comfort her, I gave her a matey nudge, such as I might give to Tanish, and said, "You need to get back to your cucumbers."

"Hardly," she said, getting to her feet and recovering something of her professional air. "I have policemen to interview and, if they'll let a humble reporter through the door, the staff of the Elitus club, where I have it on good authority that an eminent citizen of the city was horribly murdered. Has a certain ring to it, don't you think?"

"Just keep me out of it," I said, wondering if I had done the right thing. "And be careful. We're dealing with some dangerous people."

"Want to share a cab?"

"No," I said. "I'm going the other way."

CHAPTER

17

I STILL DID NOT go to Willinghouse's town house. Instead, I worked my way southwest across the city, using the roofs and fire escapes where possible to stay out of the alleys around the factories and tenements of the Thornhill District west of the Holymound market. There were still at least two hours till dawn, and there were certain parts of the city, parts ignored or forgotten by the members of Elitus and Merita, where it was not safe to be after dark. I reached the half-converted weaving shed on Seventh Street that I had once called home, went to the water tower above the ironmongers on the corner, and scaled it. I had spent many an hour up there in the past, usually hiding from the gang, and I could have made the ascent blindfolded. At the top I nestled onto a rusting metal gantry and curled up. I would sleep until the sun brought my former companions out to begin the morning shift. I had a job for one of them.

Tanish, now almost thirteen, had been my apprentice when I worked for the Seventh Street steeplejack gang. Life in the gang had changed over the last couple of months because the leader, Morlak, had been arrested and confined to Rivergate prison, where he would remain for the next eight years.

My doing, much of it, though I never actually testified against him in court.

The boys spilled out of the weavers' shed just after dawn, bleary eyed, trailing satchels of tools. I watched from my vantage as they divided into their work teams for the day, nodding their wary greetings to the familiar black workers who shared the streets with them at this time—the road sweepers, milk and coal sellers with their horse-drawn wagons, the rag-and-bone man with his half-starved orlek, the flower girls who hawked their wares outside the inns of court, and the men and women who rolled barrows of fruit and vegetables to Bar-Selehm's varying markets, some official, some less so. I was glad to see Tanish heading off down Seventh Street alone. I tailed him for three blocks, the first from the rooftops, then came down and caught up with him two roads west of the domes and minarets of Mahweni Old Town. He beamed delightedly when he saw me, then quickly doused the smile and looked away while he recovered his adolescent nonchalance. That didn't matter. It had, I realized, been a hard night in lots of little ways, and it was good to be with someone who knew who and what I was and liked me for it, however much he pretended otherwise.

Sarn, one of the eldest remaining boys, had tried to step into Morlak's shoes, but he didn't have the old gang leader's connections, and work—real steeplejack work of the kind that paid better than mere chimney sweeping—had become harder to come by. A compromise of sorts had been reached when the remnants of Seventh Street had merged—cagily—with the Westside boys, who were also short on numbers since the arrest of their leader, a man called Deveril who had, in his way, helped me in the past. The new gang was called simply New Boys, so that no one could claim precedence, and they had—said Tanish, sounding older than his years—"pooled their resources."

"Sounds good," I said, warily. I always wished he would find some other, less dangerous kind of work, though I had no idea what that might be. The factories hired black and Lani, but they didn't pay them as much as the whites and tended to keep them in menial positions.

Tanish shrugged, shedding his momentary adulthood and looking lost.

"It's not the same as it was," he said. "I hated Morlak, but it was better before. In some ways. When you were there. I wish . . ."

But he was too kind a soul to actually say it. He knew how miserable

I had been in the gang, and how much Sarn still hated me. Like it or not, my life had carried me away from them.

"They think you left the city," he said at last.

"Probably for the best," I replied. "Let's not tell them otherwise, all right?"

He nodded.

"I went to the Drowning yesterday," he said. "Saw your sister and her family."

"And?"

"Nothing," he said. "Just thought you should know."

"Why did you go?"

He shrugged, but I could tell he was being evasive. He looked young and embarrassed, but also a little sad.

"What is it?" I asked. "Tanish?"

"When you were in the gang, it felt more like a family, you know?" he said. "Now it's just a gang."

But Rahvey has a family.

I nodded.

"I'm sure they're glad to see you," I said.

"The kids are," he said significantly.

I grinned. If Rahvey felt any tenderness toward the boy, he would never know. My sister prided herself on her flinty exterior. She had always confused hardness with strength.

"Where are you working today?" I asked.

"Winelands bell tower," he said. "Just a cleanup job, but it will take a few days."

"Can I help?"

His face lit up.

"Really? You can come?"

"Something I want to talk to you about," I said. "A job. Earn you an extra shilling or two."

"Yeah?" he said, hope taking another year off his face.

"Yeah." His relief surprised me. "You are doing all right, Tanish, yes? Sarn isn't being too hard on you?"

"I'm fine," he said, so spontaneously that I believed him, though he looked away and added, "But there is something. Not about the gang."

"What?" I asked.

"Promise you won't laugh?"

"Promise. Go on."

"People have been talking. The Westsiders, mainly, but some of our boys too. They say they've seen . . . the Gargoyle."

I didn't laugh, but it was a near thing, and he pouted at me.

"The Gargoyle is a made-up story," I said. "You know that. It's a steeplejack myth that kids like Sarn use to scare the new boys, the one you get round to late at night when you've already told every Crane Fly legend *and* the one about the time Daven Saide got forgotten and was hanging for three days in his bosun's chair on the backside of the Dock Street clock tower. It's not real."

"The Crane Fly was real," he said, as if that proved him right.

"Supposedly," I said. "But the Crane Fly was an actual person, even if we don't know who he was. The Gargoyle was never more than a way to give little kids nightmares."

"I know!" he protested. "And I didn't believe in it, but Javesh, who was, like, second in command of the Westsiders before they joined us, said he saw it two nights ago way up on the old candle factory stack on Oatshill Road. Said it looked right at him. Scared him half to death, it did."

"It's not real, Tanish. He's trying to wind you up."

"He didn't say it to me. I heard from his apprentice. All thin and gray, it was, bald too, and its teeth were like . . . I don't know, like broken fangs."

He shuddered, and I put a hand on his shoulder.

"I'll come see you on the Winelands bell tower," I said, "and if I see the Gargoyle, I'll give it a smack on the nose. Sound like a plan?"

He smiled grudgingly and shrugged the moment off.

"What do you want me to do?" he asked.

"On the south bank there are some warehouses and factories owned by blokes called Markeson, Horritch, and Montresat. Three different businesses."

Tanish nodded immediately, the Gargoyle forgotten.

"I know them," he said. "Down by the potteries. One of them burned, right? Horritch's."

"Right."

"What do you need?"

"Just information," I said. "Anything. But don't ask a lot of questions. I'd rather you just watched them when you get a spare few minutes. See what they're making, what their schedules are, who they deal with. Anything really."

He frowned.

"Sounds a bit vague," he said.

"Yeah," I agreed. "It does, doesn't it?"

SOCIETY MURDER! BLARED THE headline. I peered quickly at the paper that Willinghouse had flung down on the low-slung coffee table in his tasteful withdrawing room.

> The cream of Bar-Selehm's social elite were astonished to find that one of their number——Mrs. Agatha Markeson, wife of Thomas Markeson, the well-connected shipping magnate——was brutally beaten to death within the confines of one of the city's most exclusive clubs.

Sureyna's work, and more lurid than I would have liked.

"How did they find out so quickly?" Willinghouse asked.

"They keep watch on the police stations," said Inspector Andrews sagely. "Come snooping around the moment officers are dispatched."

I said nothing. Willinghouse had been his usual taciturn self since my arrival. He had scowled thoughtfully at the news that Markeson had been the sponsor of the assassin calling himself Barrington-Smythe, but the death of the industrialist's wife—and the speed with which it had made the paper—clearly muddied the waters, as far as he was concerned.

"You shouldn't have slipped away like that," he said. "It looks suspicious."

"What would you have had me do?" I protested. "I couldn't be interviewed as Lady Misrai, could I?"

"It would have been awkward," agreed Andrews. He had arrived at almost the same instant I had, and Dahria had come down moments later, agog to hear all that had transpired. "The investigating officer is Inspector Walter Defries: a good man in his way, but absolutely by the book," Andrews continued. "When I left, he was looking for a contact address for Lady Misrai. He knows she—which is to say, *you*—couldn't have killed Mrs. Markeson, but he wants to talk to you about why you left."

"Sooner or later, he's going to show up at the Istilian embassy," said Willinghouse, squeezing his eyes shut till the hooklike scar on his cheek blanched, "who will say that they've never heard of such a person. It's a mess, and if we're not careful, it will lead back to us."

"Do you not know anyone at the embassy who might—" I began.

"Derail a murder investigation?" snapped Willinghouse. "No, I bloody don't."

"Language, Josiah," Andrews scolded. "There are ladies present."

"Oh, for crying out loud," Willinghouse returned, pointing at Dahria and me in turn. "*She's* my incorrigible sister, and *she's* a Lani steeplejack."

We both stared at him.

"Which just means they've heard worse," Willinghouse added hastily. "I didn't mean they weren't . . . you know . . . ladies."

His embarrassment, even in the circumstances, was almost funny, but I glared at him anyway. Dahria yawned.

"I apologize," he said curtly. "I am frustrated. This was a great deal of effort and expense for so little reward."

"It's a start," I said, then turned to Andrews. "Has Inspector Defries spoken to Violet Farthingale?"

"The Markesons' governess?" said Dahria. "Pretty girl? Breasts like the snow-capped peaks of Mount Zana?"

I grinned at her.

"He got her details, but I don't believe he asked her anything particularly probing," said Andrews, tearing his stunned gaze from Dahria. "Why?"

"He should," I said.

"Governess?" asked Willinghouse.

"Lady Agatha had a child late in life," said Dahria. "A boy, I think. Or a girl. I don't really care."

Andrews checked his note book, "A girl called Hyacinth," he said, "twelve years old."

"Hyacinth," echoed Dahria, making a sour face. "See? I was better not knowing."

Andrews ignored her.

"Violet Farthingale is employed to teach the girl music, needlepoint, Feldish," he said. "The usual. Why would Defries particularly want to interview her?"

"Because she was having an affair with Thomas Markeson," I said. "Or people thought she was."

"Good God, how on earth do you know that?" exclaimed Dahria.

"Gossip," I said, "and a slightly embarrassing incident before dinner."

"How delicious!" said Dahria. "And, now that I think of Markeson, repulsive. Oh, that poor girl!"

Andrews looked at her in surprise.

"If there is even a hint that she has any connection to the murder, however indirect," said Dahria, "our upstanding society friends will cut her dead."

"Meaning?" I challenged.

"They won't speak to her or acknowledge her in any way."

I rolled my eyes, but Dahria cut me off.

"No, for one used to evading killer street gangs by climbing up chimneys, that might not sound like much," she said. "But she will lose her position, her friends, her connections, and that means she will not find similar employment in the city. Ever. Whatever training or schooling or expertise she has will cease to have any value for those who might give her work. She will either have to leave Bar-Selehm entirely, or—since she will probably not be employable as a servant by any respectable household—she will have to find employment in a factory. You see, my dear steeplejack, the mere whisper of scandal just made her working class, and her aspirations for the future should now be calculated as if she were a black woman from the terraces of Morgessa. And no, brother, that was not a criticism of their worth, but an assessment of their opportunities."

Humbled, I said nothing. Willinghouse, however, was undaunted.

"So this may all be a nasty little family squabble, and nothing to do with the stolen plans after all?" he said, even more dissatisfied.

"I'm not so sure," I said, thinking about what Sureyna had said about the oddity of coincidence where Elitus was concerned. "I doubt Violet Farthingale beat Agatha to death, even if they were rivals for Thomas Markeson's affections, something which is—frankly—hard to believe."

"Hard to believe?" Andrews prompted.

Dahria and I looked at him.

"Markeson is a rich and respected man," said Willinghouse. "Those are powerful attractions to young women."

"Know a lot about what attracts young women, do you?" I asked.

He flushed.

"Markeson looks like a newly spitted pig," said Dahria. "If Violet Farthingale was having any kind of relationship with him, it was to feather her own nest. More likely the great shipping magnate wanted to dock one of his barges in her—"

"Dahria!" exclaimed Willinghouse, genuinely shocked.

I bit back a laugh. Dahria was unabashed.

"It's true," she said.

"You shouldn't impugn other ladies with your sour attitude to the male sex," muttered Willinghouse.

"It's not my attitude that's sour," said Dahria, her lips pouting in a moue of distaste.

"Perhaps if you were a little more accommodating," said Willinghouse, nettled, "you'd have more suitors."

"Then God keep me less accommodating," said Dahria.

In the circumstances, I was surprised that Willinghouse allowed himself to be drawn into so private a spat in our presence, but he couldn't seem to stop himself.

"I swear, Dahria, that you delight in tormenting men," he sputtered.

"If so," she said, "it is well deserved. But no, dear brother, the torment is all mine." She smiled privately, mischievously, as if at some secret joke, and as she lowered her face, her eyes met mine and held them. Her hazel eyes twinkled significantly, though I was far from clear what she meant and was almost relieved when Andrews pulled us back to the matter at hand.

"Miss Farthingale would never admit to any involvement with Markeson, actual or imagined," said Andrews. "Not to the police. It would destroy her reputation either way."

"Maybe she would talk to Dahria?" suggested Willinghouse. "Assuming my sister could keep a decent tongue in her head."

"Confess her indiscretions to a fellow society lady?" Dahria scoffed. "One from whom the very existence of Merita has been carefully kept secret? I swear, Joss, I wonder sometimes what world you actually live in."

I considered her. She had made light of the discovery that Elitus had a secret sister institution, but it made certain truths about Bar-Selehm society uncomfortably clear, and I felt sure she was, in her own way, upset by it.

"Violet might speak to me," I said.

The others stared at me.

"You?" asked Willinghouse.

"Not Anglet Sutonga," I said, "but Lady Ki Misrai, an esteemed person who witnessed her humiliation but is not part of Bar-Selehm society."

"I thought that identity had gone down the river?" said Dahria.

"It will," I said, "but it will take time for the police to get to the embassy and more time for whatever they learn to become public knowledge. If I change now, and Inspector Andrews were to take me—"

"Go," said Willinghouse.

CHAPTER

18

VIOLET FARTHINGALE HAD ROOMS above a draper's shop on Saint Helbrin Street in sight of the statue of King Randolph II on his charger. It was a pleasant street lined with tantu trees, where hornbills and fire-eyed grackles called to each other. The apartment itself was compact, elegant if a little old-fashioned, and scrupulously clean: good, white, middle-class housing, modest in its way but safe and comfortable, the kind of place in which few of the city's black or Lani population could ever realistically expect to live. The curtains and chairs looked older than the lady herself, so I guessed the place came prefurnished. Violet Farthingale had been reluctant to speak to Andrews and had kept him at the door, claiming to be too busy to see him, till he said that he had not come on police business.

"I have brought a lady who wishes to speak with you," he said, carefully hiding any doubts he had about what we were doing.

The young woman was clad in a simple and uncorsetted tea gown of soft mauve, which made her look, if anything, even lovelier than she had the night before, though her eyes were shadowed and still showed signs of weeping. She had cracked the door open a little, and blinked in surprise at the sight of me standing in my Istilian finery in the hallway. She had let me in more out of bafflement than decision, and I had done my part by giving Andrews a pointed look, till he—reluctantly—stepped back outside.

"If you wouldn't mind, Inspector," I said, "take the police vehicle around the corner and wait for me there."

Andrews opened his mouth to speak, but then just nodded stiffly and left. Violet looked relieved.

"Would you care for tea, my lady?" she asked, nervous and confused. She was perhaps five or six years older than me, but looked suddenly like a child, hesitating in front of the bay window and watching the police coach roll away. Its departure seemed to calm her nerves, and she turned back to me, gesturing to a chair.

"No tea, thank you," I said, in my Istilian lilt. "I will not be staying long."

"I'm afraid you've caught me rather . . . I mean, I did not expect visitors. . . ."

"There is no reason you should," I said as kindly as I could. Whatever her crime, I doubted she deserved the crippling malice of Bar-Selehm's high society as Dahria had painted it. Unless, of course, she really was involved in Agatha's murder. "I wanted to speak to you about what happened last night."

"Why?" she asked. She had a small girlish mouth without makeup.

"Partly my own curiosity," I said, "and because I suspect that you are being badly treated in ways you do not deserve."

"Whether that is so or not," she said, clasping her hands together in her lap, "I do not believe there is anything you can do about it, though your kindness is appreciated."

"Perhaps not," I said. "But then the support of a lady such as myself . . . Well, you know best."

An unworthy trick, playing on the woman's hope and despair, particularly when I knew my status in Bar-Selehm society would likely evaporate within the hour, but a part of me wanted the idea that I could help her to be true and I privately vowed to make it so. For it to work, I had to play the thing through. I got to my feet.

"You are upset, and I am intruding," I said. "I will leave you to your thoughts."

I took one step toward the door. Another. Then she spoke.

"Wait," she said, looking at her hands. "What is it you wish to know?"

I sat down again and smiled at her.

"Did you like Mrs. Markeson?" I asked.

"Yes!" she shot back, a quick, thoughtless answer given in fear. A moment later, she shook her head sadly. "Not really."

"She seemed quite a forceful woman," I said. "Opinionated."

"Yes," she agreed, softer this time.

"Probably quite hard to please."

"Sometimes," said Violet. "But she was fair. Mostly."

I took a fractional pause to digest that last word.

"Mostly?" I prompted.

"She was quite strict with Hyacinth, her daughter. As well as me. In what I taught Hyacinth, I mean. She always wanted to see the girl work, hear her play."

"Is Hyacinth an agreeable child? Talented?"

"Oh, most agreeable," she answered, smiling suddenly in ways that lit up the little room. "Not, perhaps, the most academic of children, but exceedingly pleasant and good-natured."

"Was that enough for Mrs. Markeson?"

Violet looked at her hands again. "I think she would have liked her to have more obvious gifts. She was very critical of her piano playing and said I did not push the child hard enough."

"She was a good player herself?"

"Not at all!" said Violet, indignation pinking her cheek. "She could not play a note."

"I see," I said. "Sometimes it is the faults that parents see in themselves that they most want to correct in their children."

"Indeed," said Violet. "That is very true."

"So Mrs. Markeson was strict with you too?"

"Not at first," said Violet. "But in the last few months, she became quite hard on me."

"Why was that, do you think?" I said, still taking it slowly.

"I really couldn't say."

That was, I thought, her second lie, and it was more an evasion than a flat-out untruth.

"Mr. Markeson continued to value your contribution to the household, I take it?"

"Yes," she said, and something of the smile was back, though it flickered and died like a spent candle.

"Perhaps Mrs. Markeson resented his support of you," I said as if I was merely thinking aloud.

Violet nodded fervently.

"Once, when Hyacinth had painted a charming watercolor of the flowers on her windowsill and Mr. Thomas was admiring it, Mrs. Markeson came in and began to say quite unpleasant things about the picture so that Hyacinth began to cry. When Mr. Thomas said she was being too hard on the girl, Mrs. Markeson became very angry indeed and accused her husband of terrible things."

She broke off, her eyes bright with tears. I waited for a moment, nodding thoughtfully.

"Things about you," I said.

The woman's tears spilled down her cheeks, and she hung her head.

"There was nothing to any of it," she said between her sobs. "Sometimes older gentlemen take a fatherly interest in younger women. It was all quite harmless if a little silly, but nothing ever . . . *ever* happened."

"I understand," I said. "Tell me about the shawl."

She looked up at that, surprised, and it took her a moment to realize what I was talking about.

"Did she say something after I had gone?" she said.

"No, but I surmised."

"Well, it's true," she said with weary resolve. "I had only been to Merita once before. Mrs. Markeson did not approve, but Mr. Thomas said he thought it was good for me to mix with ladies of my own station. They weren't, of course, but it was kind of him, and after our first visit, he said I needed some new finery so that no one would sneer at me. That was how he put it. I being merely a governess and all.

You see, Mrs. Markeson had already said things, scandalous things, about me, and most of the other ladies had not been very welcoming."

I nodded and let her finish, though I fancied I knew what she was going to say.

"So yesterday evening as I was putting Hyacinth to bed, Mr. Thomas came and said he had a gift for me. 'Something to make them all jealous,' he said."

"The shawl."

"Exactly. It was quite beautiful. I had never seen anything like it."

"But Mrs. Markeson took it from you," I said. "Didn't she?"

Violet put her hand to her mouth and began to sob again. She nodded, speechless for a moment, then managed to say, "She was so angry. I had never seen her in such a rage. She snatched it off me and asked how I dared parade the fruit of my . . . my *strumpeting* in polite society! I protested, of course, but she would hear nothing of it, and for once, Mr. Markeson did not dare to contradict her. So she wore the shawl, and showed it off, and I could not abide to be in the room and—"

She broke off.

"There, there," I said. "I understand. Where did you go?"

"Outside at first. I needed some air. Then, once the fireworks began, I went to the Markesons' withdrawing room on the second floor, three doors down from yours."

"You knew which one mine was?"

"Everyone did. One of the maids told us before you arrived. Everyone was so excited to meet you, even the ones who usually . . ."

"Yes?"

"Well, some of the ladies have few good things to say about people who are different from them."

"But not you."

"No. I am, as they like to remind me, not one of them, and there are many things on which we do not agree."

I took in this note of solidarity without comment.

"You stayed in the Markesons' room until the police came?" I asked.

She nodded.

"Alone?"

"No," she said. "Constance went with me to let me in. You will be surprised to hear that she can be very sweet. We often talk together. She can be most amusing when discussing the other ladies and their silly ideas and small-minded hatefulness. . . ." She almost laughed at the recollection, then remembered why I was there and came back to the matter at hand. "She had seen me during the fireworks and could tell I was upset. She brought me lavender water to cool my temples."

"She let you into the Markesons' retiring room?"

"Yes, Mrs. Markeson kept the key to herself, but Constance also had a room so she could let me in."

"I don't think I understand," I said. "Why did Constance's key open the Markesons' room?"

"All the retiring rooms are the same," she said. "That's the sort of place Elitus is. They assume the bad people are all outside. Once you're in, no one worries very much about security."

She said it wryly, and I found I was warming to her all the more.

"What did you do after the alarm was raised about the intruder?" I asked.

"I went back to the Merita parlor with the other ladies."

"All of them?"

"No. Lady Alice never came, and several of the others only arrived later. Is that when it happened?"

"I think so, yes. And you did not see the shawl again?"

"The shawl? No. Why, is that relevant? Did she not have it on when she . . ."

"No."

"You think someone killed her for her shawl?"

"That seems unlikely," I said, "though its disappearance is strange."

"It was very unusual."

"Expensive?"

She shrugged fractionally. "I had never seen anything like it in the shops. The fabric was quite remarkable. It was like wearing water."

"Where did it come from?"

She hesitated and bit her lower lip.

"Was it a secret?" I asked.

"It doesn't feel very important now," she said, "it being just cloth, after all, but Mr. Markeson did say I shouldn't talk about where it came from."

"And did you?"

She shook her head fervently.

"Absolutely not. I may not have been what people said to Mr. Markeson, but he was kind to me and I sought to deserve his trust. But now . . ." She paused and looked at me. "Why do you want to know?"

"I think it might help reveal who killed Mrs. Markeson."

"Really? I don't see how. It was pretty, but surely . . . surely?" She faltered again, then blurted out, "Mr. Markeson's friend made it, Mr. Horritch."

"Nathan Horritch?"

"Well, not he himself, but people at one of his factories."

I considered this.

"Have I helped?" she asked.

"I believe so," I replied, smiling. "Have I?"

She beamed at me.

"Most definitely," she said.

CHAPTER

19

THE WINELANDS BELL TOWER was the most decorative part of an ornate shopping arcade two blocks north of the Trade Exchange, a stone's throw from the opera house. As such, it drew the fashionable society ladies and their servants, even the latter being mostly white, all brandishing elegant parasols to keep that whiteness pure. There were, so far as I could see, only two Lani in a quarter-mile radius: Tanish and me, and we were seventy feet above the street.

The tower was accessible by rungs fastened into the masonry above the arcade's roofline, but they only went as high as the clock gallery, and the gang had rigged a series of diagonal ladders to a scaffold gantry giving access to the cupola. It was good work, tight and regular, and I commended Tanish for it.

"Can't take all the credit," he said, cleaning one of last season's wood-stork nests out of the dammed up gutters with a hand rake. "Sarn insisted that the owners pay extra for a scaffolder. I know you don't like him, but he's looking after us better than Morlak did."

"Wouldn't be hard," I said, brushing the mildewed mortar and eyeing it critically. "Looks like you caught this just in time. Another wet season, and this would all need repointing."

"Strictly cleaning only," he said. "If we see damage that needs repair, Sarn said he'll renegotiate the contract."

I raised my eyebrows, grudgingly impressed, and said nothing. From here we could see Berrit's Spire over the Exchange where the Beacon sat in its new lantern. Even in daylight, it made a hard prick of white light that you couldn't look at directly without squinting. Around it the roofs of buildings rose above ornamental treetops, lamp posts, and the scattered statues and monuments of Bar-Selehm's for-mal self-consciousness. This was the city at its most orderly, its most classical and regular. Its most Panbroke. It had a kind of noble restraint in defiance of the rest of the city and the wilderness at its edges, so that even the grackles and bee-eaters seemed out of place and dream-like.

"Looking for the Gargoyle?" asked Tanish, grinning down at me from his work.

"Hardly," I said.

"A policeman came to Seventh Street asking about it," said Tanish.

"The Gargoyle?" I said. "Don't they have better things to do?"

"Wanted to hear all the old stories," said Tanish, clearly enjoying himself. "I told him the one about the mean old baker who wouldn't pay the Lani chimney sweeps, so the Gargoyle came down his chim-ney and pushed him in his oven."

He grinned and made a noise that was supposed to sound like someone breathing his last. As Gargoyle stories went, this was one of the more benevolent ones, because it made the monster a guard-ian of the lowly steeplejacks. Most of them were rather less moral, and tended to involve unwary steeplejacks straying into the territory of the Gargoyle atop some spire or high chimney and paying dearly for their trespass.

"Did the copper say why he wanted to know?" I asked.

"*Pursuing inquiries,*" said Tanish, grandly. "I'm telling you, Ang. There's something to it."

"What about Mr. Montresat and the rest?" I asked. "Any word on what they've been up to?"

"Maybe," said Tanish slyly. "What might be in it for a young steeplejack who is trying to make an honest living in a cruel world?"

I shook my head, grinning, and fiddled in my pocket for a half crown. I flipped it to him, and he caught it deftly, whooping with de-light when he realized what it was. I had been in his place not so very long ago. The fact that I didn't have to worry about money for now was a constant source of amazement to me. And, if I was honest, pride. You never forget being poor. Not really. Though I was happy to share what I had with Tanish, I was still careful with my money, always coppering up before I made the smallest purchase as if I didn't really believe there'd be anything in my purse tomorrow.

"You sure?" he said, suddenly abashed because it was Tanish and he was too sweet to be conniving, even in play. "Not sure I've earned this much."

"Let's hear what you have."

He stopped what he was doing and dropped carefully to the gantry, setting his tools down and sitting.

"To tell you the truth," he said, "I haven't seen much. For Montresat and Horritch, it's business as usual. They don't like people prying around and keep watch according-like, but there's nothing odd, at least from the outside."

I scowled.

"What about Markeson?"

"A bit more there," he said. "Once when I got close, I got moved on by a big bloke with a boat hook who looked about ready to bust my head open, and that rather cooled my interest, you know?"

"Understandable," I said.

"But, I'll tell you this. Markeson's in shipping, right? So most of his fleet when they're not at sea are in the main docks south of the estuary, but—and this is the interesting bit—he also has a warehouse right on the river, corrugated iron roof painted blue and big doors opening onto the water with a dock *inside*. It stays open at night, careful-like. Not many lights, but there are people there, and I'm pretty sure he takes boats in when the coast guard aren't looking."

"Smuggling."

"That would be my bet," he said.

"That is interesting, Tanish. Good work."

"One other thing. That factory what burned? One of Horritch's, right? Wasn't empty. Wasn't disused. Mate of mine swore he had seen lights in there too the night before the fire."

That made no sense. If the factory had been active, why make no attempt to save it when the fire took hold? Why not report the damage? Horritch must have been insured.

"You sure?" I asked.

"Archie Jenkins, white kid who joined the gang a month ago. Ran away from home and needed work."

"And?" I prompted.

"He was poking around looking for scrap he could flog to the rag-and-bone man. Some of those old warehouses and factories just leave their machinery when they close. That's a lot of steel if you can find a way to get it out."

"What did he see?" I said, pushing.

"Well, like the warehouses, it don't sound like they want people to know there's anything going on. The windows are all shuttered up, and there are chains on the main doors, 'keep out' signs and such. So Archie was looking to bust in, and he said he could hear machinery inside. Went up close to see if he could look in, and guess what?"

"What?"

"The brick wall was hot."

"It was already on fire?"

"Nah," said Tanish scornfully. "This was the night before, remember? Only one bit of the wall was hot. Guess which bit."

"The base of the chimney," I said, seeing where he was driving.

"Right and correct," he said, pleased with his little reveal. "During the day, cold, at night, hot. What does that tell you?"

"That whoever was using the factory didn't want anyone to see smoke coming out of the stack, so they were only running a night shift."

Tanish nodded sagely.

"I'd say you should go have a look, but there's nothing left," he said.

"The whole place was gutted. They're already lining up bulldozers to push what's left of the rubble and ashes into the river."

I frowned thoughtfully, picturing pale ash on boots.

"Did you tell anyone else about this?" I asked.

"Nah," he said, shaking his head.

"Let's keep it that way, shall we?" I said, fishing out another half crown and holding it up till a smile lit his face. It was worth the money just to see that.

"THE MASK WORK HELPED," I said to Madame Nahreem at our next training session in the remote estate's private gymnasium. I had met Namud in the household carriage on the edge of the Drowning and had ridden all the way with a shotgun beside me and my eyes peeled for clavtar and elephant.

Madame Nahreem looked startled by the admission and gave me a cautious look, as if I might be tricking her.

"It was supposed to," she said. "With the aristocratic bearing, or with the climbing?"

"Both," I said, a little reluctantly. She had received my veiled compliment without so much as a smile. In truth, I was still not sure how good I wanted to be at the mask work if, as Madame Nahreem had said, it was about being rather than playing: a change in who I was, rather than a role I put on like a costume. I saw the value of the mask—or the memory of the mask—if it gave me more physical control, and I supposed I even saw the use of suppressing my more powerful feelings, however strong I thought they made me. I felt, however, that she wanted more, as if my becoming the mask was really about erasing what I had been before, scratching out who I was. That felt wrong. I was, after all, still Anglet Sutonga, Lani steeplejack of the Drowning and Seventh Street, even if my job had changed. I could not just erase those things. They were part of me. I would wear the mask, but I could not become it. Not yet.

Madame Nahreem just nodded.

"Imagine how much better it will be when you are good at it," she said.

I stared at her in disbelief.

"I was being nice!" I said. "You could at least—"

"What?" she shot back, stone-faced.

"Be more encouraging, supportive! Something less obviously critical and disappointed."

"I see," she said, her mouth turning into a half smile, but her eyes still hard. "You wish me to return your politeness with the kind of pleasantries that would make you think you are further along in your studies than you are, a dangerous mental habit that might result in your working less hard or facing an adversary with less focus. You want me to assure you that you are ready to deal with a world of trained assassins who will not hesitate to use every ounce of skill, strength, and duplicity in their control to kill you if the chance presents itself? This is what you want?"

I glared at her for a long moment, speechless.

"Well?" she demanded.

"No," I said.

"Good. Mask on."

NAMUD RODE WITH ME in the carriage back to the city, the shotgun in his lap and a wry smile on his face that suggested he knew how I was feeling about Madame Nahreem. I scowled at him.

"I don't know how you live with her," I said.

"You can put up with a lot from people you admire," he said.

"You admire her? For what? Wait, let me guess. She caught you—a guttersnipe kid—with your hand in her purse or with your lock picks at her door, but she opted to bring you into her stern but instructive service rather than turn you over to the constabulary, since when you have flourished, earning her respect and a comfortable life."

I said it sourly, and his smile was indulgent.

"Wrong in every specific," he said, "but the gist is not so very far off."

"So you feel that you owe her your life," I said. "Does she deserve so much of your admiration?"

"She took me in, as you put it, gave me a life when she did not have to."

"Why?"

He hesitated.

"She has been fortunate herself," he said. "This is her way of creating a little balance within the universe. Call it atonement."

It was an odd word, but when I gave him a swift look he pretended to be checking the shotgun, so I snorted. He was holding something back. In my book, such half deception stripped you of the right to be sanctimonious.

"So she took in a fellow Lani to make herself feel better about marrying into riches," I snapped.

He glanced at me quickly then, and there was fire in his face, anger and something else that I couldn't place.

"That's not it," he said tightly.

"Then what?" I pressed, getting irritated again. "What else makes her so bloody special? Was she a concert pianist? A diplomat? A circus act: Madame Nahreem and her amazing hyenas?"

His turn to scowl.

"I think we should save this conversation for a time when you are more . . . receptive," he said.

"Fine," I snapped, and sulked the rest of the way to the city.

THE MARKESON WAREHOUSE SQUATTED on the south bank of the river in Dagenham Steps, five hundred yards seaward of the great incomplete suspension bridge. It was squeezed in between an old-fashioned tanner's shop and a massive grain silo with hoppers that fed the river barges on the one side and the railway sidings on the other. I knew better than to wander alone around the alleys that ran between the squalid tenement buildings and the industry yards where the inhabitants worked. It was an area as poor as you could find within the city proper, and it had an ugly reputation for being, in every sense of the term, cutthroat. It stank of cheap gin, seaweed, and a heavy industrial sourness with origins I could not guess. The whole area was cluttered with every size and style of chimney belching a thick, foul smoke at all hours. The air was thick and acrid, and no light from moon or stars fought through to lessen the unwholesome night. Among the various conventional stacks were some two dozen bottleneck kilns that marked the potteries and brick ovens: strange bulbous structures, some in the open, some sprouting from the roofs of sheds and factories like baby cuckoos grown too big for their nests. They were round at the bottom and as big as a house, swollen in the middle and tight at the top, where they smoked constantly and were hot enough to make the air above them shimmer even in the dead of winter. I was used to them, but they still had a strange unearthly feel quite unlike the straight, regular chimneys that stabbed up into the smog elsewhere in the city.

I kept to the riverwalk occasionally leaving the raised concrete rampart and descending to the stony shore, always alert for snakes and crocodiles. The tide was out, and the river was low enough to expose the oyster beds and the gray, silty mudflats. The hippos remained on the north bank, and there was no point down here close to the great marine estuary where the river was shallow enough for the beasts to cross.

But animals were hardly my concern. If what Markeson was doing was illegal, as seemed likely, he would have men on watch. Perhaps even one I had met before.

Barrington-Smythe.

It was strange. This was one of the lowest, most dangerous and disreputable parts of Bar-Selehm, but it was, it seemed, central to the income of men who frequented the city's most exclusive club. You'd think that by now I would have been unmoved by the paradox of wealth and power bound to poverty and destitution, but the sheer fact of it was still confounding. None of the men who roamed the streets here would ever be allowed across the threshold of Elitus, but it was their labor on which the club was built. It was one of the truisms of the city that it was generally best not to think about too deeply.

I watched the warehouse with the blue corrugated iron roof for fifteen minutes from the vantage of the silent grain silo, waiting to see what kind of security patrols might show themselves, but there was nothing. Or nothing obvious. The boom of the silo's hopper stuck out over the river downstream of the jetty, and I crawled closer to the end, remembering all too keenly my struggle with Barrington-Smythe on the crane the night Darius died. Below me the river surged toward the sea, and to my right the shadows of the dockyard structures groaned and clanged with the noise of industry, so the sound of the warehouse doors opening onto the dock were quite muted. If it hadn't been for the soft spill of light from within, which made the black water suddenly a drab olive-brown, I would never have noticed. I peered into the darkness toward the river mouth and could just make it out, a small steam-driven barge, its running lights out, laboring against the current as it approached, belching smoke from a single squat chimney.

The boat was pulling hard toward me, the riverbank, and the open doors of the warehouse. It was going to slide quietly in, and then the doors of the warehouse would close over it, like a crocodile taking an unwary flamingo. I had seen no other way into the warehouse except doors that were surely watched and locked, and that meant that if I was going to see inside, I needed to enter with the boat. I had no time to think. In moments, the barge would pass under the hopper and be swallowed by the warehouse.

I uncoiled my rope, eyes locked on the approaching vessel, then lashed one end to the girders of the hopper arm, hastily calculating how much free rope I had to play with.

Not enough.

I was going to have to drop the last few feet to the deck. By the light from the warehouse doors, I saw the flat expanse of the boat's top side, a single pilot's cab located midway along the deck just in front of the chimney stack, and in it a solitary and shaded lamp. I could just make out the silhouette of a figure at the wheel staring at the prow through a brass-rimmed porthole.

I dropped into a squat and waited for the boat to slide beneath me, its engine rumbling and hissing, and as the cab with its lone crewman passed under the hopper, I looped the rope around my waist. Gripping it with both hands—one in front of my face, the other in the small of my back—I closed my mouth and eyes against the smoke and, when I was sure the hot chimney had gone by, jumped. The cord slid through my hands as I dropped, heating fast as I clenched my fists around it to slow my descent. Twice I did it, staring down as the bow of the boat came into view. Go too slowly, and I'd miss the barge entirely and fall into the river. I relaxed my grip and dropped the last fifteen feet, running out of rope and falling the last five to the deck with an ungainly thump that left me on my back.

The surface was wood and wet and smooth, which was a blessing. It knocked the wind out of me and left me momentarily stunned and breathless, but I had only narrowly missed a mooring cleat that would have done rather more damage. I rolled into a crouch and kept very still a few yards behind the chimney, watching and listening for any sign of alarm my arrival might have raised. In that moment, the river slipped below me and the rope was left hanging in our wake.

The prow was already nudging its way into the warehouse. There was a juddering of gears, and I felt the engines reverse as we left the main flow of the river and drifted in through the doors. It was light inside, and I would be very obvious to anyone who was watching, though the air was thickening with blue-black smoke. I scanned the deck, spotted a hatch only a few feet from where I had fallen, skulked over, and flipped the heavy metal hasp. Seizing the handle, I dragged the hatch up and open, casting a glance around the inside of the ware-house as the barge slowed, bumping up against a jetty hung with rubber tires. Two men were working to secure the prow. I had to get below fast.

And that was when I looked down into the hold and saw, with horrified surprise, a dozen faces, thin, tear-streaked, sickly, and black. Women and children all. They had been revealed as a cloud of coal smoke billowed out of the belly of the ship, chased by a wall of stench sour with the appalling aroma of excrement, vomit, and hot unwashed bodies, and they looked up at me with a mixture of dread and relief.

CHAPTER
20

I WAS NOT WHAT they expected to see. A dozen empty hands reached up from the hold, fingers splayed so I didn't know if they wanted me to pull them out or give them something—money, I thought first, then changed my mind.

Food. Water.

Gods knew how long they had been aboard. Days? Not in this shallow-draft vessel, which could be little more than a short-range ferry from whatever larger ship had brought them. For a moment I just stared, one hand clasped thoughtlessly over my nose to keep the foulness out as I took in their stained and ragged bits of clothing. I couldn't tell if they were Quundu, Delfani, or Zagrel, but it seemed certain that they were members of one of those tribes from north of the desert, and that meant my estimate was wrong. They would have been at sea for weeks.

I was still processing that thought when a man's voice called out from the quayside, a wordless cry of menace and alarm that straightened me up.

"Get back below till you're called!" he yelled.

He thought I was one of the refugees, caught in the act of coming above deck. He had a rifle on a strap over his shoulder, and he swung it round purposefully. I lowered my face so that he would not see his mistake, and glanced back to the doors through which the barge had come. They were already closing, drawn into place by a winch-and-chain system operated by another man on the jetty. The doors extended only a few inches below the lapping black water.

But I couldn't swim.

I hesitated, feeling the presence of those upturned hands and faces at my feet like the strange swelling pressure you sometimes feel before a downpour, and then there were footsteps on the quay. The rifleman was coming, squinting at me in the low and smoky light, head lowered, the muzzle of his weapon coming up.

"*Nxephe,*" I muttered, one of the few Mahweni words I knew— *sorry*—then turned, took three long strides and vaulted off the back of the boat before the gunman could get off his first shot.

The water was thick and warm, smelling of the ocean and of the oil that trailed after the rusting vessel. I braced myself for a floor of weedy rock underfoot, but there was only water. It closed over my head, and I felt the full horror of what I had done before the bullet slapped down a foot from my shoulder. I surfaced again, panic hot in my throat as I gasped at the air, bobbed briefly, and went under again. Water filled my open, staring eyes, flooded my nose and mouth so that I rose coughing.

I heard the snap of the rifle being reloaded and forced myself to thrust my head down under the noxious water as I lashed out for the doors, arms and legs flailing, my saturated boots terrifyingly heavy. I made little headway and broke the surface again, blind with the stinging river in my eyes, shrinking powerlessly as I heard the second report of the gun. This time he hit the door itself, spraying splinters as the slug buried itself in the wood.

Again I dipped, launching myself forward as best I could, too scared of drowning to hate the feeling of vulnerability as I turned my back on the gunner. I splashed ineptly in the direction of the doors, and this time, caught in some strange backward current, I felt my body carried forward. With scrabbling fingers I reached the thin fissure between the doors, stabilized my frightened drift against them, then reached below the surface for their lower edge. I did not look back at the gunman, who was now only a few yards away, feverishly reloading his weapon. With a breath—no more than a gasp that took in water as well as air and didn't come close to filling my lungs—I dived once more, levering myself down under the warehouse doors and pulling myself out.

I broke the surface with a great, shuddering breath, sucking in the night air as I fought to hold on to something—anything—that would give me a purchase on the structure. I was lucky to have lived this long. If I drifted off into the river, that luck would quickly run out.

Behind me I heard raised voices and the clank of the winch as the men inside struggled to get the doors open again. I had only seconds to get ashore and escape into the alleys of the dockside. I blinked back the oil-smeared water and—I suspect—some of my own tears, and reached for the shore, using my arms as I had seen swimmers do, stretching, plunging my hands into the water like I was grabbing it, pulling myself forward, kicking wildly.

Only then did I see the log that seemed to be drifting toward me. Drifting against the current. I saw the bumps on its topside blink, and suddenly they were bright as green glass.

Crocodile.

I cried out, lunging and flailing as before with a new desperation as the animal picked up speed, halving the distance between us in a single, breathless moment. Another leaping, desperate surge, and my knee struck painfully—blessedly—on something hard and immobile. Stone. Concrete. A last blundering thrust, and I was stumbling in waist-deep water, one hand tugging a chisel from my work belt as I spun to face the crocodile. I slashed the water, weeping, backing up still farther, waiting for the attack.

The chisel cut through the black water of the Kalihm, but the croc had gone under. I stepped back, feeling the stony and uneven ground below my soaking boots, and saw the warehouse doors open, saw the gunman, who had leapt into the water as he forced himself through the widening gap, gun barrel first. I felt his eyes lock onto me in the dark, saw his wide-eyed terror, heard his shriek of agony before the crocodile pulled him under.

"HUMAN TRAFFICKING?" EXCLAIMED Willinghouse. "Markeson? He's a pillar of the community!"

I had told him the story twice already, but he still seemed incapable of processing its implications.

It had taken me almost two hours to make my circuitous way back to the town house, crossing the river by the catwalk on the incomplete suspension bridge and skulking through the streets, one eye always open for a patrolling officer who would arrest me on suspicion of being Lani in the city at night and therefore Up to No Good. It was a warm night, but I was soaking and miserably cold, unable to shake off the fear of the gunman, the crocodile that had surely killed him, and the river itself.

Something else too, that was harder to put my finger on. There had been a second, when the gunman had first seen me, when he had thought I was one of the refugees. I thought back on that moment as I made my cautious way through the city, and I came to a strange, nagging sense that he was almost right. I *was* one of them, as I had been in the dream of the rice festival when the Drowning flooded, and we were suddenly all homeless, lost and fighting to stay afloat. I turned the idea over in my mind as if I was explaining it to Mnenga, the one person I thought might understand, momentarily fingering the sorrel nut in my pocket. But the more I imagined picking my way through the words, the more I saw his listening face in my mind, the more I concluded that I was being absurd, that thinking of myself as a refugee was ridiculous and grotesque. I might not have a home I called my own, I might not have a clear sense of where I belonged in the world, and my new life might seem to be a series of continuous and dangerous attempts at pretense—hiding behind one of Madame Nahreem's masks—but I had food, security, even money. I wasn't a refugee, and their suffering, their powerlessness in their own lives, was not mine.

Also, my thoughts prompted in Mnenga's voice, *your life was saved by a crocodile. This is very strange. And good. Think about that and celebrate what you have instead of weeping for what you don't.*

I had to grin at that.

So I relayed my news to an excited Willinghouse, who had emerged in a dressing gown over pressed pajamas.

"Thomas Markeson," he said for the fifth time. "You're sure?"

"He wasn't there himself, but it was his place, yes," I said.

We were sitting in a police carriage, waiting for Andrews to finish giving orders to the squad of armed officers he had summoned from Mount Street. At the inspector's kind insistence, I had washed hurriedly and changed into clothes last worn by a young footman. Willinghouse had been surprised by this, as if he had somehow not noticed that I had arrived dripping wet and stinking from the filth of the river.

"Markeson," Willinghouse mused, gazing at the gas lamps outside the police station.

"You're glad," I said, as the realization dawned.

"What?" he said.

"You're glad that he's involved," I said.

"Nonsense," he said, quelling the smile I had seen ghosting his twisted lips.

"You are," I said. "A political enemy, a member of the elite, implicated in human smuggling in violation of everything his cronies say about Bar-Selehm looking after its own and staying out of foreign affairs that don't concern us? Of course you're glad."

"He's not a politician," said Willinghouse.

"But he has friends who are," I answered. "Friends who sit on the opposite side of the house than you do."

"There is that," he conceded, and suddenly the smile was back and sprawling into a grin he did not bother to conceal. "There is certainly that. Those hypocritical, isolationist, flag-waving liars. This will wipe the supercilious grins off their nationalist faces! I can't wait to see their response when the newspapers get hold of it, and they *will* get hold of it if I have to dictate the story myself."

"So, glad then," I concluded.

"Maybe a little," he said, then surprised me by laughing once, a single bark of delight hastily stifled. "Good work, Miss Sutonga. Very good work indeed."

The carriage door opened.

"You find nocturnal raids amusing?" asked Inspector Andrews, climbing in.

"Mr. Willinghouse was just reflecting on the discomfited condition of his enemies," I supplied.

Willinghouse glared at me.

"A politician does not have enemies," he remarked. "Just colleagues with whom he has a difference of opinion over the betterment of his country."

"A politician's answer if ever I heard one," said Andrews, taking his seat. "On, driver," he barked through the window. "Dawn is upon us."

HE WAS RIGHT ABOUT the dawn, and that meant a long time had passed since my little adventure at the secret quay. Too much time. The warehouse was empty, the barge deserted and hosed down. The duty foreman swore blind that it had been moored there for three days having brought in a load of coal mined in the southern cape, as he could easily demonstrate from its logbook and manifest. The bullet holes in the inlet doors had been caused during events leading to the tragic death of one Albrecht Imsenga, a Mahweni barge worker who had been attacked by a crocodile. . . .

I waited in the carriage, but the moment between receiving the news and returning to me had only given scope for Willinghouse's furious disappointment to bloom.

"Why did it take you so long to get back to the house?" he demanded. "They knew someone had been in and seen what was in the boat."

"*Who*," I said.

"What?" sputtered Willinghouse.

"They were people," I said, stupidly. "Someone had seen *who* was in the boat. Not what."

"Do you think that's the major issue at the moment?" Willinghouse snapped. "Grammar?"

"I'm just saying," I remarked with a gesture of weary surrender, "that our failure to catch Markeson red-handed is perhaps less important than our not knowing what happened to the refugees."

Willinghouse deflated.

"You are right, of course," he said. "Yes."

"I will say," said Andrews addressing me, "that you might have saved time going directly to the first policeman you saw."

"Right," I said, "because the worthy constabulary of Bar-Selehm think so highly of Lani women who emerge from the shadows with seaweed in their hair." I sniffed it and made a face. My hasty ablutions had not gotten rid of the tang of oil.

"You could have given my name," he said, slightly put out at what he took to be my impugning the reputation of the police force.

"You will recall that we're trying to get Miss Sutonga to keep a low profile," said Willinghouse, as if I wasn't there.

Andrews scowled and looked away.

"Politics," he muttered.

"I don't suppose we could go back and search properly in daylight?" Willinghouse ventured.

"No," said Andrews shortly. "I'm going to catch an earful from the commissioner as it is without further alienating the esteemed Mr. Markeson. And how am I going to explain myself, Willinghouse? Tell me that. There is such a thing as an evidence chain, something

I can present to document why I acted as I did. Hunches from anonymous sources do not qualify."

I looked at Willinghouse in the early morning light cutting soft and warm through the slats of the carriage window. Apparently I wasn't the only one whose name was to be kept out of the official record—and the papers.

"I am sure you are a man of great invention," he said.

Andrews snorted but did not dignify the remark with a response.

"GOOD GOD," SAID DAHRIA as I entered Willinghouse's hallway, "you smell like you've been dead a week. Go upstairs and do not return until you can approximate a human being."

"I may go to bed for a few hours after I've properly bathed," I said. "I'm exhausted. But I'll come down and eat first."

"Of course you will," she said. "I'll have Cook roast you a warthog or two."

"Most amusing," I said.

"I'm so glad you think so. Remember your good mood as I pass along a piece of information."

"What?" I said, instantly on my guard.

"Madame Nahreem is expecting you for a full day of training at the estate."

The noise I made in response did not, strictly speaking, contain words.

CHAPTER
21

I HAD NEVER BEEN to a white person's funeral, let alone that of a society lady, and I was only able to attend Agatha Markeson's by reprising my role from a few months ago as Dahria Willinghouse's maid, complete with demure frock and coal-scuttle bonnet. It looked frightful and amused Dahria to no end, but it kept my face hidden, which would be especially useful since I would be rubbing elbows with the same ladies who had last seen me as Lady Ki Misrai.

"Did you like Mrs. Markeson?" I asked, as the fly taking us to the church rolled off.

"She was a spiteful harridan," Dahria said, "but I believe we should not speak ill of the dead, so let us merely say that she was like many of the women of her generation with whom my social circle frequently intersects."

"That's a depressing thought," I said, watching the city go by.

Dahria shrugged.

"When you know what to expect, it's harder to be disappointed," she said. "Sometimes you meet one or two who are surprisingly pleasant and thoughtful, people who do Good Works for hospitals and schools, people who arrange the church flowers or volunteer at the local museums or orphanages or whatever. Some of them are quite nice. A few of them are even—dare I say it?—politically sensible."

She grinned mischievously, and I couldn't tell if she was being serious or not.

"I didn't meet many at Elitus," I said. "Apart from Violet Farthingale. I quite liked her."

"The maid."

"Governess."

"Right," she said, as if we were in agreement. I bridled, but she beat me to it. "Snob," said Dahria.

"You, you mean?"

"No!" she protested. "You."

"I beg your pardon?" I shot back. I had been called a lot of things in my life, but *snob* was not one of them.

"Inverted snob, then," said Dahria. "Brimming with class loyalty and always ready to find fault with your betters."

"I would be happier if they didn't assume they were my betters," I said. "Besides, you just said I was right."

"I'm entitled to say it," she said. "I'm one of them. It's like family. If you are part of it, you can criticize it to your heart's content, but if you're not? Keep your mouth shut or face my wrath."

"I'll remember to keep my feelings on Madame Nahreem to myself," I said.

"You do that," she said. "And for heaven's sake, don't agree with me. Nothing good ever comes from that."

"That, I had already discerned," I said.

"My dear steeplejack," she said in her silkiest voice, giving me her most feline smile, "when did you discover all this vim and vigor?"

"We lowly steeplejacks call it piss and vinegar," I said. "I've always had it. It just used to stay in my head more."

"Pray God it does for the rest of the day," she said, putting the back of her hand to her forehead in mock horror, as if my language had made her faint.

I grinned at her, and she, almost in spite of herself, grinned back before turning to face the window. I enjoyed being alone with Dahria like this. She could be infuriating: condescending, shallow, glib, and prejudiced. But in her heart she liked me, and not just for whatever entertainment value she thought I provided. Despite the difficulty of my assignment, the dour purpose of our journey, and the stifling confines of the dim carriage, I found I did not want to get out.

Here we could spar, matching wits in our own peculiar version of a salon debating society, but out there I would have to be the silent servant, and she the imperious mistress. I hadn't thought it before, but all of a sudden, I found myself wondering which of us enjoyed those roles least.

"And you're not," I said. "Not really."

"Not really what?"

"One of them."

She smiled, grimly this time, and conceded the point with a shrug that registered only in her eyebrows.

"Because my one-quarter Lani brother and I have not been welcomed into the heady, northern climate of Elitus, you mean?" she said. "Perhaps not."

"I like you the better for it," I said.

"It's not like I have a choice," she said. "My parentage is my parentage."

"Still," I said, flushed.

"Then I will take that as a compliment and wear it safely and secretly in my heart." She said it softly and without any of her usual arch humor, so that I watched her, waiting for what the music hall comedians called a "punch line." When none came, and she simply gazed at me, a strange and intimate frankness in her warm hazel eyes, I just nodded and returned to looking out of the window, my face inexplicably hot.

The ceremony—Dahria called it a *service,* a term I did not understand in this context—was grand and dour and white, and therefore was, as Dahria observed at its conclusion, a pretty good approximation of Agatha Markeson herself. The vaulted church, adorned with fluted columns and elaborate tracery around stained-glass windows that might have been beautiful if the fog outside ever permitted the sun to shine through them, rang with the strains of a great, overblown organ. It blasted its weighty anthems over the heads of the congregation so that it was all I could do not to shrink away from sound so ponderous and smothering that I felt I might reach up and touch it. I imagined it would feel hard as a coffin lid.

Thomas Markeson wore black, of course, but he looked as leaden as the music, and though there was an ironically healthy crowd for the event, there wasn't much grief, though I suppose that people of Agatha's station prided themselves on showing little emotion. Even her daughter looked stunned and overawed rather than actually sad, though perhaps she had just been well trained in self-control. She stood beside her father like a child pushed to the front of a crowd to shake hands with a visiting dignitary she had never heard of. Her governess, Violet Farthingale, veiled and in mourning black like the rest, sat on the other side of the aisle, never taking her eyes off the priest. I saw people watching her, occasionally nudging each other and whispering, and I thought that it would be ironic indeed if Violet was, in fact, the only person there who was truly sorry that Agatha was dead.

I was not in black, or not entirely. Dahria's wardrobe for her imaginary maid did not, she said, extend to attire befitting *every* social eventuality, so I had donned black gloves and a matching shawl and added black ribbon to my bonnet. I'd thought it would do, but I was mistaken.

"Who do you belong to, girl?" snapped a voice I had heard before. "I want to give them a piece of my mind. Dressed like this for a funeral? It's scandalous."

Serafina Dearbeloved. Of course. I shrank into myself, partly my old natural diffidence and partly panic that I was about to be recognized. Except, of course, the woman hadn't really looked at me, except to determine what I was. Though we had met only days ago, she showed no sign of connecting me to the glamorous foreign dignitary with whom she had spent much of the evening the night Agatha Markeson died.

"She doesn't *belong* to anybody," said Dahria, turning to her and giving her a brittle smile. "She works for me."

"Oh," said Dearbeloved witheringly. "Of course she does. Well, you should have seen to her better. Unless, of course, you were *trying* to be disrespectful?"

I hung my head, so I did not see the play of emotions in Dahria's face, but her response came out clear and sharp as birdsong.

"Believe me, Mrs. Dearbeloved, if I wanted to show disrespect, you would be in no doubt about it."

She seized my arm, turned on her heel, and gave the woman her back, marching us away and opening a black lace parasol like a shield, while Mrs. Dearbeloved sputtered, "Really!" in our wake.

"I would cheerfully kill that woman," said Dahria. "I'm inclined to think that her name is one of the bleakest jokes in the universe, aren't you?"

I glanced up just enough to smile at her from under my bonnet, but I looked down again hurriedly. Another woman I knew from Merita—elegant and gray-eyed—was making a beeline for us.

"You seem to have outraged Mrs. Dearlyloathed," said Constance under her breath. "I swear, Dahria, you can cheer up the most miserable of events."

She grinned impishly, leaned in, and kissed Dahria briefly on the cheek, an act that made Mrs. Dearbeloved huff some more and blunder away.

"My one delight, dear Connie, is giving you pleasure," said Dahria, returning the grin. She half turned to introduce me, and I lowered my head, face set. Mrs. Dearbeloved wouldn't recognize Lady Misrai, but I had a feeling "Connie" would. Dahria hesitated, then changed course. "Is there to be a lunch? I swear churches make me hungry."

"I'm amazed you didn't burst into flame as soon as you came in," said Constance, archly.

"You know," said Dahria, "so am I. Would have livened things up a little, at least."

"What hypocrites we are," Constance muttered, scanning the bustling crowd. "How many of these people actually liked Agatha. Half? A quarter?"

"Less, I'd say," said Dahria. "With good reason. I wonder if the one who did her in is here."

This time Constance really was shocked, though she almost giggled.

"Who's your money on?" she asked.

"The governess," said Dahria. "I believe there was something of a triangle going on."

Constance shook her head.

"She was with me," she said.

"You were there?" asked Dahria, delighted. For all the talk of who I had met and what lines of work they were involved in, I realized I had never mentioned Constance.

"Father insisted," she said.

Father? Not only had I not mentioned her, I hadn't even wondered who she was.

"I was consoling her," said Constance. "The old battle-ax had unleashed some of her usual venom at the poor girl, and I was drying her tears. Wasn't her."

"The husband, then," said Dahria. "He looks the type."

"I don't know what that means," said Constance, eyeing Markeson, who was big, red-faced, and barrel chested as ever but, somehow, diminished by his mourning, if that was what it was. "I wouldn't have thought he'd have the nerve, to tell you the truth. He's a blusterer and a behind-doors operator, but not, I think, a man of action."

I risked a half look at her at that. She looked shrewd and a little pink in the face, as if something about Markeson annoyed her.

"Maybe he paid an assassin," whispered Dahria with wide-eyed glee.

"One of the servants said they were overheard squabbling just before she died," said Constance. "In the hallway outside the room where she was found. They were told not to say anything to the police. The club would prefer that it looked like the work of an intruder."

"Maybe it was Richter," said Dahria.

The Heritage party leader was also in attendance, patting Markeson on the shoulder in a manly way. He was dressed in his familiar almost-uniform, though his red and silver armband had been replaced with simple black. Now that the crowd were clustering around the bereaved husband like flies around carrion, I could see that they were all there: Richter and his party cronies, including Barrington-Smythe, his usual smile empty as his eyes; the mongoose-like arms manufacturer, Montresat; Nathan Horritch, sepulchral in a black silk top hat; and Lord Elwin, looking like he was en route to a very gloomy ball. Vandersay and Rathbone were brooding quietly together, and even the doorman, Wellsley, was in evidence, crisply precise in his formal mourning wear. The only one of the prominent men from Elitus who wasn't there was the Grappoli ambassador, which was perhaps why Lady Alice seemed to be floating off by herself, looking out of place and eager to be gone, like a winter butterfly.

"The company you keep, Connie," said Dahria warningly. "You need a better class of social life."

"I'll tell Father," Constance answered.

As she bustled away, I nudged Dahria hard. "Who is her father?" I asked.

"Nathan Horritch, of course," she said. "The textiles man. I'm surprised you didn't say she was there."

I frowned, trying to process the idea that Constance was the daughter of one of the men who seemed most deeply involved in the whole messy business, only to be taken aback by Dahria stooping to peer under my bonnet.

"Civet got your tongue?" she purred.

"What?" I asked.

"Connie must have made quite an impression," she cooed. "But then she's a very beautiful woman. I've always said so. I'm just a little surprised you didn't mention meeting her."

I gaped at her stupidly, trying to make sense of her implication, and then she snapped on her usual smile and said, "Joking, my dear. Only joking."

But I didn't think that was entirely true.

"You're very . . . focused on this case, aren't you?" she added after a moment.

"It's my job," I said, pleased to move to matters I understood.

"Yes, but it's more than just a way of putting money in your pocket and food on the table for you, isn't it?"

"Isn't that enough? Maybe if you'd ever gone without food on the table—"

"Yes, yes," Dahria cut in. "You were very poor and life was hard, but it's not now, is it? I mean, you might fall from a great height or get shot, but you'll die in better clothes."

"It's all I hope for," I said, matching her dryness.

"But that's just it, isn't it? It's *not* all you hope for. It's not about money, food, or clothes, and this time it isn't even personal. When you first came to work for my brother it was about that Lani boy."

"Berrit," I said.

"Exactly. You were very driven and passionate about it all because he was one of your own. But you're just the same on this case when you have no personal connection at all. So what, my dear steeplejack, drives you?"

It was true that I felt little for the dead cat burglar called Darius or for the odious Mrs. Markeson, and the shuffling of secret plans between hostile nations felt like so much political abstraction. But I thought of the faces belowdecks in Markeson's barge and of the sandals with the flowers by the riverbank, the shrill cry of a woman splashing back to a listing raft. They were not me, these people, and their miseries outshone mine like the Beacon does a candle, but in one sense at least, my nightmare about the flooded rice festival, when we had been united in tragedy, had been right. I knew something of what it was to be displaced, to be ignored, to be a tool when useful and an inconvenience when not, to be not quite a real person. It wasn't so very different from Berrit. The crux of the matter came down to a question: if I, who shared the plight of the discounted, the abandoned, the repudiated, would not stand by them, stand *for* them, who would?

But I could not say such things to Dahria. Not here. Not now.

"I need to know," I said. "The answers. The picture. We live in a city of shadows and lies. A constant, poisonous fog. I have to see light around the corner. I need truth."

She gave me a long look, amused and thoughtful, then nodded once and said, "Then you have work to do."

CHAPTER

22

THERE HAD BEEN NO report of the women and children I had seen in the barge: no complaints to the police about suspicious people or minor thefts, no grumbling among the street gangs about foreigners on their turf, nothing in the papers about newly arrested people put in the deportation camps. The more I thought about it, the more I could imagine only one of two scenarios. Either my presence in the warehouse, coupled with the death of one of their men as they came after me, had made the smugglers whisk the refugees away to where they had been intended to go very quickly indeed, or the refugees had taken advantage of the confusion to escape. I wanted to believe it was the latter, but my heart told me that if they had fled, guideless, into an alien city, someone would have seen them.

"What happens to refugees when they come here?" I asked Sureyna.

She shook her head.

"They mostly have nothing when they arrive because they give what money they have saved to the pirates and smugglers who bring them," she said. We were eating a lunch of samosas and starfruit purchased from a Lani bakery a block from Szenga Square. "A very small number may have family here already, but few of them are legal immigrants, so while they might hide out with them, it's a short-term solution. If they are caught, they will be shipped back and whatever belongings they have confiscated to meet the cost of their shipping. They can't legally work in the city, so some of them will try to get out into the bush, get positions working on farms or ranches where they will be asked fewer questions, but it's risky. They don't have the money to pay for counterfeit papers, though I've heard that some of the black gangs will take them in anyway."

"To do what?"

"All the things no one does by choice," she said. "Mostly illegal. The boys handle whatever the adults don't want to be caught dealing with—drugs, weapons, whatever. The girls—"

"Yes," I said. I knew what the girls would be made to do.

"And they never get out. Ever. The gang is the only thing between them and the law—deportation, imprisonment, or worse—so they become slaves. The Mahweni have a phrase for it: *inkambu-mtoti ingwane.*"

I raised my eyebrows, and she shrugged self-consciously.

"I don't really speak the old language," she said, "not fluently, but I remember a lot of what I hear. The phrase is the name of a plant which has a sweet and fragrant flower surrounded by sticky tentacles. Pretty from a distance but very large. You see them out in wetland parts of the bush. Flies are drawn to the nectar, even small birds. They get caught and slowly dissolved. The Mahweni name translates to something like 'sweet field octopus.' They—we, since the city blacks have adopted the phrase as well—use it to describe the appeal of the city to foreign refugees. Anyway, once here and enslaved by the gangs, they are trapped. Some of them run away, but they rarely get far, and punishment from the gangs is terrible."

She didn't need to tell me that. I'd seen enough of it on Seventh Street.

"What if they are captured by the authorities?" I asked.

"Returned at their own expense to their homeland, if they have any money at all," said Sureyna. "Otherwise, the journey will be shorter. They are packed onto trade barges and dumped midway up the east coast."

"Wouldn't that put them on the edge of the desert?"

"Saves time and money," said Sureyna darkly.

I pictured the low-slung boats, their smoky innards jammed with starving, desperate people. . . .

"Wait," I said. "Barges? Not naval vessels?"

"Clippers if they go all the way to the north coast. Several of them together may take a frigate for escort, but generally no, why?"

"So these are privately owned boats?"

"Yes. And it's quite lucrative. That's one of the reasons the so-called business community doesn't want to see the city's antirefugee policy changed. The owners are paid by—"

"Government contract," I said, realization dawning. "Markeson had one. So he was being paid by the smugglers at one end to bring refugees in and by the government to ship them back out again."

Sureyna met my eyes, and we just looked at each other, feeling stupid and powerless, as if we were trapped in our own version of the sweet field octopus.

"Perhaps I can ask around in the docklands. Someone might know where those people have been taken," I said.

Sureyna shook her head. "They won't talk to you," she said.

Because I was Lani, she meant. Apart from the owners and the senior foremen, the docklands was an almost entirely black area, which meant that Lady Ki Misrai wouldn't be any help either. I gave her a sidelong look.

"Too bad I don't have a black friend who speaks a few words of Mahweni . . . ," I said.

"I'M NOT ENTIRELY COMFORTABLE with this," said Sureyna. The alleys and roughly cobbled streets of the docklands were thronged with people in the early dawn light, a long snaking line of silent black men and women dressed in the tough, drab clothes of factory laborers. They spilled out of terraced houses, filed over the fishwharf bridge, disembarked from slow, sleepy ferries, and processed toward the looming smokestacks of Dagenham Steps as if on some somber pilgrimage. "It feels like deception," she added. "Manipulation."

"It is," I said. "But I swear no one we talk to will be hurt by what they tell us."

"You can't promise that," she said. "Not if the people we are up against are as dangerous as you say."

"Then we will do all we can to make it true," I said, adding—before she could register her dissatisfaction with the halfhearted compromise—"and we'll weigh that against the lives of the refugees we are trying to save."

"They may be long gone," she answered.

"Anything we learn about the smuggling ring may save others who haven't even arrived yet."

"So they'll be stuck in their own land, forced to fight a losing war against the Grappoli," Sureyna replied. She wasn't being argumentative. She was thinking it all through. "What a mess," she concluded lamely.

I just nodded, watching her eyes.

"All right," she said. "But we do everything we can to keep these people out of trouble."

"Agreed," I said, pulling the scarf I was wearing up around my head. We joined the dour line to Horritch's weaving factory in silence, trudging with the crowd like fish borne on the current.

The decision to explore Horritch's place had been a simple one. Montresat's munitions works was too heavily protected, and not just by his own people. As a military supplier, the factory had a complement of armed dragoons at each corner, and entrance required official papers. Markeson's dockside warehouse was closed up by day, but guarded less officially—and therefore more menacingly—than Montresat's. Horritch's weaving shed was located a stone's throw from both, just beyond the cluster of strange, bulbous chimneys of the pottery and brick oven kilns. There was a good chance someone working there might have seen refugees in the area. Moreover, I could not shake the idea that the three businesses were connected by more than club cuff links.

At first the workers seemed to me a uniform mass, ageless, sexless, a single body in slow, determined motion; as we moved along, however, I began to see the differences in face and clothing. Some were my age or a little younger, but most were older, men and women both, their hair tied back or pressed down with flat woolen caps. They wore trousers and dresses of thick canvassy stuff. The shirts below their overalls had spots of color or hints of decoration: a tiny embroidery here, an ornate button there, each a hint of something private and individual within the mass of humanity. They carried tin lunch pails and cloth packages with shoulder straps. They wore sturdy leather shoes and boots, or wooden clogs with hobnailed soles. Some of them—men and women—wore scent that gave the procession a strange and unexpected air of spice: another kind of privacy hinted at beneath the worker's guise. Though I was not one of them, I felt a sense of something shared, a secrecy they kept beneath their clothes that prevented them from becoming part of the machines.

Or tried to.

They produced cards from jackets and purses and ran them through the clock-in machine that stamped the time of their arrival. Luckily, no one questioned me or Sureyna for not doing the same. Above the flow, like an angler by a stream, the white foreman, a mug of something in one hand and a newspaper open on his knee, watched absently as we entered. Occasionally, he looked up and checked a clipboard or told the crowd to slow down or hurry up. I couldn't tell why.

I was almost at the door before I realized that I had been to this place only a week before, in the company of Sergeant Emtezu and his wife. She had said she would be starting a fortnight later, so she would not be here yet, but I remembered the other woman, her neighbor, who was probably inside somewhere. Rummaging through my memory, I pulled out a name.

Bertha.

The shed was cavernous inside, but while the ceiling was tower-ing, it was not, I thought, as high as the building itself, though I saw no stairs. Most of the available space in the main chamber was filled with the looms themselves, which sat like great mechanical insects in serried ranks, waiting. The whole was lit by tall arched windows in the stained brick walls, but the glass was soot-smeared and the air had a thick, gray quality that felt strangely sepulchral.

I caught Sureyna's eye, but we did not speak. A moment later, the looms came on, and conversation became impossible. I had not dreamed there could be such bedlam anywhere on earth. I was used to working outside the factories. Inside, the roar of the steam engines and the looms they powered was a constant staggering blast. The texture of the sound changed, becoming more shrill or more guttural, full of hissing or clanking, and there was the regular clock-ticking rhythm of the mechanisms sending the shuttles back and forth, re-setting, and advancing like great metal heartbeats, but taken alto-gether, they made simply a wall of noise, hard and impossibly high. I tried to speak, to shout, but could make out nothing of that slim private self I had just been celebrating, as if I had been rolled beneath the wheels over which the leather belts ran, flattened out, and made part of the engine itself.

The workers were herded into their familiar stations and set to their tasks, standing, reaching, feeding the relentless machines. Around them the air stood hot, still, and smoky, as the great looms breathed their endless, deafening bellow like hungry beasts that could not be satisfied.

Deafening was no exaggeration. As I looked around, I saw how communication took place between the workers: not with words, but with twittering gestures of their hands. I remembered how hard it had been to communicate with Bertha, and I found myself think-ing back to the eerie silence in which the workers had filed along the street and into the mill. They were all deaf, or close to it, made so by the steady roar of the machines.

As they took up their positions, Sureyna and I were left alone on the little free area of concrete floor. Keen to avoid the attentions of the patrolling foremen, Sureyna started to walk over to the closest loom. I caught her arm and mouthed, "Wait!" at her, my eyes flashing around for Sergeant Emtezu's neighbor. I found her over by the wall on one side, her hands moving fluidly over the loom as the shuttle flew from side to side. She gave us a blank look, her eyes lingering on me, trying to place my face, and continued working.

Sureyna began speaking, but her voice was drowned out by the sound of the machine. When she reached out to touch Bertha's sleeve the woman turned on her, anger flaring in her face. Words spewing from her lips, though I could not catch their sense.

Scowling, she pushed a large red lever and the loom disengaged from the driving engine. She tilted her head up enquiringly, her gaze switching to Sureyna, till the newspaper woman motioned vaguely that she wanted to talk. Bertha glanced hastily around, then nodded across the floor toward a door with a glass pane in the upper half.

Sureyna nodded and the woman led the way. She was large and solid, though her back hunched from bending over the loom, and her arms and hands were powerful. She wore a white kerchief knotted around her head, and an oil-spattered apron over her oddly formal-looking dress of brown worsted.

The door led to a locker room, and the woman strode through it and another door without hesitation, turning the moment it was closed behind us. They were good, well-fitting doors, and the noise of the machines dropped by at least half.

"*Yini?*" she demanded, her voice very nearly a shout.

Sureyna began with a few words of Mahweni, but the woman clearly couldn't hear and made a face. Sureyna tried again, louder this time, but she seemed far from sure of herself.

"Feldish," Bertha roared. "I speak it."

"Right," said Sureyna. "Good."

"What?" roared the woman, exasperation tightening her features.

"I just . . . good," Sureyna shouted.

The woman nodded and looked at me.

"No more jobs," she shouted.

It took me a second to realize her misunderstanding.

"I'm not here looking for work," I said.

"What?"

"I'M NOT HERE LOOKING FOR WORK!"

"You are Tsanwe's friend," she said, considering me beadily.

"Yes," I said.

"And you?" she said, turning to Sureyna.

"She is my friend too," I said. Bertha raised her eyebrows, then shrugged fractionally, waiting for more.

"I work for the newspaper. The NEWSPAPER," said Sureyna, reading the woman's confusion. "My name is Sureyna."

It was the first thing to soften Bertha's fierce demeanor. She smiled at the word, transforming into a different person entirely as she nodded approvingly. "Bertha," she said, putting one large hand on the middle of her chest.

Sureyna and I both relaxed visibly. This was progress.

"We are looking for some women and children from another country," said Sureyna.

"Another country?" echoed the woman, puzzled.

"Quundu, Delfani, or Zagrel," I said.

Bertha considered me warily. For several seconds, she said nothing, and the words, which I had said loudly, seemed to linger in the air between us like the ever-present noise and oily smoke of the machines. If I had to put a name to what I saw in her face, I would call it caution. She shook her head, but said nothing.

"They are refugees," I added.

"They are in trouble," said Sureyna, simply. "We want to help them."

Bertha looked doubtful, then considered me.

"You worked with Tsanwe," she said. "Helped him."

I shrugged.

"A little," I said. "He helped me too."

Bertha nodded thoughtfully.

"Yesterday," she said, at last. "Men came. White men. Looking."

"Police?" asked Sureyna.

Bertha looked away and bit her lip, then shook her head with grim decision.

"Who?" I asked.

She shrugged.

"Did you see any of the women? The children?" Sureyna followed.

Another head shake from Bertha, another half check over her shoulder before saying, "But. Maybe someone saw."

"Who?" I asked, but she avoided my eyes. She wasn't going to tell us that.

"What did they see?" tried Sureyna.

"Children," said Bertha, and now her face was closed as if she did not trust herself to show any emotion. "Hungry. Frightened. They were in the street but ran away before morning."

"Where did they go?" I asked.

Again the shrug, the head shake. She didn't know, and not knowing hurt her a little.

"How many?" asked Sureyna.

Bertha tipped her head on one side.

"Ten?" she said. "Twenty? I don't know."

"All right," said Sureyna. "Thank you."

I said the same, and when the woman gave me a nod of acknowledgment, I added, "The cloth you make here for Mr. Horritch, it is cotton? Wool?"

"Cotton, yes," she said nodding and smiling, and this time there was a glimpse of the private self again, a hint of pride and pleasure.

"Not Bar-Selehm silk?" I said.

She gave me an odd look, confused, then shook her head as if I had said something slightly ridiculous. I looked around the room.

"What is upstairs?" I asked.

"Nothing," she said. Her eyes flashed to a heavy door, and when she realized I had seen, she added, "Locked. Always. We don't go up there."

"But there is a steam elevator," said Sureyna, nodding across the room to where a pair of metal screens covered the front of a great platform hung with slack, heavy cable. A squat steam engine sat beside it.

"Not used," said Bertha.

There was something in her face when she said it that seemed careful, noncommittal.

"Never?" I asked.

Again the half glance over her shoulder.

"They say not," she remarked.

"But?" I prompted.

"The water gauge on the tank," she said, leaning forward and lowering her booming voice a fraction. "Sometimes full, sometimes not. And the coal bin. Sometimes full, sometimes not."

And then it—whatever it was—was done. Her manner became businesslike again.

"Now you should go," she said.

"Thank you," said Sureyna.

"Thank you," I agreed. "You've been very helpful. Your Feldish is excellent."

"Not much use here," she said, unsmiling. "I went to school. Wanted to be a teacher. Wanted to talk to people. But now I am stuck here in a place where we can't talk at all."

As if to make the point, she opened the door to the main shed and the roar of the machines hit us like thunder, deafening and relentless.

"Would you like to?" I asked on impulse.

"What?"

"Would you like to teach?" I said. "I know some children who need a teacher."

CHAPTER

23

I NEEDED TO GET a look at the upstairs of Horritch's factory, but that would have to wait till dark, and until I had a better idea of where to look for the refugees, I could do nothing on that front. Given how heavily guarded Montresat's munitions works were, I really had no choice as to where to go next, though I went reluctantly. Norton Richter made steel, and he believed Bar-Selehm should be more closely tied to the Grappoli. If anyone had motive for the theft of the machine gun plans, it was him. The fact that he repulsed me, that he frightened me, could not be allowed to derail my investigation.

Remember the mask. Be composed. Neutral.

I knew his factory complex, though I had never worked on its chimneys. It was only a few blocks from the Seventh Street weaving shed in the area of the city known unofficially as the Soot. Richter's Steelworks was a large, modern facility with a number of distinct parts, all red brick, all efficient and smelling—in a grimy sort of way— of progress. I thought I knew what to expect, so the scene as I reached the factory gates came as a surprise. A stage of sorts had been erected, and the area thronged with white people waiting for something to begin.

I hesitated, feeling uneasy, out of place.

My first thought was that this was some kind of protest, but I was quickly disabused of that notion by the cheering and clapping as Richter himself took the stage. He was clad in his gray and black almost-uniform, and flanked by similarly dressed impressive young men who stood like standard-bearers with a pair of flags, one for Bar-Selehm, one the red and silver lightning-fist of the Heritage party.

Standing beside the stage in the same uniform, half master of ceremonies, half sergeant major, was Barrington-Smythe, and hanging at his waist in a purpose-built leather holster was a familiar little pickax.

I suppressed the urge to run.

Instead I lowered my head and pushed my hands into my pockets, skirting the edge of the crowd and trying to make myself inconspicuous. That at least was not hard. All eyes were focused on Richter, who had started to address the crowd like a general surveying his troops, speaking in sharp, clipped sentences punctuated with broad gestural flourishes like an actor in one of the larger theaters where you need to be big and loud to reach those in the back. I had never seen anything quite like it. There were torches set into the stage, and the foggy haze of the city seemed to glow about him like an aura, making him a figure of power and magic.

And there was the voice, ringing, precise, and sure of itself.

"Let me draw your attention to the marvelous edifice behind me. Ten years ago, the plant on this site produced three percent of the city's steel. Three! Now we produce fifty-one percent! And the city's overall consumption of steel has gone up by three hundred percent. A remarkable achievement made possible by what has come to be known as the Richter Conversion Process. Now, my competitors, such as they are, would have you believe that my contribution to the industry is all about quantity, but in this they are, as in many other things, mistaken. Yes, I produce a great volume of steel, more than they ever will in their wildest dreams, but how do I do that? What is the true heart of the Richter process? I will tell you. Because it isn't about quantity. Quantity is a *by-product* of what we do here. The heart of the process is quality and, more particularly, purity.

"I see there are ladies in the audience, so I won't bore you with a lot of confusing technicality, but the Richter process is about converting pig iron to steel. Now, don't get me wrong, iron is a good material. It's hard, and it—with luxorite—is the bedrock of Bar-Selehm. It's what the city is built on, what it was built *with*. But iron is also full of impurities like carbon, and that makes it brittle. Give me a girder cast from pig iron, and I, if I find the right spot, could shatter it with a hammer.

"Not steel, though. Steel is strong and flexible. Steel is pure. And to make it, all I need is some of that pig iron, with all its imperfections, and a little hot air. Now, some of my critics will tell you that I have nothing but hot air, but I'll tell you this for nothing: I know how to use it."

The crowd cheered, but he waved them down and went on.

"I pour that molten, low-grade pig iron into one of my converters and blow the hot air up through the liquid metal. My competitors say, 'You can't do that! You'll make the metal cold!' And I say, '*Really?*' And you know what? It isn't true. It doesn't make the metal cold. You blow the air through, and it makes the molten metal hotter still, and as the air comes out of the top of the converter, it blows out all the carbon, which burns up in a great blue flame like a torch, and all the manganese and silicon float to the top as slag, but the metal underneath is pure steel, and you can pour it off and make it into anything you want. It's tough, it's workable, it's fifty times stronger than iron."

More applause, though I found the speech a little baffling. Was this a political rally or a lecture on metallurgy?

"The city we know was built from iron, and like that iron, it is full of impurities which make it brittle, so that one day, when someone hits it in just the right spot, it will shatter. I offer you a new city, purged of its impurities, the blacks burned off like carbon, the Lani so much manganese slag to be tipped away, the half-breeds, intellectuals, homosexuals, and other deviants all purged in the fires of the process, leaving only what is strong and pure and bright as steel. That is the future! It's what we want, what we need, what we deserve. Thank you for your attention and vote Heritage, vote Richter!"

The audience cheered and applauded, and I, suddenly cold and fearful, had to fight down the urge to slink away. I got ahold of myself and thought fast. Then, while Richter—guided through the crowd by Barrington-Smythe—shook hands and waved and kissed babies, I moved quickly around the perimeter wall, found a suitable spot, and with the aid of a dustbin, climbed over and in.

Some of the crowd were workers, presumably given time off to hear their employer's political theatrics, which meant that the factory would be quiet, even deserted, but not for long. I chose the building which looked most like an office and made for it at a flat run across the cathead cobbles. In other circumstances, I might have hesitated, but the more his words resonated in my head, the more Richter stoked my rage. I fished the crowbar from my satchel with trembling fingers.

The impurities that would be burned away, the slag tipped out and discarded . . .

I thrust the head of the crowbar between the door and the jamb, and leaned on it till the lock splintered. What I was doing was criminal. Again. And I felt the terror of doing it in broad daylight and in this place where—more even than Elitus—I felt the venom directed at me and my kind like smog on the air. I shouldered the door in and made for the filing cabinets, levering them open with the same blind and unreasoning fury.

The murders, the human trafficking, the military support of the Grappoli. Richter was at the heart of all of this. He had to be.

There were books, great binders of work orders and contracts, inventories of raw materials and finished product, and I ran through them with unsteady hands, sweating with panic at the idea of being caught, but also with a kind of wild and dangerous desire for just that, as if I wanted a reason to turn the crowbar on whoever came through that door after cheering Richter on.

Purification . . .

I found those jobs commissioned the day after Darius's theft of the War Office's plans, the men and machines assigned to each, focusing not on the raw steel production—which was most of the plant's output—but on the individual projects made on-site in Richter's own milling, turning, and forging workshops. The largest order was for locomotive rails, placed by the Bar-Selehm West Transport Corporation. There were three others for reinforcing rods for use in concrete, one for bridge girders, and another for a made-to-order steamboat hull. Two other orders stood out. One was labeled BOLTABLE SUPER-STRUCTURE/TURRET, and I would have ignored it except that it had been commissioned by Montresat Industries, the arms company charged by the War Office to produce their machine guns.

Coincidence? The natural overlap of companies involved in related businesses? Or something else entirely? I couldn't say, but then the other order seemed more telling anyway.

It was for a small project calling for only two hundred pounds of steel. It was labeled simply FIREBRAND: PROTOTYPE, and if it had been commissioned by someone outside Richter's firm, that detail had been left out of the ledger.

It could, of course, have been anything. But my furious and terrified heart told me it wasn't. It was a machine gun. Faster and more lethal than any made to date.

Firebrand. A flame-spewing tool for eradicating people as his converter eradicated impurities from metal.

The fear and anger that had been hot and swirling in me since I had heard Richter speak chilled and hardened into certainty.

Yes. This was it. The most deadly weapon Bar-Selehm could produce, in the hands of the man who wanted to see the likes of me eradicated.

The White Man's Dilemma. . . . Which was what? When to shoot? Who to shoot? When to stop?

All of those.

But now I knew. For all his clever speeches, all that snide talk of metallurgical refinement applied to people as if they were so much industrial by-product, I knew, and I was going to stop him.

But why a prototype?

Why would Richter need to build a model of something already being produced for the military by his friend Montresat as if the weapon was still at the development stage? I drummed my finger on the book irritably and looked at the entry for Montresat Industries, mouthing the description softly to myself.

"Superstructure/turret."

Meaning what?

Seeing the work itself might give me a clearer sense of what was going on. The projects were all assigned a number and a factory location. This one was designated B-3.

I slammed the book shut and left the office. I couldn't conceal the damage I had done to the lock, so my break-in would be evident the moment the workers returned from Richter's rally . . .

Which was now.

I saw them pouring in through the main gate, flowing up the railed drive toward the sheds and foundries. I came out into the cobbled yard, looking around for identifying marks on the various buildings around me, and spotted the designation B-1 painted in white over the door of one of the construction sites. I forced myself to walk rather than run, head bowed, as if I worked there, striding past the building to the second—marked B-2—and stopping at the next—B-3.

The structure was apparently half workshop, half transit depot and sat astride its own railway siding, the locked double doors designed to close a few inches above the rails and sleepers. I dropped to the track, shoved my satchel under the doors, and crawled after it as quickly as I could.

Though I could hear work going on close by—the ringing of hammers, the clank of machinery, and the drawing of heavy chain—this building was, at present, deserted. Stacked against one wall were large wooden packing crates branded with Richter's lightning-fist emblem awaiting cargo, but the rest of the shop was an open assembly area cluttered with riveting and welding tools. There were bundled lengths of steel beams, buckets of nuts and bolts, vices, anvils, racks of hammers and pliers. The place was dominated by a small crane, beside which a gravity elevator gave access to an upper work station only a few feet below the roof.

The two pieces under construction—three of each, in various stages of completion—were what the logbook had labeled "superstructure and turret." Each consisted of a girder frame closed in with thick steel plate. The one I took to be the turret was a slightly irregular box with a hole in the front and open underneath. There was a hinged hatchway in the top just big enough for a man to climb through. It looked vaguely nautical, like it might be the command tower of a steamship, though there were no windows or portholes. The bottom of the turret was flanged and seemed to fit into the other, larger piece, which I assumed was what the ledger had called the superstructure. It was also boxlike, though much shallower than the turret, and it too was missing its lower side. It was as long and wide as a two-horse carriage and did not look remotely boatlike. I was standing there, my head tilted one side, trying to make sense of what I was seeing, when I heard the sound of a heavy lock turning over.

I spun round in time to see the doors over the track pushed open and half a dozen white laborers coming in. One of them pointed and shouted, and then they were running. I did what I always do when life on the ground turned menacing. I went up.

CHAPTER

24

I STEPPED ONTO THE gravity elevator, threw the lever, and felt the counterweight drop, dragging me up toward the pulley in the ceiling. I hopped onto the work gantry and moved to an open vent, leaning out over the cobbles of the factory yard and reaching for the ladder I knew would be there. I had worked an almost identical structure at the Dyer Street cement factory a few months earlier.

I pulled myself out and up, conscious of the noise from below that suggested the complex had been less deserted than I had assumed, then sped along the ridgeline of the roof, hopped across the gap, and landed on the gable end of the next structure.

Unseen?

I thought so. Ducking behind a chimney stack, I surveyed the layout of the yard below, strewn as it was with offcut steel, barrows of coal and coke, and piles of refuse. The architecture around me formed a kind of courtyard, though it was less an open space than it was a central, roofless workshop, and at its heart sat a great pear-shaped metal structure around which men were gathered clutching chains, as if they were restraining a wild animal that was threatening to burst free. The Richter Converter. It looked like a strange, bulbous kettle, its massive spout canted at an angle where it met the smoking outlet of a neighboring furnace. The whole thing was mounted on an equally massive stand, and as I moved around the roof looking for a place to get across to the next building, the men around it pulled their chains so that the whole thing pivoted till it pointed almost upright.

I moved quickly along the roof, getting closer to the spout of the converter, lowering myself over the edge and dropping a few feet to the adjacent roof as I heard the clanking of machinery below. There was a sudden hiss of air like a bottled cyclone, and then the sky caught fire as the converter roared, shooting a great column of orange flame only feet from where I stood. I fell back, stunned by the heat, which seared my skin and crinkled my hair, so I was lying down as the jet turned from amber to blue, a fierce torrent of burning gas hard and sharp as a blowlamp. I rolled onto my belly and drew my arms and legs in, shielding myself from the heat as best I could, then crawled away, deafened and humbled by the blast.

At the edge of the roof, I peered over, found a set of rungs in the wall only a few yards away, and loped over to them, my elbow hooked across my face to stave off the heat. Seconds later, I was running again, like I was fleeing hell itself, too scared to look back, too dazzled by my own stupidity at coming here, and too relieved at getting out alive to think further about what I had seen.

THE EPISODE AT RICHTER'S plant left me cautious, frightened. Risking my life out of righteous indignation had served only to remind me of my vulnerability. This was not, as Madame Nahreem had been quick to point out after the day's exercise and mask work, a productive lesson.

"I thought the hyena incident had already taught you to be more judicious with the risks you take," she said, as one of the maids applied balm from a mortar and pestle to the burned and blistered skin on my right cheek and arm. She made me sit a half hour with the ointment smeared over my face and a handkerchief taped over it, so that catching my reflection in the looking glass on the nightstand it appeared as if I was wearing some new form of the neutral mask.

Without warning, it was three months ago and I was back in the opera house, pursuing the figure who had tried to kill me, a figure that had turned out to be my sister Vestris. She had been wearing a strange, featureless mask. . . .

I touched the makeshift bandage, suddenly cold, and stared at my unfamiliar reflection. The eyes looking back at me were mine and not mine. I could almost have been my dead sister.

"Is everything all right, miss?" asked the maid.

"What?" I said vaguely, coming back to myself with a strange sense of disorientation, as if I had just woken from an unsettling dream and was not yet sure where I was. Madame Nahreem was watching me, her face blank. She was quite still. "Yes," I said to the maid. "Thank you. I'm fine." Feeling Madame Nahreem's eyes on me, I turned to her and, to change the mood of the moment said, "Can I borrow a pistol?"

Dahria had lent me one once before, but I had returned it to her, intending never to use one again. Madame Nahreem knew as much and scowled.

"I thought you didn't like guns," she said.

"I don't," I said. "But I think perhaps I need one."

I didn't like guns because I had killed two men with one. It had been, I was quite sure, the right thing to do, but I had never gotten over the fact of it, and I still dreamed of that night in the dockside warehouse three months ago: the smell of the smoke, the noise, the blood.

"You will need to show me that you can use it," said Madame Nahreem.

"I don't have time for that."

"If you want to carry a firearm, you will make the time," she said.

Half an hour later, she led me to the courtyard, where Namud set up targets and told me how to stand to stabilize the weapon. Unlike the heavy revolver I had borrowed from Dahria, Madame Nahreem had presented me with a much lighter and simpler pistol, which had to be reloaded after each shot. It was silvery, elegant in its way, with a gracefully curved handle inlaid with mother-of-pearl, and it was clearly designed for a woman. I made a face at it, and Madame Nahreem raised an eyebrow.

"Problem?" she prompted.

"It's not very functional."

"It works perfectly well."

"I'd rather have less pretty and more bullets," I said.

"While I'd rather we perfect your shooting before we give you anything that will spray projectiles all over the house," she observed.

I thought of Sergeant Emtezu and his disdain for the lazy inaccuracy of machine guns and sighed, watching Namud's hands as he walked me through the laborious readying of the weapon. I aimed, sighting down the barrel as he had shown me, fired, broke open the barrel, inserted another cartridge, snapped the barrel back into place, cocked the hammer, and fired again, hitting the target squarely both times.

"Not exactly a battlefield weapon, is it?" I muttered.

Madame Nahreem's batlike ears somehow picked up the comment.

"Then it's a good thing you have no plans to enter a battlefield, isn't it?" she said. "One shot at a time. Make each one count."

Actually I was almost relieved that the gun forced me to be so deliberate, because it felt like I could do nothing rash: rushed decisions made in anger were one of the things that scared me most about guns. They were just too easy to use, too deadly in effect. But the more I practiced, the slower the process seemed, and my frustration mounted. If I really had to face down someone who wanted to kill me and I was armed with nothing but this antiquated thing, I had better kill them with the first shot. I doubted I'd get another.

So I fired and reloaded and fired again, while Namud adjusted my posture and told me when to breathe. For her part, Madame Nahreem watched critically, correcting me without gentleness or encouragement, and as my irritation increased, my shooting got wilder.

"No!" she exclaimed. "Don't yank the trigger like you are plucking a chicken. Squeeze it gently."

I bit down on my anger and fired again.

I should be out looking for the refugees instead of wasting time here with
this maddening woman—

"Worse!" she said. "If you cannot learn to shoot more accurately,
I cannot let you go armed. You are a danger to yourself and others."

I fired twice more, furious, and the target did not so much as move
as the bullets sailed wide.

Madame Nahreem stepped up close and put her palm on my chest.

"Your heart is racing," she said.

"I need to go," I said. "And you annoy me on purpose."

Namud took a discreet step away.

"Yes," she said. "Yet my words are nothing to what someone will
do to you if they mean you real harm. I thought your experience at
the opera house taught you that. Put away your fury and your fire,"
she said, handing me the hot pistol. "Remember the neutral mask."

It was a monument to my composure that I slid the gun into my
satchel without shooting her first.

THE REFUGEES HAD TO be my highest priority. I could still see
their upturned faces in the boat, their hollow cheeks and glistening
eyes, their hands outstretched for something they could grab hold of,
some way to pull themselves out of all they had been forced to en-
dure. I did not know where they might be, but I would find them.

I just didn't know where to start.

"There must be empty buildings where they would hide around
Dagenham Steps or in the railway sidings," I said to Dahria after dinner. I had felt the need to confide in someone, but could not bring
myself to confess my plans to Willinghouse in case he demanded I
focus entirely on Elitus and the stolen plans. "Abandoned factories.
Warehouses."

She looked dubious.

"My dear steeplejack," she said, "you are thinking like a city girl.
These are people from villages and farms. Some of them may be

itinerant herders. Their first experience of Bar-Selehm was being mistreated and imprisoned. The last thing they would do was seek refuge in the city."

"You think they'd retreat into the bush?" I said, not liking the idea.

"They wouldn't cross the river," said Dahria, considering an old tea-colored map hanging on the parlor wall. "That would be too conspicuous, as well as leading into the heart of the city."

"So they'd head west along the south bank," I mused.

"Avoiding ranches owned by whites, looking for the closest thing to their own people."

"Unassimilated Mahweni," I said.

Mnenga, I thought, and his name brought a rush of comfort, as if I had been waiting for a reason to seek him out and it had finally appeared like an impala, peering at me from behind a bush. I suppressed a smile and said, "Herders and bush people, neither of which are easy to stumble upon down there."

"Which they wouldn't know," Dahria said, "so they'll wander upriver."

"That would put them opposite the Drowning," I said. "Someone there might have seen something on the far bank."

"Well, that's good, isn't it?" said Dahria brightly. "Somewhere for you to start looking."

"I'm not allowed in the Drowning, remember?" I said.

She frowned.

"What's on the other side of the river?" she asked.

I shook my head, feeling suddenly uneasy, like a child waking from a nightmare and knowing that discussing it wouldn't help—or uneasy and stupid, because I knew that what I wanted to say made no more sense than Tanish's tales of the Gargoyle. But Dahria's critical stare got to me, and the words came out anyway.

"The haunted place," I said.

"What?" she exclaimed, mockery lighting her face.

"I know," I said miserably. "It's what they always used to say to stop us crossing the river. It's ancient Mahweni land. Sacred, I think. There's some sort of ruined temple there, and a burial ground."

"Didn't you grow up around temples and burial grounds of your own?" asked Dahria.

"Lani temples, yes," I said, feeling ridiculous and ashamed. "But this is . . . I don't know. Different. Foreign. Weird. Don't look at me like that. I didn't say I wouldn't investigate."

"Ah, yes," said Dahria smugly. "Investigating. Like a professional detective or spy or whatever my brother thinks you are. I'll try not to tell him you're afraid of ghosts."

I gave her a baleful look and hoped to all the gods that she wouldn't.

I GLOWERED MY WAY past the *Standard*'s doorman, asked Sureyna about reports of unassimilated Mahweni on the south bank, and explained why I was going to the Drowning so that someone would come looking if my trip across the river went badly. Or so I told myself. I think I really wanted her to talk me out of it. But she nodded noncommittally, and as soon as I stopped talking, she changed the subject.

"So here's a thing," she said. "I spoke to the people at Elitus, who did everything they could to tell me nothing at all and threatened to have me arrested for trespassing. But the neighbors had told me that the night Agatha Markeson died there had been fireworks and the Elitus staff eventually confessed that there was a reception in honor of the Grappoli ambassador and a visiting dignitary from Istilia. One Lady Ki Misrai. A princess, no less."

"Really?" I said carefully. "I'm sure a club like that hosts those kinds of events all the time."

"I thought so too," she said, clearly pleased with herself, "but, being the responsible reporter I am, I thought I'd get my facts right before printing anything. So I went to the Istilian embassy, and you'll never guess what."

"What?"

"They have never heard of this Lady Ki Misrai."

"Really?"

"Really," she said, giving me a level look. "I got to thinking about how you said you had been there, how you had seen the old woman's body and all, and I began to wonder. Guess how many female Lani work as servants at Elitus?"

I sighed.

"How many?" I said.

"None," she said. "So I'm wondering how someone like you—"

"All right," I said. "That's enough."

"You really are quite the chameleon, aren't you, Ang? Assuming that's your actual name."

"Oh, shut up."

She grinned, glad that her hunch had been right and, in a grudging sort of way, impressed.

"One more thing," she said. "Since, despite your shape-changing, you really are both a Lani and a steeplejack—"

"Or I was," I said, half joking.

"Or you were. What do you know about the Gargoyle?"

I rolled my eyes.

"Not you too," I said. "If you want to be considered a serious journalist, I wouldn't even bother asking about it."

"Didn't say I believed in it myself," said Sureyna. "But other people apparently do, and that makes it news."

"People have always believed in it, but it wasn't news before. The ones who believe in it now are no smarter, so why do you care?"

"The people who believe in it now aren't just Lani steeplejacks."

"Ah," I said with a bleak smile. "What was a quaint and silly folk belief becomes a major news item when white people believe in it."

"Not just white," said Sureyna. "Some of the reports are coming from the black shanties by the docks. That's not the point, though, because this isn't just about rumor and spooky stories. Not anymore.

The police have three bodies—all with their throats cut—which they are linking to sightings of a strange, hairless figure seen scaling high buildings."

I stared at her.

Three bodies?

"They're sure it's not an animal?" I asked. Weancats and leopards are both climbers, though they rarely venture near the city.

"Seem pretty sure," she said. "Animals rarely take your money."

"Where did the attacks take place?"

"All over. Two on the south bank, one in the Financial District, one outside the Trade Exchange, one on Fifth Street. The fatal attacks were . . ." She pulled out her notepad and, for once, had to check the details. "By the South Road fish market, in Mahweni Old Town, and under the suspension bridge   north bank. You think there's a pattern?"

"Not one I can see. Who were the victims?"

"A corrupt banker called Jeremiah Walpole, who had business deal-ings with the disgraced secretary of trade, Archibald Mandel," she said, off her notes again. "A street thug called Jarvis who ran an opium and prostitution ring, and an unidentified white male who was killed, according to a witness, while threatening said witness with rape."

"So not huge losses to society," I said.

"Interesting, isn't it?" said Sureyna, raising a finger as if I had just hit the nail on the end. "Multiple sightings, multiple robberies, but only three killings, and all of people the city won't—not to put too fine a point on it—be sorry to see the back of. So now while some people are terrified of the Gargoyle, others are starting to see him—it, whatever—as a hero. A vigilante."

I shook my head.

"The Gargoyle's a fairy story," I said. "Or I always thought so. Maybe someone is copying the old legends. Or maybe it's some home-less crazy person. There are good secret places to hide out in the city if you have a head for heights. I suppose if you were looking to attack and rob people, dropping on them from above would work pretty well. You'd be amazed how little people look up, even when they're on their guard."

It was Sureyna's turn to make a face.

She said, "I'd keep insights like that to yourself."

I grinned. Still, the idea that the Gargoyle story might contain a germ of murderous truth gave me pause. I was glad I had Madame Nahreem's pistol in my satchel, even if it did feel more like an ornament than a weapon.

"One more thing," I said. "You have a copy of that story about Darius's identity?"

"Sure," she said. "Why?

"Something I want to check on my way to the Drowning."

VANDEMAR PAINT AND SIGNAGE was located above a tobacconist's facing the South Road fish market, on a narrow, soot-blackened terrace once quite respectable but long since gone to seed. Several windows had been replaced with permanent shutters, and the mbeti nest on the chimney suggested it had not been swept in a season or more. The proprietor, a skinny, fiftyish man in a suit a little small for him, threadbare at the elbows, looked up from his desk with a welcoming air that faltered tellingly when he took in my appearance.

"Mr. Vandemar?" I asked. "I'm from the *Standard*. I was wondering if I could ask you a few questions about the late Karl Gillies?"

"Karl," said Vandemar, sitting back and removing his spectacles with a wistful expression. "I was wondering if you people would come back. One minute he was the talk of the town, the next . . . nothing. I thought I'd have a line of customers right round the corner."

He seemed quite indignant about it.

"Well, I'm here to fix that," I lied, smiling. The fact that the man saw the death of his employee as an opportunity to promote his business sickened me a little. "You told the police you were surprised to learn that he was Darius the cat burglar."

"Astonished," he said.

"He never gave you any reason to suspect he had a separate source of income?"

"Never, but then he was very private, Karl was. I didn't even know he had a lady friend, let alone a fiancée."

I remembered the newspaper reporting that the woman to whom he had been engaged had been the one to identify his body.

"You didn't meet her till after he died?" I asked.

"Still haven't," he said.

"Not even at the funeral?"

"There weren't no funeral," he said. "Not that I were invited to, anyways. I figured it were a family-only thing."

"Did he have a large family?"

"So far as I knew, he lived alone. Parents were dead."

I paused. Something about this felt wrong.

"Was Karl good at his job, Mr. Vandemar?" I asked.

"Oh, yes," said the proprietor, breaking into a real smile. "Wonderful brushwork, Karl had. Best I've ever seen. Met . . . met . . . What's the word? Careful, you know. Painstaking."

"Meticulous?"

"Exactly. *Meticulous.* Fancy a person like you knowing a big word like that! Anyways, yes. Meticulous. That's what he was. If I had to describe Karl's work, I'd say it was meticulous."

"And a good climber?" I asked.

"Climber? Oh lord, no!" said Vandemar, chuckling.

"No?"

"Couldn't go more than two rungs on the ladder without freezing up. Scared of heights! All the high boards had to be brought down so he could work on them. Doubled the cost, of course, but some people still wanted him."

I stared at him. The man I had pursued over the rooftops had been deft, confident.

"So it must have come as a shock to hear that he was Darius the cat burglar," I said.

"Exactly so," he answered. "Must have been some kind of mistake. That's what I told the police when they came round. A mistake of some kind, I told them, but they didn't want to know. Well, they wouldn't, would they? Like the papers. Present company excepted, of course. But then someone like you might think differently about people like us."

"People like me?"

"Lani," he said. "No offense meant. Speak as I find, me. Never had any cause to gripe about the Lani. But the society types, they wanted their cat burglar to be Baron Such and Such. When they found out it was just Karl, well. Didn't want to know, did they?"

He frowned again, and I realized he hadn't just been indignant about missing out on some business. He resented the way Karl had been ignored and, by extension, how he—we—were always ignored by what he called the *society types*. When this was all done, I would have to ask Sureyna to write some version of the article I had promised.

"You said he had no girlfriend that you knew of," I said. "Was he not popular with the ladies?"

Vandemar's manner shifted, and he was suddenly on the defensive.

"Nothing was ever proved," he said.

"I'm sorry?"

"Those girls who said he . . . that he made unwelcome advances," said Vandemar, his color rising. "All charges were dropped, and I'd thank you not to bring the matter up again. Slandering a dead man on the word of some gin-totting floozy? It's not right."

"I see," I said.

"He was a good lad, was Karl," he answered, daring me to contradict him. "Liked his bit of fun is all."

"Thank you, Mr. Vandemar," I said, with less compassion than I had felt only moments before. "I am sorry for your loss."

CHAPTER

25

I GAVE RAHVEY HER money while the children were about their games, and she vanished it into her purse.

"Aab is still playing with Radesh," I observed, watching the disconcerting deaf girl. There was a lack of self-consciousness about the child that felt wild, feral. Rahvey shrugged wearily.

"Nothing else for her to do," she said, adjusting Kalla who was nursing.

"They come down here most days?" I asked.

"Yes. Why? You think they should be in school learning about Panbroke and reading books?"

"No," I said, ignoring the edge in her tone. "I just wondered if they had seen other children. Not Lani. Maybe on the other side of the river."

"Over there?" asked Rahvey. "What would anyone be doing over there? Where the old temple is, you mean? No one in their right mind would go over there. You know there's a clavtar? Been there at least a year. We hear it roaring at night all the way across the river."

"Do you mind if I ask the children?"

Rahvey shrugged. "Why would I mind?" she remarked. It was a challenge rather than a real question.

"Wouldn't want to intrude," I said.

"Just because you pay me doesn't mean we're not sisters anymore," she remarked stiffly, avoiding my gaze.

I smiled and, emboldened by her concession, said, "I hear Tanish has been visiting."

"Always under my feet, he is," said Rahvey, though she couldn't quite suppress a grin. "Still, makes a change to have a boy around. So long as he doesn't get ideas about my girls. I don't want Jadary marrying some two-bit steeplejack. No offense."

"None taken," I said. I bit my lip. This seemed as good an opening as I was going to get. "You want good things for your daughters," I said. "I understand. So how would you feel if I brought a teacher here? Paid her myself. Just for a couple of hours in the evening. You wouldn't mind that, would you?"

Rahvey got that watchful look of hers, as if I might be up to something, but she shrugged, still looking away.

"I don't see why not," she said, her eyes on the infant at her breast.

I nodded, then stood up and waved up to what passed for a road so close to the Drowning's uncertain ground. Bertha got to her feet and began to plod her way toward me.

"You brought someone?" asked Rahvey, turning back to me aghast. *"Today?"*

"I thought you wouldn't mind," I said.

My sister was flustered, torn between indignant speeches about how it was her job to make decisions about what was best for her family, even about involving non-Lani in the life of her children, and something softer, something grateful and pleased, even thrilled, which flashed through her unwary eyes. Before she could resolve the conflict, Bertha was there, and she was big and beaming, and Rahvey was embarrassed into nodding and smiling graciously.

"I am Bertha," said Bertha, so loudly a bittern that had been motionless in the reeds took startled flight.

"Her hearing is not the best," I said quickly to Rahvey, who had nearly fallen off her rock, "but she has training and she speaks good Feldish. She reads and writes. Knows math and geography—"

"Rahvey," said my sister, offering her hand.

The black woman shook it once.

"Where are the children?" she roared, loud as the putative clavtar.

Rahvey nodded down the bank, and as Bertha followed her gaze, she gave me an uncertain look. I shrugged and left my sister sitting on her rock with Kalla, and Bertha followed me down to the other children.

The four of them, made five by Tanish, who had been half adopted by the girls as a kind of strange, dashing brother, were in a sandy hollow surrounded by long grass. Radesh was singing to the rest, and her sisters were clapping along, laughing to themselves. Aab was fiddling with something in the sand, barely aware of the others, as if trapped in a bubble of glass.

They gazed at Bertha wide-eyed when I introduced her as Miss Dinangwe, but she showed no self-consciousness or irritation, even when they giggled at her booming voice. In fact, she seemed to expand with patience, generosity, and goodwill, and it occurred to me how hard it must have been for such a person to spend her days slaving over a loom.

When they had introduced themselves, I said that I would leave them to get to know each other. While Bertha was producing a few ragged picture books from her bag, items which the children treated as exotic treasures from some distant land, I asked them if they had seen any black children in the area. The Drowning was exclusively a Lani district, and it was a matter of some concern on the rare occasions that Mahweni were glimpsed near the shanty. The girls shook their heads.

"On the other side of the river?" I tried, dropping to my haunches so I could look them in the face.

They stared at me.

"In the haunted place?" asked Radesh, standing up and turning to stare across the river. On the far bank you could just make out the rough stone top of an ancient, moldering structure through the marula trees. "No one goes there."

Bertha was watching closely, studying our lips.

"Sometimes we see baboons or hippos," said Jadary. "They come down to the river to drink, but we tell the village if the water is shallow enough for any to come across. The hippos, I mean. The baboons don't cross, but we have them on this side too."

"But no children in the last few days?" I said.

"There's a clavtar over there," said Radesh. "And ghosts."

"Ghosts aren't real," said Jadary.

"The clavtar is," said Radesh, as if that closed the subject.

"What about Aab?" I asked. The girl was watching me intently. "Have you seen anything?"

The child looked to Radesh, who was gazing across to the fragment of temple on the far side of the river looking fearful. Bertha extended a hand and touched her gently on her shoulder so the girl turned and looked at her.

As Bertha repeated my question, she gestured with her hands, making pictures and symbols with her fingers, which the girl considered seriously.

Small person. Over there. Seen?

Gazing at Bertha with a kind of wonder, Aab nodded once.

"You saw someone?" I asked.

The girl pointed emphatically over the water.

"She doesn't know what you mean," said Jadary. "She can't hear, and she gets things confused."

"No, she doesn't," said Radesh. "She's not stupid."

"She understands," said Bertha, loud as ever, but soothing. "Don't you, sweetness?"

Aab made a noise and pointed again at the distant temple, then stabbed with her index finger at each of her friends in turn.

"Children?" I said. "That's what you mean, right? You saw children over there?"

"It was probably just monkeys," said Jadary, sounding uncannily like her mother.

"How many?" asked Bertha, holding up her fingers to Aab and

counting them off. She had gotten as far as six when Aab reached forward earnestly, her eyes serious, her body uncannily still, and grasped her hands.

"Six?" I said. "When?"

Bertha repeated the question carefully, signing instinctively, indicating the sun and then thumbing over her shoulder. *The past.*

Aab nodded, fascinated by the woman's hands.

"One day? Two?" I tried, holding up my fingers as Radesh had done.

Aab reached forward and bent one finger back into my fist.

One.

"Yesterday," I said.

I DID NOT KNOW the south bank side of the river once you left the docklands, and I set out uneasily, beginning with a railway journey by Blesbok class locomotive with nothing but third-class carriages and half a dozen open haulage trucks. I sat in the rearmost car facing backward, scarf bound round my head, and my old work satchel in my lap with the strap looped over my head and one shoulder for safety. There was an old Lani man who I thought might have been a village elder sitting up front, two white ranchers, and a dozen Mahweni laborers, most of whom slept the whole way. No one spoke, and everyone ignored me, which was how I liked it.

We went directly west, crossing the river at a narrow canyon four miles from Bar-Selehm on a single-track girder bridge, arcing south for another mile before I disembarked at a platform that hadn't so much as a canopy to shade travelers from the blistering sun, but that did have a small steam crane with its own coal bunker for loading freight. The place was named only by mile marker, and I was the only one to get off there, startling a pair of female nyala grazing on the weedy ballast beside the track.

I took a path east past a cotton field and a ranch where tsobu grazed and then there was, for a while, nothing. On either side was tall, wild grass and stands of acacia and nikorel trees throbbing with hummingbirds. I moved carefully, quietly, constantly looking about. There could be all manner of animals in the area, everything from elephants and one-horns, to weancats and hyenas. Birds whose names I did not know swooped and called overhead as I plodded on, sweating heavily, feeling the weight of the pistol stowed in my satchel but knowing its single shot would be of little use against anything large that decided to investigate what I was. Or tasted like.

Not helping, I thought.

In fact I saw nothing but a pair of giraffes in the distance and a single mud-caked warthog, which minced away when it caught wind of me, its tail in the air, indignant and absurd on its little trotters. It reminded me a little of Agatha Markeson in her high-heeled shoes.

I didn't know how far I would have to go exactly. I was following little more than a hunch bolstered by the reports Sureyna had shown me and what I could glean from her office's maps about the land this side of the river. I didn't know I would find what I was looking for, and a part of me wasn't sure I wanted to. But about a mile from the railway, I came over a low rise and saw, off to my right in an open swath of wild grassland dotted with thorn trees, a flock of nbezu.

There were perhaps fifty of them, smaller and more goatlike than antelope, and they were tended by three men and a small dog, which patrolled the group watchfully. The men were young and black, dressed in the traditional skirt and shoulder-draped robes of the Unassimilated Tribes.

They were brothers, men who had saved my life once before. One was called Wayell, the other was Embiyeh, and the third, the one who came striding toward me and clasped me in a strong embrace to his bare, smooth chest while the others bowed and smiled as to some foreign dignitary, was Mnenga.

CHAPTER

26

I SAID HIS NAME, then broke from the embrace and gazed at him, smiling.

"How are you?" I asked.

He shrugged and beamed, his face alive with joy as he took my hands and gazed at me.

"Well," he said, "we had good rains and there is new grass, so the nbezu are very happy."

He laughed then at the absurdity of what he was saying and hugged me to him again. I was overcome with relief, not just at seeing him, but at his easy acceptance of me, his pleasure that we were together again. I had feared he would be indignant, even angry with me, after our long silence. Now, feeling the warmth of his arms, his smile, I closed my eyes and clung to him.

But that was too easy, and I did not deserve easy. Not yet.

"I'm sorry," I said, pulling away once more. "I meant to write to you, started to, but I couldn't think what to say and wasn't sure how to reach you so . . ." It sounded so stupid and ineffectual that I fished desperately in my pocket and pulled out the sorrel nut, showing it to him as if it was some luxorite gem encased in gold and crystal.

He frowned, baffled.

"Thank you," he said. "I have some."

"No," I said. "This is one you gave me. I saved it to remind me of you. When I felt lonely or was missing you, I would take it out and hold it."

"This nut," he said.

"Yes," I answered, feeling more idiotic by the second.

He tipped his head on one side thoughtfully, and we were suddenly conscious of his brothers watching.

"That is . . ." He sought for the word. "Nice?" he said. "Sweet. Yes. Sweet. Thank you."

His gratitude pained me, his very kindness exposing my paltry gesture for what it was. I was getting it wrong again. The disappointment showed in my face, and he put his palm against my cheek. Tears of frustration were gathering in my eyes, but his touch stilled them, and I realized with a shock that he was smiling broader than ever. He leaned in close.

"You know," he whispered, "that you can find these nuts everywhere."

"They are not rare?" I asked, stunned out of my other confused feelings. "Hard to find?"

He took his eyes from mine and glanced quickly round, his gaze alighting on a shrublike tree covered in new leaves.

"Some there," he said, turning and nodding to his left. "Another bush over there."

I frowned again, eyes brimming, and then he was holding me again and laughing till I joined in, till my guilt and anxiety melted in the simple joy of being with him once more.

"Better?" he said at last.

"Yes," I said. "Thank you."

"Now," he said, "tell me why you are here."

I hesitated, but there was no critique, no judgment in the remark, so I took a breath and told him about the refugees, who they were, why they had come here, and how I had tried to find them. He nodded gravely without asking why I was looking for them. That accepting disinterest was part of his special kindness and grace, and feeling it, like the warmth of his smile, I experienced another ripple of shame that I had—again—sought him out only when I needed his help.

I took his hand, smooth on the back, calloused on the palm, as if he were the brother I never had, and in doing so, I remembered wondering if for him home was less about place and more about people. I could not read his smile for subtleties because it contained nothing more than happiness that I was with him, and for a moment—a wonderfully content and uncomplicated moment—I felt the same.

At last, I released his hands.

"We have heard of these people, or some like them," he said, after consulting with his brothers in their own language. "Quundu, I think. We think they are closer to the river that way." He pointed east, back toward the city, toward the ancient temple over the water from the Drowning.

I nodded grimly. The haunted place. For all his pleasure at seeing me, he couldn't hide the ripple of unease that thinking of it gave him. It was at least as dreadful for him as it was for me.

"I need to go and look for them," I said. "But I cannot speak to them. I was hoping—"

"I will come," he said.

And that was Mnenga. Whatever fear of the place he might have, however inconvenient it would be, however dangerous, he would come. No hesitation.

"Thank you," I said. "I do not deserve your friendship."

Rarely had I said anything that felt more deeply true, though he rubbished the remark with a wave of his hand.

"My brothers must stay here with the nbezu," he said. "They are too stupid to leave alone. The nbezu," he clarified, "not my brothers. Although . . ."

His face split into that wide grin of his, and he turned to Embiyeh, translating quickly till they were both laughing, heads thrown back, roaring with delight. Wayell just smiled, and when he spoke, he looked concerned. Mnenga answered him shortly, again waving away whatever concerns his brother had raised, touching him on the shoulder and speaking slowly into his face, till Wayell pursed his lips and nodded with solemn acceptance.

"These people," Mnenga said. "The Quundu. We were also looking for them. The elders of my village have heard of them coming
here from the north. Those who try to cross the desert die, so some
have come by boat around the coast. But if they are caught by the
city people, they are sent back, even though where they come from
is very terrible, and many will die. You know there is a war there,
yes?"

"Yes," I said.

"But the city sends them back anyway," he mused, shaking his
head.

I nodded, thinking of the way he divided the world not by tribe,
class, or race but by "city" and "not city."

"If you found them, what were you going to do?" I asked.

"We were supposed to tell our village elders where they were.
That's all," he said, dissatisfied. "I think we should do more. Help to
keep them safe from the city."

"Some people in the city want to help them too," I said.

He gave me a doubtful look.

"Not many," I conceded. "Some."

He nodded at that and managed a smile, which said that was as
much as could be hoped for. Then he shouldered a roll of fabric lashed
with twine and suspended from a hide cord, and picked up his short-
shafted assegai. I hovered awkwardly while he said his farewells,
then I shook his brothers by the hands and followed Mnenga as he
checked the position of the sun and headed east.

"They did not want you to go," I said.

"The temple is an old place where many dead are," he said. "We
like to leave it to them. And to the animals."

"I heard there was a clavtar in the area," I said, hoping he would
laugh the idea off.

"There is," he said, hefting his spear thoughtfully. "We have heard
it. Let us hope we do not see it."

"And if we do?"

"We will die," he said, with a shrug and a half smile at my astonished face. "Probably," he added, as if that would make me feel much better.

"Probably?" I said, giving him a pointed look.

"Possibly," he said. "We may survive. Only be very badly injured."

"I think you can stop now," I said, giving him a grin. "I missed you," I added on impulse, realizing just how much even as the words formed.

"I also," he answered. "Every day."

He smiled, but sadly, and I had to look away. It was several minutes before I asked him to tell me about the temple.

"It is very old," he said. "We call it *Umoya ithempeli*. Long ago it was a place of . . . like a village where everyone comes for festivals."

"A place of community?"

"Community," he said. "Yes. Before the white people came. The dead were left here."

"Buried?"

"Only the chiefs of their tribes would go into the ground," said Mnenga. "The rest were left to feed the animals." He caught my look and smiled. "It is the spirit that matters for us. The body is just like a . . . *embewini*. The outside of a seed or fruit."

"A shell? A husk?"

"Husk, yes," he said. "It is not important."

The idea was not so very far from those I had been raised with in the Drowning. We burned our dead, but sometimes the fire was only a token gesture, and there was a lot left for the jackals and crocodiles.

"So why does the place upset you?" I asked.

"We remember our ancestors," he said. "We keep them in our thoughts, and we celebrate them in festivals. They watch out for us from the spirit world. But if we forget them, they become angry, dangerous."

"The people buried by the temple have been forgotten?" I asked.

"Who is here to remember them?" he asked. "All the people here died when the white men came. Died, or were moved to other places, their dead left alone. For three hundred years, they have been left alone: no festivals, no sacrifices, no one to remember what they did."

"This will make them angry?"

Mnenga shrugged. "I do not know. Perhaps. Perhaps none of it is true."

He looked sad and annoyed at himself, at his confused and diluted faith, as if he had lost something but was not sure how. Without thinking, I took his large hand in mine again, so that he gave me a quick, startled look, then nodded in acknowledgment, and walked in silence beside me.

It was over an hour before we began to cut north toward the river. I felt Mnenga's unease deepen as we did so, particularly as the land began to descend and the vegetation grew thick, lush, and pulsing with the life of the wetlands below. Insects whined about our heads, and Mnenga paused to pick broad green leaves from an unremarkable-looking plant, which he crushed in his hands and smeared on my face and arms. The juice was slightly sticky and smelled of oranges and spice.

"Keeps the mosquitoes away," he said. "Mostly." He frowned as he looked about him, and I was conscious that he had raised the tip of his spear as if he might need to use it at a moment's notice. "Stay close," he said, "and stay quiet. There are many dangerous animals here as well as the clavtar."

I had never seen a clavtar and knew few of my age who had, though some of the Lani elders had stories of days before they had been confined to the south bank of the Kalihm. I had seen pictures, of course, but the animals themselves were rare, hunted close to extinction during the initial conquest by Belrand when Bar-Selehm as it was today had first taken shape. They had retreated into areas where people were few and game was plentiful, but their names were still whispered with awe and horror throughout the city. The clavtar is a kind of lion unique to the region, gray as steel and very large, three or four times the body weight of the most impressive weancat. Exotic though they were, I could live a lifetime without seeing one in person.

The first sign that we were entering what had been the old temple grounds was a collapsed ring of stone that looked like it may once have been thatched with reeds from the riverbank. The ground was scorched in parts as if by lightning strikes or brush fires, and the whole had an air of the desolate and abandoned. The air was still, and I heard no birdcalls, so that the silence felt weighted and significant. I drew the ornamental pistol from my satchel and checked that it was loaded, drawing a doubtful look from Mnenga. I shrugged, but—feeling no more comfortable for holding the weapon—said nothing. We both knew it wouldn't stop a clavtar.

The temple itself, if that was what it was, was an uneven stone pyramid made of steps, rounded and irregular on the sides. It was flanked by tumbledown alcoves sporting roughly carved faces, all eyes and teeth. It wasn't clear if they were human or animal, but they leered with undeniable menace. Mnenga made a private gesture, both ceremonial and fearful, an instinctive flicker of the hands to ward off evil. If it was intended to make me feel better, it didn't.

The place was eerily silent, the air itself dead, though I also felt an unsettling presence as if the very stones had eyes. With each step we took, the quiet menace of the place swelled, but I heard nothing beyond our own footfalls in the dry grass, as if something was holding its breath, waiting. Maybe it was the wildness of the place getting to my urban heart. Or maybe it was the past, all that had once been here before the whites came and reduced it to ghosts and echoes. Whatever it was, it was dreadful, and I stayed close to Mnenga, wishing I could hear his breath, his heartbeat in this strange dead place.

The top of the pyramid was a crag so that it was almost possible to believe that the structure had not been made by human hands at all, but was an accident of geology, a part of the earth that had speared up through the ground. It was the portion of the temple visible from the Drowning. If the lost children were still in the area, this was where we would find them. I felt a sudden and powerful urge to get them and go, run back to the city and never look back. Mnenga's tales of angry spirits haunting these stones seemed far more plausible now that we were among them, the light softening as the sun began its descent in the west.

Should have set out earlier—

Somewhere off to our left, a twig snapped.

Mnenga stopped in his tracks, hefting the spear. I froze, the one-shot pistol in my hand feeling dangerous, like a badly trained dog as likely to turn on me as it was to protect me. For a long moment, we waited like that, feeling the standing heat of the day singing in the dry bushes, and then I caught movement in my peripheral vision, a slight and cautious shifting followed by a sudden stillness. I turned slowly toward it, feeling the sweat running down the back of my neck, and looked.

It was no larger than a jackal, but stood on spindly legs, tan striped vertically with thin white lines. A nyala female, lacking the male's powerful neck and intimidating horns.

I breathed out with relief, and the nyala walked on, revealing, behind it, a motionless black boy who was staring directly at me. He was wearing a ragged, dirt-streaked smock, and his feet were bare. He might have been eight or nine, though his eyes were older. He was gaunt, the skin of his face tight so that the skull showed through, and he was watching me, not moving one iota. He stared as the nyala had, gauging the threat, poised to leap into sprinting retreat.

Slowly I reached behind me and pushed the pistol into my waistband, bringing my empty hand back where he could see it, fingers spread. Following suit, Mnenga lowered his spear and raised his free hand in a gesture of calm.

The boy still stared, eyes moving between us, then widening with horror.

"It's all right," I said soothingly. "We're here to help. Mnenga, tell him."

But Mnenga was processing what I had missed, that the boy's terror was not about us. It was about what was behind us. With a surge of dread, I forced myself to revolve and look into the face of the clavtar that was stalking toward us through the grass.

CHAPTER
27

IT WAS MASSIVE. ALMOST as big as a rhino. Its mane was the color of steel, and its eyes were a cool, uncanny blue.

Mnenga lowered into a half crouch and raised his spear once more, but I had never seen anything so clearly futile. In that half second, in a moment of sudden and awful clarity, I knew that he was going to die and that it would be my fault. I reached for the gun in the small of my bank and drew it fumblingly.

The clavtar sniffed the air, the muscles of its great silver shoulders shifting, its tail lashing gently from side to side as if it was languidly considering its options. I cocked the pistol, and the snap as the hammer locked in place stilled it, focused its attention.

"Where are the others?" I breathed to Mnenga, my eyes locked on the clavtar. There were no rules I knew for how to survive the situation. Running was obviously pointless, but whether I should be staring the beast down, talking, or playing dead I had no idea. Presented with the size of the creature, I was suddenly sure that shooting it would only make it angry, though the noise might frighten it for a moment. Through my sweating terror, I heard Mnenga murmur in his own language and, seconds later, heard the boy respond in his.

I only hoped they could understand each other.

"Behind the temple," said Mnenga. His voice was low and hoarse. "Back away slowly," he said.

Cautiously, my gaze still fixed on the clavtar, I picked up one boot and reached back, a long, careful step that moved me a couple of feet away from the huge lion. It lowered its head, tail swishing, raised one colossal paw and held it in midair as if considering taking a step. Or leaping into an attack.

Still watching it, I took another step away. The clavtar blinked and set its paw down in the grass. I took another step, Mnenga at my elbow, spear pointed squarely at the watching animal. The evening seemed to be descending on us even as we stood there, so that it felt like we had been locked in place like this for hours.

Another backward step, and the clavtar gave a low, coughing snarl. Another, and now I wanted to turn and run as fast as I could, even though I knew the beast would be on me in seconds. Mnenga was muttering to the boy again, and I thought I heard him move more quickly away. The clavtar's ears flicked and it roused itself again, its head almost level with mine. The pistol was slippery in my sweaty hand, but I dared not try to wipe it off.

"Keep moving slowly," said Mnenga. "Go to the temple. Climb."

For a second, I thought that high ground would stop the clavtar's advance, but while it was marginally safer, harder for the lion to attack us there, I was fairly sure that all cats but cheetahs were confident climbers. We were the interlopers here. This was the clavtar's world, and no ancient relics of a dead human past would change that.

I didn't mean to move faster, but I couldn't help it. I backed toward the temple pyramid, the gun waggling ineffectually in my hand like something whose purpose I had forgotten. Mnenga matched my speed, putting himself between me and the great cat, and I was dimly aware of footsteps behind me. Lots of them.

I turned, startled out of my mesmerized eye lock with the clavtar.

There were children pouring up the steps of the pyramid in a wild scramble. A dozen or more. There were young women with them, all draped in once brightly colored robes, now torn and filthy. They looked back to where the clavtar took a single bounding step, halving the distance between me and it.

I fired without thinking, shooting over the beast's head so that it winced away from the deafening report. For a moment, the clavtar seemed to shrink in on itself, then it took a wary step back, and in that moment, I bounded onto the foot of the pyramid and began my panting, blind, and blundering climb to the top. Mnenga brought up the rear, tracking the lion's movement with his spear.

I skinned my shins against the rock, and the great stone heads seemed to shriek my silent pain and fury.

"Up!" I said to the children, gesturing clumsily, herding, corralling, and they stared at me, too desperate to feel the horror they ought to in the swelling gloom of the early evening. At the top was a vast stone basin, coarsely hewn from the rock and long since fractured by the elements. I looked down. The clavtar had skirted the base of the pyramid and was padding through the grass, gazing up at us. For a second, I thought it was leaving, but then it paused and turned back around.

It was only a matter of time before it came up.

I gave Mnenga a feverish look. He was dragging brushwood, dead leaves, and ancient, shriveled vines up the stone steps, and was babbling to the children to do the same.

I knew what he was thinking, even if I didn't see how we could do it fast enough to make a difference. I unclasped my satchel and pulled out the tin box containing a three-inch steel bar, a piece of flint, and a wad of cotton soaked in methylated spirit. My nostrils flared at the heady aroma and, somehow, brought me to my senses, focusing my attention as if I was looking through the folding telescope, all the details suddenly sharp. I made it to the stone basin in half a dozen steps. It was already half full of sticks and dead leaves. I added the cotton and struck the steel with the flint, making sparks fly. In three strokes, the cotton had begun to smoke, and in five it was ablaze.

One of the boys fed twigs into the basin, and a girl dumped a handful of leaves, which caught and billowed with sudden flame. In the same instant, Mnenga cried out.

The clavtar was coming.

It reached the base of the pyramid in a bound as long as a coach and horses, and was halfway up before Mnenga could shout at the children to get back. He lunged with his spear, but the clavtar swatted it aside like it was a match. At my back I felt the flare of light and heat in the basin, and the clavtar saw it too, the orange glare reflecting in its pale eyes. It roared, a deafening bellow of sound that showed its knifelike teeth and a maw wide enough to take me headfirst, then winced away, and in that moment, Mnenga pulled back before it could strike him down.

I turned and dragged the largest branch out of the basin and brandished it, its leaves blazing, smoke trailing in a long plume as I ran down the steps of the pyramid to meet the lion.

"No!" Mnenga yelled, but the clavtar was wary of the firelight, and as I came at it, it turned and leapt down, loping away, head turned balefully toward us.

For now, we were safe.

"It will be back," I said, watching the cat sidle into the underbrush, "and we don't have much to burn."

"Thank you," said Mnenga.

"Least I could do." I shrugged.

His face wrinkled with confusion at the phrase, so I smiled and shook my head.

"It doesn't matter," I said. I looked down. One of the children—a girl, no more than six or seven—had taken my hand and was gazing up at me wonderingly. I stared at her, embarrassed and unsure what to do or say. In the end I dropped to my haunches and smoothed her hair. When she hugged me, sobbing with what I took to be relief, I just squatted there. I had faced the clavtar with better instincts.

Mnenga spoke to her, then to the others, experimenting with dialect words till he found what was closest to their own language, and I busied myself feeding sticks into the fire and watching for the clavtar as darkness fell on the bush. We had wood for maybe an hour. After that we'd have to go foraging on the forest floor which, as night fell and the clavtar continued to lurk close by, was suicide. I caught Mnenga's eyes flicking to the woodpile and knew he was thinking the same thing.

But somehow, somehow, he had the children laughing. First two little boys who looked like they had been through hell, and then three more, till almost all of them were talking loudly and happily about the horrors of their journey through the bush. I don't know how he did it.

But it wasn't all of them. One of the women, rail thin and wrapped in a swath of coarse fabric that might once have been sailcloth, was weeping inconsolably even as the rest came to life, sitting very still and staring at her gnarled fingers as if looking for something. She wasn't the only one. Reluctantly they gave up their stories to Mnenga, who nodded solemnly and smiled with understanding and compassion as they quietly, matter-of-factly, rehearsed the horrors of their journey and all they had lost, so that—selfishly—I found myself glad that I couldn't understand what they were saying.

The girl who had taken my hand sat beside me, staring at the fire as I scanned the shadows of the trees for signs of the clavtar.

"Her name is Ife," said Mnenga. "She has no family here. Her mother was lost, I think, but I do not know how. They are Quundu, and their language is like Sanweeti, which I know pretty well, but not quite the same. I do not understand everything they say."

I smiled at the girl, and she linked her arm through mine in silence, the firelight flickering on her face. In the glow I saw pink and glistening blisters on her cheek and neck, which I had not noticed before. For a second I wondered if she had fallen into the stone brazier, but these were not new injuries, though they were not old either.

"How did this happen?" I asked.

She flinched, turning away as if embarrassed, but said nothing.

I looked to Mnenga. "Ask her about these burns."

He squatted next to her, considering her injuries and then whispered smilingly. At first she just grunted in monosyllables, before uttering a phrase which clouded his face and made him turn to me in puzzlement.

"She did not just arrive with the others," he said. "She has been here a month."

"A month?" I repeated. "Doing what?"

More whispering and then he nodded.

"What?" I asked.

"Later," he said.

I held his gaze, read the concern for the child, who looked suddenly distraught, then nodded. I reached for the thickest branch I could see, and shoved it into the fire. The sun was down now, and beyond the stone basin of flame, I could see nothing. Somewhere in the bush, the clavtar roared, and the sound seemed to come from everywhere at once, so that the children's laughter died and everyone huddled closer to the fire.

I shot another glance at Mnenga and saw the concern in his face before he snapped on his grin for the children. Someone asked him a question, and he made soothing noises, deliberately avoiding my eyes. I patted the girl he had called Ife on the head and stood up, climbing to the highest point of the step pyramid and turning my back on the fire. For a moment, I closed my eyes tight in the hope that I'd see more when I reopened them, but I could make out nothing beyond the difference between the blue-black of the horizon and the deeper shade of the trees.

I turned to face the river and caught my breath. There were two pricks of soft light out there on the water. Lamps. I kept my eyes on them until I was sure they were moving, coming closer.

Boats.

I called to Mnenga, pointing.

"Get everyone down to the river," I shouted. "Now! Take some of the burning sticks."

In fact carrying burning sticks was harder than it sounded. They tended to go out as soon as you started to run with them, but they smoked and glowed, and maybe that would be enough to make the clavtar wary. In seconds, we were at the base of the pyramid and picking our way through the reedy wet ground at its base, eyes flashing around for animals.

The lights from the boats were nearer now, and I could see oarsmen pulling against the water, backs taught. Lani men. Only one per boat, which meant they had come to get us.

I pushed my way to the front, babbling thanks as I splashed into the shallow water, but stopped abruptly when one of them turned and I recognized Rahvey's husband, Sinchon.

"How many are there?" he said in Lani without preamble.

"About fifteen," I said.

"We'll have to take two trips," he said. "Youngest first."

Even in the panic of the moment, listening for the clavtar's approach and trying to herd the children aboard the slender boats, I found myself humbled and amazed. I had never thought much of Sinchon.

"Keep the rest here," he said. "We'll bring one more boat when we come back."

"Thank you," I said, but he was already pushing off and clambering in, so I was not sure he heard.

The river was wide, and the boats were overloaded and undermanned, so their crossing seemed painfully slow. At least with the lights on their prows we could track them, and though we returned to the brazier on top of the pyramid for a few minutes, it wasn't long before we were back by the river and sloshing through the water as the boats returned. I was the last aboard, and we had just pushed off when I heard the roar of the clavtar close and echoing off the stone. Turning, I saw it pacing the upper tier of the pyramid, the dying flames from the stone basin painting its sleek gray hide with amber and gold. It looked like a feral king, an ancient and terrible force that might have been there for a thousand years, and I privately decided that Mnenga was right: this was no place for the living.

CHAPTER

28

FLORIHN, THE DROWNING'S MIDWIFE and the closest thing I had to an enemy who was still alive and at liberty, met us at the shore of the Drowning. Her expression when she saw me was rigid but unsurprised, and I knew why. The rescue of the refugees was Rahvey's doing. She had known I was here and why, and when someone reported seeing the fire on the temple, she had realized I was in danger. When I saw my sister giving cups of water to the children, bustling about with the other mothers who were loaded down with blankets and pots of curried dal or rice, I rushed to her and threw my arms around her.

"Thank you," I whispered into her hair. "Thank you."

"You thought we would leave you there?" said Rahvey, separating herself from me and giving me a hard stare. "We are not monsters."

"I know," I said. "I'm sorry. I just didn't think. . . . Thank you."

"Help me with the food," she said, matter-of-factly. "There is naan in the basket over there."

I did as I was told, avoiding the way Florihn watched me with that supercilious smile on her face, as if my return in the company of a Mahweni herder with a horde of homeless black children was no more than she had expected.

"You can't stay here, you know," she said. "Neither can they. We will feed and clothe them as best we can, but in a few days, they will have to move on. You will have to go sooner."

"I know," I said. "I appreciate your help."

She stared at me then, as if trying to decide how much to say, all the things she had stored away since our last meeting when the rules of the Drowning about fourth daughters had changed at my insistence and in spite of her objection. In the end, she just nodded curtly and walked away.

I turned to see Tanish coming into the shanty with Bertha at his side, a shawl drawn around her shoulders and a hat with flowers on it, as if she was on her way to church.

"We heard," she boomed, smiling. "We came to help."

Tears of joy and gratitude started to my eyes as, for once, the world turned out to be the way I had always hoped.

MNENGA MADE ALL THINGS better. The children flocked to him, forgetting all they had been through in their delight in food and firelight and his infectious company. He taught them old Mahweni songs and told them stories of life in the bush, and though they did not understand everything he said, they felt his warmth, his compassion, his spirit. Even the Lani who generally kept a safe and suspicious distance from the Mahweni seemed to take to him. The women brought him food, and the men—Sinchon included—brought him drink. I watched, smiling, confused by old, uncertain feelings and by the surprising and inconvenient wish that it would all go on forever and that I would be part of it.

I slept for a few hours on Rahvey's warped and creaking porch and said my farewells an hour before dawn.

"When will you be back?" asked Mnenga.

"Soon," I said. "I promise. If the authorities find out the children are here, they will be shipped back."

"I will send a message to my village," he said. "We will help as much as we can."

Of course.

"They listen to you, don't they?" I said. "Your people in the village."

He looked away, and I caught something I rarely saw in his face. It was not deception, exactly, but there was a reluctance to speak, and when he just shrugged, I asked him directly.

"Who are you really, Mnenga? I know you are a herder with your brothers, but there is something more, isn't there? Something you haven't told me."

"Nothing important," he said.

"That's not a no."

He sighed in resignation.

"My people—the Unassimilated Tribes—have different ways of choosing their leaders. In my village, the oldest men and women give jobs to the younger people according to their talents. I am the Outward Face of the village. I travel. I talk to people from other places. Even the city. One day I will be on the tribal council. I did not choose this," he said, and his tone suggested he would not have done. "But it is my job, and I must do it. As well as looking after the nbezu," he added, finding his smile once more.

I nodded. I thought of his facility with Feldish, his composure under pressure, and his knowledge of the political world. That he should have been earmarked as a kind of ambassador, possibly even a future leader for his people, made sense to me, perhaps more sense than it made to him.

"I don't know what will happen to the refugees," I said, "the Quundu, and I know they can't stay here forever, but if your brothers can spare you—"

"Spare me?" he said, puzzled.

"If they can work without you, I'd like you to stay with them for as long as you can. They like you."

He shrugged and smiled at that, as if it was a great mystery he had come to accept.

"And you?" he asked. "You like me too?"

"Always," I said. "You know that."

He considered me and smiled shyly. It wasn't quite the liking he wanted, perhaps, said the smile, but he would take it. Then his face darkened.

"The girl," he said. "Ife. The one with the burns. She was working in a factory near the docks. They worked only at night. It caught fire. Her mother did not survive."

It was as if I had been experimenting with Namud's lock picks, twisting, rotating each one in turn, fingers focused but mind wandering, till the snap of one of the lock's tumblers seized my attention and held it.

I HAD LESS THAN an hour of darkness left to me by the time I had made my way into the city and crossed into the docklands of Dagenham Steps. There were no streetlamps in the back alleys, and the darkness was thick and dangerous between the tenements and factories. The area smelled of urine and machine oil, coal smoke, and the sour edge of the river where pools stagnated, dammed up and glistening with industrial filth. The air was thick with the peculiar tang of the smoke from the pottery kilns whose swollen, bottleneck chimneys stood like a huddle of fat, blank-faced men. Horritch's factory—which is to say Horritch's *remaining* factory—where Sureyna and I had met Bertha, was so dark that for a moment I thought I had been wrong. The windows showed no signs of life, the doors were locked, and the sky was still too gloomy to see if there was smoke coming out. I moved cautiously, watching for guards, skulking from coal hutch to the deep shade of a container car with roughly cut vents near the top and marked with a large yellow *M*, seemingly abandoned on a nearby siding. Two night watchmen were on duty, one covering the door through which I had last entered the building, one patrolling the perimeter. I had almost decided that getting closer was not worth the risk when I heard the distinct whine of machinery followed by a hiss as steam burst from a vent on the second story.

The elevator.

Someone was working inside on the "off-limits" upper floor. I scoured the building for signs of a ladder to the roof, but if there had ever been one, it had been removed. I knew that the interior stairwell was carefully locked, so the only way up was by the steam elevator, or at least up the shaft through which it ran.

The patrolling guard was lazy, predictable. After I had watched his circuit a couple of times, languid, whistling the same music hall tune in incompetent snatches, I knew how to time my approach. I remembered the stifling heat of the warehouse and knew there would be ventilators communicating with the outside. Some would be on the roof, but others were visible in the walls. They would be tight, and I may need to force a grating or two, but they would be no worse than climbing the inside of a chimney.

As the watchman rounded the corner, heading toward the river, I sprinted from my vantage and scaled the bars on the outside of one of the great oval-topped windows. From there I was able to reach over to the downturned pipe that emerged from the brick like a great faucet. Its internal diameter was about two feet and, for the first time in a while, I wished I was a couple of years younger.

I swung across, thrust my left arm up the pipe till I could hook it over the bend, then let go of the window bars and flung my right hand up there as well. For a second or two I just hung, before I worked my aching shoulders in, drawing my weight through and over. My satchel snagged on the pipe, but I wriggled, shrugging off the claustrophobia and fighting my way in till only my legs stuck out. As I paused for breath, I heard the distinct sound of whistling.

The guard was coming back.

It was too much to hope that he wouldn't see me dangling a few feet above his head. I squirmed and fought like a snagged fish on a line, pulling, tightening my belly, rolling joints and muscles against the hard seams of the metal. The whistling got louder as the guard rounded the corner so I drew my legs up at the knee to try and get my feet out of sight.

Somehow that was the one wriggle I hadn't tried, and I slid over the bend in the pipe and fell headfirst into an iron box fitted to the inside wall of the silent factory. I kept very still and counted to fifty. The whistling never stopped, and as it faded away, I focused my attention on the wire mesh fastened across the front of the box.

The wire was no match for the bolt cutters in my satchel, and in under a minute, I had snipped enough that I could brace the soles of my boots against it and push till it opened like a hatch. I slipped through, hung from my fingers, then dropped, bending my knees and rolling out the impact of the hard concrete floor.

I scuttled into the shade of one of the great crablike looms, listening, but there was no sound of anyone there, though I could feel a steady hum reverberating through the empty air. It was coming from above. The massive structure of iron beams, concrete, and brick insulated the sound well, but there was no doubt. Someone was running machinery up there. A lot of it.

The elevator had gone up, but the gate at the bottom was open, revealing the shaft and the cables that linked the elevator platform to the throbbing engine beside it. I put my hand to the boiler and felt its heat. Whoever operated it had gone up on the platform, but he wouldn't leave it unattended for any length of time, and I wouldn't be able to get up there, even if I could scale the inside of the shaft, so long as the elevator was locked in place on the upper floor. I was going to have to wait for it to come down.

I looked around for somewhere to hide, and in that moment, the engine gasped, the great steel wheel began to turn, and as the cable rolled out, the platform began to slide down the shaft.

I ducked hurriedly behind a pallet of bundled fabric and dropped into a crouch, hands on the bales of cloth.

The fabric was unusually soft.

I kneaded it with my fingers in the dark as I listened to the descent of the elevator, felt its extraordinary smoothness and elasticity, and even in the low light, I thought I caught a slight sheen, an inner glow like what I had seen on Agatha Markeson's shawl.

Bar-Selehm silk.

The steam elevator thunked into place, and someone grunted, dragging another bale of cloth for the pile. As I knelt breathless behind the stack, he heaved it into place and then sauntered off along the long aisle of the factory, wheezing from the exertion.

This was my chance.

I got to my feet and slid round the heaped fabric and onto the elevator platform. The inside of the shaft was a girdered cage, the cables that bore the elevator running up to a great pulley system high in the tower. I jumped, grasped the bar over my head and swung my boots onto the girders in the wall. Gripping the cable above me with both hands, I began to walk my way slowly and silently up the shaft.

The gate at the top was latched but not locked, and in seconds, I was on another concrete floor, behind another door with a glass pane in it through which I saw the illegal night shift finishing their work.

Women and children, all black, mostly wearing the same inadequate and ragged robes I knew from the kids who had been taken in at the Drowning, the same thin arms and legs, the same tired, desperate eyes. Dozens of them. Fifty at least, judging by the arrangement of the machines, some as young as six or seven.

The upper story was half machines—smaller than those in the shed below, finer somehow—and half pallets of bedding and boxes containing the workers' bits of things. It was no wonder they looked so weak and sickly. They probably hadn't seen sunlight in weeks. I cracked the door a fraction and was hit by heat and by the stench of machines and bodies intertwined, fused till one became the other.

Now I was here, now that I had seen them and understood the horror of their endless prison, I found that I did not know what to do. My instinct was to kick the door wide, pistol in hand, and urge them out in a great riot of liberation that would sweep the guards under our feet. Even as I wondered how to get them down by the elevator or break through to the staircase, I knew that getting them out of the building was only solving the beginning of the problem. I could not get them to the Drowning from here unseen, particularly now that the morning shift was about to begin and the streets would be packed with workers. Trying to do so would only lead to their arrest, after which they would be packed onto ships and sent back to war and devastation.

Suddenly it seemed that all I could offer was a choice of miseries, different places in which to live in exploitation and die in poverty. What had Rahvey said?

Life, eh, sister mine? It's no place to be poor.

I stood there, paralyzed by indecision, like one of the shuttles waiting to be sent one way, then the other, endlessly hurried back and forth, my movement under someone else's control. One by one, the looms were shutting down, and I realized, too late, that the foremen would be coming to inspect the work.

The elevator whirred into life, and the cables started to run as a snatch of speech drifted up to me.

". . . package it all up and crate it for Georgie May by midnight."

Horrified, I looked down and saw the bowler hats of three men, two in shirtsleeves, one in a jacket. They were coming up.

I pushed through the door, pulling the scarf over my mouth and nose to cut the stench as much as to hide my face. One of the women who was standing up with weary relief as her loom shut down, spotted me, and gave me a long baffled look. The room was lit with the soft amber light of oil lamps, which hung over the looms, and the walls were so dark you could barely make out the shuttered windows. I moved toward them, fishing in my satchel for a crowbar, conscious of the elevator's steady, squeaking ascent up the shaft, and then came a voice, loud and accusatory, shouting in Feldish.

"You! Stop where you are."

He was burly and black, but one look at the heavy stick in his hands said I should expect no help there.

"Stop," he roared again, "or I swear I'll beat you to death right here!"

He had an accent, and not of the city. One of the smugglers, perhaps, who had brought the people here and had been paid to stay on to badger them in their own tongue. I didn't doubt that he meant what he said.

I moved quickly to the nearest window, but realized too late I would not get the shutter open before he caught up to me. I worked one bolt free, but had barely got the crowbar under the padlock when I saw him appear around one of the looms, head lowered and bullish. He wore sea boots, and his face was scarred on both cheeks, as if branded. The stick in his hands looked iron-hard, and he tapped it meaningfully in one large open palm, grinning like a jackal.

I wasn't sure where the cry started. It was one of the women. I didn't see who was the first to move. Suddenly there was a throng around him, thin arms and hollow cheeks, pushing and shouting words I did not understand, their anger unmistakable. One of them looked at me and urged me with a cry and a gesture. They could not delay him for more than a few seconds. Already he was fighting free of their slashing nails, laying about him with his club.

Horrified, I wrenched at the lock, and it popped open. The shutter juddered and swung, and I used the crowbar to smash the glass in one of the panes behind it. It was a long way down, and there was no ladder.

I shot one agonized glance back into the shed. The man with the stick was shrugging the women off, but he looked angry, even as the three white men came hurrying over to him from the steam elevator. I leaned back against the window, reached through the frame with both hands and hoisted myself through. There was no way down, but the inset patterning of the brick was as good as a ladder up to the roof. Using only fingers and toes, I scrambled up the fifteen feet or so to the top and hauled myself over the gutter.

The roof was pitched steeply, like an engine shed, but there was a walkway along the side, and I moved quickly, one hand on the slates, hoping that my memory was right. At the back of the factory where the warm chimney pointed into the sky like a gun, still smoking in the first light of day, was an access platform and, across a narrow ginnel between the buildings, a work shed connected to the pottery yards with a flat roof, only ten feet below.

I did not break stride. Running full pelt, I vaulted through the air, rolling on the roof next door, the satchel clutched to my chest. I landed among the uncanny brick landscape of the bottleneck kilns and paused to look back, to see if any of Horritch's men had dared to give chase, or if they were going down by the stairs in the hope of catching me at the bottom. If so, they would be disappointed. I had a clear route over the pottery works, shielded by its hot, bulbous chimneys, the blast furnace on Wharf Street, and the tanner's yard shed, and could drop to street level at any point.

But my flash of confidence and triumph lasted only a second, and not because they were coming after me. The black man who looked like a pirate was leaning out of the window, looking wildly around, but they had lost me as I went over the roof, and I had a good lead on them now. No, it wasn't them who made my breath catch.

Perching on the top of the chimney forty feet above me was an outlandish figure wrapped in torn fabric. It was crouching froglike, a pale, gangly creature, hairless and strangely gray so that it looked barely human.

The Gargoyle.

CHAPTER

29

THE THING I HAD thought was the Gargoyle—the *person,* my rational mind insisted—watched me for a moment, then vanished round the far side of the chimney. I blinked, feeling the strangeness of a tremor in my reality, but I did not wait to see if it reappeared.

I also did not go straight into the city. Instead, I went down to the river and made my way through the tangle of back streets till I reached the remains of Nathan Horritch's burned factory, thinking of the one I had just left where low-grade oil lamps hung perilously over the exhausted laborers. It wasn't hard to find the place. The buildings on either side were scorched and sooty, and one—a ceramics factory with a particularly large and irregular kiln chimney—had lost part of its roof in the blaze, but of Horritch's place there was barely anything: blackened and twisted steel beams, heat-fractured brick, and shattered roofing slates, all blue-black from the fire.

I glanced around, but I was sure I had not been followed, either by Horritch's thugs or by the strange figure I had glimpsed on the chimney, something I had almost managed to convince myself had been a large vervet or baboon . . .

Almost.

I squeezed through the wooden barriers that had been erected by the fire department and picked my way through the wreckage to where a pair of yellow steam tractors with great bulldozer blades fitted to the front sat ready to push the remains into the river. Each was marked with a stenciled letter *M.* Their drivers had not yet arrived, and it occurred to me that this might be the last look anyone got at the ruined site. I wandered cautiously about, my boots kicking up clouds of white ash with each step. In places glass had pooled and solidified in swirls of black and bubbling color. It had been a hot fire.

There was metal too, far too much of it to have been part of the building's structure. This was machinery. If the factory had been abandoned, as Horritch had claimed, there had been a lot of valuable equipment left sitting in it. I stooped to the ash and sifted it with my hand, wondering what that action reminded me of, scattering flakes of blackened brick, twisted screws and bolts, and something charred that looked like . . .

Bone.

A jawbone, human, set with broken teeth.

The dream—the one about the flooded rice festival—came back to me in a flash, that final moment when the island beneath my feet had turned to human skulls. . . .

I dropped the bone fragment in horror, then picked it up again and stared at it, turning it over in my hands and trying to tell myself that it was not what it appeared to be.

But it was, and with the rush of exhilaration—that what I had found, what there would surely be more of, was evidence, proof of a terrible crime and its subsequent cover-up—came a deep and penetrating sense of failure and grief. I slipped the fragment into my satchel, wiped my eyes with a dusty hand, and set off for Willinghouse and the police.

I CROSSED THE RIVER on the Ridleford pontoon bridge and hailed a ride from a skeptical cabbie who wouldn't let me in till I showed him the coins in my purse. If I was quick, I thought, I might catch Willinghouse at home before he left for Parliament, but even so, I took no chances, and as Namud answered the door, I stepped inside and barked out my order without pausing for breath.

"Get a message to Inspector Andrews. Have him meet us at

Horritch's factory in Dagenham Steps, fast as he can get there. He'll need armed support."

"What is it?"

I told him, quickly, and his face set like concrete, his dark eyes flashing.

"I will join you there," he said.

"There's no need," I replied, not wanting him to risk his life or position. "I'm sure the police can—"

"I said I'll join you there," he answered.

I nodded, and he managed a smile.

"Can't have you spreading mayhem and destruction without me to clean up after you, can we?" he concluded, closing the front door behind him.

I raced down the hallway calling Willinghouse's name. He trotted down stairs, dapper in his dark, conservative suit and cravat, a buckled briefcase in his hand. He looked mildly irritated by all the shouting but stopped when he saw my face, then the fragment of bone and teeth which I held out to him.

"What is that?" he asked, his green eyes bright, hawkish.

"Horritch's factory wasn't empty when it burned," I said. "It was full of refugees, most of whom did not make it out alive. He has another factory in the same area where more are working right now."

It was easier to say it like that, simple, without outrage or any other emotion, and now that I had his attention, I didn't even shout.

THE FACTORY'S LOWER FLOOR was in full and deafening use when we arrived, the looms pulsing, clacking, and roaring so that Andrews had to lead his men back out to give them instructions. Willinghouse clamped his hands over his ears and looked to me. I pointed toward the locked door that led to the only staircase, and he made for it, Namud at his heels, only to be intercepted by a blustering white foreman in a flat cap. The man attempted to bar our passage, but when he saw the uniformed officers, truncheons in hand, he gave up the cause as lost. I passed the empty steam elevator shaft and joined them as the foreman took an iron ring off his belt and unlocked the heavy door.

"There's another at the top," I shouted over the din.

"What?" bellowed Willinghouse.

"Another door," I yelled back. "At the top."

He still couldn't hear me, so I snatched the keys from the foreman and led the way up four flights of fifteen steps that brought us to another concrete landing and, as expected, an identical door. I thrust first one key in, then another, checking Andrews's pinking, anxious face before turning the key and putting my shoulder to the timber.

The door scraped, then flew open.

I knew immediately we were too late. The air, which had been heavy, hot, and rank the night before was clear and comparatively fresh. Every window had been unshuttered and opened, and the room was quiet.

I ran among the still and silent looms shouting, "No, no, no!"

The machinery was all still there, but the workers and their poor bits of things were gone. Andrews sighed, and Willinghouse shouted a single curse, and then there was only the throbbing of the concrete floor as the looms in the hall below lumbered on.

"I came right to you!" I yelled at Willinghouse. "How could they have been cleared out so quickly?"

"The machines have been running recently," said Andrews, who had stooped to a patch of oil on the ground.

"Of course they bloody have!" I shot back at him. "I was here. I saw them!"

"Well, the workers are not here now," the inspector returned.

"I can see that too!" I shouted. "Get some men on the ground asking what people saw. The morning shift must have seen them leave. It's been less than an hour since I was here. How could they have been cleared out that fast?"

"We have nothing!" roared Willinghouse. "Again."

"We know there was an illegal operation working out of this space," Andrews conceded.

"We can't prove it," Willinghouse said, turning on him. "We had to catch them red-handed."

I closed my eyes and put my hands to my head as if the looms were running and I was trying to shut out the noise. Behind me, Willinghouse continued to bicker with Andrews. I walked to one of the windows and looked out over the river to the city proper.

Bertha, I thought. *I'll ask her.* Maybe if she was early, she might have seen something, or heard from someone who did. . . .

The ting of cable under tension struck my consciousness, and I turned. I'd heard it before, but it hadn't registered. Now it did, and I strode to the steam elevator, whose gate was closed, though the platform was not there.

But it hadn't been at the bottom either. The shaft had been empty.

So it was in the middle, suspended between floors, and that meant that someone was on it. It wasn't anywhere near big enough to hide the refugees, but it was hiding something, or someone. I rejoined the others and told them.

Andrews arranged all but two of his men around the room. Willinghouse, Namud and the rest, one of whom had a shotgun, took the stairs down. As we reentered the cacophonous lower hall, Namud drew a revolver from his jacket pocket, and I—reluctantly—fished the single-shot pistol from my satchel and cocked it. Willinghouse motioned the women at the nearest looms to stop working and go. They frowned, deaf to what he was saying, but they saw our weapons, and soon the machines were shutting down one by one and the workers were pushing for the door. The din of the machinery and of anxious voices gradually subsided, and the shed lapsed into an eerie calm as I knelt behind one of the silent looms, my pistol trained on the elevator, the memory of my last gunfight stampeding through my head like a wild orlek.

Namud went to the steam generator which served the elevator, threw a lever, and turned a handle. A valve opened by the water tank and, with a great serpentine hiss, the steam blew out in a long jet, which became a cloud and drifted away. I saw the red needle on the gauge slide slowly round to the left, and then the elevator was creaking and groaning its way down.

The gate was open, so I saw the platform descend. It was heaped with boxes of blankets and dirty clothes, everything they had not been able to clear out in time. It was evidence, of a sort, and it had been left to one man to take care of.

The burly man in sea boots, the one with the heavy stick, his face slashed from the nails of the women who had slowed him down as I made my previous escape, rose up from behind the crates, a black and heavy pistol in his hands. He knew what being caught here now meant, and he had no intention of coming quietly.

The gun flashed once, twice, its cannon roar filling the uncanny silence of the mill before the policeman's shotgun knocked him down. I had fired but hit only the wood of the crate. The bellow of the weapons, the sudden rush of acrid gun smoke, filled my nose and ears completely. For a moment I was stunned and terrified, even though I had seen our foe go down. I shrank back behind the frame of the loom, muscles tight, a full body cringe away from the carnage and into myself which is, perhaps, why it took so long for me to realize that the villain in sea boots had not been the only casualty.

I was the last to reach Namud's body.

He had been hit only once, but the bullet had gone through his chest and his back was slick with blood when I put my arms around him. He looked not so much afraid or in pain as stunned, his eyes wide, lips parted but still, breath coming and going in shallow gasps. Willinghouse dropped to one knee and took his hand.

"Hold on, man," he said in a bluff, hearty way. "Help is on its way."

"Not, I think, quickly enough," whispered Namud with a bleak smile at me.

Behind and above me, officers barked commands about bandages and where to put the pressure, and then a strong hand gripped my shoulder and started to pull me politely but inexorably out of the way. . . . Or would have, were it not for Namud himself, who suddenly seized my wrist and pulled me toward his face as his mouth sought to form words. I shrugged off the policeman's grip and lowered my head to his. He moistened his lips, and there were flecks of blood in the saliva.

"Namud," I whispered.

"Don't," he began, then hesitated, fighting through a cough that brought more blood up from his lungs. "Don't . . . be too hard on her."

"What?" I asked, my eyes swimming. "On who?"

But he was smiling vaguely now, and his words, when they came, were dreamy, as if coming from far away.

"You were," he managed, "a damned fine steeplejack."

And then he was gone.

CHAPTER

30

SOMETIME LATER, WE MADE a grim procession to the site of Horritch's burned-out factory but were too late there as well. The yellow steam-driven bulldozers emblazoned with the stenciled *M*'s were sitting by the riverbank, and the shore, which was usually black with oil and coal dust, was white with ash. Of the factory, its equipment, and—most important—the remains caught inside when it burned down, there was almost no sign. It could have been that some of the bones had not yet been washed downstream, but finding them would take time and resources, and proving who they were and how they had died was next to impossible.

NAMUD HAD BEEN MORE than a helpmate in my planning for the Elitus episode, and inside the club itself, when things had lurched toward disaster, he had kept me safe. I had thanked him in a cursory sort of way and had meant to say more at some later time. That would never come now. He had, I realized with mild surprise, been as close to a male friend as I had had of late, a Lani from the streets, like me, taken in and made . . . what? Useful? Family? I wasn't sure, and his loss made my isolation sharper. That he had known things, things I had hoped he would eventually share with me about my employer's family, things that seemed to touch me in ways I could not explain and that had died with him, burned within me like acid.

And I had liked him. Not romantically, of course, but with the instinctive closeness of people who have taken similar paths through life and wound up in the same place. He was clever and funny, humble and—in his way—kind. That I had only realized these things after his death felt like an especially bitter failing of my own.

We returned to the city in stunned, defeated silence. Andrews and Willinghouse said nothing and, unable to bear the restraint of their grief, I slipped down from the coach at the westernmost point in the journey and told them I would rejoin them at the town house later that morning.

Don't be too hard on her, Namud had said.

On who? My heart said he was talking about Madame Nahreem, but the words made no sense to me, and the idea that he had died offering me something I could do nothing with made losing him all the harder.

I HAD NO PLAN, but a possibility had occurred to me, and I needed to do something to get out from under the sense of loss and failure. I had been asking myself over and over how someone had spirited a large number of women and children away from the factory without anyone noticing but then I remembered something.

The container car.

As I had crept into the factory last night, I had hidden behind a single rail truck parked on one of the numerous sidings that served the docklands. It had ventilation slits cut in near the roof. In the morning when we had returned, it, like the children, was gone. There was no system for tracking privately owned railway carriages, and without a serial number to go by, there was no point in asking for police assistance, but there were other ways of finding such things, other people who kept their eyes on what moved through the industrial hinterland of the riverbanks.

After laying flowers for Namud on a shrine at the old monkey temple on the edge of the Drowning, I went down to the river and found the children sitting around Bertha, who, the factory being closed for the day, had opted to throw in an extra lesson. She managed to be somehow deafening and serene at the same time. The children were gazing at her, laughing and signing. All of them. Tanish, all his city swagger abandoned, was joining in with great enthusiasm while Aab gazed on him, shyly fascinated. When I beckoned, he came away reluctantly.

"You want me to find a container car?" he asked, recovering his worldly skepticism.

"It was marked with a letter *M*," I said.

"That's nothing," he said. "There are hundreds of them."

"It had holes cut in near the roof. Vents."

"No one's gonna notice that."

"You can't do it," I said. "All right."

"Didn't say that, did I?" he said. "I'll ask around. Got a mate who works round there. If things move off schedule, like, unexpected, so to speak, he might have noticed."

"Thanks, Tanish," I said. "You like being here, don't you?"

"The Drowning's all right," he said, shrugging, like he didn't really care one way or the other.

"I mean here with my sister's children and the others."

"Yeah," he said, unable to completely suppress a grin, as he glanced back to where Aab was twittering with her fingers, beaming and full of life, a person I had never seen before. "Family-like, you know?"

I nodded, wondering vaguely if Namud had also been a Drowning boy once, if there might still be people here who had known him. Someone should tell them what had happened. Someone should weep for him.

TWO HOURS LATER, SITTING in Willinghouse's town home parlor, we received word from a police runner that Nathan Horritch was blaming whatever had been going on at the factory on his subordinates, mostly on the black man who had died that morning. Expensive lawyers were already making his case, and Willinghouse had been cautioned by senior members of Parliament to drop the matter, lest his involvement look like politically motivated interference.

And that was that. Horritch had been released on bond. There was no sign of the missing refugees. Namud was dead. It was more than defeat. It was an inversion of that feeling I had had in the Drowning only the day before, that sense that the world was how it should be.

"It wasn't your fault," said Andrews.

I nodded absently, wondering how many times I would hear that and if it would ever feel true.

Andrews had brought a piece of the fabric they had found snagged on a wheel in the steam elevator in Horritch's factory. It was a strap, three inches wide with a slimmer piece stitched along its length, but bunched to form a series of narrow pockets, open at each end, just wide enough to take a pencil. Though it was stained with oil from the machinery it was, like Agatha's shawl, sheer as gossamer but remarkably strong.

"It wasn't just looms up there," said Andrews. "There were cutting tables and sewing machines too, so whatever they were making was coming out as a finished product."

"No dye vats, though," I said. "So unless they were coloring the fabric elsewhere—"

Willinghouse cut me off. "Color? We're worrying what color it was?" he spat.

"Actually," I said, as patiently as I could manage, "I'm saying the opposite. Whatever they were making, I don't think they cared what color it was."

"It doesn't make any sense!" Willinghouse exploded, launching himself to his feet and pacing the room like a caged clavtar. "Horritch and Markeson are extremely wealthy men. All this risk for a smuggling ring? For cloth and cheap labor? There has to be more to it."

"Does the name Georgie May mean anything to you?" I asked.

They shook their heads.

"Sounds like a woman's name," said Dahria. She had been sitting with us the whole time, but had not spoken till now, and I felt that Namud's death had hit her much harder than any of us would have expected. Even Dahria. "I know a few Georges, but none of them go by Georgie, not publicly anyway. I know one Georgiana, though, and all her friends call her Georgie."

"What's her last name?" I asked.

"Svenhold," she said. "She's a twenty-four-year-old debutante who spends all her father's money on making herself look beautiful. Mr. Svenhold, alas, does not possess the necessary means." She attempted a bleak grin, but her heart wasn't in it.

"The machine gun plans," said Andrews. "That's where this started."

"Yes," said Willinghouse, pointing at him emphatically. "There has to be a connection."

"Elitus," I said. "They are all there: Horritch with his fabric factories, Markeson with his boats, and Montresat with his guns. If they are smuggling weapons, he has to be involved, and using Markeson's private shipping would be a way to sidestep military and governmental oversight if he's dealing guns illegally."

"Elitus doesn't connect to Darius," said Andrews. "He was a nobody."

"Connects to his killers," said Willinghouse. "This Barrington-Smythe character and his cuff-linked friends."

"It's more than that," I said. "I don't think the sign writer Gillies was Darius. Gillies was afraid of heights and had a history of violence against women. I think he died during an attempted rape, and that his body is in the morgue. Get a picture of the corpse to David Vandemar, his boss, and I think he'll confirm it."

The two men stared at me.

"Then who was Darius?" asked Andrews.

"A man called Ephraim Sandringham, another frequent visitor at the club till he recently went missing," I said.

Dahria reacted to that, a momentary look of surprise, hastily doused, and I caught her eye, thinking of the way her friend Constance—Horritch's daughter—had been romantically linked to the mysteriously absent Sandringham by the Merita ladies. If he had indeed been Darius, then Constance was another link between the theft of the plans and her industrialist father and his friends. How much of this Dahria read in my face, I couldn't say, but she looked sadder and wearier than I had ever seen her, and I resolved to say nothing about Constance for now.

"So the body was deliberately misidentified?" said Andrews.

"To divert attention from Elitus, yes," I said.

"By whom?"

"A young lady with blond hair, according to the papers," I said. "Darius's alleged fiancée."

"Who was really . . . ?" Andrews prompted.

"I'm not absolutely sure," I said, "but I think it was Lady Alice Welborne, who is romantically involved with the Grappoli ambassador."

It was a mark of Dahria's depression that she barely reacted to this piece of news, but Andrews looked up, and there was a light in his eyes.

"Is that the link?" he asked. "The machine gun is being smuggled to the Grappoli? They'll hang for it."

"We have to prove it," I said, not hopefully.

Willinghouse flicked open the paper to its society pages and showed an image of what looked to be a glamorous party in which elegant people—many of whom I now knew—milled around a familiar black-eyed man with a sash and epaulettes on his evening wear.

"*Count Alfonse Marino, royal Ambassador to the court of the Grappoli Empire,*" Wilinghouse read aloud, "*is currently spending all his free evenings at that most sophisticated and private of Bar-Selehm clubs, Elitus. They are all in it together.*"

"I thought the ambassador was going back home?" I asked, snatching up the paper.

Willinghouse shook his head.

"Changed his mind," he said. "Matters demanding his attention, according to the Foreign Office. I don't know what, but they weren't very happy about it. Maybe the mysterious slowing of the Grappoli advance in the north."

"Why didn't you tell me?" I demanded.

"Does it matter?"

"Well, now we can arrest and question him," I said.

"No, we can't," said Andrews. The next two words came out of his mouth at the same time Willinghouse said them: "Diplomatic immunity."

Another inversion of how things ought to be.

I slammed my fist onto Willinghouse's elegant coffee table so that the untouched tea set that had been brought to us rattled alarmingly.

"There's no link to Montresat," said Willinghouse. "I don't like the man, but I find it hard to believe he would knowingly manufacture weapons for the Grappoli."

"Maybe it's not him," I said. "Maybe it's someone else who works in metal production and has a known liking for the Grappoli."

Andrews gave me a quizzical look, but Willinghouse's face lit up with a feverish inner glow.

"You mean," he said, "*Richter*?"

"He could do it," I said. "No one produces more steel than he does. If the plans were sufficiently exact, he could build a prototype. He's working on something he calls Firebrand."

"Which is what?" asked Andrews.

"I don't know," I said. "It may be connected to some metal box structures he's producing for Montresat."

"How do you know this?" began Andrews, but he caught himself. "No, don't tell me. I don't want to know."

"Oh, please let it be Richter," muttered Willinghouse in a kind of dark ecstasy that drew Andrews's amazed stare.

"But even if we can tie Montresat—or Richter—to Markeson's

smuggling, that still leaves Horritch and his fabric," said Andrews. "What's the connection?"

"Maybe he's a separate issue," I said.

"Or a coincidence?" said Willinghouse.

"I dislike coincidence," said Andrews.

I nodded in assent, but said, "I don't see how cloth can be part of it. What could a textile factory be making that would be worth all this subterfuge?"

I thought of Agatha Markeson's shawl that had first been given to the family governess.

"Speak to Violet Farthingale," I said to Andrews, getting to my feet. "She will be able to identify the body of Darius as Ephraim Sandringham."

"What are you going to do?" asked Willinghouse.

"Something else you don't want to know about," I said.

CHAPTER

31

THE GRAPPOLI EMBASSY LOOKED out upon Szenga Square from treelined Fullerton Lane, the heart of Fulwood and, outside the Government and Finance Districts, one of the most expensive pieces of real estate in the city. The embassy was faced with white marble, and its portico boasted fluted, gilded columns. It was set back from the street and surrounded by iron railings whose ornate leaf pattern almost concealed their sharpness. Guarding the gates were soldiers in emerald green tunics and pith helmets trimmed with long, golden feathers that might have come from the tail of a king pheasant. There was nothing ornamental about their rifles, however, and it was said that the pair of decorative field cannon that flanked the entrance were kept loaded. It was, after all, only a few months since there had been rioting in front of this very building as Bar-Selehm had braced itself for a war with the Grappoli that had been narrowly averted.

Again.

We always seemed to be close to a war footing with the Grappoli, and whatever personal and business intimacies the current ambassador had built with his Elitus friends, I had to assume that security would be extremely tight. I had spent an hour watching the building from a series of accessible vantages, but I had another set of eyes rather closer to my target. Sureyna was camped out as close to the building as the soldiers would permit, and peppered anyone who approached with questions: nothing difficult or political that would have gotten her moved on. Just fluff for the society pages. She was brushed off twice by visiting dignitaries before some dry-looking secretary came out to give her the tidbits it would take to get her off their property with the least trouble.

The Grappoli had no desire to cause upset where it could be avoided.

Ten minutes later, she joined me on the roof of the Harrison Art Gallery, her paper-stuffed reticule clasped firmly in both hands, though she kept a safe distance from the edge.

"He's taking tea at home this afternoon," she said. "Entertaining."

"Good," I said. "Servants? Body guards?"

"Minimal," she said. "Most have been given the day off."

"Meaning he wants his privacy," I said. "Better still. I think I smell the heady perfume of Lady Alice Welborne."

"Will you be swanning in as Lady Ki Misrai?"

"I don't know whether that identity is still secure," I said. "Either way, it wouldn't get me in. I plan to take a more direct approach."

Sureyna winced playfully, then caught herself. She looked into my face and what she saw clearly worried her.

"This is personal for you," she said.

"For lots of reasons," I said.

"Like what?"

I didn't know how to answer that. I wasn't a refugee and never had been one, so perhaps my sympathy for their plight should have been distant and intellectual. It wasn't. My own separation from where I grew up, my sense of unbelonging, the drifting unmoored feeling I had felt in my gut like a knot or a stone ever since the rice festival dream all weighed on me.

We are the lost, I thought, *the discarded, the not quite human. We are the rejected, the unwanted, the detritus of other people's comfort and profit.*

Richter's speeches and Namud's death had made this feeling hot, angry, though I didn't know how to say any of that to Sureyna. I shook my head, eyes lowered.

"What are you going to do?" she asked.

"That depends on the ambassador," I said.

SUREYNA WAS THE DIVERSION. She went back to the front door with more questions ten minutes after Lady Alice had pulled up in her coach, and while she did that, I jumped the wall at the back and shinned up the downspout on the one corner the rear guard couldn't see. I pulled myself over the balcony and took a sink plunger and a glass cutter—a simple metal thing with a diamond tip that I used to use for scoring tile—from my satchel. I squatted at the window and spat on the plunger's rubber head before pressing it onto the glass. Pushing the diamond point of the glass cutter against the pane with one hand while I held the plunger with the other, I traced a circle around it, over and over, biting deeper with each revolution. At last I felt the glass snap, and I lifted the circle out with the plunger, leaving a hole broad enough to reach through and unlatch the window from within.

I had chosen the third story because I expected security to be tighter downstairs. Now I slipped inside and kept very still, listening. I was, I realized, behaving like a cat burglar, and the memory of Darius, the gentleman thief who had befriended Constance Horritch and who crept around in people's bedrooms as they slept, came unsettlingly to mind.

Technically speaking, I was in Grappoli territory, so while I was armed, I knew that attempting to deal with the embassy's guards would likely get me killed. Whether it was on the spot or at the end of a rope a week later didn't make much difference. I was going to have to be careful.

As I took in the well-appointed bedchamber, I heard shouts from the street, and for a second, I thought I had been seen. I dropped out of sight, listening but unable to see whoever had been yelling. The voice came again, two brief shouts suddenly cut off, and though I could not catch the words, I thought I knew the voice.

Sureyna.

She had been caught, or—and this seemed more likely—she was trying to warn me, to put me on my guard, and that could mean only one thing. Someone had arrived. Someone I had not been expecting had come to the front door of the embassy.

Who?

Her voice had been shrill with more than panic. It had been angry, and I knew only one person who may have come to see the ambassador who would incite that kind of rage in Sureyna. I thought of the way she had looked when I had left her, the reticule clasped tightly in her arms and in it, almost certainly, the Heritage party's pamphlet on *The Dilemma of the White Man.*

Know your enemy, she had said.

Richter was here. He had to be. Fear only kindled the fire in my own breast, like the terrible heart of his famous converter. I reached for the pistol in my satchel and checked its chamber. Crossing the room swiftly, I cracked the door, listened, then stepped out into the hallway. Suddenly, terribly, I realized why I had asked for the gun in the first place.

Voices below.

I moved carefully to the stairwell, conscious now of the Grappoli ambassador's rich, fluid tones on the floor below me, then there was the opening and closing of a door, and the voices became muffled. I looked down the stairs, saw no one, descended lightly, found the door they had gone through, and pressed my ear against it.

At first there was only muttering, low and indistinct, so that no matter how hard I focused, I could not catch the words, but then the ambassador's voice cut in sharper and louder, and it was so clear I almost recoiled.

"Again?" he barked. "How can it have failed?"

"I cannot say, my lord." Richter's voice. My fists balled till the nails bit into my palms.

"Then find out! Make another."

"There is no point in making another, my lord. The flaw is in the design."

"Nonsense. It works," the ambassador shot back. "We know it works. You must not have built it correctly."

"The parts were made with the greatest exactitude," he said. "I oversaw the boring of the barrel myself. Everything fit together precisely, just as the first prototype did. The weapon simply does not work."

"Then how do you explain the death of Grappoli soldiers at the hands of men armed with exactly such a weapon?"

It took a second for the impact of this demand to hit me. Grappoli soldiers were being killed by the machine gun Richter was trying to build? The Firebrand was being used *against* them? How was that possible? Who could be using it? I could not guess, though I wondered if this was an explanation for the mysterious slowing of the Grappoli advance.

"I cannot explain it, my lord," said Richter, "but I assure you—"

"What do you mean it doesn't work? In exactly what way does it not work?"

"It jams, my lord, just as the other did," said Richter.

"Then the measurements are wrong."

"No," said Richter, more forcefully now. "The measurements are precisely as indicated in the plans, and the problem is not that the bullet won't fit in the chamber or go through the barrel. The first shot is fine. But there is no second shot. It misfeeds every time. The problem is not the steel or the workmanship. It must be the design."

"How many times do I have to tell you that our generals have seen the weapon in enemy hands and in action?" bellowed the ambassador. "It works!"

"The belt snags or shreds no matter what we make it out of," Richter protested. "We've tried canvas, cotton, leather, even silk. They either tear away from the bullets, or they pucker and jam the mechanism."

The belt?

I thought of the strap we had recovered from Horritch's factory with its little pockets each just large enough to hold a pencil.

Or a cartridge.

There it was. Another tumbler of the lock turned over in my head.

The Firebrand had replaced the older machine gun's hopper loading mechanism with a fabric belt into which the bullet cartridges were inserted, but the belt only worked if it was made of Bar-Selehm silk. I thought of the awful guns I had seen shredding muscle and bone all those months ago in the dockside warehouse the night Tanish had been hurt, and I thought of this new weapon, spewing bullets at twice the speed or more. For a moment I was so overcome with the sheer fact of the thing that I heard nothing as the theater in my head played out the whole awful truth of the weapon and how it worked.

"Either way," Richter continued, "it does not work, and I would advise you that I have some expertise in mechanical engineering, expertise which you—for all your titles and flunkies—do not have, so kindly stop questioning my judgment and workmanship!"

"How dare you!" exclaimed a new voice. A woman.

Alice.

"My dear," said the ambassador, "I pray do not concern yourself."

"He insulted you!" Alice riposted.

"Go upstairs!" snapped the ambassador. "Wait for me there, and don't presume to meddle in things you do not understand."

This time I did recoil. I leapt for the stairs and was halfway up when I heard the door snap open.

"Constance is right," Lady Alice spat. "You don't take women seriously."

She slammed the door and stomped toward the stairs as I vaulted the top, turned the corner, and opened the bedroom door as quietly as my haste would let me. I made for the bay window through which I had come and turned into the long and heavy curtain, my heart thumping.

I was barely in place before the door opened again and Alice barged in. As she threw herself onto the bed, sobbing, I kept very still, shielding the broken window with my body lest she discern the draft and come over to investigate. The curtains were long and heavy. Enough to keep me concealed unless someone attempted to draw them closed.

As her weeping subsided, I heard Alice light the oil lamp by the bed. I heard the argument below rumbling confusedly through the floor. I heard the slam of the door on the lower floor and footsteps on the stairs. I heard the bedroom door open and the ambassador enter.

"I hate you," snapped Alice.

"My dear—"

"I defended you, and you treated me like a fool. You always do."

"That's not true," he said. He was trying to soothe her, but he remained angry about Richter. "Let's not talk about it anymore."

"No," I said, unfurling the curtain and stepping into the half-light, my pistol extended. "Let's talk about it some more."

"Who in God's name are you?" snapped the ambassador, peering at me. I had the window behind me and my face wrapped as before, and was confident they would glimpse nothing of Lady Misrai in me. He took a half step toward the door, and I snapped back the hammer of the pistol. In the silence, it resonated like a bell. The ambassador became very still. Alice was sitting wide-eyed on the bed like a discarded doll, her hands clasped girlishly in front of her chest.

"What do you want?" asked the ambassador. He was calculating. I could hear it in his voice.

"From you?" I said. "Nothing. But I would like to ask Lady Alice a question."

"What nonsense is this?" spat the ambassador.

"Sit down and be quiet," I said.

Reluctantly, his eyes on the muzzle of my gun, he did so, perching on the edge of the bed.

"You wanted to ask me something?" Alice said in a breathy whisper that contained an edge of excitement.

"Two things," I said. "First, who is Georgie May?"

Alice's thrill died immediately. She looked confused and disappointed.

"Never heard of her," she said.

"Ambassador?" I prompted.

He shook his head too, his eyes blank.

"What else did you want to know?" asked Alice, determined to contribute something to the air of mystery and intrigue she apparently saw in me.

"Why did you say that the body of the man they called Darius was Karl Gillies, sign writer from Hastingford?"

Alice took a breath, and all the curious glee drained from her face.

"What?" sputtered the ambassador again. "She didn't!"

"She did," I said. "Didn't you, Alice?"

The woman said nothing. She was close enough to the thin glow of the lamp that I could see the fearful calculation in her face.

"Alice?" prompted the ambassador. "What is she talking about?"

I believed him instantly. Whatever Alice had done, he did not know about it. As the silence unfurled like smoke from the lamp, I said, "She gave her name as Leticia Jones, the dead man's fiancée. Isn't that right, Alice?"

The woman still said nothing.

"I don't understand," said the ambassador. "What did you do?"

"I had to," she said, turning to him suddenly. "To protect you. So no one would know about . . . you and that awful man."

"Don't say another word," said the ambassador, panic overwhelming his confusion. "I don't know who this person is—"

"It doesn't matter who I am," I said. "What matters is why Lady Alice did what she did, because I do not believe it was her idea."

Another shocked look from the ambassador. He turned to Alice with horror.

"My God," he whispered. "Who did you tell?"

Alice looked away, and in that instant, all the ambassador's studied composure left him.

"You stupid girl!" he shouted, seizing her by the shoulders. "Who did you tell?"

But I already knew.

"Let go of her," I said. "Now."

He released her, and she shrank away. As he buried his face in his hands, she began gathering her things in silence. By the time I heard her close the door behind her, I was already out of the window and making my way down to the street.

CHAPTER

32

SUREYNA WAS WAITING FOR me at the corner. She was not alone. Tanish was with her and, trailing shyly, adoringly behind him, was Aab.

"You're all right," said Sureyna, relieved. I nodded, and something in my face got her attention.

"I found your missing railroad car, Ang," said Tanish, proudly.

"I knew you would," I said.

"It's owned by a company called Montresat," he added.

"But you already know," said Sureyna. "Don't you?"

"Most of it," I said. "I need one question answered and then . . ." I hesitated. "Then we finish this."

Again Sureyna studied my face and drew her own somber conclusions.

IT TOOK ME TWENTY minutes to find the house in Morgessa, which I had visited only once before, and it would have taken much longer than that if I hadn't used the underground, much to Aab's speechless delight. She had taken to practicing her sign language with her fingers and hands whether the people around her could understand her or not. Tanish had learned a few words, and they played games, ignored by the other passengers, while I thought it all through and Sureyna scribbled feverishly in her notepad. Once she looked up, considered the others, and said, "I hope you have other reinforcements in mind. The four of us give new meaning to the term 'irregulars.'"

I gave her a bleak smile but didn't say anything. I was hoping there wouldn't be any need for force, not from us, anyway. If there was, we'd lose, even with a dozen armed policemen to back us up.

TSANWE EMTEZU OPENED THE door himself. He had shed his dragoon's tunic, but was still wearing his uniform trousers. He was surprised to see me, doubly so when, having stepped aside to invite us in, I shook my head.

"I can't stay," I said. "I just have one question."

"What's that, Miss Sutonga?" he said, stately and calm, so that Aab, reverting to her pre-Bertha self, took shelter behind Tanish, peering up at the soldier warily.

"That morning you went to meet Clara after her interview," I said, "you were in uniform. Had you just come off duty?"

"Yes," he said, thinking back. "Why?"

"Am I right in thinking that you had been ordered to cordon off a burned-out building?"

"Yes," he said, more than a little amazed. "How did you know that?"

"You had ash on your boots," I said. "But not your trousers, which I assume means you didn't actually go into the site."

"That's right," he said. "We were just to secure the perimeter as a matter of public safety. Didn't want people wandering in and falling through burned-out floors or anything. What is this about?"

"Who gave that order?" I asked.

"It came through the usual chain of command," he said, cautious now. "I was under the impression that it came from the War Office itself, though I believe the message was initiated by the cabinet secretary."

"Abel Rathbone."

"Yes," he said, confused and a little anxious. "Is that not correct?"

"Yes," I said. "I think it is correct."

"It seems that this is not good news," he said, considering my face. I managed a half smile and shook my head.

"Thank you for your help," I said. "Oh. One last thing. Does the name Georgie May mean anything to you?"

He smiled suddenly.

"A friend of mine is a marine," he said, "so yes. Georgie May is the slightly disrespectful name for what the rest of us call the *Georgiana Maria*, a heavy steam clipper, named after the late empress consort. She's a trader with a small military complement."

Of course she is.

"Thank you," I said again.

He watched me in the doorway, and for a moment I wanted to beg him to come with me, but I had put his career in jeopardy before, and I would not do so again, whatever the peril. I walked away feeling at least that I had done him a kindness, even if it was one he would never know to thank me for.

"You're going to the docks," Sureyna said.

"I'm going to the docks," I agreed, not looking at her.

"The oceanfront, right? Not the river," she said. "A heavy clipper needs more depth. Do you know exactly where?"

"No, but it's a large freighter. Shouldn't be hard to find. I believe she sails at midnight."

"I'm coming with you," said Sureyna.

"No," I said, turning abruptly to her. "Go to Willinghouse. Tell him where I've gone. Have him meet me there in an hour and a half. Tanish, take Aab and go with Sureyna."

"What?" said Tanish. "Not a chance. I'm coming with you."

I squeezed my eyes shut. I did not have time for this.

"No," I said. "It's too dangerous. You go with Sureyna. And look after Aab, you hear me?"

The fierceness in my face drove all the swagger from him, and he managed only a nod.

"Tell Inspector Andrews too," I said, "though I suspect he may already have been summoned."

"What?" said Sureyna. "Who by?"

I scowled, and a great dread knotted around my stomach like the chain of a huge anchor so that the last thing I wanted to do was keep walking forward.

"Richter," I said.

THE OCEANFRONT DOCKS NEVER really slept, but by the time I got down there, it would be about as quiet as it was likely to get. I crossed the river on the catwalk of the unfinished suspension bridge, past the work camp there, and pushed steadily southeast, making for Blackstairs, walking briskly, eyes scouring the darkness ahead. I could cut through the alleys of the Warehouse District or work my way along the riverbank itself all the way to the sea, but both routes were dangerous after dark, and I did not know the docklands skyline well enough to trust to my skills as a climber. I followed the railroad tracks south, then cut east to the docks proper at Stallings Junction, watching every shadow, listening for every paw or footstep, and I reached the deepwater jetties of the oceanfront with a swelling sense of alarm.

There were half a dozen ships moored at the harborside, but only one was a bustle of activity in the dark. It was a massive vessel, iron-hulled and three-masted, with a pair of great slanted chimneys set fore and aft of an engine room which, in the absence of visible paddle-wheels, had to drive screw propellers below the waterline. I climbed the ladder to the roof of the closest warehouse, whose huge front doors opened onto the harborside, and watched with my spyglass. By the light of four oil lamps suspended from spars, a half dozen dragoons with rifles were overseeing the loading of the ship: crates with rope handles carried by pairs of soldiers up a gangplank and taken to a hold belowdecks, while three much larger crates were being loaded by steam crane from a train of flatcars on a track that ran to the very brink of the quayside. Among the flatcars were a pair of open goods wagons covered with tarpaulin and a familiar container wagon marked with a stenciled yellow *M*.

The refugees.

If they were still in there, then they were to be shipped back where they had come from. I watched the crane move the last of the three large crates out over the water and onto the deck where it was chained in place. I'd recognized those crates before I spotted the lightning-fist brand. These were the strange metal superstructure and turrets I had seen at Richter's factory. They were coming from Montresat's works, which meant that they had been fitted to whatever had been waiting for them. The letters painted on the sides said TRACTOR PARTS.

I remembered the yellow steam tractors that had bulldozed the remnants of Horritch's factory—and the people who had died in it—into the river and recalled Sureyna saying something about Montresat's nonmilitary merchandise.

He has another factory that builds agricultural machinery, but unless we plan on defeating our enemies by riding over them with steam tractors, I suspect that's a blind alley. . . .

It wasn't a blind alley. I pictured those hulking, steam-driven bulldozers overlaid with the armored shell made at Richter's foundry, and in my head I added a Firebrand machine gun to the front of each turret. The hair on the back of my neck rose, and a chill stole through my limbs in spite of the warm night. A terrible new weapon was being loaded onto that ship, a kind of mobile, bullet-spitting fortress, unstoppable by anything but the most powerful artillery.

Watching the work were three men and a woman: Thomas Markeson, who provided the ship; Eustace Montresat, who provided the tractor and the machine guns; Nathan Horritch, who provided the fabric belts for those guns; and his enigmatic daughter, Constance, who provided . . . what? The inspiration? A cool head for business and secrecy? It was surely Constance who had manipulated silly Alice Welborne into diverting police attention away from Elitus as well as providing an open ear for whatever the Grappoli ambassador and his Heritage friends might be planning.

Because that much was clear. I had mistakenly assumed that everything that had happened had been a single plot orchestrated by a prime villain—the theft of the plans; the deaths of Darius and Agatha Markeson; the moving, hiding and, ultimately, sacrificing of dozens of refugees; the far-right maneuvering on behalf of their racial allies, the Grappoli . . . all of it orchestrated by a single leader or organization. But it wasn't. There were, I thought, three separate crimes that were related only tangentially, through overlap at a fashionable city club.

Some of the details were still coming into focus in my head, but I was pretty sure now that I had a solid grasp on the main facts. One of the most important was right in front of me in the form of that great hulk of a ship, looming out of the evening fog that sat on the bay like a faded fur mantle. The *Georgie May* might be bound for Belrand, but those armed tractors would be dropped off en route, not to serve the Grappoli but to fight them. Some of the machine guns were already in the hands of the northern tribes or the drug cartels who were doing the bulk of that fighting, much to the ambassador's chagrin. That was why the Grappoli advance had slowed drastically over the last week or so. Where they had previously met resistance only in the form of spears and hide-covered shields, the Grappoli's imperial forces suddenly found themselves up against state-of-the-art weaponry supplied secretly, and in violation of the nonintervention treaty, by Bar-Selehm.

I had wanted to know the truth, but now that I had it, I wasn't sure what to do with it. Indeed, even though I had alerted Willinghouse and Andrews, a part of me wanted to see the ship leave now before it could be stopped, to complete its journey and deploy its illegal cargo to stop the further extermination of the northern tribes by the Grappoli's colonial war machine.

But only a part of me. Because I also knew what was in the hopper car. The refugees had been shuttled back and forth in their misery and despair, from a war zone to a cramped and brutal factory to do the work no one in the city could know about. Had Constance known and condoned that particular horror in the name of a greater good? I wanted to believe she had not, though I didn't know what difference that would make. For all the tension and anxiety I had been feeling, the dread of what would happen next, I found what I felt most deeply in this moment was a drab and weary sadness.

The jib of the steam crane swung back to the railway siding, and one of the black longshoreman clambered onto the roof of the container car and stood there like a statue or a beacon, one hand upraised as the crane's hook wound down toward him. He took it and began securing the cable harness that would lift the container off its truck bed.

It was dark on the quayside, and the gas lamps were too far apart to make much impression on the night smog, creating smudged patches of yellowish gray among the shadows, so it took me a moment to realize that the laborer on the train car was not alone. A small brown figure was clinging to the side of the wagon, just out of his line of sight, balancing on tiptoes on a latch at the back, tiny hands gripping the bars which had been welded over one of the makeshift ventilation slots.

It was Aab.

The deaf girl had followed me. Too intent on where I had been going, and too caught up in the confused implications of everything that had happened, I had not noticed her, and now she would be caught, thrown in with the refugees, perhaps. Or worse. I looked desperately around but saw no sign of Tanish. Had she given him the slip, or was he here too, hiding in the shadows? I got to my feet, dimly aware of the way she was twittering with her fingers at whoever could see her inside the train car, and ran back to the ladder.

Heart throbbing, I slid down to the ground and rounded the cor-

ner of the warehouse at an incautious dash. Under the thin glow of
the gas lamp, I could see Aab, now squatting on the roof itself, gesturing repeatedly to the longshoreman who stood frozen in his task,
staring at her. As I got closer—no more than fifty yards from the rail
car now, but still hidden by the darkness that pooled around the warehouse—he hesitated, glanced around him, then stooped to the roof
of the container. I was close enough to hear the creak of the panel as
he unlatched and opened it. For a moment, he gazed down into the
metal box, one hand over his mouth, just as I had done when I had
stumbled upon them in Markeson's barge. In that instant, I realized
that he had not known what he was loading onto the *Georgie May*.

He came up shouting in some Mahweni dialect, and others came
flocking to the car, leaping up to the vents to look in, and then turning angrily on the huddle of white overseers.

"*Machinery!*" yelled one in a bold, accusatory voice. "You said we
were loading machinery. This vessel is not licensed for passengers.
Your paperwork is void!"

His fury came from something far deeper than irritation over a
bureaucratic technicality.

"That's not your concern," said Markeson imperiously.

"The hell it isn't!" the longshoreman roared back. He threw down
the long-handled wrench he had been holding, and it clanged on the
dockside like a bell.

"Passengers?" said Constance. "What does he mean?"

So she didn't know.

I felt it like relief, though I knew it would not help.

"None of your concern, my dear," said Horritch. "Migrants. Illegals. They have to go back now."

"Migrants?" she repeated, incredulous. "You were going to ship
refugees back to that war zone? Where did they come from?"

"It doesn't matter," her father said.

"What?" she gasped. "How long have they been here?"

"Who do you think did the work?" Horritch demanded, all paternal care for her evaporating as he turned on her. "Citizens couldn't do it. Who knows who they would have told! This way we keep our costs down and serve the city in multiple ways. Several birds, one stone."

"You *knew*?" she asked, still struggling to catch up to what he was saying. "All along, you knew? What about when the factory burned?"

"Casualties of war," said Montresat.

She put her hands to her mouth as if she might throw up.

"I helped you," she said, appalled. "I covered for you, spied for you, because I thought you were *helping* the refugees, equipping them against the Grappoli, but all the while you were no better than the monsters we were fighting against."

"Nonsense," said her father. "This was never about the Quundu or the other tribes. We were fighting the Grappoli on behalf of the city."

But Constance was picking up her skirts and running down the gangplank to the train car. She found the main hatch padlocked and turned back to the ship, bellowing, "Open this at once!"

Markeson spoke up, nodding to one of the remaining soldiers, who was uneasily watching the longshoremen, his rifle gripped tightly in his hands. "Move her off," said the big man I had last seen at his wife's funeral, "and have those men complete their orders."

As the dragoon moved warily down the gangplank, Horritch turned on the shipping magnate.

"Leave her out of this, Markeson!" he snapped.

"We should have. All the way out," Markeson replied.

Constance, meanwhile, had snatched up the longshoreman's wrench and was now hammering the padlock wildly. The lock snapped and fell, but before she could get the hatch open, the soldier had jabbed her in the midriff with the butt of his rifle and she sank to the concrete of the dockside, wheezing. Her father shouted his outrage, but the soldier was too mindful of the longshoremen—at least half a dozen of them—who were looking mutinous. They were picking up what had been tools—boat hooks, crowbars, spanners—but were now weapons. Aab had dropped to the ground and was watching fearfully as the tension thickened like the smog, promising violence.

Moments before, I had been half hoping the ship would set sail before the police arrived, but now I would have given anything to have Andrews and a squad of constables with me. The ship had to go, but it had to leave the refugees here, and it had to do so without costing any more lives.

I stepped out into what passed for light on the quayside, unsure of what I was going to do beyond getting Aab out, but before I could make myself known to the deaf girl, I became aware of running feet and raised voices.

The police!

I turned, and for a second or less, I thought my wish had been granted. But then I realized that the uniforms were wrong. The alley behind me was full of grim-looking men in gray with red armbands, several of them armed with pistols and shotguns. At their head were Richter and Barrington-Smythe. The former slowed to a cockerel strut, strode past the longshoremen as if he hadn't seen them, and pointed a long, pale finger at Markeson and the others.

"Citizen's arrest!" he proclaimed. "Take those men into custody on charges of treason against the laws and ordinances of Bar-Selehm."

CHAPTER

33

THE HERITAGE MEN MOVED with cool efficiency, their black boots almost in lockstep as they strode up the gangplank and laid hands on Montresat, Horritch, and Markeson. "You'll hang for this," said Richter, smiling, "and so will anyone at the War Office who has turned a blind eye to your treachery."

"How dare you!" barked Horritch. "You jumped-up little nobody. We are patriots, not traitors."

"You're the worst kind of traitor," Richter shot back, distaste showing through his glee. "You're *blood* traitors. Race traitors. But for once in this city of appeasement, you'll swing for it. When that happens, when the newspapers tell your story, the way you've supplied savages with weapons they are barely intelligent enough to operate against your white brothers—"

"Against the Grappoli!" exclaimed Montresat. "The city's oldest and most recalcitrant enemy!"

"Your *white* brothers," repeated Richter, unmoved. "When the people hear what you have done in violation of your own laws and treaties, your party will crumble, your government will collapse, and Heritage will take its rightful place in the ruling of Bar-Selehm."

The longshoremen looked cowed and desperate, as if Richter was about to begin his rule at once, and they had no more than a few moments to stop that from happening. I realized with horror that they would attack him, and that in the process, they would be cut down. As if to make the point even sharper and more terrible, I heard the splintering crack of one of the great tractor crates, and looked over to see where Barrington-Smythe had levered open the front panel, revealing the dreadful machine inside.

It was just as I had imagined it, an armored monster with great tracks around its wheels and a turret from which sprouted the sleek new barrel of one of Montresat's belt-fed machine guns. Barrington-Smythe gave his bland, terrifying smile, climbed onto the steel shell Richter's company had unwittingly built, and threw open the turret's side hatch. He assessed the interior quickly, then clambered inside and opened another hatch in the top, sticking his head up so that he could look along the barrel of the gun as he slewed the turret round experimentally.

"My work," said Richter, more obviously angry now. "Steel made at *my* plant turned into a weapon to be used against my white Grappoli brothers. Did you think I would never learn what you had done with it? It's an abomination." He seemed to think for a moment, and something of his reptilian calm returned. "But I am curious to see it in operation, and there are so many low-value targets on hand whose loss might be easily explained away as having occurred in the chaos of the moment."

He looked at Barrington-Smythe, and the blond man adjusted the weapon of the armored tractor so that it pointed directly at the container car packed full of refugees. The longshoremen dropped back, spreading out, their eyes locked onto Barrington-Smythe with horror. Several of them dropped their tools and raised their hands, though I doubted that would make any difference. Even the handful of dragoons looked uncertain whose side they were on or what version of the law they were supposed to enforce.

"You think we don't know that it was you and your Heritage goons who stole the plans for that gun?" demanded Montresat. He was trying to sound outraged, but there was a wheedling, anxious tone in his voice, and I knew he was scared and stalling for time, as if he knew what Richter's men were capable of. "You were going to build it and sell it to the Grappoli."

"You can't prove that," sneered Richter, "and if you attempt to try me in the court of public opinion, I will emerge a national hero."

"Not to everyone," said Constance.

Richter looked at her as if noticing a fly that had drifted into his living room.

"Everyone?" he said. "Since when did everyone matter? You people are all alike. No common sense, and no real principles or strength of character. I'll be a hero to the right people, and this is, let me remind you, an election year."

I didn't see the other ship till it was pulling alongside the *Georgie May,* and only saw it then because it unmasked a luxorite lamp with a mirrored lens that sliced through the fog and flooded the quayside with sudden light. It must have cut its engines some way out and coasted silently in.

"Put down your weapons!" The voice was round and echoing, as if it had come through a bullhorn, distant but somehow full at the same time. Andrews? It might have been. I couldn't be sure, but I felt relief wash over me.

Thank the gods. We will live out the night. All of us.

"Stand where you are and raise your hands," said the voice again. "This is the Bar-Selehm coast guard, and I say again, put down your weapons."

The unexpected appearance of the boat looming out of the fog cast a strange spell over the docks, paralyzing everyone. Then Barrington-Smythe called down to Richter.

"Don't listen to them!" he said. "Coast guard. War Office. Government agencies. The National party and their industry cronies. Collaborators in the great race war! They are all in it together. We stand guard over the evidence here or we go down fighting."

For the first time, Richter looked uncertain, even a little afraid, and I wondered with a surge of panic just how much of a hold he had over his primary attack dog. I remembered the night Darius had died, when Barrington-Smythe had come after me with his little pickax, glad of the chance to use it, and all the relief I had felt burned off like river mist under a hot sun. Richter shook his head.

"Lay down your arms," he said. "We have the evidence we need."

But I heard the whirring of a hand crank, saw the turret on the armored tractor turning in its crate.

"Purify!" yelled Barrington-Smythe.

The gun came to life in a blare of light and noise that cut the timber to ribbons as it rotated to face the coast guard vessel.

CHAPTER
34

THE CHAOS WAS INSTANTANEOUS. I couldn't see what was happening on the coast guard cutter, but around me people dropped to the ground or scuttled crablike for cover. Men grabbed weapons or flung them down and ran, and then came the whir and screech of bullets in the air as the coast guard returned fire. Amidst the noise and thickening smoke of the battle, I saw Constance wrenching at the hatch of the container truck, and I loped over to her, wresting the door open, so that its frightened, desperate contents spilled out. They ran too, and in the confusion, I turned to Constance and, for the first time, I saw the light of realization in her eyes.

"Lady Misrai!" she gasped.

It was absurd, and now, with gunfire careening off metal and stone and concrete, I would not waste an ounce of strength on pretense. Before I could say anything, I saw something in her face, a hazy desperation, like one transported into a nightmare.

Or a memory.

"It wasn't me," she gasped. "I told him to take it off his stupid wife, but I didn't know . . ."

She hesitated, and in that instant seemed to come back to herself, to this place and the real danger of gunfire all around us, and she was stricken with a new horror at what she had told me.

"Go," I said. "Take the children and go."

I seized the thin wrist of Aab as she blundered past and slapped it into Constance's hand.

Constance ran as best she could, hunched over, her long skirts trailing in the oil and coal dust, arms spread wide, herding the children back toward the warehouses.

The Heritage men had turned their weapons on the coast guard, Richter behind them, drawing an ornate pistol from its holster. I hit him from behind, barreling into him, and bringing the butt of my own gun down hard across the back of his head. He landed face-first on the concrete, but any satisfaction that might have given me dissolved when two of his uniformed thugs rounded on me. One raised a shotgun, but just as he was about to shoot, one of the longshoremen leapt on him, brandishing a length of pipe.

I scrambled to my feet, but shrank down again as the night was torn apart by the blast of the coast guard's cannon. The remains of the crate around the armored tractor shattered in a hale of splinters and the tractor itself rocked free of its mooring, kicked sideways by the blast, even as its machine gun continued to fire its deadly stream of bullets. It tipped from the reinforced cargo platform, off balance and sliding under its own weight, so that for a moment, its weapon spewed fire wildly up into the furled sails and rigging, and then it was teetering on the very edge of the deck. Barrington-Smythe fought to get the machine gun under control and retargeted, but a second cannon blast slammed into the armored hulk, and it slewed over the stern, smashing the wooden rail. The *Georgie May* seemed to buckle slightly as part of its decking gave way, and then the armored tractor was turning inexorably over and down into the gap between ship and dock. Barrington-Smythe leapt free as it fell, but with a great turbid splash the deadly vehicle vanished under the black water.

Barrington-Smythe landed on the dockside, knocking one of the rattled dragoons off his feet in the process, and came up running, laying about him with that miniature pick to clear the way. I didn't know if he was just trying to escape or if he was looking to do some more spiteful and murderous mischief, but he went in the same direction as Constance and the children, so I went after him.

In a handful of strides, we had left the lights of the harbor behind and were lost in the sour-smelling darkness of the warehouse alleys, where jerry-rigged rooflines, gables, elevator towers, and crane booms loomed jagged and erratic out of the night fog. Sound bounced hard off the brick walls but came wreathed and matted in smoke and river mist, so the footfalls I was trailing seemed like things heard underwater, soft but percussive, close and far way all at the same time. What little moonlight had softened the blackness at the harborside vanished utterly here, and I slowed against my will, hands outstretched, conscious of the worn irregularity of the cobbles under my boots. I turned left at the corner, listening hard, then right at the next, but I knew I was losing him, losing myself in the process.

Catching the pearly glow of gaslight filtering around another corner, I made for it, pistol out in front of me like a talisman against the darkness. My sense of space had shrunk in on itself like a frightened rabbit, and I longed to be up on the roofs and gantries four stories above me. I glanced up, my eyes sucking in the merest hint of light like lips drawing in air, and as I did so, I thought I caught the black flash of movement, as if something or someone had leapt over the ginnel from one roof to another.

A fishing bat? Perhaps. Some of them were very large when their wings were spread.

My feet slowed still further, and that was bad. The children would be lost, or Barrington-Smythe would catch up to them, which would be worse.

Unless that had been him above me? He had shown uncanny composure the first night we met, as if the possibility of falling had simply never occurred to him. At the time, I had assumed that meant he was an expert climber, but now I wondered if he just thought himself special, untouchable—and not merely because he had skills. He was the right hand of an anointed people, an angel of death, beyond the reach of those ordinary mortals he thought refuse, detritus to be burnt and purged away . . .

"You," he said, as though reading my thoughts.

The gas lamp was still fifty yards away, a thin and inefficient lantern hanging over a warehouse door. Barrington-Smythe was between me and it, so he appeared only as a shadow, a smoke-edged silhouette, and the only part of him that wasn't black was the miniature pickax, which sparkled like diamond as he held it away from his body. Like he was showing it to me. He had stepped out of an alcove in the wall where he had been waiting, and was only two long strides away.

"I know you," he said, musingly. He was quite still, and though I could not see them, I could feel his eyes burning into me, skewering me so that I could not move, a nyala under the predatory stare of a clavtar.

I stabbed the muzzle of my pistol toward his chest and fired, but he was moving before the shot went off, peeling to the right and vanishing against the blackness of the wall before he came at me. I felt the sharp tang of the pick in my forearm, and the empty gun fell heavily to the cobbles. Crying out, I turned into the fight, swinging with my left fist, only to have him block it and hug me to him, a terrible, stifling action that overpowered me and threw me off balance. I fell back, and he came with me, his full weight driving me to the ground so that I gasped in wordless agony, incapable of anything as he reached for my face and snatched the scarf roughly away.

"You!" he said again, but it was different this time. The first recognition had been about the night Darius had died: now he knew me for Lady Ki Misrai.

It didn't matter. His eyes glittered, hard as the pick in his hand, and I guessed he was smiling to himself. The pain had driven any bodily control I might have from me, but my arms and legs were pinned anyway. I could think of nothing to say, and that made no difference either. There was nothing to do but die, and not with dignity and peace. I would die full of rage and grief, hot and wholly ineffectual.

I thought of the neutral mask and found an unlikely calm, a deliberation, but I had no weapon, no strategy, no strength left.

He adjusted his position so that the lamp at the end of the alley touched him with silver light, and the pick flashed as he raised it above his head. I stared into his face, refusing to close my eyes, so I saw the sudden blackness that dropped from above before he did, saw the way it snatched at his hair, dragging his face up as if about to haul his entire body weight skyward, saw the flash of silver across his throat before the hot blood sprayed.

I rolled and scrambled away in equal parts horror and relief, thrusting myself up against the far wall of the alley as the creature held him by the head for a moment, making sure, then let him slump to the ground, lifeless as the cobbles. I cringed away, feeling desperately for the fallen pistol, and the Gargoyle turned its bald head swiftly toward me, a snarl breaking from its awful lips. Its dreadful face was gray and patchy, hollow cheeked, but its strange, deep-set eyes found mine, and with a shock of recognition, I knew her.

My sister Vestris stared at me, sucking in the night air, her eyes showing no more than a hyena might when caught on a kill, but I knew that this had been no random attack. She had been watching. Waiting.

I stared, taking in the ruin of her once remarkable beauty, and even though I knew that ruin had been my fault and that she had tried to kill me more than once, I felt no threat from her now. She looked at me, still and impassive as one of the actual gargoyles that braved the smog from the cornice of the trade exchange, and then she was folding the razor into its handle with long, bony fingers.

I tried to say her name, but my lips could produce no sound, and when I did manage to speak, I could frame only a single word.

"Why?"

My sister's strange, blank eyes flickered, and her mouth opened.

The inside was black, and when she spoke, the words were strange, furred and liquid as if she had lost most of her teeth.

"Atonement," she said.

I stared at her in bewildered horror as the word echoed through my head, casting uncertain light on another dark corner, another bleeding corpse.

Don't be too hard on her. . . .

I thought of my sister when we had fought over the stage of the opera house, when she had been wearing the neutral mask.

"You trained with Madame Nahreem," I said.

The name seemed to arrest something in her face, stilling her as she was about to flee, and for a moment, it was like she had fallen into the past and was trying to find something that had once been important. When she could see me again, her eyes were lit by that animal fierceness and instinct, so that for a second I was almost too afraid of her to realize that she had nodded.

"Why did you leave her?" I tried.

She blinked, and her mouth creased slightly, so that for the briefest of moments I could almost see my beautiful sister as she had once been, smiling her elegant, knowing smile.

"I was never good at being . . . *neutral*," she said.

"You knew Namud," I said.

The smile, if it had been there, was gone now. Looking into Vestris's ravaged face was like beholding a blasted landscape after some terrible flood had subsided. It was an island of bones. She said nothing, and I knew she would stay with me only seconds more.

"He told me that Madame Nahreem also sought atonement," I said. "What for?"

The barren sadness melted from my sister's hollow eyes, driven by a heat like the heart of a furnace when the bellows blow, white and all-consuming. It was terrible to look upon.

"Ask her," she said.

And suddenly she was away, leaping like an antelope down the alley and up the wall, sure-handedly pulling herself up on pipes and lintels and the broken irregularities that were a steeplejack's salvation. At the top she looked down to where I still lay motionless, disbelieving. Then she was gone.

CHAPTER

35

"I DON'T THINK MARKESON meant to kill his wife," I said to Inspector Andrews. "Connie told him to take the shawl from her, but—"

"Connie?" Willinghouse said sharply.

"Constance Horritch," I said. "Agatha was drawing attention to the shawl, and Connie told Markeson to take it from her. I think he was already angry with her and that they argued about Miss Farthingale. They were overheard by the servants. If I had to guess, I'd say that he snatched the shawl from her shoulders in the hallway outside my room. She was wearing new shoes with very high heels, not designed for a lady of her age: a response, perhaps, to her husband's admiration of the lovely Miss Farthingale. As he took the shawl from her, she fought back, overbalanced, broke her heel, and hit her head on the stone plinth of a floral arrangement when she fell. I smelled the blood on my fingers shortly after touching it. I think he panicked, put the body in my room because it was handy and his key opened it, and then went to join the others, taking the shawl with him. Probably burned it later. Horritch was furious, of course, thought he'd risked drawing attention to the one thing Richter and the Grappoli didn't have: the fabric that they used for the machine gun belts, without which their guns were useless."

"How much did *Connie* know?" asked Willinghouse. He was watching me carefully, as if I might be making excuses for Constance because I—or Dahria—liked her.

"Not sure," I said. "Nothing about the refugees. She thought her father and his friends were working to save the northern tribes from the Grappoli advance, rather than just trying to thwart the Grappoli by whatever means they had, and she helped them cover their tracks. I don't think it occurred to her that her principles were irrelevant to the War Office and that she was being used."

"I doubt she'll be prosecuted," said Andrews. "The courts will assume she was coerced by her father, and her attempt to help the refugees escape from Richter's gunman was noted by the coast guard."

"What about her father and the others?"

"Hard to say," said Andrews, displeased. "The War Office was operating in secret and contrary to their own laws and treaties, trying to circumvent scrutiny by relying on private contractors. The prime minister is blaming the civil service—the cabinet secretary Rathbone and his cronies in the War Office. Though it's hard to believe the higher-ups in the party didn't know what was going on, I doubt we'll be able to prove it. Rathbone will fall on his sword—a few years in prison and a fine—and he'll emerge, good little soldier for the government that he is, exonerated and with a well-paying position set aside for him. He might not even serve time if he can convince the courts that he was acting in good faith—a misunderstanding, an overextension of his authority, but not actually criminal, surely . . . ? You know how this goes. Everyone involved is already claiming that they were serving the national interest by working against the Grappoli, but there are a lot of red faces in Parliament now that the story has broken."

"I really wish you hadn't told your friend at the newspaper," Willinghouse cut in.

"I had to," I said. "She helped, and I promised her a story."

Anything rather than have her write about the Gargoyle of Bar-Selehm.

No one knew who had killed Barrington-Smythe. I think Andrews thought it was me, but he had been careful not to ask the question. The man had been a killer, and he had put two of the coast guard's cutter crew in the hospital. No one was looking too closely at who exactly had delivered his death blow in the chaos. I had said nothing about the Gargoyle, and absolutely nothing about my presumed-dead sister, Vestris. I intended to keep it that way until I had thought it all through.

"Richter will make hay out of this," said Willinghouse darkly. "He's already crowing about the government's lying to the people and supporting *savages*. We haven't heard the end of it. While I'm normally pleased to see the Nationals suffer a setback, I fear that any ground they lose will be made up by the Heritage party."

I shifted in my seat.

"What will happen to Horritch and the rest?" I asked.

"Markeson will probably be charged with manslaughter over the death of his wife," said Andrews, "assuming he confesses to a version of your account of the matter, but he'll certainly face charges for smuggling and involvement in illegal immigration. Horritch will have to answer for the deaths of the illegals in his factory, and though proving the case against him will be harder, I think we'll get him in the end. He'll serve time for it. Montresat will be charged as an accessory, but I'm not sure what else. He'll lose his government contracts, which will hurt him more than any criminal charges, since that effectively puts his munitions factories out of business. All three of them could face conspiracy charges, but I doubt they'll be convicted of treason."

"And Richter?" I asked.

"I don't think we can touch him," said Andrews. "The coast guard's evidence will say he did not fire upon them and he told Barrington-Smythe not to. His attempt at a citizen's arrest, however paramilitary, was quite legal. Since he did not actually steal the machine gun plans himself, I think the most we could charge him with is collusion, and that would be shaky. We are not, after all, actually at war with the Grappoli."

"So he'll walk free," I said, wondering—not for the first time—what we had achieved.

"His sympathies have been exposed," said Willinghouse. "He'll be watched."

I snorted derisively.

"His *sympathies,* as you call them, are the subject of every speech he makes," I said. "He shouts them from the rooftops."

"I meant his leanings toward the Grappoli," said Willinghouse.

"I know what you meant," I said, my face getting hot.

"He won't have made any friends among the nonwhites of the city," said Andrews, "but I doubt he's unduly concerned about that."

I gave him a hard look.

"But he'll gain ground with the whites?" I said.

"Not all," said Andrews, hurriedly.

"Then those people, the ones who see his hatemongering for what it is, have a responsibility to stand publicly against him, don't you think?" I said.

"Well, it's complicated, isn't it?" said Andrews. "People are afraid of alienating their neighbors, their friends and family. Being considered a kind of traitor to your own as Constance Horritch is. I think she'd testify against her own father."

"I would hope so," I said, my jaw clenched. "She should."

For a moment Andrews just looked at me, then nodded hastily.

"Well, yes," he said. "If you put it like that. Quite so."

THE REFUGEES WHO ESCAPED from the train car were mostly rounded up and relocated to the Blackstairs camp pending repatriation, but local assimilated Mahweni community leaders had launched an amnesty campaign on their behalf, which the Brevard party had taken up, arguing that they should be permitted to stay and join the local workforce. Richter spoke against the idea, of course, but the National party members who would usually block such measures had been humbled by the War Office's underhand dealings, and they did not feel, according to Willinghouse, that they could mount a suitable opposition without seeming to be hypocrites. I was visiting Rahvey's family, sitting by the river in a patch of grass that smelled of wild onions and garlic, close to, but not technically in, the Drowning when Tanish brought the news.

"Passed," he said, unable to keep the grin of his face. "Narrowly, but it passed. They get to stay."

Aab signed to the Quundu, and there was an explosion of delight and relief that began as shouts and laughter, then became dancing, and ended in silent thoughtfulness with not a few tears. I watched Rahvey bustling around with pots of goat cheese flavored with cardamom and hot peppers, listened to her cheerfully complaining about how many people there were and how the Lani could not possibly afford to keep feeding them. They were the things she always said, and they were true, but she smiled as she watched them eat.

Championed by the Brevard party, the newly approved measure—which carefully emphasized the fact that offering amnesty to those already here in no way opened the country to others who may come in the future—granted a stay of deportation and potential citizenship to upward of a hundred souls, mostly women and children. It offered no provision of housing or employment, so there were still hard times ahead, but they would be hard times here or close by, not in slavery, not clinging to sinking rafts, and not in their war-torn homeland. It affected only a few, and it was but a partial solution, but it was as close to success as I could see for the moment, and I celebrated with them.

I also successfully petitioned Willinghouse for a small increase in my stipend, so that I could pay Bertha more. Her class size had almost doubled, and she was considering reducing her shift load in the factory to spend more time teaching. They had no schoolroom per se, and continued to meet on the riverbank with a few ragged books between them and a half dozen pencils, carefully passed out and collected at the end of each class, but it was another partial victory.

There would be no total victories, not for people like them or, for that matter, people like me. Not for some time yet. But maybe one day, when the partial victories were pooled, we would find that we had done enough to make something more complete at least possible.

Was it worth the loss of Namud? I could not say, but I thought he would approve.

Mnenga took several of the children under his wing and offered to show them his village. Some—in spite of the horrors they had endured—had already fallen in love with the city and wanted to be like Bertha, reading and wearing northern clothes, and buying food from shops with money earned in the factories. Others saw in Mnenga a version of the past they had left and wanted to return to the bush, to herding and hunting and planting.

"We will see," he said. "My village has lost many young people to the city, so we have room. If we will be happy and they will be happy . . ." He shrugged and smiled. "We will see."

"I will come and visit them," I said.

"And me," he replied.

"And you."

He reached into the pouch he wore at his waist, plucked out a hide bag with a drawstring, and gave it to me. I opened it, and sorrel nuts spilled into my hands. I grinned at him.

"This is a magic bag," he said.

I gave him a quizzical look, and he smiled mischievously.

"If you keep filling it up," he said, "it will never be empty."

I nodded solemnly, then studied his face.

"Thank you," I said. "For everything."

He made a shrug and a head shake that said there was nothing to thank him for, and then we caught the strains of children singing, a high, lilting lament, sad and beautiful and strangely knowing.

We turned to follow the sound.

By the river, the pyre with its heap of flower-strewn sandals blazed. The children stood stalwart, singing good-bye, and we sat in silence watching the water flow down to the sea.

SUREYNA WAS FEELING PLEASED with herself.

"Junior reporter assigned to follow up parliamentary deliberations on the refugee crisis," she said, brandishing a note from her editor. "I'm not the lead lioness by any means, and I'll probably only get to write up the bits no one else cares about but—"

"It's a step up from cucumbers," I said.

"That it is," she said. "I had another idea too."

She fished inside her desk and pulled out a sheet of paper featuring a box of close type. It read *Lady Ki Misrai wishes to extend her thanks for the hospitality shown to her by the people of Bar-Selehm and hopes to return very soon.*

"Why?" I asked, lowering my voice. "She's done. I can't play her again."

"I'm not so sure," said Sureyna. "The Istilian embassy concedes that there are lots of aristocracy in the Lani homeland, including some who style themselves princesses, who are unknown to them. They aren't about to expose Lady Misrai as a fraud, particularly if people continue to say nice things about her. She was, I think you'll find, quite the hit in polite society, and lots of people have already claimed to have been with her at events all over the city."

"They can't have been," I said. "I didn't go anywhere as her except Elitus and Violet Farthingale's apartment."

"Exactly," said Sureyna. "But people want to be in her orbit, as it were, so when one person lies about seeing her somewhere, all her friends agree and become a kind of royalty by extension. I'm thinking that if I occasionally imply that someone claimed to have seen her at some fashionable gala or other, that will keep her in mind for when you want to reuse the disguise. Ethically it's borderline, but it might be useful."

"Sounds risky," I said.

"Not compared to climbing out of windows and running along roofs," she said.

"But people will know it's not real," I replied. "If you post something about her attending an opera when no one there saw her—"

"They'll say they did, and that makes it true," she said with a sly grin. "After all, it was in the paper."

MADAME NAHREEM GAVE ME a long look. In response to her inquiries I had recounted everything that had happened on the docks, talking her through it all as it happened and in detail. Almost everything, anyway. There were things I was not ready to discuss, questions I was not ready to ask. I had not mentioned Vestris.

"This Barrington-Smythe frightened you," she said.

"Yes," I said. "He was a killer."

"But it was more than that, was it not?"

I paused to wonder.

We had just finished Namud's cremation, a private affair on a hilltop in sight of the estate, and were sitting in the drawing room, a sunny, spacious chamber made formal by the straight-backed chairs. Somewhere outside they were grilling meat over a fire lit with a brand from the funeral pyre in the Lani way. I could smell the smoke, sweet and fragrant on the air, and distantly I heard the clatter of pans in the kitchen. Madame Nahreem seemed to hear it too, and for the slenderest of moments, I caught in her face something wistfully sad, and knew she was thinking about Namud. I had seen so little tenderness in her that I was startled by the fact of her grief, even more so when I saw her eyes bright with unshed tears.

Don't be too hard on her. . . .

One of the pet hyenas slumbered at her feet, its black muzzle inches from my leg. It grunted, shifting, and her attention came back to the room and to me. It was as if she had thrown a veil over the person I had briefly glimpsed in her face, and she looked upon me as her old self, stern and a little irritated, awaiting my response to her question about Barrington-Smythe. I scowled at the Lani rug on her polished wooden floors and tried to find the words.

"It's like he was sick," I said. "In his head. He didn't do what he did because he was paid to or even because he hated people like . . . like us." She squinted slightly as if about to qualify that last remark, but said nothing. "The intrigue, the military posturing, even the racism, all of that was just an excuse, a way of justifying hurting people, breaking them apart. It's what he enjoyed."

"That scared you?"

"Yes," I said. "Because you can't reason with such people. You can only beat them, and I did not have the strength or the skill to do so."

She nodded again, but there was something thoughtful in her face, and I realized I had revealed more than I meant to.

"So who did?" she asked.

"What?"

"You did not have the skill to overpower him, but someone did," she said, watching me, hawkish and unmoving. "Someone cut his throat. I checked the autopsy reports through Inspector Andrews. He did not die in the melee, hit by a stray bullet. He was killed by someone standing behind him. Would you like to tell me who that person was?"

I just looked at her.

"One of the children," she said, "reported seeing someone clinging to the struts of a water tower in sight of the docks. Some*thing*, I should say, since the child did not think it was a person. The police dismissed the observation as hysteria, but there have been other such sightings in the city, have there not?"

"I think I've heard something about it," I said, trying—and

failing—to sound casual. She may as well have been wearing the neutral mask, while I felt my confused anxiety was painted all over my face. "I thought it was just a folktale. A scary story."

"Told particularly," she said, "by steeplejacks."

"Yes," I said.

"Interesting, isn't it, the way people invent monsters to scare themselves? As if the real world isn't terrifying enough."

She smiled faintly and left it at that, but I knew that the tales of the Gargoyle had given her something to think about, something that made her distant and reflective again, as if she was remembering something from long ago. Whatever it was, it involved my sister. I was sure of that. My beautiful older sister who had once—for all I knew—trained at this very house. Had Willinghouse known? Had he hired her as he had hired me? Whose choice had that been: his or his grandmother's? Why this strange, obsessive interest in my family when the training I was now undergoing had failed so spectacularly with my sister?

"Namud liked you," she said suddenly. "So do my grandchildren. I do not always see eye to eye with them, but I think their estimation of your character broadly sound."

It was as indirect and understated a compliment as I had ever received, but it cost her something to say it, and I lowered my head, giving in to my old diffidence.

"Thank you," I said. "I endeavor to give satisfaction."

"You're not a servant," she quipped, something of her more usual sharpness returning. "Don't talk like one. And never think like one."

Another critique that sounded like she was coaching me to play Lady Misrai, though I think her advice was supposed to be more than that. I wondered if she had ever said something similar to Vestris before she had become . . . whatever she was now.

You could ask her. You could demand why she sought to replace Vestris with you, if that's what happened, and what she is trying to atone for.

Not yet. I didn't want to just ask. I focused on the neutral mask and, when I felt ready, looked up, met Madame Nahreem's keen gaze, and nodded once.

DAHRIA MET ME IN the garden.

"I thought you hated it out here," I said, admiring the treelined walkway where the rollers gathered and the fire-eyed grackles squabbled.

"It's not so bad at the moment," she said, giving me a sidelong look.

"Perhaps it's the company."

"Perhaps."

"You're a bad influence," I said.

"Me!" she exclaimed. "What about you? You'll have me eating with my hands out of a trough and going to my bedroom via the outside drainpipe. If my friends in the city could see how I live out here—"

"You worry too much about a society you secretly despise," I said.

She raised an eyebrow, but conceded the point with a half shrug.

"Sometimes you cling to what you have, whether it fits or not," she said. "I would think you of all people would understand that."

I looked around the grounds of the great house, one of the many places in which I did not truly belong, and smiled ruefully.

"Speaking of your society *friends*—using the term loosely," I remarked, deliberately shifting the direction of the conversation. "What can you do for Violet Farthingale?"

"What do you mean?" asked Dahria.

"You said she was in danger of losing everything. Her job. Her position. All because of a scandal in which she was quite guiltless."

"You want me to ensure that her position in Bar-Selehm society goes untarnished?"

"Yes," I said.

"I don't think I can do that."

"You need to think more like an aristocrat," I remarked, grinning. "You can do anything once you put your mind to it."

She matched my grin.

"Perhaps the Farthingale woman will be gainfully employed in the service of other people's unpleasant little children."

"Perhaps twist your brother's arm a little, and she might be paid a little extra to teach occasional classes at a fledgling school that meets in the Drowning."

"You think she would?"

"I do, actually," I said. "I think she has a good heart."

Dahria cocked her head on one side, eyeing me curiously.

"You want to see the best in people," she said.

"I need to try," I said.

Before she could respond, Willinghouse came strolling out of the house, tieless and in a suit of light gray that made him look buoyant and youthful.

"Ladies," he said, "I have been told to inform you that dinner will be served in half an hour."

"You may consider your mission complete," said Dahria.

"Mr. Willinghouse," I said.

He stopped in the act of walking away and turned to me.

"Please," he said, "I think you have earned the right to call me Josiah."

"Thank you," I said, fairly sure that I would not do so except in the most extreme of circumstances. "I never got a chance to say that I was sorry about Namud."

His jaunty manner clouded over, and he nodded.

"Yes," he said. "We all are. Thank you."

"You will need to hire a replacement," I said.

"I suppose so," he replied. "My grandmother will want to be involved in that. Her requirements are quite particular."

"Imagine that!" said Dahria.

"Perhaps you might consider some of the Quundu," I said. "They are not all children, and they need work. They would not be able to take Namud's place, of course, but perhaps they could do some of his duties."

He seemed to consider this.

"I wonder if having so many black servants sends the right message?" he mused.

"To whom?" asked Dahria. "Your electorate? I think that if they want the work and you pay them well and treat them with respect, that is the only message you need to worry about."

He looked at her, blinking in the sun, as if one of the hyenas had just given him precise instructions on how to prepare its dinner, and then nodded vaguely.

"Perhaps so," he said. He gave us an equally vague wave and returned to the house, lost in thought.

I caught Dahria watching me as he left.

"You like him," she said.

"He's a good employer, who has trusted me when no one else—"

"Yes, yes," she snapped, "but that's not what I meant, and you know it. You *like* him."

"Why do you make every conversation so difficult?" I said, flushing. "You're always . . . probing, making fun."

"Not at all, my dear steeplejack, not at all," she replied. "If I play, it's because I like you. You know that."

"Yes," I said, grudgingly, avoiding her eyes.

"I just mean that you're going to have to choose. At some point."

"Choose what?" I replied.

"Who you like best, me or my sainted brother. *Which* you like best."

"Why?" I said and, with a private smile at her baffled exasperation, turned back to the house. "Come on, Dahria. We have to get ready for dinner. I'm sure your sainted brother has matters of urgency to discuss, new threats to the security of Bar-Selehm that he wishes me to investigate."

"You are the most maddening person I ever met," said Dahria, linking her arm through mine and leading me up the stairs to the house.

"That, my dear Miss Willinghouse," I observed, pushing open the door and catching the scent of roasted meat on the warm air, "is why we get along."

ACKNOWLEDGMENTS

Thanks to Diana Pho and all at Tor Teen; to my agent, Stacey Glick; to Stephen Melling, Finie Osako, and Sebastian Hartley.